D1483788

Praise for the Empire of the House of Thorns Series

Shadows Over London
"Klaver dazzles with an adventure rooted in complex feelings about family loyalties, and magically full to the brim with faerie mystery."
— **Tobias S. Buckell, World Fantasy Award Winner and** *New York Times* **Bestselling Author**

"An enchanting and enthralling series opener."
— *Kirkus Reviews*

"Fantasy at its most fantastic. Monsters, mystery, and magic in a beautiful and frightening world all their own. Justice Kasric and her strange family are a delight from first to last."
— **Steven Harper, author of The Books of Blood and Iron series**

"This first title in a new series slowly builds into a magical adventure in a world that is dark and unique . . . the plot and world building are sure to enthrall readers."
— *School Library Journal*

"Klaver's rich, lyrical descriptions augment the fantastical source material in this engaging series starter."
— *Publishers Weekly*

Justice At Sea
"[T]hose who enjoy epic fantasy will find much to enjoy here . . . Sweeping and intricate."
— *Kirkus Reviews*

"Christian Klaver's delightful fantasy novel *Justice at Sea* blends faerie magic with historical elements to spectacular effect."
— *Foreword Reviews*

ARMADAS
IN THE
MIST

CHRISTIAN KLAVER

ARMADAS IN THE MIST

CamCat Books

CamCat Publishing, LLC
Brentwood, Tennessee 37027
camcatpublishing.com

Hardcover ISBN 9780744305159
Paperback ISBN 9780744305166
Large-Print Paperback ISBN 9780744305173
eBook ISBN 9780744305227
Audiobook ISBN 9780744305296

Library of Congress Control Number: 2022938691

Book and cover design by Maryann Appel

5 3 1 2 4

To Katie and Kimberly, for believing.

KASRIC FAMILY
· HOUSE OF THORNS ·

Rachek Kasric   Martine Kasric

Joshua

Lord of Thorns   Martine Kasric

Prudence   Benedict   Faith   Justice   Henry

Lord of Thorns   Lady Dierwyn

Temperance   Hope   Charity

Lord of Thorns   Ashmir

Pyar (Love)

ACT I

FORCES
GATHERING

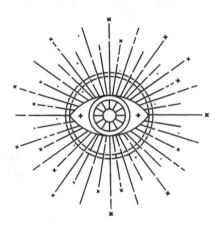

CHAPTER 1

JUSTICE
Dreams and Storms

The things I remember most about the days before the Battle of the Sevens are the storms and the dreams. Turns out, these weren't really two different things, though I didn't tell anyone that at first.

I came out on the deck of the HMS *Specter in the Mist*, buttoning Father's old, black, full-length coat against the murderous cold and squashing my wide-brimmed hat down more securely on my head.

"Captain on deck!" one of the Dwarven gunners shouted. The other Dwarves in his crew and a few of the merfolk Prowlers coiling rope nearby all stopped to salute.

"Captain Justice," the gunner said.

I waved to them to continue their work and headed for the starboard rail, where my brother and sister were. I stopped at the rail, seeing now the glowering, black, swollen mass waiting for us.

"Will you look at that?" Henry breathed.

"I don't want to," Faith said, her voice catching a little. Then they both became aware of me, and Henry's face changed, became more closed, which wasn't something I was used to seeing from my little brother at all. But he had his reasons. After all, I'd shot his father. The fact that it was *my* father too and that I'd had little choice didn't matter so much. Nor did the fact that Father had wanted me to, since it was the only way to keep him from being controlled by the Seelie Court and forced to lead the invasion against England. Oversee the destruction of everything he loved or death. Not much of a choice, but he'd made the honorable one and asked me to implement it. Not that any of that kept the nightmares away. Faith, having been with Father and me through most of it, understood why I'd done what I'd done, but Henry, even after Faith had explained the situation to him, clearly didn't, and he hadn't been right with me since we'd come back. I couldn't really blame him.

He was a little shorter than I was, and under normal conditions, had the kind of open and friendly face that people underestimated and took advantage of. Of course, Henry could also topple over a carriage full of people without breaking a sweat, but he didn't look like it.

"Some storm," Faith said. While Henry looked just the same as when all this had started, Faith had changed a great deal. The leather hood she wore was thrown back now, showing her shaven scalp. She carried the staff tipped with the fragments of Sands' magical violin and wore the sword we'd gotten from Victoria Rose at her side. Faith's expression was filled with subtle and profound knowledge that she'd received in her training, and I could only imagine how unsettling that must have been.

She wasn't exaggerating about the storm. It was four or five miles out and coming fast. The sea was gray and choppy, as if the wind and water fought each other. We were beating our way to windward, so the ship was already swooping up and down in the rollers of the channel like a wild and caged beast of the sea. You could smell the storm coming too, and feel the charged air. Rain fell in fits and gusts, thrown by a capricious wind.

And it was going to get a lot worse.

"How bad can this get, Justice?" Faith asked me.

I looked in her direction, my eyebrows raised.

She took a deep breath and let it out. "That bad?"

"You can't do anything?" I asked. Faith, as a magician, had a connection to the Wild Hunt, which allowed her some influence over the wind, but that control was sporadic, unreliable.

She shook her head. Her face and the part of her scalp not hidden by her hood glistened with beads of water. "No. Only when the Wild Hunt is near."

"Damn it," I said, then bellowed, "Mr. Starling!"

A shocked silence sprang up around me as everyone, my siblings, the deck crew, officers, even the sail crew up in the rigging, stopped what they were doing, stunned and more than a little embarrassed for me.

Mr. Starling, my old first mate, wasn't here. He never would be again. The Faerie monster known as the Goblin Knight had killed him, clubbing him down with a cudgel that smoldered and smoked but never burned.

"Mog is here, Captain," Mog said near my elbow. Another Goblin, Mog, and as different from the Goblin Knight as two people could be. Honorable and compassionate, though not exactly a master of dinner etiquette. Also Mr. Starling's replacement as my first mate.

You had to know Mog well to read his expressions, but now his hangdog frown was as clear to me as anything. Mog had been closer to Mr. Starling than anyone, and probably missed Starling even more than I did. His barrel form was hunched over morosely, his black eyes sorrowful, his long batlike ears hanging limply down past his chin.

"Mog is here, Captain," he said again, very gently. Like half of my crew, he didn't wear any uniform, but he'd become an efficient and dutiful first mate, despite working in Mr. Starling's shadow.

"Good," I said to him brusquely, trying to push through my colossal embarrassment and sense of loss, "that storm is going to knock us right over if we don't reduce our wind drag as much as possible. Reef all sails except the jib and the main. Get the sea anchor out."

"Yes, Captain," Mog said.

"Quickly," I said.

A few hours later, the storm hit our little fleet in the English Channel like falling anvils.

We struggled to maintain position while the storm wailed and tore at us. The instant our blockade slipped or the invasion fleet discovered a way to batter through, they would be able to send troops along to France and from there, to the rest of the continent. On land, they were unstoppable. England's absurdly quick fall had proved that. Only the invaders' lack of sailing prowess and our few ships kept the Faerie Invasion trapped in England. The storm was too powerful for the invading forces to try sending troops across. As long as we were here when the storm stopped, the blockade would hold.

We just had to stay afloat while winds and a heaving sea tried to tear us apart.

So the HMS *Specter in the Mist* struggled in the choppy waters of the English Channel while the wind and rain lashed all around. We used the sea anchor and shortened sail. I took the helm, with Avonstoke on one side and Henry on the other, trying to steer just enough to keep the ship moving so that the keel and rudder bit the water and we didn't flounder, but not to the point where we fought the elements any more than we had to. It was a tricky business, but with Avonstoke and Henry's strength and my feel for the sea, the *Specter* just barely succeeded at staying afloat in the howling chaos.

Spars broke, rigging tore, and the wind howled while my sail crew of Goblins and Ghost Boys struggled to contain the damage and our deck crew of Prowlers, Dwarves, and Court Faerie fought to adapt our few standing sails to the incessantly changing directions of the storm. We kept triple watch on lookout to avoid running too close to either shore. More deck crew manned the bilge pumps, and their constant squeaking, up and down, never stopped. Everyone worked grimly, with fierce determination. None of them had been sailors six months ago, and now they went about their tasks with no quarter asked or given. I used every trick I had, but I knew it wouldn't be enough. Not if the storm held.

We had to fight. We had nowhere else to go. England, my home, was now an enemy shore. We couldn't harbor with any of the foreign nations either, not even nearby France, an occasional hazy line off to starboard. Any ship of the modern world would shoot and sink any ship coming out of the Faerie mist. At least the Faerie ship *Seahome* had enough magicians capable of hindering the weather. So did the rest of the Faerie Outcast Fleet. But our ship didn't have that kind of magic at its disposal.

Faith, having no nautical duties, had taken up station on the deck, leaning on her staff and watching, just watching, the storm that battered at us. Just on the other side of the quarterdeck, she was half hidden by the rain except when the lightning flashed. She stood with her hood up over her naked scalp, peering out into the darkness of the storm as if she could stare it down.

Dawn came, but it didn't grow any lighter.

"There's more to this than weather," she called over. "I can feel it." She stared at me with elaborate gravity.

"Like what?" I asked.

She just shook her head. The storm continued to rage around us.

We went another two days this way. All that time I avoided sleep. That was partly because the *Specter* teetered on the edge of capsizing and I was terrified to leave the quarterdeck. But also, I was afraid of the dreams.

The next day I reluctantly gave orders to rest the crew in shifts. They deserved more than a few hours' sleep, but being shorthanded made weathering the storm even more dangerous. Still, driving the crew past utter fatigue had its own cost. Two of the crew had gone missing in the night, certainly fallen overboard. I'd been using the Ghost Boys more than the rest of the sail crew because ghosts couldn't drown. But they couldn't swim well enough to get back to the ship. Not in this gale. Even if they could make it to land somehow, we had no way of retrieving them. It could be years before we saw them again, if ever. I dared not drive them any further.

After the first and second shift had rested and come back into the wet, howling gale, Faith appeared at my elbow and ordered me below. My brain was too numbed and fogged to fight her.

Later, I fell into my swinging cot, briefly disturbing Enemy, Sands' cat, before he settled on my cold feet. Even then, I couldn't sleep.

I heard both the rattle and thunder of the storm outside and the screaming from below. Our prisoner, Captain Caine. He'd been bothering my sleep more and more of late. I put my hands over my ears to muffle the sounds.

When I finally drifted off, my nightmares were more of the storm, only worse.

I sailed a torn and battered ship under stormy skies the color of steel and black iron. Far ahead, silvery, luminous light broke through the cloud cover, a haven I'd never reach. The wind was tearing the sailcloth to ribbons, and we were heeling hard over to port, so that the railing was lost to view as green sheets of water shipped over.

Lightning streaked across the sky, giving me a glimpse of a black, smoldering figure the size of a volcano behind us. A man, features shrouded, with a shining crown so high up it was nearly lost in the storm clouds. Or rather his head and torso, because, waist down, he was submerged in the sea. He lifted his hands in a gesture that was part threat, part entreaty.

Llyr of the Tuatha De Dannan. God of the Sea.

All your gifts, Llyr thundered, *all your gifts come from me.* The ship ran roughly into the next wave and water sprayed up in great, cool, snowy-white fountains. The man, the god, the sea, they hungered for me. They would take my fealty or my life.

Submit, the waves sang as they pounded into the hull. I could hear wood splinter with every hit. *Give yourself to me. Become my champion, my avatar, and I shall fill your heart and your hands with powers undreamed of.*

Arawn's forces come to lay waste to our homeland, yours and mine. Become mine, and you shall be mighty enough to defend it.

Give me your gifts, I shouted at the rain, *and I shall save England. This is the desire of my heart! But I worship no one.*

Even in the dream, I could still remember Father in my mind's eye, first as a god in his own right, battling with his wits with the Faerie King in a snowy woods, then sick and confused, in bed. Just a man. I loved him still, more than anything, but now my world had no gods. Because the truth was, I just didn't trust them.

Help me, I said to the sea in my dream, *and I will save England. But I do this. Not you.*

The sea roared in anger at my audacity.

But I wouldn't relent. I still remembered, too vividly, the God of the Wild Hunt chasing us underneath a stormy sky. I could close my eyes and still taste the blood in my mouth, and the fear. My gut told me none of the Faerie gods could be trusted.

The sky flashed again, showing the God of the Sea with clenched fists, hunched over now in terrible anger. To starboard, in the center of the English Channel, I could see more shadowy figures. Three women standing so close together they might be one. Brigid, the triple Goddess of Fire and Water. Beside her, a shadowy horse. One aspect of the Morrigna, another triple-aspected goddess, only she couldn't make up her mind. I could see her two other aspects, the Crow and the Crone, and still more shadowy figures off the port side, near the English coast.

The gods were siding with the invaders.

Next to the Morrigna's two aspects was the skull-faced Arawn, the Warrior-King God, Lord of the Underworld and the driving force behind the Faerie Invasion. Far ahead, off the bow, another enormous, inhuman figure struggled, apart from the others, somewhere through the Strait of Dover. It was draped in storm and shadow, but the bulk and gait reminded me of the Soho Shark. Then I caught a flash of the head and saw the sand shark's mouthful of black teeth. Now I was sure. Formori.

I woke.

I sucked in a deep, shaking breath, like a drowning swimmer just breaking the surface. In my thrashing around, I kicked something furry. Enemy. He yowled and leaped off the cot. He landed on the deck, his orange fur ruffled and angry, and then jumped into the lap of a figure seated there. She'd been sitting so still I hadn't even noticed her.

"Bad dreams?" she said.

I sat up in the cot and stared at her, trying to decide how much she knew and how much I might be reading into her question. Truth was, Faith was uncannily perceptive, and probably it was time to tell someone. They were all suffering for my stubbornness.

"The Faerie gods," I said hoarsely. "They want me to submit to them. Still."

"And you still won't," Faith said sympathetically. It wasn't a question. I was listening carefully for judgment in her tone, but it wasn't there. Her face, hooded in shadow, was hidden to me, so I couldn't gauge her expression. Despite the fact that she was both an acolyte, of sorts, of the Wild Hunt, and a disciple magician under Drecovian and Brocara, who gave her her *own* Faerie dreams, she'd never criticized my refusal to follow the same path.

"I keep waiting for you to tell me I should listen to them more," I admitted.

"No," she said after a moment's thought. "I won't tell you that. I'm not sure if that's the right path. For you."

"That wasn't what I expected you to say," I said. I wasn't sure, considering the stakes, that I could be so objective, if I'd been in her place.

She laughed, honestly surprised and amused. "It helps that there's absolutely zero chance of your doing what someone tells you when you think it's wrong."

I laughed. "Right back at you." This was a franker discussion than we'd had on this topic before, and I found myself burning with curiosity. "But you follow them."

"I do," she said. As if to emphasize the point, she drew back her hood, revealing her shaven scalp. Once, before the Faerie Invasion and the fall of England, she'd had a long mane of golden hair. Longer, finer, and better kept than my own blonde hair, which had a tendency to tangle itself when I wasn't looking. Hers had been a truer color too, white gold to my tarnished yellow. She'd been the pretty one before becoming a magician and an acolyte to the Wild Hunt and had shaved it. No one had told her to shave it. She'd simply woken up one morning and decided that a shaved head would make her feel more like one of the arcane.

Unfair as it was, she was *still* the pretty one. She carried off the look in a way no one else could have. It made her beauty seem unnatural, otherworldly.

"Why?" I asked.

"The truth is," Faith said softly, "that you being stubborn is one of the things that allowed me to let myself go and do what I had to do. We have a lot of things we want to save. England, Benedict, the rest of our family . . ." She waved her hand indicating all the other things. "You being steadfast for England and refusing to be influenced by the Faerie gods makes it safer for me to let them in."

I frowned, remembering the Faith who had declared, a very short time ago, how little she trusted the Faerie. This was a complete reversal. "Let them in? How? Why?"

"We use whatever we have," she said. "Everything we have. You found your way to get things done. This is mine."

"Do *you* trust them?" I asked. "The Faerie gods?"

"Yes," Faith said. "But that's not the question you need to ask yourself."

"What is?"

"You need to ask yourself if you trust *me*."

"Of course I do," I said automatically.

She stood up suddenly, taller than I was and more imposing. The movement had put her under the skylight and lightning chose that moment to burn across the sky, splashing shadows down over her.

"Do you?" she asked again.

I was keenly aware that being sisters, we'd fought more often than not. There had been lots of other times in the past where I hadn't trusted my selfish, beautiful, charming, and aloof sister at all.

But I did now.

"Absolutely," I said firmly.

She stepped forward and grabbed my shoulder in a fierce grip. "Good. I feel the same way. That's all I need to know."

"What kind of place," I wondered out loud, "is England going to be after this? Even if we win, it won't go back to what it was."

"No," Faith agreed. "It won't. Whatever happens, our world and the world of Faerie are connected now. But we don't want the Black Shuck ruling it."

"No," I agreed. "We don't."

I had to find my uniform and Father's old heavy coat in uncertain light, since the only light that came down from the skylight or stern windows was flashes of lightning. Faith had lit one of the lanterns swinging from the low rafters, but it didn't show much. The wailing of the wind and the motion of the ship grew even more violent as Faith helped me get dressed.

A quick glance at the mirror was enough to see that I looked a mess. My blonde hair hung in long, wet clumps. My left eye, the ghost eye, looked more unnatural than ever in my gaunt, exhausted face.

My gaze fell to the table where I could see the maps, sea charts, newspapers, and chess board.

I picked up the most recent newspaper with a wounded heart. Sands' agents had brought it only two days ago. I couldn't read in this light, but I knew what it said already.

QUEEN VICTORIA DEAD.

I dropped the paper and fought back a cold blackness. Even if we won this war, the Faerie occupation had already changed and destroyed so much, so many. It was surprising how many of England's citizens continued under the occupation, adapting to an occupied life. The thought of the countless dead was horrifying, but equally horrifying was the idea that just as many citizens labored under their new Faerie overlords. Even if we won, the world was never going to be the same again.

The newspaper article itself didn't have a lot of information, only that the House of Lords—which now included as many Court Faerie as men—was still deliberating possibilities for the next monarch. The Black Shuck or Widdershins would be pulling all those strings and making all those decisions. The Shuck himself or a Faerie puppet-king, perhaps. The picture under the headline showed Queen Victoria's famous diadem crown, broken in half, with her hand open and lifeless lying next to it.

Sands' network of spies had culled an enormous amount of information. That was enormous compared to what we had otherwise, which was almost nothing thanks to the impenetrable fog surrounding most of the British Isles. We knew now that, contrary to expectation, a large part of England's population still lived, if under Faerie rule. We got a great deal of details and numbers on their overpowering standing armies, but less on the disposition of their ships or what plans they had next. But we didn't learn any more about Queen Victoria, and I'd give my mizzenmast to find out exactly how she'd died. Several reports came of Queen Victoria's distant relatives being smuggled over to the continent, but our information from that direction was even sketchier, since any French, Spanish, or American forces we'd seen had clearly identified us with the Faerie and shot at us on sight. We knew little of what went on in the outside world.

Surprising how the newspapers still thrived in Faerie-occupied England, considering everything. The Faerie loathed the press machines but were amused to no end by the papers themselves, so they kept a contingent of pet newspaper writers to produce them. Most of the information printed in them was pure fabrication. The Outcast Fleet, especially the *Specter*, were mentioned often, but only as pirates. We were out here fighting for England, and most of England hated us. That we were ridiculously, profoundly outnumbered was confirmed many times over—our only saving grace being the lack of any naval power among the invading forces.

It was a madhouse in London now, with the capricious, powerful, and inexplicable Faerie in charge. Rachek Kasric—the real one—had gone there a few days back. Or had tried to. He hadn't any experience with the mist, despite living in Faerie all those years, and had insisted on taking a small dingy to the English coast. Stupid, stupid, stupid. I should have had him thrown in chains if that had been the only way to keep him from committing suicide, but I hadn't had the heart. Our family had wronged him, owed him, but sending him off to his death seemed a poor way to pay it. I hoped he was somehow all right.

Hoping against hope for some kind of good news, I looked at the chess board Father had left. His oracle. It was a visual representation linked to the war that changed magically to reflect depositions and strength of troops, but only Father could read the bloody thing properly, and he was dead. Dead at my hand. I shook my head and regarded the set again. Sands had had a feel for it before he'd lost his magic, but no longer. Still, it wasn't hard to glean this much: nothing had changed and we still looked grossly outmatched. The maps, sea charts, and scouting reports all said the same.

I mashed my hat down. If my sleep was going to be plagued by Faerie nightmares, I might as well deal with real storms rather than their dream cousins. Anything was better than poring over volumes of old, bad news. I wondered where Avonstoke was now, then my thoughts turned to what he'd have to say about the Faerie gods reaching out to me.

I pushed open the narrow double doors to my cabin to see Avonstoke standing there, dripping from the rain. Over his shoulder, I could see a part in the blackened clouds, a thread of blue sky.

He grinned. I could feel his presence, one that affected me like no other, as if he were made of hot coals. I saw a brief flash of yearning in his expression before he carefully brought it under control. It had been too fast to see unless you were really looking for it.

I was, of course.

"Ah," he said. "My captain." The warmth in his voice was unmistakable, and it made me flush under my hat. "I hope I didn't wake you. I came to tell you that the storm has—"

"You shouldn't be above decks," I said, grabbing a fistful of his emerald-green Court Faerie marine uniform. "Get in here." I hauled him through the doors, which banged shut behind him.

He came willingly, moving with grace despite his blindness, and then, an instant after the doors had shut, his body was pressed against mine, and our mouths met in a blistering kiss. His breath was warm, exciting, like it always was. He smelled of wet wool from his drenched uniform and tar from handling deck ropes. Even through the wet clothes, his body was hot against mine.

I took pleasure in his heat, his solidity, for as long as I dared, four minutes, perhaps five.

Then I pushed him reluctantly away.

"I'm sorry," I said. "I need to get out there." I desperately didn't want to leave his arms and go out into the cold and wet, but these few snatched moments were all I could risk. None of the others had the same feel for the sea that I did, and every minute away from topside brought a chance of wreck and ruin.

"I know," he said, his breath ragged. Then his blank gaze, blind as he was, strayed in the direction of the rumpled blanket on the cot I'd just left. For an instant, his expression was one of desire, and I flushed, feeling an echoing desire blossom in the pit of my stomach. There was a lot more waiting for us than kisses in the dark, but I didn't dare think about that now with war and duty in the way.

I took a deep, ragged breath.

Then Avonstoke's face turned back toward me and his expression became thoughtful and pensive. "The dreams?" he asked. "They still haunt you?" His tone was carefully neutral. We'd discussed the Faerie gods before, my distrust, his devotion. We were very clear on each other's feelings there.

"Yes," I said, the feeling of warmth sluicing away, just that quickly, replaced by a cold chill.

He nodded seriously, saying nothing. His face still looked strange to me. He'd lost the black raven tattoo on his face and his sight in the same battle at Stormholt, three months ago, and I was still adapting.

There was an awkward moment of silence, filled with sounds from outside the cabin. The whistling of the wind, the creak of the ship around us, the squeal of sailors working the pumps to force out all the water the storm shipped in.

"Has the storm slackened any?" I asked, my voice sounding weak and feeble to my own ears.

"The storm continues to be . . ." Avonstoke lifted his hands in a shrug. "Terrible. I would not have thought a ship could weather it if we weren't proving otherwise, even now."

I looked at him again. He was clearly exhausted, his eyes hollow and his hands shaking. Worse than exhausted. He was on the verge of dropping, bolstered only by force of will. Had he taken any rest since standing two or three shifts at the helm with me? I didn't know.

"But then," he said with forced cheerfulness, "it is fitting for the mighty Admiral Justice and the Outcast Fleet. It'd be a dull epic if the sea were calm, would it not?"

"Admiral Justice," I said, "doesn't run the Outcast Fleet, if you can even *call* it that. Lady Rue's got a number of those schooners. Who knows how many, exactly? But she doesn't answer to me. Neither does the Faerie Council, which actually runs *Seahome*. So, the Outcast Fleet, as far as this admiral is concerned, is the *Specter*. One ship." I gave him a hard look. "You look exhausted. Have you gotten any sleep?"

He shrugged.

"You should get below," I said gently. "Get some sleep."

Avonstoke had no sailing experience, but he'd worked hard to overcome it. And had. Then he'd been struck blind, a poison scratch from a Kellas Cat, and one he'd gotten protecting me. Even after that, he'd worked hard to learn his way around the ship, *again*, this time without the use of his eyes. And he'd succeeded, again. Blind, he was still a remarkably competent deckhand. But in a storm like this, wandering the deck blindly, he might easily be washed overboard.

"I thought you might need another lookout," he said, squinting with mock intensity. "Besides, I was just coming to tell you that the repairs are done to the mizzenwhistle or spanker gun or one of those things. The sail that broke just before you came down?"

"Main topsail yard?" I said, at least 60 percent certain that he was just taunting me with "mizzenwhistle." Perhaps 70.

"That's the very one!" he said brightly.

I put a hand on his arm.

"You *need* sleep," I said.

"We all do." He shrugged again, as if the matter were of no importance.

Then I thought of slipping into his arms on my cot, or in his hammock on the lower deck, and sleeping protected and safe there . . . or, perhaps, not sleeping . . . and my face flushed all over again. How could I keep my ship and crew safe if I was constantly distracted by these heated thoughts?

"Sleep," I snapped and withdrew my hand.

He shook his head. "You need all the hands you can get."

"That's an order," I snapped, falling back into my duties. A sudden, even more violent than normal dip of the ship threw us in closer proximity, both of us leaning on the door frame for support.

He shrugged yet again, his expression maddingly mild.

"You need . . ."

"I don't need my crew falling overboard through exhaustion," I said. "*Please*. Just sleep a little. I promise not to let you do it too long."

"Perhaps a little," he relented, "just this once. If you promise not to let me make a habit of it."

"I promise," I said gently. He nodded and with another, almost imperceptible glance at my cot, made his way to the hatch to below decks.

We didn't lack for brass, my crew and me. Now we could use a little luck.

I stumbled out against the wind and slashing rain to make my way up the stairs and join Henry on the quarterdeck. Faith was with him, though I was sure it wasn't her watch.

I immediately immersed myself in the constant, bitter struggle of a ship tossed by the storms.

A sudden, particularly violent gust tore the mainsail in half with a sound like thunder and we were frantic to put some sail in to replace it before the lack of a bracing against the wind tipped us over.

We'd just finished when Henry pointed past me.

"Where's *he* going?" he said.

I turned to see Avonstoke on deck again.

He was walking across the deck, seemingly mesmerized. He didn't look blind so much as completely unaware of his surroundings. It had been nearly an hour since I'd seen him on deck and he'd left his emerald marine uniform below, braving the chill with only some kind of leather leggings.

Was that what he slept in?

Was that *all* he slept in? That was a distracting image I didn't need right now. Two Prowler crewmen skirted out of his way while he shuffled blindly past. The crewman looked to me and Mog for confirmation.

"Avonstoke!" I shouted. "What are you doing?" But he was already grabbing the shrouds and stepping up. He slipped then, something I'd never seen him do before that I could remember, even blind.

"Avonstoke!" Faith shouted. Then to us: "Is he even awake?"

That seemed a question I couldn't answer. We were all moving, Faith, Henry, and I, across the deck.

"Grab him!" Faith shouted at the two crewmen, but we'd been too slow. They rushed across the deck but weren't close enough to actually stop him.

"Raythe!" I shouted. It felt odd to call him by his first name. In fact, I couldn't remember when I'd ever done it.

But it made him pause, just a second, with one foot on the rung of the ladder, getting ready to haul himself up. But then he went on, without looking, as if the pause hadn't even happened. He was already twenty feet up, moving in a jerky, uncoordinated but quick fashion. I mounted the shroud after him, quickly moving myself to try and catch up.

The sea groaned and raged all around us, and I suddenly felt a cold touch of horribly potent fear.

Llyr. Or one of the other bloody Faerie gods. They had him. They'd been trying to get me and when they couldn't, they'd decided to strike at me through the people I loved. Even in that moment of terror, the realization that I did, in fact, love Avonstoke, for all that I couldn't tell him, was another, entirely different kind of fear.

I couldn't afford to let either master me right now. The machinations of the Faerie gods had turned Mother and Joshua against humanity. They'd conspired to take Father, until death had been the only honorable choice he'd had left. They'd taken Benedict too, trapping him as a rider in the Wild Hunt. They'd tried for the rest of us too, including Henry, Faith, and I, and had come very close to succeeding.

Now they were going after Avonstoke and they couldn't have him!

I caught up with him just as he reached the mainyard platform. From the foremast at the front of the ship, the crewman stationed at the crow's nest goggled openly at us. Some of the fuzzy Goblin sail crew were out on the yardarm, also staring at us openly. I didn't care. I was still shouting for Avonstoke to stop.

"Justice?" said Étienne, leader of the Ghost Boys. He was a young boy with blond hair and a checkered hat. One of the reefed mainsails had worked itself loose, and Étienne and a trio of Goblins were working to get it reefed again before the storm winds caught it and tore the mast off. My ghost eye, however spooky it looked, had its uses. One of them was being able to see Étienne, Percy, Emily, and the rest of our Ghost Boys.

"Where's 'e going, then?" Étienne said, gaping at Avonstoke.

"It's all right," I called back to him, though I wasn't at all sure that was true.

Avonstoke mounted the ladder to the upper part of the mainmast as I struggled through opening onto the platform. He had to turn my way to do it, so I caught a look at his slack and haggard face. His eyes were open, sightless, his hands groping for the rungs of the rope ladder. It was cold as hell up there, even with a coat. Avonstoke, in just his britches, had to be freezing.

"Let go of him!" I shouted at the sky, as if the Faerie gods would hear or care. "Avonstoke!" I shouted again, but he kept on going.

Following him was stupid. It wasn't like I could drag him down by force without causing both of us to fall, but I couldn't just watch him go up and kill himself without trying to intervene. I made the mistake of looking down. Being this high up, at least on a ship, had never bothered me before, but the deck looked dizzyingly far below now. Fitful but powerful winds tugged at us and the ship, and the unsteady rocking of the vessel, amplified this high up, was nauseating. Every time the ship rocked, we moved a good twenty to thirty feet across the storm-tossed sky. It was only going to get worse as we went up. Down below, I could hear Faith and Henry's voices calling out to me.

He kept climbing. I kept going up after him, hissing uselessly at him to stop or at least, for God's sake, slow down. I caught up so I was on the same level as his bare feet, but there still wasn't much I could do physically to stop him.

Avonstoke reached the top of the ladder just as an obscenely powerful wind hit us. He swayed and his foot slipped. He started to swing outward then, his right hand and foot loose. He would have fallen too, if

I hadn't gotten ahold of his pant leg and held on. The two of us and the rope ladder bounced and jerked a hundred feet up from the deck and I nearly lost my own grip. The wind howled and hummed through the rigging, and the cold bit like icy needles. Lightning flashed somewhere nearby, too close, and the booming of a thousand cannons followed. The black storm was all around us now, lashing wet and cold with such a fury into our faces that it felt like the entire sea had risen up against us.

I didn't have enough strength to actually hold him if he fell, but my grip was just enough to keep him from swinging wildly. Yanking insistently, over and over, I finally managed to haul him back into position so that he could get his foot on the rope ladder. I struggled up to a position level with him.

"Justice?" he said, looking over suddenly, his face wildly animated, his eyes very wide. "What, in the gods' names, are we doing all the way up here?"

He looked right at me.

Thunder crashed again, followed by a scream, and a patch of the dark storm fury dropped toward us with wings spread wide and talons reaching.

I shrieked and clutched at Avonstoke for purchase, hooking the elbow of my other arm more securely around the rope ladder, sure dragons were falling out of the sky to try and knock us both off the mast.

Avonstoke's face, looking up at the thing dropping down, wasn't scared at all.

But then, he was a man that probably *yearned* to die by dragon. He'd shown as much reverence for them as he had for the Faerie gods themselves.

But it wasn't a dragon.

It was a bird. A raven. Black as the stormy sky and landing as neatly as you please on the rigging above us.

And Avonstoke was laughing. His face was very close to mine.

"I can see how upset you are with me," he shouted happily. "That little furrow you get in your brow when you think I've gone mad, again.

The set of your jaw, your determination to deal with it, somehow. Head-on, most likely. Your complete disregard for what the wind is doing to your hair underneath that atrocious excuse for a hat."

"I love this hat!" I snapped. "More than I like you, in fact!" Fear was making me angry, but Avonstoke had a way of doing that too.

He grinned at me, meeting my gaze. *Meeting my gaze.* He was, without a doubt, *seeing* me! His gaze was focused on my face and there was a light dancing in his eyes. "Don't you understand? I can *see* these things. I can see!"

I laughed out loud and flung my arm around him again. Perhaps we weren't going to fall to our deaths right this instant. Somehow, Avonstoke could see again.

Even the storm didn't seem so terrible right now.

Then I realized, looking around, that the storm *wasn't* as bad. The thunder had come down to a low rumble and the rain had slackened, while the wind became suddenly, profoundly still.

The storm was receding.

We made our way back down to the main deck much more carefully and slowly than we'd gone up. Avonstoke's raven cawed and leapt off of his shoulder, sailing in a tight circle around us. Avonstoke gasped and gripped the rope in alarm, suddenly helpless.

"What's wrong?" I said. "Is your sight . . ."

"I can see," Avonstoke said mildly, "but it seems to be through *his* eyes." He nodded at the bird circling around us. "Seeing yourself *only* from a distance, while your vantage is in midflight, is just about as disconcerting as you'd think it would be." He spoke as if this were only a thing of light concern. He looked up at the bird. "If you would only do me the pleasure of staying in one place for a moment?"

The raven cawed and landed on the crow's nest.

"Thank you," Avonstoke said, with overwrought politeness. He resumed his descent, his natural agility and confidence seeming to reassert themselves as he went. He made it to the deck in short order.

Faith and Henry met us at the foot of the mainmast.

The raven cawed again and flew down from the crow's nest and landed with surprising grace on Avonstoke's naked shoulder. The two of them looked so comfortably balanced that there was little need for the raven to dig its claws into Avonstoke's shoulder for balance, and it sat easily, with no sign of causing him discomfort.

Faith cast a keen, narrow-eyed look at Avonstoke and the raven.

"Where did he come from?" Henry said.

"My face, actually," Avonstoke supplied helpfully, but Henry just looked confused.

"It seems," Faith said, "that not all of the Faerie gods are against us. Drecovian's shadow magic comes from the Morrigna's horse aspect and he gave you both that raven tattoo and the black fire sword you have. You even lost the tattoo and it came back to you when you needed it most. I find that encouraging."

"The Morrigna's horse side might be helping us *now*," I grumbled, "but I'd trust it a lot more if the other two aspects weren't driving the invasion."

"True," Faith said. "It's the Crow and Crone aspects of the Morrigna that give power to the Black Shuck and the Goblin Knight." The capricious, arbitrary nature of these gods made me want to scream, but she just shrugged.

"Three personalities attached to the same person," I said, "and they're on different sides. Can't even make up their own bloody minds. I just can't shake the feeling that they're constantly trying to manipulate us for their own ends."

Faith shook her head and turned back to me. "The gods have accepted Avonstoke's service. Perhaps they've also decided to accept *your* service on your terms." She gestured around at the suddenly mild winds around us. "After all, Llyr's storm has broken."

"Or he's planning something worse," I said.

"Hmm," Faith said, a noncommittal noise.

"If this Morrigna," Henry mused, "has three aspects, the Crone, the Crow, and the Horse . . . why did the horse send a raven? Wouldn't that be . . . I don't know . . . the Crow's job?"

"You're thinking in straight lines," I said. "But the Faerie don't." I longed to reach out and ruffle his hair the way I'd used to, but that wasn't a thing I could do anymore. Not after what we'd been through and with Henry not entirely trusting me. Not after I'd shot Father.

Henry looked at me and nodded stiffly.

"Captain," Mog said, appearing at my elbow. "Storm is gone, but it not natural. Mog does not like that sky." He pointed.

I turned and looked. I didn't like it either.

A late-afternoon sun burned to the west, showing itself for the first time in days. But an unnatural darkness glowered from the west too. Then the darkness shifted, got closer, and gained definition. It was big and it was coming right for us.

"Oh gods," Avonstoke breathed, and I knew they all saw it too.

Cernunnos and the Wild Hunt.

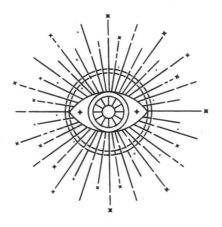

CHAPTER 2

JOSHUA
State of the Occupation

Joshua Kasric, general of the Seelie Vanguard, Counsel to the Seelie Court of New London, grimaced and crushed another ink pen to messy, stained bits. He swore and lifted a cloth off the deck behind him and tried to get some of the ink off his monstrous hands. Wasn't doing much good, that cloth, but he managed to get some of the stickiness off. He stood at the lead-glass window of his office in Dover Castle, rubbing his hand and overlooking the grandeur of the Seelie Army, packed shoulder to shoulder along the slope down to the water.

It was a staggering thing. Companies of Court Faerie cavalry, spearfolk, and archers side by side with battalions of Dwarven foot soldiers. Loose packs of Goblins gathered on the stone fortifications closer to the water. The upper levels of Dover Castle above Joshua were crammed with more Goblins, and far worse: Pix, Kellas Cats, and other monsters.

Past the shimmering heat of the working Dwarven forges, he could see movement in the trenches, the heads and shoulders of some of their larger army members. Trolls, Ogres and other Jötnar filled those trenches, many of them large enough to be seen from Joshua's position, despite the depths of the trench floors relative to the rest of the slope. There were even larger Jötnar back in London: the giants, on construction detail with the Wealdarin, the reality-altering tree folk. There was also the faintest reflection of his own image, a demonic monster in the uniform of a horse guard, a treasure chest of glittering medals on his front.

Craning his neck, careful not to break the window or gouge the wood with his ponderous horns, Joshua could even make out dragon wings in the sky. The huge black one, Brocara, with the Outcasts, had mauled and drowned one of the smaller emeralds, but their new recruit just flown in from Faerie would tip the balance of air power back in their favor, to be certain. How could something that big move so quickly? Joshua took a moment, almost against his will, to watch the deadly, sinister grace of the thing.

The dragons could all be dead if things went badly in the war. Then, the rest of the Faerie would follow. Something about the dragons, footprints of the gods, being the source of all magic.

"More tea, my lord?"

"Fine," Joshua said. He waved vaguely while one of the brownies or sprites or whatever the hell class of Faerie this particular servant belonged to, shuffled over to the large table that dominated the room.

"Not there," Joshua bellowed. "The desk." The table in the center of the room was covered with maps too important to risk tea spills. (Or ink pen accidents, which was why he did his writing at the desk.)

The servant, who was shaggy and stumpy, with bowed legs, a large nose, and not-too-many teeth, not at all bothered or cowed by Joshua's outburst, plodded over to the desk. There, it set out the tea in pale china, which was really just an excuse, because teatime also meant medicine time. There it sat, next to the tea, in a shallow earthen cup.

Joshua growled and shifted his demonic bulk away from the window, clawed feet scraping at the floorboards as he stepped across the room. Ignoring the tea, he picked up the medicine and drained it in one long, nausea-inducing draft. It burned, tasting of scorched anise and oranges left out in the sun too long and God knew what else Mother had concocted in her basement laboratory.

Whatever it was, it caused changes inside of him. He could feel it. It was also, Joshua suspected, slowly killing him.

But it would take years.

He would have years as Mother's pet demonic general, suitable for leading the battle across the channel and into Boulogne. From there, they would no longer be contained in England, and nothing in the modern world could stop them from moving through the continent and then the entire world. If he wasn't killed in battle, he could easily live long enough to see most of the campaign before his transformation killed him. Ironic that. The longer he lived, the more likely it would be that Mother's care would be the death of him. He could live another eight or nine years, perhaps. More than long enough to get through Europe. He just hoped he'd live long enough to see the Americas. Specifically California. Ever since hearing about that grand, wild, unspoiled world, he'd longed to see it. So much untamed land. There was nothing like that kind of solitude on this side of the world. Even Faerie didn't have that to offer.

That was all dependent on breaking the blockade. Justice and the rest of the Outcast Fleet kept them bottled up here in the British Isles. He had to find a way to break this blockade first. Everything else, including California, depended on it.

The servant waited long enough to reclaim the cup from Joshua, making sure he'd taken it all. Obviously under orders from the Black Shuck or Mother. Then he scuttled out. Joshua opened a drawer in the desk, pulled out another ink pen from a lacquered box filled with them, picked up another report, and compared it to his sheets and lists. Then he sighed and dropped pen, report, and notes back onto the desk. He'd already gone over all of it twice this morning.

Mother, Mother, Mother. It all came back to Mother. Mother's discovery of the Faerie world and the horrific violation that it had inflicted on her had been the start of all of this. Or had it? Mother had always longed for more power than she'd had, even with her elevated place in London society. The Faerie world, and magic, had offered her power beyond her wildest dreams. She would use magic to reclaim everything that had been stripped from her. Her husband, Rachek Kasric, her status in society, her health . . . everything.

Only it had gone so much further than that. Their decade-long sojourn into Faerie, a period of time that had only taken weeks in England, had taught both of them a great deal, but Mother had turned the tables on her one-time captor, Lady Westerly, and passed her teacher to become a magician of enormous power. But if Mother's goal had been to free herself from the Faerie, as she'd told him many times, that part clearly hadn't happened. Instead of freeing herself from the addiction to Faerie absinthe, Mother's magic now depended on ingesting it regularly. It sharpened her power and her intellect, but her focus . . . Joshua shook his head. She'd forgotten the important things. Father, England, none of that mattered to Mother as much as her own path to power.

He'd felt all along that they should be driving the Faerie out of London, not leading the occupation.

Justice probably thought she was fighting for England, trying to drive the Faerie out, but she had it all wrong. Fighting alongside the Outcasts, she was just helping one Faerie faction beat the other, and where did England fall? Either victory would be a loss for London. So, Joshua stayed with Mother. He might leave her if there was a purely human fighting force battling against the Faerie. As if such a force would have any chance. But nothing could resist the pure destructive power of the Faerie.

The entire family had been torn apart by this war: Mother and Joshua here in England, fighting for the Faerie; Justice, Faith, and Henry fighting for the Outcasts. Benedict taken by the Wild Hunt. Joshua felt a stab of guilt about his brothers. He'd been part of giving Benedict over to the Wild Hunt. Justice had tried to stop him and failed. She hadn't failed with Henry, however, pulling him out of Newgate Prison. Joshua felt real gratitude toward her for that. He hadn't wanted Henry's death on his conscience too.

He'd also learned a great deal about the Lord of Thorns, the man who had pretended to be his father and then gone on to breed Benedict, Justice, Faith, Henry, and who knew how many other half-bred monsters. And then died when Justice violated the sacred peace of the World Tree and shot her own father in the back.

And what of Joshua's father? The man actually born as Rachek Kasric? Mother had all but forgotten him, but Joshua hadn't.

The man was finally free of the Faerie curse that had trapped him in the Lord of Thorns' body and castle, only no one knew where he'd gone. He'd left Faerie with Justice, but Joshua's scouts had lost track of the man. He wasn't with the Outcast Fleet, as far as they knew. The man might have fled the war altogether. Or he might have somehow infiltrated London, looking for his wife and one actual son, Joshua. But Joshua had combed London and the English countryside, with no sign of Rachek Kasric.

Until a week ago.

A week ago, he'd gotten a report through winding channels and spy networks, that Rachek Kasric was with the Outcast Fleet, on *Seahome*. He hadn't been able to get to London at all. It had cost Joshua a lot of effort to get that information. Now, he just had to find a way to tell Mother without the Black Shuck or Widdershins hearing him. The Faerie kidnapping of Rachek Kasric had led Mother to think he was dead. Theirs had been a rare, passionate love. Getting him back would bring her back to her real family. Father, Mother, Joshua. She'd leave the Black Shuck and forget about the invasion once she found out Father was still alive.

The problem was how to tell her.

The Black Shuck and Widdershins valued Mother's magic and watched her closely. Widdershins would understand the danger of this information at once, which made him very dangerous. Widdershins' mind was a mental threshing machine, casting out and picking up fragmented bits of thoughts and ideas from everyone around him. It drove the average person mad, but Mother had flourished under it, gleaning secrets from Widdershins and anyone unfortunate enough to be around him like a weaver plucking threads.

But also going mad.

Joshua's first step had to be getting Mother away from Widdershins. Then he could tell her about Father. He just needed to keep his own thoughts away from Widdershins in the meantime. Difficult but possible with discipline. But that meant keeping away from Mother too. Until the time was right.

Joshua carefully lifted the teapot lid. His hands weren't suitable for the task anymore. Had his claws gotten longer since yesterday? He thought they had. Tea would be just the thing to make him feel a bit more human and possibly, just possibly, wash the vile taste of the medicine out of his mouth.

He took a deep whiff and nearly choked. It was even worse than the medicine had been. Something had fouled the tea. Badly. He might as well have been drinking hot urine.

With an inhuman snarl, Joshua hurled the pot at the open doorway, where it shattered like a shot, giving him some satisfaction. But the servant was long gone, and the feeling of satisfaction drained away almost instantly.

He shook his ponderous head. Until such time as he could pry Mother from the Faerie, his only safety lay in performing his duties with excellence.

Back to running the invasion.

He looked at the newspapers the servant had brought in with the tea and medicine. He picked up the top one, looking at the headline:

QUEEN VICTORIA DEAD. That was going to be a headache. They'd need to prop up some kind of new monarch to give the remaining population something to hold on to, or else they'd have to kill every remaining human in England. Who would run the newspapers then, to say nothing of the farming, waste disposal, and a hundred other menial tasks? Better to leave at least some of them alive, as long as they understood their place in the new Faerie England.

He took up a piece of foolscap and carefully dipped a pen in ink. Then, even more carefully, he wrote down Father's name and location on it. He set the pen down and regarded the paper with an odd sense of satisfaction and dread. It could get him killed, this slip of paper and the motivations behind it. But it might be possible to just slip it to Mother, when a whispered word would be easily overheard. Maybe that would be the shock she'd need to remind her of what was important, to snap her back.

"Joshua!"

Joshua jumped, not just because only a very few people called him by his given name, but also because the voice, Mother's voice, had barked at him from an unoccupied part of the room, near the fireplace. His claws clattered on the floor even through the carpet, which now had another few gouges in it. He was going to have to have this one replaced soon.

A candelabra on the mantel flared into life, all five flames showing a hazy image of Mother around the edges. This was new, disturbing magic. Mother was getting stronger all the time.

"We are here," Mother's voice said. "There are new plans that will affect the deposition of your troops. You are to come at once."

"Here?" Joshua said stupidly. Not still in London? "Where? Who's we?"

"Down in the tunnels beneath you, of course," Mother said. "Bring the maps. We'll be making the new war room down here."

The candles all flared and went out, leaving a smoldering mess of melted wax and scorched metal on the shelf. Joshua went over and put a clawed finger in the hot wax that dripped off the mantel. Mother wouldn't be using her trick on this particular candelabra again. She could have just used the fireplace, couldn't she, if she needed fire as a landing spot for her new spell? Would she set his desk on fire next time she needed to reach him? Joshua had no idea, and it wouldn't do any good to ask her.

Joshua pounded the desk with a heavy fist, splintering wood and tearing some of his documents and lists. He sighed, the momentary flash of anger already draining away, and smoothed over the torn paper. The Black Shuck and Widdershins' powers of fear and confusion had a lot to do with keeping the Faerie invasion forces from fighting among themselves, but so had Joshua's careful disposition of troops and supplies. The Jötnar and Dwarves bivouacking too closely to each other could cost them as many troops as any enemy attack. Joshua had carefully avoided all but the most random explosions of infighting. No one else seemed to understand how close to the precipice they were. Not even Mother, lately.

He realized that he was still holding the crumpled piece of foolscap in his clenched fist. Carefully, he smoothed it out and tucked it in his coat pocket.

Stifling his indignation, which also wouldn't do him any good, the nominal general of the Faerie Invasion carefully folded up a few of the least important maps from his war table and left his office, heading for the tunnels.

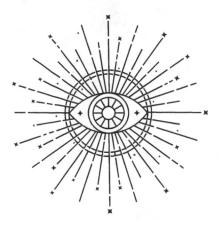

CHAPTER 3

JUSTICE
The Storm Breaks

W e stood on the heaving deck and watched the Wild Hunt come
down out of the storm-tossed sky.

In the far distance, now that the weather had calmed, we could make
out the enormous Faerie raft, *Seahome*, still shimmering with protec-
tive magic. It had probably taken every magician on board to keep the
ungainly floating city from sinking. They were our allies, but even they
wouldn't dare defy the Wild Hunt. Besides, they were too far out to offer
us any assistance.

"Clear for action!" I shouted to Mog.

Mog nodded, his eyes wide as he stared at the sky.

An instant later he bellowed orders in his guttural voice. I didn't
know if the Wild Hunt was a direct danger to us or not. They'd alternately helped us and tried to strike us down in the past. But I'd been thumb-
ing my nose at the Faerie gods for days and now the sight of the most

feral and unpredictable of their number filled me with a sharp, nearly debilitating dread.

"Treachery!" a harsh voice said.

I turned, having almost forgotten about our prisoner.

Down in the vessel's waist, ex-captain Caine, the previous commander of this ship—back when the ship had been the HMS *Rachaela*—stood in shackles.

He was a man beaten by imprisonment but not broken. You could see that. His back was straight and he stood vary tall. But his once-broad frame was thin and wasted, and his clothing and person frayed and dirty. His gray, dirty curls were in disarray, and his beard, also dirty gray, was as long and unkempt as I'd ever seen it. But his robin's-egg blue eyes were hard and unflinching.

"Treachery!" he said again. He'd raised his voice to be heard by everyone on deck. "Treacherous captain on a ship filled with traitors. Your father would weep!"

"Get him below," I snapped, my voice tight. There had been a bit of waver in the command and I could see the people around me notice. They hastened to obey anyway. The shackles clanked as they dragged him back to the hatch that would lead down to the brig. I'd had to assume command, and Caine would have stopped me if he could. Would have killed, stillborn, the only hope England had. I couldn't allow that then, and I couldn't allow that now, but it still pained me to keep a loyal officer in the brig.

Avonstoke was standing next to me now, moving easily with his raven on his shoulder. He always seemed to be doing that. Appearing next to me when I was most upset. He'd been fulfilling the same role to the ship too, since regaining a semblance of sight. We didn't have anything as formal as actual leftenants, but if we had, Avonstoke would have been the clear choice for second leftenant, after Mog. He was already doing the job, and everyone knew it and approved. I also had no question about Mog or Avonstoke getting along.

They already spent time together when the ship's schedule permitted, usually drinking honey wine on the forecastle, a tradition that Mog and Mr. Starling had started, before Mr. Starling's death at the hands of the Goblin Knight.

"Mog," I called. "Roll out the guns. Maximum elevation!"

The Dwarves had modified the gun carriages of our long nines to allow the cannons to fire at anywhere from a zero- to a sixty-degree angle, far greater than other cannons. Of course, there was only so much they could do to support the wooden deck below, so repeated firing would break the deck into pieces all around us, but with enemies that could fly, like dragons, we had to have the option.

Of course I'd told no one, no one at all, that I was also thinking about firing cannons into the Wild Hunt. Dragons were sacred enough to the Faerie, but an actual Faerie god was even more so.

So, I'd expected a murmur of dissent from the crew, or at least some grumbling, at this last order, but was surprised to see them all jumping to the defense of the ship with alacrity.

"Are you really surprised?" Avonstoke said. Apparently, my attempt at a neutral expression needed a little work. He'd had his sight back for all of ten minutes and could see right through me

"What do you mean?" I said.

"Don't you know how they talk about you?" Avonstoke said. He seemed honestly surprised and a little amused. "To them, you are the captain that faces dragons, and they would face that and twice as much under your command. They tell stories down in the gun deck and the mess about your raid into Faerie territory and how you dragged your brother out under the noses of the Faerie powers. They'll do anything for you! You're the captain who rides with the Wild Hunt and thumbs her nose at the gods' will. Who fears nothing!" He looked somehow inordinately proud of me.

I could feel my mouth standing open and hastily shut it, staggered by what he was telling me. "You're not serious?"

"Of course I am," he said. "There's even a ballad, poignant, thrilling, lyrical, and magnificent, that tells of your exploits. *Mighty Ghost-Eyed Justice Sails the Seas.*"

"Mighty Ghost-Eyed Justice?" That couldn't possibly be true. Whoever wrote it clearly hadn't been there when I'd failed to save Benedict. Or when the dragons had nearly sunk us. Or when . . . when any of it happened.

"When I find whatever myopic, addle-brained, misguided, and idiotic nobody wrote the bloody thing . . . Ghost-Eyed Justice indeed!"

"Well." Avonstoke sniffed. "It's a working title. I haven't quite got the three-part harmonies down yet either. But when I do, Faith can sing them all! Won't that be lovely?" His grin grew even larger as he saw my mortified expression.

"You?" This was all too much.

"Justice!" Faith shouted. She was still on the forecastle, looking back at the two of us with exasperation all over her face. She jerked her head in the direction of the Wild Hunt rampaging down out of the sky, which I'd all but forgotten during this ludicrous conversation.

"Ready the upward carronades!" I bellowed. "Loaded with grape! And the upward cannons!" The dwarves, after our encounter with dragons and all other manner of flying beasts, had rigged carriages for the four carronades and another eight of the larger nine-pound cannons, in order to aim them nearly ninety degrees upward, as well as swivel on their mounts. I had small hopes of them being able to fell dragons or any other maneuverable flying threat, for the mechanisms for aiming them moved too slowly for that. In addition, the wider spread of ammunition like grapeshot would have a lesser impact and do little past taking off some dragon scales. A dozen shots would, however, shatter the wooden planks beneath them, despite the additional reinforcements worked out by the ships' Dwarven carpenters.

Also, I had no idea if cannon of any kind would injure Cernunnos himself.

But I'd seen enough during the attack on Newgate prison to know that the riders and beasts of the Wild Hunt could be injured. Grapeshot would be devastating to them.

"Lor!" Henry said. "They're coming right at us!"

"Fire a warning shot, Mr. Mog! As fast as we can aim one well off to starboard, but I want all the elevation you can give me. Show them what we can do."

"Mog is just Mog, Captain," my first mate said promptly. "Not a mister."

"Mog!"

"Yes, Captain." He turned and bellowed commands at Render, the head gunner.

Of course, cannons wouldn't kill them all and nothing would stop the surviving members of the Wild Hunt from dismantling sails and masts in short order. They'd tear the ship to sinking pieces in minutes. Mutual destruction, probably. Ten minutes from now, both the HMS *Specter in the Mist* and the Wild Hunt might actually cease to exist. But I wasn't going to let them tear up my ship without a fight, and I wanted them to know that.

Render had altered the carriage in cunning Dwarven fashion for just this kind of occasion. He now had portside bow chaser aimed precisely at a forty-five-degree angle, which should answer nicely.

"Fire!" I bellowed.

Render echoed the command and the team did their jobs quickly and efficiently. The lighting torch descended and the cannons fired, belching out smoke. The glyphs and sigils glowed on the side. Father's work. The magic that allowed the cannons to penetrate through the Faerie protection against normal weapons.

The shot was well aimed. Impossible to see near the darkness of the Wild Hunt, but the screaming cry of the cannonball hurtling past would alert the entire hunt of its presence.

Cernunnos, leading the hunt, turned away from the cannon shot, angling off to our starboard but still coming. Black, oily, billowing thunderclouds rolled out before the Wild Hunt while crackling lightning lit them from above and below. Flurries of storm crows flew in and out of the storm, screaming fit to wake the dead. As the cloud unfurled in the sky, dozens of bone-white hounds, their ember eyes flashing, their red, red tongues lolling horribly, ran along the advancing edge, always on the verge of outstripping the cloud and falling off, only they never did. The baying of the hounds added mournful notes to the crash of thunder. They weren't coming at us anymore, but circling, which wasn't exactly a comfort.

Behind them came the riders themselves, on steeds the color of soot with red eyes to match those of the hounds. The riders, most of them, were little better than beasts themselves, with pale, naked flesh and wild manes of hair, howling and screaming fit to drown out the crows, the hounds, even the storm itself.

The vanguard of the Wild Hunt, however, was something else.

The leader was Cernunnos, the heart of the Wild Hunt, shaggy but somehow noble and grand for all that. His great, tined antlers cut through the sky as he rode on. Man and beast both, with the body of a massive stag, charging as he led the way.

Behind him rode the two kings, the King with an Eye Patch, holding a wide-bladed spear, and the King with the Sword, bearded face grim. Both the spear and the sword had runes that shimmered in the half-light, seen one moment, then gone the next.

And after that came someone even more familiar.

Benedict, my brother. Or at least he'd been once. Now regal and haughty and inhuman, with his red eyes and cruel, laughing mouth, he was as wild and dangerous as any rider in the Wild Hunt.

"God," Henry breathed next to me. "Look at him! He looks . . ."

"He looks like one of them," I said, my voice rough in my throat. "Taken from us and now given over to them." I'd been nearly paralyzed by fear, but now, seeing my brother brought a hot, angry power welling up inside of me. The anger freed me and I set my feet wide and glared up at them. If I ordered cannon fired into the attacking horde, how likely was I to kill my brother? And yet, I couldn't hesitate if they threatened to fall on us.

Faith was standing on the other side of me. She nodded grimly, still looking at Benedict. "He does. He looks like one of them."

"Damn it to hell!" Henry snarled softly. "It's all my fault too." The Wild Hunt had helped us free Henry from Newgate Prison, but they'd taken Benedict at the same time.

Faith shook her head, still staring upward. She looked a lot calmer than I felt. It was more than a little irritating, this newfound fearless mastery of hers.

"It's not your fault, Henry," she said. "They were going to take Benedict no matter what. Part of Father's transgression. Having them free you was the only good choice we had." She didn't sound bitter about that. Not angry either, the way I was. It was just a statement of fact.

Henry was clenching his hands on the railing, which looked splintered from where he'd treated it too harshly.

"Benedict isn't your fault," I said, glaring at him, "but breaking my ship is."

He swore and let go of the railing.

"Why are they here?" Faith said. "What do they want?" I'd been wondering that myself.

The hatch to below slammed open and Sands struggled up out of it. Clearly he'd been told what was in the sky, because he looked up at once. But telling hadn't prepared him. He gawped in open wonder, and the yellow wisps of his blond mustache and beard quivered.

Then he pointed, one hand outstretched, the other to his face, which was twisted in purest surprise.

"Sands' horse!" Henry said, his own misery and guilt momentarily forgotten in his own surprise. "She's still with them!"

"Acta Santorum," I breathed. Behind me, I could hear Sands do the same.

She's still with them. Henry's exclamation laid a heavy weight of betrayal on me and I closed my eyes, leaning heavily on the railing. I was going to pay for this now, and should pay, because I'd done Sands wrong in the most profound, personal, and hurtful of ways.

Henry and I had ridden on Pavor Nocturnus, my own magical nightmare, with the Wild Hunt on that same terrible and wondrous ride that had ended tragically but had started with Henry's rescue from Newgate Prison. Cernunnos had agreed to ride with the Wild Hunt, through the sky, but there had been rules.

Rules we had broken. I'd seen Acta Santorum then, Sands' steed, a magical artifact attached to Father's chess set, a sister to my own Pavor Nocturnus. Acta Santorum had been lost to Sands when he'd broken his magical bond with Father, shattering his connection to Acta Santorum in the same stroke. Sands had given up magical power and insight, become someone less than he'd been, so that Faith and I could succeed Father and him. Everything he'd gone through and it was our fault. Of all the things he'd lost, I thought that Acta Santorum had been the one he'd missed the most and seeing my chance, I'd been determined to somehow get him back for Sands.

Through my own eagerness to capture her, and through Nocturnus's own rambunctiousness, we'd strayed too far from the hunt and fallen into the sea, almost to our deaths.

And I'd never told Sands the first thing about it.

I'd wanted to, meant to, but he'd been trying so hard to put his loss behind him, and he was so fragile that it had never seemed like a good time to strike him down with the news that we knew where Acta Santorum was. I'd been afraid that he'd obsess about the Wild Hunt, over which we had no control, instead of helping Faith learn her new role as magician. And then, when Brocara the dragon had taken over Faith's magical tutorage, Sands had wavered, then come out of his black depression and thrown himself into his unique spy network, bringing us the only news we had of England under Faerie occupation. I'd needed him to keep his mind in that work and again hadn't mentioned Acta Santorum's whereabouts.

Now, Sands knew. Knew that I'd had information about his deepest yearning and kept it from him.

"She's beautiful," Faith said, bringing me back to the glory in the sky.

And she was. A glittering form in motion with mane and tail trailing like falling stars, shining brighter for all the darkness around her.

◁▷◁▷◁▷◁▷

Faith was still watching the hunt. She'd pushed her hood back, now that the wind and rain had gone, and the sun shone on her bald scalp.

"The gods sent you dreams," she said to me, "and then they sent you storms, both of them designed to press you into their service."

"You'd have me follow them, wouldn't you?" I said. Certainly, Faith had done so. The Wild Hunt was where her magic came from. The other magicians on *Seahome* had started calling her an avatar of Cernunnos. She learned from dragons and other magicians, was almost Faerie herself now.

"No," Faith said evenly. "Clearly, it's not the right path for you."

I blinked in surprise.

She went on. "But the gods sent two coercions, neither of which worked. Now the storm breaks and in the exact same moment, the Wild Hunt comes on us. That's not a coincidence."

"Could Llyr have sent them?"

"Hard to imagine," Faith said. "No one sends Cernunnos. Being wild is his defining characteristic in the stories."

"In the stories," I said, "has anyone ever withstood the Wild Hunt? Beaten it and turned it back?"

"No."

Cernunnos of the Wild Hunt turned. He dropped down another thirty feet so that he ran parallel to the ship's course, his man's torso and stag's body moving with a liquid grace, his hooves gracing the tips of the waves. The Wild Hunt followed in his wake with the ponderous certainty of death.

Then Cernunnos, the Faerie god of the Wild Hunt, did three more things.

The first was that he turned, angling to cross our bow and pass fifty feet off the port side. The second was that as he rode, the God of the Wild Hunt threw back his head and put his horn to his lips. The last was that, as he rode past us, he produced a heavy, wide, curved sword and lifted it in salute as the Wild Hunt thundered past. Following his lead, the two Kings in his wake lifted a wide-bladed spear and a rune-covered sword and shouted in triumph. The entire hunt followed suit, giving a wild ululation as they pounded past.

I saw Avonstoke and Swayle bring their weapons up to return the salute, but most of us, myself included, were too stunned to do the same. Sands had taken off his hat, his wild yellow hair, cut short, plastered wetly on his skull. I had my pistol out, pointed uselessly, but finally managed to sketch a belated salute in return as the last of the Wild Hunt pounded by. Already, Cernunnos was leading them up and away.

Faith was watching them go, looking about as helpless as I felt.

"You ever hear of them doing that before?" I asked.

"Yes," Faith said. She didn't look happy about it. "It's happened in a number of stories." She stopped, reluctant to say more. I thought I understood that reluctance. So many of our stories, our myths, came from imperfect reflections of the Faerie from our past, warped, twisted, mashed, and muddled over time, that it made interpreting the stories a hopeless task.

But when Faith spoke, she didn't sound uncertain at all.

"Some say," she started, her voice heavy with meaning, "that King Arthur saw the Wild Hunt after the Battle of Camlann, just before he passed across the water to Avalon. Others say Wotan, or Odin, will see the Wild Hunt just before Ragnarök, the end of the world. Or has viewed . . . before the end of the last world. It depends on the story. There are some versions of the story where Cernunnos and the Wild Hunt will be part of the world ending."

I thought of the King with the Sword, bearded, with a runed sword that might have been called Excalibur and with what looked like the weight of the world on his shoulders, and the taller King with the Eye Patch and the wide-bladed spear. King Arthur? Odin? Now bound to Cernunnos along with my brother? The ramifications made my head hurt.

The sky brightened and allowed the afternoon light back in. It was starting to make my ghost eye ache.

"It means," Faith went on, "that Cernunnos isn't a puppet to any other Faerie god. He's marked us, and the other gods won't interfere with us again. You've won your face-off with Llyr and the Morrigna. I don't think they'll be sending any more dreams or storms our way."

"Then why don't you look happy?"

"Because it's also a warning," Faith said grimly. "There's still an old debt to be redressed between Cernunnos and Father, and I think this is a reminder of that. Father stole magic from the World Tree, a place sacred to Cernunnos, and Cernunnos decreed that his life would be forfeit to the Wild Hunt. But Father escaped that by leaving the world of Faerie and entering our world, where Cernunnos couldn't reach him. Cernunnos wants that debt paid. One way or another, someone is going to be claimed by the Wild Hunt. Soon. Very soon."

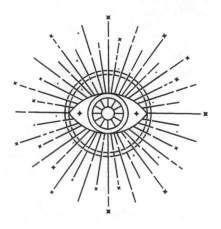

CHAPTER 4

JOSHUA
War Room

A large group of Goblins stood in the hallway outside Joshua's office, but they scattered as he stormed through them. There was no moving quietly with his new shape. He was as much a monster as anyone there. Goat's fur, ram's horns, yellow, burning, vertically-slit eyes, and clawed hands. He was unrecognizable as human anymore, but he had to admit it was a magnificent shape to express anger with. He stomped, inches from crippling one of the slower Goblins, and swiped a long, ragged, but satisfying scar into the stone wall with his bare hands as he passed. A better shape for war, to be sure.

Lesser, smaller monsters scurried out of his path the entire way down to the tunnels.

Once in the tunnels themselves, which were occupied, like all the darkest places of the occupation, by the Hanged Dogs, he took a moment to let his eyes adjust to the darkness. His night vision was better than it had been before, but it was very dark. Dank water smells and the sweet, pungent rotting scents of the dead rolled out from the depths. That made it very clear which Faerie power had been responsible for this profligate display of magical power: the Black Shuck. A clamor of voices came from behind him, up in the castle proper, but no sound at all came from farther below.

A stone arch, carved with unsavory markings that Joshua couldn't read, yawned open, exposing a downward-sloping tunnel. It was very old and no longer man-made the way the tunnels underneath Dover Castle had all been yesterday. The Faerie had reshaped this too, for their purposes. Joshua wondered what had happened to the supplies and creatures that this new tunnel of the Black Shuck's had displaced. Nothing good.

The instant he lumbered into the archway, two of the foul Hanged Dogs materialized out of the shadows. They looked like enormous Irish wolfhounds from a distance, but this close, you couldn't help but see the gray, tattered flesh, bloodless wounds, or the lifelessness in their eyes. Each of them invariably had a noose and three or four feet of old, frayed rope still hanging from their bruised, mangled throats.

Joshua still didn't know the origin of these foul creatures, but Lady Westerly had told Joshua that they'd all been living men or women once, criminals who had been wrongfully hanged. Widdershins had intimated the exact opposite, however, and this Joshua believed: that the Black Shuck, and then the others after him, had been the worst of the criminals. Hanged, yes, but guilty a dozen times over. Wielders of knives in back alleys, highway robbers who reveled in the darkest aspects of their trade, rapists, torturers, poisoners, abusers of children. Just being a robber, harlot, or opium-seller or any other part of the criminal world wasn't enough. Greed, immorality, and lawlessness weren't motivation enough. Malice and a lust for violence had to be there as well. And then they had to be caught and hanged. Something about choking on all that murderous hate.

His drive to understand how the Hanged Dogs were made was simple: a war between himself and the Black Shuck was coming. If not before the conquest of the modern world, then certainly after. He also knew the Black Shuck was making more Hanged Dogs down here. Even now, as the Hanged Dog guards moved silently out of his way, Joshua could make out the distant moaning sound of dungeons. Victims waiting for their transformation.

A small percentage of the British citizenry continued with their lives nominally unchanged. Farmers, milkmen, carpenters, masons, butchers, carriage drivers, even a few of the royalty and politicians. Some of the farmers and tradespeople were actually better off, for their large-scale competitors had gone out of business. Factories ground to a halt and now stood as dark, empty shapes, pools of darkness in the bustling city. Nothing by way of machinery continued.

The factory workers, train conductors, engineers, and machinery people had all disappeared.

Some of them, Joshua had long suspected, had been arrested by the Hanged Dogs, the Black Shuck's agents, and brought here, or to places just like this: dark tunnels or abandoned buildings controlled by the Black Shuck.

And now Joshua passed heavily through a large, vaulted underground chamber that confirmed his theory in the most blatant manner possible, because it held a dozen rough-hewn, squat gallows. The room was empty and none of the Hanged Dogs had followed him, so it fell to Joshua to find his way across the darkened room. He did so slowly.

The wood was stained dark and the place reeked of blood and excrement, which Joshua could also taste on his forked tongue every time he dragged in a foul breath. There was no sound at all except for his own footsteps.

The cluster of black shapes was so closely packed that Joshua had to weave his way through them, searching for a door or passage on the other side. Once, the space between two gallows scaffolds was so narrow that he was forced to clamber over the moldy, splintered wood. Finally, he caught sight of another torch on the far side of the room and got clear of the Black Shuck's death factory with a desperate breath of relief.

Down the next hallway was a flickering spill of light and the murmur of a small crowd.

Just stepping into the room was like stepping into a cold, underwater cemetery where ghosts whispered on all sides. The combined, treacherous effects of the Black Shuck and Widdershins.

The voices, Widdershins' voices, hit him the instant he was in the room.

Death . . . taste of a woman's skin, the scent of her . . . warmth of blood slipping through gloved hands . . . whimpering sounds of a woman dying, dying, slipping slowly away . . .

Joshua forced himself through the doorway with a deep breath, ignoring how his bowels went icy. He focused on the mental exercises Mother had taught him, the chant: *I am me and no one else. I am here now, and nowhere else. I am me and no one else . . .* It didn't help much, but it usually helped a little, if he didn't get too close.

At first, he thought the mental exercises weren't working at all, because of the whispering that echoed all around. He stopped just inside the room. Then he realized that other voices hovering in the shadows, not Widdershins, were actually whispering.

Joshua steeled himself and went the rest of the way into the room.

The powers of Faerie were all waiting for him, gathered around a stone table. Lady Westerly was idly poking a lumpy, bloody smear on her side of the table. A bowl of water, several stained cups, and a cloudy mirror littered the table too, but most of the others were glaring at a wooden chess set in the middle. Fire danced in a pit a short distance behind them. Off to one side, the firelight reflected off the surface of a black, still pool.

"It's a feeble force," the Black Shuck growled. "Pawns and knights, all of them. They can't hold us off forever."

The hulking, macabre presence of the Black Shuck was easily the most terrifying of all of them, a wolf twice as big as any of the undead Hanged Dogs, with ragged holes where his eyes should have been and a puckered scar on his neck.

Widdershins was near the Black Shuck like a gentleman's shadow, with his round glasses, silver-tipped cane, and white gloves shining in the partial light. There was a suggestion of a top hat above the glasses, but the rest of his black suit was nearly invisible, even to Joshua's keen eyes.

"What of this one?" Mother asked.

"We could remove it," Widdershins said in his cultured voice, "but it would cost us several major pieces. More than we can afford."

No one had looked up when Joshua entered the room. The perimeter was filled with a crowd of some sort. It was they who were whispering in the background. The Black Shuck's court, filled with Unseelie and even a few Seelie courtiers, all them keeping well to the shadows near the walls. Joshua caught unsettling glimpses of skeletal faces and gleaming eyes. Talons, tentacles, and hands of all shapes and sizes, most of them holding weapons.

"The maps you wanted, Mother," Joshua said, trying to approach the table obliquely so that he might get close enough to Mother without getting any closer than necessary to Widdershins. It was the long way around and he moved slowly, desperately trying to run through the mental exercises—old folk tunes, mathematical tables, other silent recitations—to try and occupy his mind.

"Maps!" the Goblin Knight, the closest to Joshua, snarled. Joshua hadn't gotten more than halfway around the table before the Goblin grabbed them out of Joshua's hands. "Maps stupid!"

The maps fell onto the table near Lady Westerly, fluttering half open so that they landed in both the bloody mess and the bowl of water. Westerly hissed like a stoat at the both of them and dealt the stone table a surprisingly powerful blow with her small, elderly fist. She clawed the maps out of the way, letting them fall carelessly, dripping, to the floor.

Joshua stopped, more relieved than anything, since this gave him the excuse he needed to avoid getting any closer.

Mother frowned at the stained, ruined maps, then made a slight moue of distaste at Joshua, perhaps in commiseration. Then she shrugged and went back to looking at the chess set.

"As if maps could help win a war!" Widdershins tittered. "What a quaint notion!" He leaned close to Mother, far too close, in fact, his hands brushing hers on the table.

Joshua felt a rising wall of red rage at the sight, only to be replaced, in a whirlwind rush, by a sickening fear that Widdershins might have picked up Joshua's thoughts.

Widdershins did, in fact, lift his head suddenly and regard Joshua with those gleaming lenses behind which only darkness and danger and shadow lurked. The sinister gentleman chuckled, amused, then went back to the board. An amused murmur ran through the shadowy figures of the court too.

Joshua took a few careful steps back, hoping it looked more like respect than fear. He could feel just that small distance ease the constant, cold, oily assault on his mind.

Then he took in the board, which wasn't set up like any board he'd ever seen before.

For starters, the board wasn't even square, but an irregular parallelogram that Joshua realized, after a moment, was an imprecise coastline of England, the English Channel, and the northern coastland of France, all overlaid with black and white squares like a chessboard. The pieces seemed to be from several different, unmatched sets. One long line of black knights, pawns, and the occasional stronger piece sat in the water. White pieces were arrayed, a great many of them, on the English side, greatly outnumbering the black side. But then, if this reflected reality at all, the problem was the water more than anything. It was no good having superior forces that needed to cross the English Channel when most of them couldn't so much as tread water.

"Where is he?" The Goblin Knight growled. His voice, with its broken English, sounded fierce, but there was a note of fearful agitation in it. Joshua could feel the waves of fear, revulsion, and confusion that rolled out from the combined presence of the Black Shuck and Widdershins, and the resulting clench of fear throughout his entire body. The Goblin Knight, despite his fearsome bone mask and smoking club of power, was clearly feeling these things too.

"Soon," Widdershins said mildly. The Black Shuck didn't answer but continued to stare at the board with a growl of frustration.

Mother was still standing too close to Widdershins, which was conspicuous, when everyone else was trying to keep a healthy distance between themselves and both the Black Shuck and Widdershins to avoid the worst of the Shuck's fear effect, as well as Widdershins' projected aura and scattered thoughts. The combined effect of these two, like flame and gasoline, was what kept the Seelie Vanguard too cowed and enslaved to start bickering among themselves. That and the possibility of Widdershins picking up any thoughts of betrayal from those around him. No one in their right mind purposely exposed themselves to the full force of that.

Except that's exactly what Mother was doing. She was close, far too close, to Widdershins' side. Almost familiar. That made Joshua more nauseated than all the rest put together.

Westerly looked haggard, drawn, and ancient beyond reckoning. Her corruption of Lady Martine Kasric, now Martine Scarsdon, Mother, had been her crowning achievement and a terrible blow against England, but she'd made herself a terrible rival, and Joshua knew that Mother had secretly employed enough poison and circuitous curses against her old nurse to sink a battleship. But the old enchantress endured . . . for now.

The Black Shuck, Widdershins, the Goblin Knight, and Lady Westerly were four of the Faerie Sins, arrayed symbolically against England's Virtues. It was a curious thing, but even responding to Virtues with Sins seemed like it should have been an anathema to the Faerie, a concession to human religion. When the Faerie had been driven out of England, modernization as much as human religion had been responsible. But England had raised Virtues, and so the Faerie responded with Sins. The symbols caught the imagination and attention of the Faerie gods, and so they fought with symbols, like duelists choosing pistols or blades at dawn.

The fifth Sin in the room was John Brown. He looked, in comparison to the others, so staggeringly normal as to be laughably out of place in this company. That is, if you didn't notice the dark, saffron-spotted salamander on his shoulder, or the fanged pix leering out of his waistcoat pocket. He'd been the one to prepare things the most for the invasion, neatly counter-stepping the Lord of Thorns and the Outcast defenses, and also infiltrating the British government for decades, undetected by anyone. He wore his trophy of such in the open now, a broken fragment of Queen Victoria's diamond crown, crowing his direct involvement in the death of England's monarch.

There had been two more, of course: Victoria Rose and the Soho Shark. But Justice had shot both of them. Joshua had, in fact, put his axe into the Shark's back, giving Justice her opening, a fact he needed to keep out of his thoughts if he wanted to keep sucking air. He took another automatic step backward, but it didn't matter. Everyone, including Widdershins, had forgotten all about him. He carefully pulled the scrap of foolscap out of his uniform coat pocket, still looking for a chance to get Mother alone long enough to slip it to her.

Why were they all gathered, and why here? Until now, the lot of them had been more intent on finding two more Faerie powerful and dangerous enough to replace the Soho Shark and Victoria Rose, leaving all the management of their forces to Joshua.

"He's here," Widdershins said. The shadowy court voices rose slightly in expectation, though still remaining inaudible.

"And so," a cultured voice said, "it came to pass, on a cold November night in the heart of England, that the Emissary of Lughus, last of the sacred Formori, came into their presence to carry the vengeance of Lughus on to those that so richly deserved it."

The voice echoed around the room, amplified somehow. Most of them jumped, startled by the suddenness of it, despite Widdershins' announcement. Joshua felt his claws flex and his teeth bare in a reflexive snarl. The Goblin Knight brandished his smoking club. Only the Black Shuck and Widdershins kept their composure.

"For lo," the voice, still unseen, continued, "the mighty god Lughus was profoundly wroth for the transgressions that had been heaped on his blessed people, and so, onto his own divine person. Lughus had held to his sacred vow to take no part in the affairs of either the mortal or Fey worlds, but the callous slaughter of his blessed people has tipped his hand."

The voice was coming from the pool.

A shape stepped from the flames, slender, of average height, with a cloak and a staff. The shape was clear, as the flames cascaded off the body and guttered out, but not at all human. A crocodile's face with dun-colored goat's fur all over, reptilian eyes, and a mouthful of predator's teeth. Clawed hands clutched the staff of bone, and clawed, unshod feet scraped the dirt floor.

A Formori, like the Soho Shark, which Joshua had thought was the last of his kind. Clearly not so. The newcomer was not the behemoth that the Soho Shark had been, but there was no doubting his nature.

"The crafts of the sea are the province of two gods," the Formori went on, "Llyr of the Sea and Lughus, Master of the Twenty Sacred Crafts. But Lughus had forsworn, at the urging of Llyr and the other gods, retribution on the world that had cast the Faerie out, so the lore and crafts at his disposal—shipbuilding, for instance—were not at the invaders' disposal.

"And so . . ." The Formori waved a clawed hand, palm up, in a gesture of theatrical oration. "The cult of traitors led by that sordid by-blow of a traitor's seed, Justice Kasric, was able to keep the invasion contained on the group of isles from which most of the Faerie spawned. With the ability to cross the channel now in their grasp, and the final of their Seven Sins gathering in this, the place of their power, the fate of the world would now be changed forever."

This all came back to the Faerie gods, Joshua knew. It was said, among magicians, that dragons had been the first intercession of the gods, and that the second had been prophecies. Prophecies like the Seven Virtues versus the Seven Sins. Through prophecies like this one, the gods had voices. That is, if you didn't count the Wild Hunt. Joshua crept around the edge of the chamber, still holding the scrap of paper in his clawed grip.

The Formori continued. "And lo, the Artificer of Lughus came into their midst, his grand personage ready to crush all that stood before them."

Lady Westerly sneered and audibly scoffed. The old crone's eyes blazed a livid, viscous green, and she opened her mouth to say more, but the Black Shuck growled low and she closed it without making a further sound.

"What about the Formori god?" John Brown muttered darkly. "Will Lughus give us its support?"

Urguag's answer was a toothy smile. "He will. Now that we are seven, none will stand before us."

"Excuse me," John Brown said carefully, looking at the Black Shuck, "with all due respect, perhaps I've missed something. We only have six Sins, counting our new pontificating friend."

And here, something clicked in Joshua's head that really, really should have clicked long before this. Mother's reckless pursuit of revenge and ambition, and her soaring magical powers. Her inclusion in this company, not to mention her unsettling chumminess with Widdershins. The slip of paper with Father's name and location on it was in his clenched fist now, crumpled into a hard ball.

"Tut, tut," Widdershins said. "You've deduced our lovely surprise." He nodded, lenses gleaming, at Lady Westerly.

Lady Westerly hesitated just a fraction of a second too long, her jaw clenched, and the Black Shuck started growling, very low and deep in his chest.

"The Lady Martine Scarsdon, formerly Martine Kasric," Lady Westerly intoned quickly, "newly blessed champion of the Morrigna's Crow and Crone aspects." The "formerly Kasric" part had probably been meant to be a not-too-subtle insult, perhaps the "new" part too. Westerly obviously didn't like sharing her status of power, but no one seemed to care. Westerly bowed her head low. "Welcome, sister." That muscle in her jaw was twitching so it looked ready to snap and fly across the room.

"Much appreciative thanks," Mother said sweetly. The court applauded raucously around them.

"London will also need a king and queen," the Black Shuck said, cutting effortlessly through the noise. "I can think of none better than the two standing before me."

"You do us honor, my lord," Widdershins said.

"It is a paltry thing," the Black Shuck said, "of little consequence compared to being one of the Seven Sins in our blessed war, but important, nonetheless. We shall hold the marriage ceremony and the coronation together the day after tomorrow."

Then Mother and Widdershins were kneeling in front of the Black Shuck to receive his benediction and blessing, renewing their fealty to him in preparation for their new roles. Two days. The words kept rolling around in Joshua's head. *Two days.*

When they rose, Joshua realized, to his pure and unadulterated horror, that Mother and Widdershins were holding goddamn hands like the betrothed couple they now were.

Joshua had gotten, in his maneuvering, very close to the pool of black water, so when he dropped the slip of paper, it fell into the water and slowly, quietly, disappeared from sight.

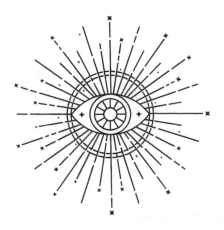

CHAPTER 5

LORD OF THORNS
Gloaming Hall

The wind groaned outside, audible even over the roaring fire in the hearth. The room was stiflingly hot but had nearly every comfort and overwrought luxury that this corner of Faerie had to offer: thick, sumptuous rugs running through with colors of gold, walnut, and blazing saffron, glorious tapestries that shimmered a tableau of moonlit woods, and a bed carved of thick, ornate cherrywood, worked with almost identifiable figures that danced when you weren't looking straight at them. A table, also of cherrywood, stood laden with fruit and roast chicken enough for three or four. The dishes were glazed pottery crafted to look like moving water. The utensils were made of copper and probably danced or wove baskets when you told them to. Three large, overstuffed chairs lay scattered around the room, all positioned to face the bed so that visitors could, presumably, watch him while he slept.

What the room didn't have, it seemed, was a way out.

No door, no windows. There was no feeling of magic from the fire, so someone had to be feeding it. There must be an exit somewhere.

Lessard du Thorns, who had been the Lord of Thorns for eons, and then, more recently, Rachek Kasric, lay in bed.

He'd been sick, no, injured, for a very long time and was just coming back to himself. He'd also been a father to a number of extraordinary children, perhaps still was, if they were still alive. First Temperance, Hope, and Charity here in Faerie with the Lady Dierwyn, his wife. Then he'd left Faerie and fathered Prudence, Benedict, Faith, Justice, and Henry with Lady Martine Kasric. He had been a powerful influence setting enormous forces in motion, the outcome of which he still didn't know.

But his children were going to be caught up in the churn of war. Trapped as he was in this place, he was in no position to assist in the war that would destroy not only the human world but also allow the Black Shuck to continue his campaign back into Faerie worlds.

The Lord of Thorns didn't know this room, but he knew where he was. Who else would the Seelie Court trust his imprisonment to but Lady Dierwyn, his dear, devoted wife? But they didn't call her that now, did they? The Lady of Sorrows. His mind skittered away from the guilt—deserved guilt, he knew—that lay behind that title. Startling how easy that was, actually, in his Faerie shape.

How long had he been here? How was time flowing here compared to England? That last would depend, he knew. It fluctuated, like so much here in Faerie.

He could feel himself thinking more clearly than he had in some time. She'd been shrouding his mind. He could feel that now. Easy enough while he was wounded. But somehow, he'd recovered enough to break free.

He sat up carefully in his bed, but not carefully enough. The motion ground the bullet still lodged in his back against some part of his spine, causing shooting pain to lance through him. He cried out, even braced for the pain as he was, and flopped heavily and helplessly to the floor. The rugs weren't as soft when you hit them face first.

He lay there, twitching and whimpering as convulsions and waves of pain went through him. It felt like someone pulling strips of flesh slowly from his back. His antlers and horns tore the carpet into strips, and near the end of his seizure, he vomited onto the entire mess. It was a good ten solid minutes before the pain receded and he could climb to his feet.

He stood, leaning on the bed, trying to regain his breath. His right hand, large and heavily clawed, probed tentatively and awkwardly near the center of his back, where the bullet was. He propped himself up with the left hand on the bed. That hand, far, far larger, had claws large enough to disembowel a horse in one swipe. He was a hulking monster again, half again as tall as a man and six times the weight. Careful fingers reminded him of a face like a wooden mask, heavy beard, a crown of thorns around his brow, and sweeping antlers spread wide above that.

He remembered with a pang how pleasing the ease and symmetry of a human body had been and a wall of depression loomed up from deep inside of him. He pushed it down.

The pain in his back was gone now, as if it had never been. He couldn't even feel the bullet, but he knew it was there. Exactly what motion had set his back on fire? No idea.

Another realization dawned slowly, as he came back to himself. He'd made noise, a great deal of it just now, but no one had come. He'd been watched carefully and now he wasn't being watched at all. Something had happened. Something had distracted the Lady Dierwyn du Thorns and the rest of his wardens. But what? How long would that last? That last thought overcame his caution and he started moving.

First, he stripped off his bedclothes and used them to wipe the sick from his beard and fur. All the time he moved, he kept expecting the pain from the bullet in his back to come back, but that didn't happen. He probed with his smaller right hand and still couldn't feel any kind of wound at all. Did they leave the bullet in on purpose? No. The bullet was crafted from silver and black iron, with spells and sigils to thwart even the most powerful magic. So, they'd undoubtedly healed him as best they could. But removing it would be impossible for the Faerie. He should know. He'd crafted it. He'd just never expected to be the one shot with it.

He discarded the soiled bedclothes on the floor.

Finding the hidden door was easy when he thought to look for it. It was hidden both by a glamour of a bookcase and, behind it, a heavy tapestry with the obligatory hunting tableau worked into it. It would have been far harder to find if they'd just used one or the other. He waved away the gossamer bookcase glamour and ripped the tapestry down with one quick yank.

The door was locked, both physically and magically. He squinted, examining the telltale dark shimmer. He was sufficiently recovered to deal with this kind of magic too, but this was sturdier stuff and Dierwyn would be able to feel it miles away. He flexed his back, which still felt fine, then his huge right hand, which was six or seven times the size of his left. He needed to test the wound in his back, to know the limits of his movement and what might set off another flash of pain, and this was as good a time as any to find that out.

The masonry next to the door was solid but old and shifted with the first blow. Amazingly, there was no pain from the bullet. He couldn't even feel it. Three more blows and still no pain, but the chunk of masonry had shifted enough to be pulled free, his clawed hand digging into dry, crumbling gray mortar and white stone fragments. Five more minutes, and he'd cleared a hole large enough to squeeze through. He was out.

Fog rolled down the silent stone corridors, dreary but normal for Gloaming Hall. Probably part of why he'd loved London so much. Behind him, the sight of the door, unmoved and with the shimmering wards still pristine right next to the rough, crude hole in the wall, forced out of him a dark chuckle.

He didn't recognize this part of the castle. The room next to his held some clothes in a plain, uncarved wardrobe. There was a rough tunic made for someone smaller, as well as leggings, several belts, and assorted small clothes. He put the tunic on, tearing it a bit to make it fit, and cinched it with a leather belt he found, ignoring the rest. There was a sword too. More like a large knife to him, but he picked it up with his left hand and tucked it into his belt.

When he turned around, his wife was standing in the doorway.

She was as tall as he was, but willow thin and hard. Her midnight skin and ivory hair gleamed, even in this uncertain light. Her dress lay short enough that he could see her legs, furred and backward bending like a beast's. She had a grace and monstrous beauty to her, but he also found her wild and strange after so many years in London. Her eyes, most of all, were remorseless and unsettling, even through the black mourning veil she still wore.

She'd always been in mourning, he realized, even before he'd left, but he couldn't remember why. He found that he could no longer remember their actual wedding either; it had been so many lifetimes and eons ago. But his memory of their life together was still vivid. Lord and Lady of Gloaming Hall and all the duties. Duty to his land, duty to his people. So many tasks and rituals and audiences and politics, all of it so pointless. A tedious, endless, trap he couldn't bear to go back to. Besides, he had a more pressing obligation calling to him.

"You're leaving," she said. It wasn't a question.

"Yes," he said.

"Why?" she said bitterly. "No, wait." She held up a thin, overarticulated brown hand. "I find that I actually don't care why anymore."

"I wouldn't want you to have to take off the veil," he said, and regretted it at once. None of this was her fault. But he also knew that he'd never make her understand.

He had been one thing. Static, lifeless, caught forever in the trappings of Faerie. Then he'd taken on the shape of Rachek Kasric, a seemingly whimsical action that had changed his life forever. Shape changing was a slippery business. Once you'd lived so long in one shape, you were never really rid of it. He could feel human thoughts, ideas, feelings, roiling deep inside his Faerie skull. They wouldn't have, couldn't have, expression here. He'd have to go back to feel that part of himself again.

"Your duties are here, my lord," she said, echoing his own thoughts. "Not in some foreign, human world."

"No one," he said sadly, "will suffer here at my absence. Not in any way that really matters. Not even you. Especially not you."

"What about our children?" she asked. "Hope and Charity have been watching you, as I have."

"Imprisoning me, you mean," he snapped. "Shrouding me to keep me unconscious."

"Only until all this is over," she said. "You make poor decisions when we allow you. No longer."

The Lord of Thorns sighed. Hope and Charity had never forgiven him for abandoning them, and still held to that grudge as only Faerie could. He had hoped, before coming back here, that Rachek Kasric might have taught them something of the lessons that humanity could teach the Faerie, while he was here, but they had barely spoken to him all those years.

Now things would get worse. The invasion, the conquering and remaking of England into a Faerie nation, if it wasn't already. Justice, Faith, Prudence, Henry, Benedict, all of his children in the human world would be killed if he didn't help them.

All of his children . . . Something tickled at the back of his memory. He'd meant to create all of the Seven Virtues, his main defense for England, to be seven powerful symbols. Female, because most of the truly terrifying magical beings in Faerie history had been female, though perhaps that hadn't been necessary. The Seven Virtues worshipped in England: Justice, Faith, Prudence were all in danger in the human world. Hope and Charity were here.

He looked at the Lady Dierwyn, barring his way.

"Have you not heard from Temperance in all these years?" he asked.

The Lady jerked as if slapped, then spat. "We do not speak her name here."

No, they hadn't.

Not since she'd left her and denounced them all. But he had kept track of her travels. Until the last few years, when, horribly, he'd lost her. She still had to be found, but he no longer had time to search for her. He would just have to hope.

"I suffer," the lady said, breaking into his thoughts. "When you are not here."

He shook his great, shaggy head, his massive antlers swaying. He had much to answer for, but this woman and this place was the least of them.

"Your pride suffers," he said, "and not very much at that. We play at emotions here, but they're theater, long, drawn-out dramas that go on for ages. Not the real thing. You can't know the difference until you've tasted it."

She opened her mouth to make the scripted, tedious retort, but he moved suddenly, reaching out and grabbing her with his left hand. He moved fast, for all his bulk.

"Your mourning attire," he said. "The black. Do you even remember who you mourn for?"

Her eyes had gotten wide. He'd surprised her, frightened her. He regretted that, a little, but it made her seem more human for an instant. Maybe he could reach her, make her understand.

"I grieve for my father and brothers," she said automatically, "dead these long years, butchered at the Battle of Regalash."

"Yes," he said. "But what were their names?"

She looked confused.

"What color was your father's hair?" he insisted, shaking her. The violent motion had brought her face within inches of his, a more intimate posture than he remembered being with her in memory's lifetime.

"His eyes?" the Lord of Thorns pressed. "Was he tender? Cruel? What was he like? What about your brothers? How many were there?"

"Three," she said, but sounded uncertain.

"What were their names?"

He could see by her face that she didn't remember.

"You hold to the grief," he said, "but you've forgotten who and why. I can't go back to that kind of existence. Especially when there are truly important things happening. Don't you see?"

But the dark eyes and hard expression were back. "Unhand me," she said.

The moment when he thought he might reach her had passed. Perhaps it had never been. He let her go.

"I could kill you," she said haughtily. She had magical powers of her own. She was a lady and a significant power in Faerie. Spells of dark, moonlit woods and blood.

"You could," he agreed. "But I'm awake now and come back into my powers enough to fight back. You'll have to kill me to stop me." He tried to measure her expression, predict if she would strike him down or not. Who knew this woman's thoughts? Certainly not him. It didn't really matter. There was no going back to that sickroom for him, and they both knew it.

"The Seelie and Unseelie Courts have minions watching the border," she said. "You've no hope of breaking through."

"I have to try," he said. "There are people depending on me."

She let loose with a bitter, fragile laugh. "Everyone in the human world thinks you are dead. Yes, even your poor daughters trying to lead a failed defense against the Faerie occupation."

He could feel himself sag in place at that news, and he saw the exultant glee in her eyes. She'd hurt and rocked him with that news and she knew it.

He forced himself to stand up straighter, shoulder the extra burdens. It was fair, with all the burdens he'd asked others to bear for him. So be it.

He pushed her gently aside and moved past her.

"They'll kill you," she hissed. "You know that. Only my promise to keep you prisoner persuaded the courts that you should be allowed to live."

Another burden, that. He took it with all the rest.

He kept going. She didn't try to stop him.

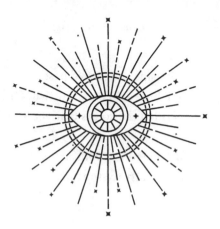

CHAPTER 6

JUSTICE
Rue and Revelations

Beneath the main deck on the *Specter* lay the gun deck, like on most ships. Being the smallest ship with three masts, the *Specter* had only one gun deck, so the deck below that, the orlop, held the slew of rooms and miscellaneous compartments needed on board, the most unusual of these being the makeshift pen where we kept Pavor Nocturnus.

My nightmare, or so Henry called her. Another gift from Father, she was a demon summoned from a wooden horse chess piece. One of the same pieces that belonged to the chess set in my cabin, in fact.

Nocturnus nickered at me softly, a sound barely audible over the crash and bang of the storm outside. I made my way over in near darkness, lurching from beam to beam as the ship slewed wildly. I lit a lantern and hung it from one of the rafters.

"Hey girl," I said, nuzzling her face. She blew out, her breath warm, earthy, and normal in a barnyard comfort sort of way as she pranced happily in her stall. When I put a hand on her warm face and neck, she leaned into my touch, almost knocking me over.

"Easy, girl," I said, laughing softly. Her eyes danced merrily.

Keeping Nocturnus in these quarters was a decision few of the crew understood, though they didn't seem to mind caring for her, since they all knew I could summon and unsummon her at will. Why bother to stable a horse, especially on a ship, when you could use magic to make her disappear at will? But shape changing was a tricky business, as Father demonstrated, and I was convinced that staying here was profoundly beneficial to her. Taking the shape of something also brought with it the properties of that thing. The longer you stayed in a new shape, the more of yourself you began to lose as you became that thing, a change that went far more than skin deep. This was something Father had had to suffer, losing his Faerie powers as he stayed human year after year.

With Pavor Nocturnus, however, it was a blessing. Neither Sands nor any of the magicians could tell me what kind of demon Nocturnus was, but it had multiple shapes and a murderous disposition. One of those shapes had almost killed Henry and me after we'd all fallen in the water. Probably whatever pocket of Faerie she returned to, in her demon shape, was absolutely horrible. So I didn't send her.

She was a horse here and clearly enjoyed it. Three months ago, she'd seemed only half alive in this stall. She hadn't slept, merely stood stock-still, even with the motion of the ship. Like a statue. But now, having kept her horse form for three months, she moved like a living horse. I'd even found her sleeping—and snoring! Her affection grew each day. She ate happily, though I got the impression it was more from pleasure than need. Her eyes looked more and more alive each day. But you could still bend a pitchfork tine on her skin without leaving a mark on her, and I had the sneaking hunch that her phenomenal strength and endurance were undiminished.

I only wished I had a better place to keep her in than belowdecks on a ship, one that wasn't so constrained. Dropping her into the water would be disastrous for everyone, and we were on a ship at sea. At war. Sometimes, ships sank in war.

"She likes you, my captain," Avonstoke said from behind me. "You have a way with them." He moved forward. The deck had a low ceiling, so that a normal person his height would be forever cracking their skull on the rafters, but Avonstoke had a way of gracefully avoiding them without seeming to.

"With demons?" I said, feeling a smile curl my lips despite my pensive mood. Avonstoke seemed to have that effect on me.

"With everyone," he said, moving closer. When I had time to think about it, fear that he, or anyone else, would look closely and see me for an imposter always seized me. Nepotism and luck had gotten me this far, and any instant, everyone would see it and things would come crashing down around my ears. But his admiration shone on his face and I could not doubt it.

Then Avonstoke was in my arms. His hot mouth met mine. His hands buried themselves in my loose hair and my own went to his back, crushing my body to his.

"All the ship," he breathed into my mouth. "They respond to you. We . . . respond to you."

The bird on his shoulder, always with him now, made a soft noise and we could hear movement in the next room. Avonstoke disengaged himself with a wry smile that had something of an apology in it, even though he was taking care to avoid public displays of affection only on my account.

The footsteps went on past, some member of the crew on one errand or another. But the reminder of people nearby and some stubborn scrap of the proper dignity that every captain or admiral needed to cultivate wormed their way between us, and the moment was past.

Avonstoke turned and made a small adjustment to the lantern, just keeping his hands busy. Funny thing, the blind man adjusting the light. His raven fluttered slightly on his shoulder. His eyes, strange and

Faerie and golden, looked a little different now than they had. Before he'd lost his sight, you could always tell what he was looking at or thinking about, even though the surfaces of his eyes were featureless. Something about the edges of the eyes, the tiny expressions of his face. They hadn't seemed expressionless, those eyes. Then he'd lost his sight and you could tell that too, just by looking at the blank expression, even though his actual eyes hadn't looked any different.

Now, though still blind, he could see the world through his raven's eyes, and his expressions were something between blind and not blind. He noticed and paid attention to things, saw them, but there was a slightly distant expression to his face when he looked carefully at something. Of course he was still beautiful, and that mercurial mind still moved through thoughts and ideas faster than anyone's, all of which crossed his face, so that reading his thoughts on his expressive face wasn't the difficult part, but rather parsing out the flashes of fifteen different thoughts, emotions, and ideas that passed in a remarkably short time.

Now he reached out and let Nocturnus nuzzle his hand. Once she was satisfied, he pet her nose softly. "Don't trust the gods," he murmured. "Only their gifts."

"What?" I said.

"Something a court philosopher said between meals of people stew. Terrible person, by all accounts, but a brilliant writer. He was talking about a gift given to him from Morrigna, the triple-faced goddess."

"Triple-faced goddess," I said. "That's a great title for building trust."

"It means all her statues and paintings cost three times as much," Avonstoke said helpfully. "Three faces. Drives artists mad."

"I know what *triple-faced* means," I snapped.

"But think of the legend to be made if you can navigate this storm," he said. "Justice Kasric. She'll be the stuff of legend. I think *Mighty Ghost-Eyed Justice Sails the Seas* might only be one of many ballads written about her. I'll have to write at least one other."

"How many miles can you swim?" I asked darkly, but he just laughed.

A second later, footsteps scuffed the deck behind him, and Faith and Henry rushed in. Henry had a drawn cutlass in one hand and a lantern in the other, his face very pale. Faith, behind him, looked nearly as terrified, which, in turn, frightened me.

"You're all right," Faith said breathlessly.

"Yes," I said. "Why? What happened?"

"Bad dream," Henry sputtered. "Horrible dream. You, drowning one deck down. Right here. There was water everywhere and Nocturnus screaming and . . ." He looked around, his eyes wide with fear.

"A vision, I think," Faith said, frowning. "I had the same dream, at the same time. I'm still not sure how. I thought you were . . ." She took a deep breath. "I thought you were in terrible, hideous danger."

"Hideous," Avonstoke said, his eyebrows lifting. "Really?"

Faith shot him a withering glance. "Not from you, idiot."

Avonstoke opened his mouth to respond, but never got the words out, because then a voice in the darkness said, "Good. You're all here."

I yanked my pistol from its holster. Avonstoke was suddenly between me and the voice, almost by instinct. Nocturnus reared up slightly and pounded on the stall, shaking the deck underneath us.

The corner the voice had spoken from was still in the dark, which didn't make much sense with two lanterns going. Avonstoke pulled the lantern down and moved closer, but still the corner lay swathed in darkness.

"Assassins," the voice said dryly, "would hardly announce their presence before they strike. There is no need for weapons."

The unnatural darkness seemed to ooze away, like syrup through a sieve, revealing a figure sitting in the corner.

"How did you get in here?" I said.

She was sitting in a chair of dark wood and silver inlay, a chair that had no business being there. She wore the silver mask on the upper part of her face, like always, with her cruel, red mouth uncovered below it. She was dressed sumptuously in layered robes, vivid silks of crimson and sable. Her black, silky hair was up in the crown of spikes she always wore, dripping with jewels, most of them valuable enough to buy the *Specter,* or any other ship, ten times over. She looked regal and unimaginably wealthy and glamorous. As out of place in the rough cabin as a sapphire dropped into a bucket full of entrails.

The Lady Rue leaned forward. "Not an assassin. An ally, in fact. A friend."

"Friends don't jump out at you in the dark," I said.

She made a rueful grimace. "Perhaps there's truth in that. I apologize, but I had need of secrecy."

The retort I had ready died in my throat. I could feel my eyebrows shoot up at that. I couldn't remember the Lady Rue ever apologizing. For anything, to anyone, let alone me. She was also looking pointedly at my drawn pistol. Her expression held no fear, only exasperation.

"Secrecy?" I said. "For what?" But I put the pistol away.

"That message," Faith said, her voice still shaken. "That . . . image you sent me. That wasn't real? It was just a way of getting me here?"

The Lady Rue shrugged as if it were of no consequence. "I would hold council with you. Close the door. I have a great deal to tell you."

The door, as it were, was a sailcloth curtain strung between two bulkheads. There wasn't much to close. Henry twitched the cloth shut and shrugged. Faith's expression hardened and she took a step forward. She looked ready to chew nails and murder children, or at least murder a Faerie noble. Lady Rue didn't even notice.

"Now then," the lady began.

"Wait," I said.

"Wait?" The lady's voice was incredulous.

I turned to Henry. "Send word for Sands."

The lady's voice was icy. "The exiled magician?" She spoke about him as if he were something you'd scrape off your shoe. "Very well."

"I might," I said sweetly, "need his advice regarding throwing you overboard later, if you don't have an absolutely brilliant reason for these shenanigans."

Lady Rue stared incredulously at me for a long few seconds, her mask, of course, blank, and then she burst out in a peal of laughter.

"You never disappoint," she said with a delighted chuckle. "Very well. Send for the soiled and broken-down magician."

I looked at Henry and he nodded and slipped out of the room.

There was an odd moment of silence while the Lady Rue and I regarded each other, she still seated in her ornate chair, me standing. Faith moved closer to my side. Avonstoke relaxed slightly and moved out of the center of the room, his eyes never leaving the Faerie noblewoman. The silence stretched out. We could hear the sloshing of the ocean waves against the hull, feel the always-present corkscrew rocking motion of the ship.

"It's impressive," Lady Rue said, seemingly just for something to say. She gestured around. "Your ship. Your enchanted steed. You should be proud."

I blinked. Was Lady Rue making chit chat?

"Um," I said slowly. "Thanks?"

"And that scent," she said, sniffing delicately. "Delightful. What is that?"

Faith and Avonstoke both shot me glances, clearly confused. This deck didn't have much for fresh air. It had sweaty people, sweaty livestock, including Nocturnus's brimstone scent, powerful in close quarters. Also the wet, dank smell of every ship belowdecks.

"I think you mean the bilgewater," I said. "The whole ship smells like that below."

"Ah," the Lady Rue said, sucking her teeth. "It's . . . nice."

Faith and I gave each other the eye.

"Yeah. Thanks," I said. Avonstoke's expression was priceless, his mouth open, completely stupefied. His raven shifted on his shoulder and made soft clicking noises.

A few more awkward minutes ticked by, and then the curtain swished to one side and Henry came in with Sands behind him. Sands had a wine bottle to his lips as he came in. When he saw the Lady Rue, he stopped, choked, and sputtered wine down his front. Lady Rue withdrew her slippered foot, some kind of black silk, which had been in some danger of getting wet. Sands stared at her, aghast.

Henry pulled the curtain closed. "I shooed everyone off this deck," he said. "Best privacy we can get, I guess."

"No one will overhear us," Lady Rue said. Normally, a curtain wasn't what I'd call perfect protection against eavesdropping on a ship, but the lady seemed sure.

"Well," Faith said. "What's this all about?"

"Gods, you're all so insolent!" Lady Rue sighed. "I knew this would be difficult, but you people make everything so much worse than . . ." For the second time in two minutes I watched the Faerie noblewoman master what was clearly a towering temper. Whatever she wanted here, she wanted it badly.

She took a deep breath. "Let us begin at the beginning. I am not truly the Lady Rue as I have led you to believe." She fingered the edge of the silver mask that ran along her cheekbone. Her red mouth, below the mask, twitched into a wry smile.

Avonstoke, already in a near state of shock, now rapped his head against one of the rafters so hard it made a hollow sound, like a ball hit with a cricket bat. Most of us had met Lady Rue this year, during the war. But he'd known of her, at least, all his life. He'd never spoken directly with her before this year, but she had a terrible and ruthless reputation among his people. He'd feared her since childhood.

"Who are you, then?" Faith said. Of all of us, she seemed the least stunned.

The woman stood up and pulled off the silver mask, letting it fall carelessly to the wooden floor with a muffled ringing noise. Some kind of enchantment seemed to peel off of her along with the mask, one far too powerful and sophisticated for my ghost eye to penetrate. The illusion slid slowly down from her head like melting snow.

The spiky urchin hair was unchanged, but that was all. Foot long, curved horns of bone graced her head, looking very sharp. Her face was the color of polished oak now, smooth but just as angular, haughty, and inhuman as the silver mask had been. Her elven ears were longer than any I'd seen and studded with wondrously delicate silver decorations. At first, I thought she wasn't Court Faerie at all. But a second look at her face gave me the idea that she was Court Faerie, but ancient to a degree I'd never seen before.

The glamour continued to slowly fall away, revealing the rest of her. It pooled in mercurial wisps of magical power at her feet before dissipating entirely. She wore a diaphanous dress of gray and black translucent lace that swirled around her, leaving far too much of her skin revealed. She didn't look ancient there. I blushed and the woman breathed a shameless chuckle. Then the black gossamer trails of her dress flexed and unfurled, and I realized that the black parts weren't a dress at all, but enormous wings.

"Lor..." Henry whispered.

The wings moved again and I could see now that they were a quartet, like butterfly wings, only these were leathery, something between bat, bird, butterfly, and dragon. Her hands were clawed, and her feet bare.

"My name," she said, "is Queen Mab d'Noctis, Empress of Shadow and Darkness, monarch of the Unseelie Court, sovereign of all those in Faerie that shun the light."

I caught myself sucking in a deep breath in surprise and had to make myself unclench my fists. I hadn't expected this. I'd spent all this time wondering, and now...

"All this time," Henry said, "you were wearing a mask that looked exactly like the face underneath? No one recognized you?"

I turned to ask Henry if he'd lost his mind, then took another look at her face and the silver mask on the floor. Even with my ghost eye, they looked the same. The illusion, possibly linked to the mask, had hidden her ears, the spikes, and the nature of her face, but the shape of it, the features, eyes, brow, cheekbones, were exactly the same as her real face. Her mouth and chin, red and cruel, hadn't been hidden at all.

"The mask served its purpose," Queen Mad d'Noctis said. That wry smile was back. "There aren't that many people who remember what I looked like when alive, and I haven't given any audiences as queen for many, many years."

That sounded sinister.

So much now all fit together. Faith looked even more shocked than I felt, which was saying something. Avonstoke gripped my arm protectively, though it seemed a futile gesture in the face of something like this.

"Don't," Faith said, slowly, "expect us to bow."

The Queen of the Faerie gave us a feral grin. "I did not expect that, as it happens." Her voice made the insult clear, as if we were too stupid and ignorant to know the proper way to do anything.

"How is this possible?" Sands said.

"A better question is why," I said. "I would have expected you to side with the invasion."

"Because you don't understand us at all." She shot a pitying glance at Avonstoke. "How do you put up with them?"

"It's the Black Shuck," Avonstoke said, smiling winningly. "Isn't it? Everyone's afraid of something."

Her glare might have withered stone, but Avonstoke merely beamed. Finally, the Queen of the Unseelie Court made a sad, dismissive moue at him.

"Is he wrong?" I asked, knowing he wasn't.

"Not . . . entirely," the queen admitted slowly. "The Seelie and Unseelie war on each other, but when it comes to our feelings about humanity and England, there is little agreement in either court."

"Most of the legends," Sands said, "human and Faerie, agree that the Unseelie Court has always been dangerous to humanity."

The queen smiled. "We're dangerous to everybody."

"What about the Seelie Court?" Henry said.

Sands shrugged helplessly. "Slightly less dangerous to humanity."

"Stories are just that," the queen said. "Stories. I do not hate humanity, or England, the way they might have you believe."

"But why join the Outcasts?" Faith asked. "Why hide your identity? What purpose does that serve?"

"And why block us at every turn?" I said, even angrier now than I was when I thought she was just a Faerie noble. "You've been doing everything you can to slow us down."

"Was it to sabotage the Outcasts?" Faith said. "Curry favor with the Black Shuck, make him into an ally? Is he from the Unseelie Court?"

"That beast!" the Queen spat, her ferocity as sudden as it was surprising. "I'd rather bow to one of your English street vendors than see him in the court. But the Black Shuck and Widdershins now have powerful allies there. No, I wanted to make certain you made proper use of the prophecy, which you seem intent on ignoring."

I looked at Faith, then the others, to see if they were buying this. Faith shrugged. It was certainly possible. The Black Shuck and Widdershins, with their mental control over other Faerie, had to be an enormous threat to her, and she'd made no secret about her opinion on the prophecy, favoring it over all other considerations.

"The Seven Sins disturb the natural way of things," the queen said. "They were meant to rise up in response to, and to challenge, the Seven Virtues. They were not meant to conquer England or to seize power in both courts the way they have."

"Wait," Henry said. "Seven? I thought Justice killed two of them?"

I didn't quite flinch at this statement, but it felt like a strange thing to be proud of, and I wasn't, exactly. I had to settle for a blank expression. Then I counted. We knew about the Black Shuck, Widdershins, the Goblin Knight, Madam Westerly, and John Brown. Who were the sixth and seventh?

"Your mother has become one of the Sins," Queen Mab said.

"That bitch," Henry said quietly, echoing what we were all thinking.

Or what most of us were thinking, anyway. Faith didn't look as angry as I felt, only infinitely sad. "That poor woman," she said, almost to herself. "There's no coming back for her, is there?" Then she shook her head, visibly forcing herself to move on. "We don't have Seven Virtues. Or any way to get them."

"Even worse," Mab said. "In addition to your mother. They have been joined by an avatar of Lughus. He is the last of the Formori, a creature called Urguag. He will give the Black Shuck what the invaders need to build a fleet to take them across the channel, batter through our blockade, and gain entrance to the lands beyond. We must resist them with the means we have now or fall. The entire world will lie open to them if they reach the mainland."

So Lughus's sudden change of mind was because of me. Lughus was Formori. The keeper of his race, which had all but died out long ago. I'd thought that the Soho Shark, who I'd killed, had been the last, but now there was another. Still, considering that the last of the Formori, the Soho Shark, had been trying to murder me at the time, it wasn't like I'd had a whole lot of choice.

"What is it you want from us?" I said.

Mab faced Faith. "I can no longer afford to wait for our Seven Virtues. They are not all here, may never be here. But the Seven Sins have gathered with an avatar and champion of Lughus in their midst. Lughus was not part of the war, but now he is. Thanks, in part, I think, to you." She looked hard at me so that there could be no misunderstanding.

"Lughus will give them crafts of the sea," Sands said, his voice unsteady. "They'll have the means to build and sail ships. Sail them with arts humans have long forgotten, or never knew."

Faith caught my eye and I lowered and then holstered the pistol. This was bigger than Mab or me, or my guilt.

"The only reason we've been able to hold them in this blockade," I said grimly, "is because they don't have sea magic, and haven't had enough decent real sailors to overcome that weakness."

Faith looked at me and nodded.

"How long do we have?" I said to Queen Mab.

"Three days," Queen Mab said grimly.

"What," I asked, "kind of fleet could they have ready in three days?"

"Four large ships," she said. "The *Emerald Demise* and three others of similar size."

"So, ships of the line," I said.

"Yes," she said. "With cannons that have been rebuilt after your attack on the shipyard. The best they could salvage, but they didn't have enough seaman to sail her." She grinned at me, a ghastly expression on her inhuman face. "It seems the terror of Justice's naval campaign has paid off. Anyone capable of being pressed has gone into hiding."

Was that . . . a compliment? This queen behind Lady Rue's persona was going to take some getting used to.

"But now," the queen went on, "with Lughus's support, they have access to magical means of sailing them."

"Windshrikes," Faith whispered.

I caught Faith's eye, trying to ask, without actually asking out loud, if her ability to suppress magic might be employed against this new threat. She caught my meaning plainly enough, shrugging. She had no idea. I could have spoken the question out loud, but some part of me still didn't fully trust this queen, and I thought keeping the details of our abilities a prudent caution.

Queen Mab was staring at Faith, her eyes behind the mask wide in surprise. "Your learning surpasses my expectations."

"Dragons," Faith said primly, "are most insistent teachers. Brocara sends me dreams. All night. Every night."

The queen pursed her lips. "Ah. I did not know that." She cocked her head and looked at Faith for a long moment. "What are dragon dreams like?" A rare note of curiosity had crept into her normally icy voice.

"They're exhausting," Faith blurted out immediately. "I feel like I'd murder someone for a decent night's sleep."

I was surprised myself. Faith had told me a little but had never spoken about it this openly before.

"Ugh," Faith said, her hand rubbing her temple. "I'm not supposed to talk about it."

"What are Windshrikes?" Mr. Sands said. I could tell it pained him to have to ask. There had been a time when Sands had been our deepest source of information on magic and the Faerie, and now he was no longer a magician. He still knew a great deal, but it was also clear that Faith had outstripped him in many areas. Avonstoke, too, looked keenly interested in the answer. He clearly hadn't heard of these Windshrikes either.

"Elemental spirits of the wind," Faith said. "Magicians of Lughus used to chain them to ships to do their bidding." She looked at me. "Like the storm serpents the Outcasts use, but much more powerful. They'll be much faster than any ship without them. They may even be able to turn them on us directly. Imagine a localized hurricane filled with barbs and thorns. Very nasty. I do not know their full power, but it will not be good for us."

"How do you know all this?" I asked the queen. "About Lughus?"

In answer, the Queen of the Unseelie Court stood up. She pulled a small, curved knife from a hidden pocket inside her voluminous sleeve. It must have been very sharp, because she swiped it effortlessly and casually across the tip of her finger and it began to drip a slow but steady stream of blood. She held the knife so that some of it pooled on its blade. She used this impromptu tool to pour some of her own blood onto the floor.

She stepped back expectantly.

At first, nothing happened. The blood shivered slightly with the motion of the ship, but that was all. Everyone watched, listening to the creak of the ship and the ocean outside.

Then the pool of blood expanded. We shuffled back, startled, with a scraping of bootheels.

"I will show you," the Queen of the Unseelie Court said, "what I have already seen."

She dipped her clawed, elegant finger into the blood, which rippled. When the ripples had passed, we saw shapes.

It was the shoreline near Dover. I could see the fortifications going up the hill and the white cliffs off to the side. We were looking from a vantage point on the water. I could see the *Emerald Demise* moored at the docks, and also the three other ships the queen had told us of. They were, indeed, ships of the line, large and looming high above the water. They looked ready to sail too, with yards crossed and sail going up. Myriad Faerie were mounting the gangplanks, boarding the ship: Goblins, Trolls, Dwarves, Kellas Cats, and more of the loathsome Hanged Dogs. Lots of Faerie.

Four ships of the line, packed to the beams with an army ready to land in France. Any one of those ships held troops enough to make a beachhead and hold it. From there, it would be a simple matter for the Faerie to overpower France's physical defenses and move deeper into the continent. An invasion fleet, ready when we thought they couldn't possibly be ready.

And I had no idea how I was going to stop it.

"This was just yesterday," Queen Mab said.

There was movement on the shore too, in the image. The Faerie invasion army. The queen wasn't wrong. They were loading entire battalions into those ships.

The queen waved a hand and the vision dissipated.

She turned back to us and continued without comment. "Now, if I do nothing, the Black Shuck will usurp my throne and very likely my life." She frowned, apparently struggling with new thoughts. "So I must make peace, which is why I come to you now. My way back to Faerie is blocked, as is all of ours. We are bedmates in this, whether I would or no."

"Make no mistake," she continued. "The Black Shuck means to cover the world in darkness. Once he has this world, it will just make him hungrier to conquer Faerie too. This is bigger than just your monarchy. If the Black Shuck completes his rise to power, there won't be much left of the Seelie or Unseelie Courts. They'll follow humanity into a blackness, and none of us will ever come out again."

I took a deep, deep breath. "So," I said. "What do we get?"

Queen Mab's eyes blazed. Clearly she was not used to anyone talking to her like this. It all made more sense to me now. She'd acted so much like a queen all of this time that it should have been obvious.

"What?" she said.

"You've laid out the danger," I said, my voice hard, "and what you want from us. What I'm trying to understand is what use you can be." I'd taken about as much abuse from this woman as I was willing to take, regardless of the usefulness of her information. If we were about to be in the fight of our lives, a monarch that blocked my every move was just going to get in my way more than ever.

"What would you say," the Queen of the Unseelie Court said, "to unimpeded, complete authority and control over *Seahome*, as well as the *Blood Oath* and the rest of my ships?"

"Congratulations, Admiral," Faith murmured. "You have your fleet at last."

"It's a start," I said. Up until now, every duty I'd wanted to assign to one of the Court Faerie-controlled schooners invariably involved so much negotiation that it was hardly worth it. "But it's not nearly enough."

"What else would you have?" the queen said coldly.

"It's not a matter of negotiation," I said. "No amount of schooners are going to stop four ships of the line. At least not with normal tactics." A schooner carried only four twelve-pounders and a crew of twenty. Hardly a threat to any ship of significant size. *Seahome* was enormous, but much too ponderous to catch or cut off any of those ships. Any one of those four ships could end the blockade, and then all would be lost. Still, it might give me something to work with. With the proper tactics, there might be a chance. A long one, but even that was something.

"I haven't given up on the prophecy," the queen said. "The prophecy is true. Uniting the Seven Virtues is the only way to beat the Seven Sins. But until our path to the Seven becomes clear, we need to have a plan."

"This again," I said. "I'm not going to run an entire war by ignoring military tactics in favor of some nursery rhyme!"

"Is there a rhyme?" Henry said. "I didn't know that."

"No," I snapped. "There's no bloody rhyme."

"Just a story," Faith said, pondering, "that the Seven Virtues and the Seven Sins will meet in a mighty battle and decide the fate of the world."

"More than a story," the queen said. "It is a spell decades in the casting. Your father was one of the great powers of Faerie and a general unmatched. There is much power there still, despite his death."

"Father knew this much," Faith said. "He knew the Faerie would someday come back to our world and we would need magic of our own to fight them off. He wanted to gather the symbols together and then empower us, through his prophecy, to help us deal with whatever dangers came.

"Didn't exactly go according to plan, did it?" I said. Father's death, and his Virtues scattered. What if I had agreed to continue banishing Rachek Kasric? Would Father's prophecy have been enough to stop the Black Shuck now if I'd hadn't had an attack of conscience?

Queen Mab nodded at Faith. "That was my understanding too. With that much power gathered behind them, the Virtues should be able to do anything. I have wagered much on this."

"You've been hindering everything," I snapped, "our entire military campaign, in the hopes that all this groveling and supplication would win us favor from the gods?"

"I grovel to no one," the Queen snarled. "Not even the gods. But why not curry their favor? They are supremely powerful forces."

"Because they lie!" I shouted. "They make promises and don't keep them. You of all people, deceptive as you are, should know better than to trust any of the Faerie! Even their gods."

"Oh, Justice," Faith said softly. "This is about Father, isn't it?"

Everyone was looking at me suddenly. My hands were shaking. I couldn't get enough air in the stuffy cabin.

"She is not," the queen said softly, "entirely wrong. The legends and arcane sources make it clear that the gods are, intrinsically, two things. Powerful beyond comprehension, but also capricious. They would not be Faerie gods any other way."

Something about my finally losing my temper so badly seemed to have cooled her anger. She sat, primly, gracefully, and there was nothing else for the rest of us to do but sit again ourselves. Even seated, my hands were still shaking where they lay on the table.

"You have been wronged by the Faerie," Queen Mab said slowly. "More than most. I understand this. But . . ."

"No," I said. "It's not that." My gaze flickered, against my will, to Avonstoke. I'd expected anger, knowing I deserved it, but he just looked sympathetic and sad.

I turned back to the queen. "I'm not saying I don't trust any of the Faerie. I'm just saying," I finished, "that I don't trust your gods."

"Do you trust the gods?" Avonstoke asked the queen. "Truly?" The relief I felt that I wasn't the only one with some reservations on that point was like a lifted weight, and I flashed him a grateful smile.

"Sooner ask a starving wretch if they trust food," Queen Mab said sadly. "What other choice is there?"

<hr/>

Faith, Sands, and Henry all left quickly after Queen Mab departed, each on their own errands, leaving Avonstoke and me alone for a brief moment, if you didn't count Nocturnus. I rubbed her velvety soft muzzle and suddenly, without any warning, I was sobbing openly.

"Justice?" Avonstoke said, he put his hand on my shoulder and I turned into him at once. He wrapped me in his strong arms.

"I didn't mean you," I sobbed. "I didn't mean that I didn't trust you! You've always been here for me. It's just everyone else."

"Your Father," he said, pulling me closer. "And everyone else you've ever met among my people. It's no wonder we've left you cautious."

"It's not just that," I said. "It's everything. It's all happening. At last. I've been fighting this war with both hands tied behind my back, just waiting, and now all the terrible things I've been waiting for are finally happening and I've actually got the ships I need to stop them and . . ."

"Isn't that good?" he said, his voice curious. "I mean, except for the war part, of course. But all the rest?"

"Yes," I said, wiping my nose on his uniform lapel. He pretended not to notice. "Yes, it's good. It's what I wanted."

"Then why?"

"Shut up," I said.

And he did. He held me until I'd cried myself out.

ACT II

BATTLES
AT SEA

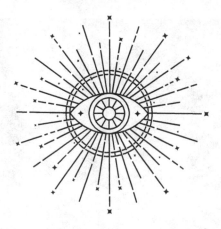

CHAPTER 7

JUSTICE
A Conversation with Avonstoke

I leaned on the rail, unable to keep the image of four ships of the line out of my mind's eye. Nearly four hundred guns, and heavier guns than the *Specter* carried, at that. I could play a distance game with our long nines, but we'd be hard pressed to sink one ship, let alone four, that way before it could reach France's coast. And that was discounting the possibility of two of those behemoths crowding me from opposite sides to bring me under one of their devastating broadsides. A very real possibility if they could outmaneuver me using Lughus's Windshrikes.

Dusk was starting to glower on the horizon. If Queen Mab was correct, and we were sure now that she was, the enemy fleet would be coming out the day after tomorrow. A bitter wind threw droplets of icy rain into my face. It was a sudden comfort to think that I could start crying now and no one would even know. The *Specter* rode easily at sea, but spray still burst over the prow with every dip.

A calm sea. For now. I had a feeling this was the respite between two storms.

Avonstoke stood at the rail with me. My rock. Always there. That might not be true in a few days, with the Black Shuck's new fleet coming out. A cold pit opened in my stomach as I envisioned being on this deck without them. The idea of dying tomorrow, or worse, being crippled and humiliated by a screaming cannonball, was bad enough to make my hands shake, but watching that happen to Avonstoke, or Faith, or Henry, or anyone on this ship, hurt even more. It had nearly unmade me when Avonstoke was blinded. How much worse would this next battle be?

How much would we lose?

With that thought foremost in my mind, I put my hand very deliberately on Avonstoke's arm and, when he turned to look at me, a question in his eyes, I jerked my head toward the captain's cabin. I could feel the question and tension in my own eyes ease when his face split into a delighted grin.

I thumped him in the ribs, wishing he weren't so damned obvious. His face immediately fell into a deeply insincere expression of profound sobriety. All the times when he'd been thoroughly enigmatic, and now I only wished he was. His faux-serious expression was, if anything, even more obvious than his grin had been. I dragged him across the deck before he had time to send up signal flags or flares or perhaps start composing a sonnet about us and recite it on the fly.

We burst our way into the captain's cabin like a pair of drunks, clumsy in our haste. There was a slight rustle of movement and for an instant I thought we'd burst in on Faith sleeping, but she was down in the gunroom reviewing old manuscripts with Sands and Henry. But Enemy, Sands' cat was there, two glowing and sullen eyes in the half-light of the smoking oil lamp.

"Hold on," I said, breaking free of Avonstoke's embrace.

Thinking how Sands retrieved his intelligence from England through his uncanny link to the cats there, I stared at the orange cat.

"The last thing I need," I said, "is to wonder about Sands right now."

I scooped up the orange cat and opened the door to hurriedly toss him out of the cabin. He mewed plaintively, but I knew he'd be fine. He'd make his way down to the lower decks, chasing rats, where he should be anyway. I still had no idea how he kept getting into our cabin when it was usually closed up.

As I started to close the door, a slight shadow fell over me and I looked up the two stairs to the main deck to see Faith standing there. She'd clearly been about to come down and into the cabin, but also just as clearly knew exactly what was happening now, why I was kicking Enemy out. Faith's expression wasn't difficult to read. The sister I'd grown up with had been intense, quick to anger and smile in equal measure, and becoming a magician hadn't changed that.

I froze, still in a crouch, trying to think of something to say, but I couldn't think of anything, only waited for the sharp reprimand my reckless foolishness deserved.

Instead, Faith smiled at me. A brilliant, wicked grin that surprised me as much as anything else that had happened today. She moved her staff to her nondominant hand so she could pick up the offended Enemy. He glared at me from the shelter of her arms. No smile there.

"Good night," Faith said softly, and spun on her booted heel, heading for the lower deck.

I slammed the door, horrified and embarrassed, and leaned back against it.

"Problem?" Avonstoke asked.

"Yes!" I blurted out. "No. Yes. No." I took a deep breath. "No. In fact, it probably solves a big problem." Faith might have come in without knocking, but no one else would. Avonstoke and I would at least have until morning now.

And with that sudden realization, my legs weren't really working right. I'd lost my sea legs, somehow, feeling unsteady with the motion of the ship for the first time in my memory as I walked toward him. For a long, stretched-out moment, neither of us moved. The wind thrummed in the rigging far above us, audible even through the ceiling.

"Now," Avonstoke murmured, his arms enfolding me. "Where were we?"

"Here," I said, tangling my hands in his golden hair and pulling his mouth down to mine. "Right here." I shed my coat when we came in and his body, through my shirt and the stiff cloth of his uniform was strong and beautiful. The certainty that we'd be awkward lay like a stone inside of me, but our bodies fit together perfectly, as if made for each other.

"Caw!"

"Bloody hell!" I snapped, glaring at the raven on his shoulder. "Right in my ear!"

"Hold on," Avonstoke said. Using his left hand, he hurriedly tried to scoop the raven off his shoulder with his finger, which became an immediate awkward failure when the bird screamed in protest and hopped, with an angry flutter of wings, from Avonstoke's right shoulder to his head, then his other shoulder.

"No!" Avonstoke said. "I'm not getting a mouthful of feathers for your curiosity. Go sit on the table or something." He thrust a finger at the bird, but it cawed again. A clear refusal.

I tugged at his shirt. "Hurry!"

"I know! Believe me, I know!" He chased the bird with the proffered finger once more, but it just avoided him, seeking refuge in his golden hair. I'd seen this man walk a deck or climb the mast and even fight Hanged Dogs, all with consummate grace, but he wasn't getting anywhere with the bird, possibly because it seemed to know his every move before Avonstoke made it.

"For the love of . . ." I said and reached up to shoo the bird off his shoulder myself. I wasn't terribly gentle about it, and it fluttered away, screaming again in anger, a raucous noise in the close quarters of the cabin. It landed on the table and glared at me with first one eye and then the other, but it stayed there.

"Should've kept the cat in here," Avonstoke murmured into my mouth. "Finally have a use for it!" He turned his head to fire these last few words at the bird, so I had to grab his face with my hand and pull him back down into a kiss. His mouth was warm on mine and my blood started to pound in my ears. The sea crashed on the cabin walls outside.

We'd had innumerable fumbling partial encounters in the dark, but this was something else, and we both knew it without a word having to be spoken. I shed my clothes, wet from the spray of waves against the prow. I wasn't delicate about it, or graceful. Actually, I was trying to get them off and get naked, committed to the act, before I lost my nerve or somehow came to my senses. I'd been worried about propriety up until now, but we could both die tomorrow. This might be the last time both or either of us had all our limbs, and I couldn't see the sense in waiting any longer for something we both wanted.

I stood naked, dripping, suddenly cold in the center of the room, and Avonstoke stopped unbuttoning his uniform shirt, staring openly. He'd never seen me naked before, and I'd undressed with all the finesse usually reserved for slopping pigs. He was really looking, looking thoroughly, and I blushed.

"Are you getting undressed or not!" I snapped.

"Oh!" he said, as if I'd startled him. "Yes. Yes, of course." Except his fingers fumbled at his buttons without making much progress. I had to help him out of the rest of his uniform.

Finally, we both were naked. I shivered in the cold. The ship took a long, sudden, corkscrew dip in the waves and we swayed. His skin was darker than mine, almost gold, though not so golden as his glorious eyes or his hair still bound up in its queue. How could this man want me? But he clearly did.

His hands reached for me, their warmth so welcome in the cold room.

I came into his arms, reaching up for his hair. "I've wanted to do this since the very first day that I met you." The emerald cord keeping his hair bound was knotted at the lowest end, a knot decorative rather than practical. I'd have to teach him the clove hitch for this. Or just a decent square knot.

Finally, the cord was free and his hair came loose. It was a glory of golden silk and I ran my fingers greedily through its softness. He chuckled softly, a noise that turned more guttural when my fingers reached the corded muscles of his back, and then slid lower. I pulled him back toward the captain's cot, my skin hot with excitement, fear, and a little shame, but mostly excitement.

He bent and scooped me bodily up into his arms, carrying me like a child. There was a part of me that was almost offended at the implied helplessness of it, but the rest of me luxuriated in the feeling. He eased me gently into the swinging cot and then I pulled him in on top of me. The cot wasn't made for two people and the canvas and cordage creaked dangerously, but it held.

"Raythe," I whispered. It felt strange to call him by his first name, as if it were a secret that only a few held. Everything swam dangerously inside of me.

"Captain, oh my captain," he murmured back to me, his mouth hot on my neck. "So beautiful."

His compliment seemed ridiculous compared to his naked glory, but I knew he meant it too, poor fool.

His breath was warm on my shoulder when he said, "I love you, Justice Kasric."

A fearful tangle I hadn't even realized lay deep inside of me came loose, very suddenly, and my eyes teared up. I pulled his face back up to me so that I could stare into the golden eyes. "And I you, Raythe Avonstoke."

His strong body was above me now and I welcomed him.

We were awkward, a little bit, that first time, but the passion and desire sluiced all that away in short order.

The next time, we got better.

Later, still in the comfort of his arms, I stirred happily. "We can't actually lie here all night, you know," I said.

He squeezed me, hard. "I know, my captain."

Neither of us moved. Avonstoke's raven cawed softly, possibly in agreement, possibly urging us to get up.

"You ever going to name that thing?" I said, feeling suddenly uncomfortable, not with Avonstoke but with his clear admiration. I was certain that when he, or anyone else, looked too closely, they'd see me for the imposter I was. It was just nepotism and luck that had gotten me this far, and any instant it was going to come crashing down around my ears.

"It's a part of me," Avonstoke said. "So the idea feels odd. A bit like naming the left side of your face."

His fingers stroked softly along my back, stirring up distracting feelings. "You need to visit the Shimmering Seas someday. Or Lichen Bay, or sail the Caves of the Deep."

"These are real places?" I asked, intrigued despite myself.

"So I am told," Avonstoke said, his fingers still moving so that it was hard to concentrate on his words. "I have not yet seen them myself and have always wanted to. Even more so, now that I know you. The Shimmering Seas are said to pile up like bundles of glittering, coiled rope, or like a rolling, shining storm front, all of it underneath constant, tangerine storms. Very picturesque, very difficult to sail, according to the legends—old stories that I heard as a child and promptly forgot until now. But if anyone can figure out how to sail uphill, it would have to be you."

"What about knowing me makes you remember them now?"

"Your love of the sea," Avonstoke said, putting his warm mouth onto my shoulder, to delicious effect. "It is somewhat contagious. Also, you may be the only captain I would trust to get me safely through it."

"Oh really?" I said playfully, basking in both his words and his attentions.

"Unless Caine is available, of course," Avonstoke murmured. "You understand, I'm sure."

"Caine!" I shrieked, slapping him on the shoulder.

"Careful," he said, not bothering to lift his mouth more than a hair's breadth from my skin. "The crew might hear and misinterpret. Of course, if they were listening earlier..."

"Shut up, you," I murmured, but then his mouth drifted lower and it was all I could do to keep quiet again.

◁▷◁▷◁▷◁▷

"Let me ask you something else," I said, some minutes time later. "The horse aspect of the Morrigna made Nocturnus, which, if Sands and Prudence are correct..."

"This again?" he said mildly. He was behind me, snuggling into my back with his arms around me so that I felt warm and protected. His mouth was buried in my hair, very close to my ear, so his voice was a low murmur. "Was that what you were thinking about when I—"

"No!" I said. "But I was wondering yesterday. If Morrigna made Nocturnus..."

"Prudence and Sands don't agree on much," Avonstoke said, "so it's a compelling argument when they do."

"Right." I pulled his hand to my mouth and kissed it, grateful, as always, for how quickly he understood me. "That's just what I'm getting at. Neither the gods nor magic make any sense to me, which is one of the reasons why I don't trust them. But we're using so much of their magic. Nocturnus, the pistol Father made, the cannons, dragon, the list goes on. Father's magic, in fact, seems to have come from even stealing a piece of the World Tree. Faith told me that. She saw it in a dream. So even the prophecy is magic, stolen from the gods, and twisted to Father's ends."

"Really?" Avonstoke said. "He really was a first-rate scoundrel, wasn't he?" Of course, Father was the man who'd sent Avonstoke to watch over me in the first place. I wonder how much of this Father had expected. Had he planned this, even this? I hoped not.

"Try not to sound so admiring," I said, shoving him in the ribs. "Scoundrel is not a compliment." Avonstoke *oofed* appropriately and chuckled into my ear. He didn't sound exactly chastised, though.

"All the Faerie play at being scoundrels, but we are also people of rigid, unbreakable honor," Avonstoke said, wonder clear in his voice. "You have to admire someone who manages both so thoroughly, at least a little."

"So," I said, trying not to lose my train of thought, "if magic is the province of the gods, why don't they seem to have any control over it?"

He shifted and his mouth left my shoulder, so I knew he was pondering what I'd said. We both knew the stories Sands had told us. Gods made dragons and used the dragons to make magic. If the dragons all died, so would magic. A fact that hadn't stopped the dragons from getting embroiled in the war, on both sides.

"I have no idea," he said finally. "But I don't see gods, magic, and our purposes as the contradictions that you seem to. Or perhaps the Faerie, myself included, are just a far more contrary people than seems natural to you."

"You revere the gods," I said. "More openly and honestly than anyone I know, without getting any power that I can see, like the magicians. But do you trust them?"

"It's not about trust, or power," he said. "It's about love. I revere them and love them. I don't expect them to make sense, any more than you'd expect a thunderstorm to have purpose."

"That makes no sense at all," I complained.

I could feel him shrug. "There are people that worship the Christian god in England, are there not? With far less physical evidence than we Faerie have at our disposal. Do they all understand every facet of why they believe? My people in Vasyil believed, and I find it a comfort to do the same."

"Which god? All of them?"

"I revere and love them all," he said, "but make offers to Llyr and Brigid. But while I fight to defeat Arawn's minions and designs, I don't want to vanquish Arawn's existence any more than I want to vanquish nightfall."

"That doesn't make any sense either," I said. I turned in his arms to look at him.

"People don't make any sense," he said with a rueful grin. "In Faerie or in England. It is the same."

"That is not even remotely helpful," I said bitterly.

"It is . . . how it is," he said.

I glared at him.

"Let me put it this way," he said very slowly. "You, yourself, are hardly predictable. You steal, lie, cheat, murder even, to get what you want . . ."

I opened my mouth to protest but closed it again. He wasn't exactly wrong.

"But what you want is noble and selfless," he went on. "You don't always succeed, but you're a mighty force, and I know you'll fight to save England and her people to the very end, to, literally, your last breath, if need be. That's why we follow you."

"I'm not any of those things," I protested. "You're comparing me to the Faerie gods, to religion. That's ridiculous."

"Is it?" he said. "What do you call someone who defies the gods?"

I rubbed the bridge of my nose, tired and aching. "Dead?"

"Probably," Avonstoke agreed. "But if she wins . . ." He shrugged again.

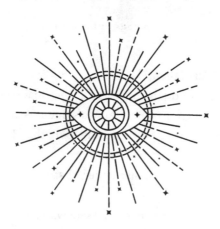

CHAPTER 8

JOSHUA
Pondering Temperance

J oshua looked behind him down the corridor and saw no one. Good. He'd scared off all the servants who might have accompanied or followed him. Once he was sure of that, he used the heavy key to let himself into the suite of rooms he'd taken for his own. They were drafty, but he'd found that he didn't get cold anymore and didn't mind. Besides, they were far enough away from the more heavily occupied portions of the place to afford him some privacy, which was what he really cared about.

The first few rooms included another desk, a bed heavy enough to support his new, burdensome body, and a small shelf of books he'd rescued from the fires. He locked the door behind him and passed through the front room and bedroom, stopping in front of a large piece of slate that leaned against the back wall. The slate could have served as a table for a dozen or so, but instead, the surface had been painted with a representation of the Faerie traveling along the Bridge of Sorrows. He'd found the slate some months ago and commissioned the work from a Goblin archer who'd been part of the Saltblood clans, until he was killed during one of Justice's raids. Joshua hadn't really cared about the painting at the time but wanted to disguise his real use for the slate. The painting, crude at first glance, had revealed surprising depths after serious consideration. It had grown on him. The mist curling around the enormous supports of the bridge, the barely visible masses—of Faerie, so distant that Goblin, Merfolk, Dwarf, and Court Faerie were indistinguishable, even the barely discernable V shapes of the dragons—all evoked a profound loneliness that Joshua understood.

Still, the slate had another, simpler, purpose.

It was a gate. Joshua grunted as he moved the two-ton piece of stone, a serious obstacle for any overly curious visitors, and slid it out of the way. Behind lay another door, to the last room. No real point locking this one, but he did anyway. You never knew. He unlocked it and went inside.

This room was bare except for a series of paintings. Paintings Joshua had had smuggled from Stormholt. The family portraits. Mother; the Lord of Thorns; Joshua's father, Rachek Kasric; and all his pseudo-siblings, the various by-blows of the Lord of Thorns. Justice, Faith, all of them were here, and Joshua liked to come and look at them and think of times long gone. He even looked wistfully at his own, for the hints of his own monstrous changes. The fangs, the horns, were already there, but in the portrait he was still mostly human, particularly in the face. His limbs still looked like human limbs. Gloves and boots could still be worn. Not so, now.

He turned his focus to a portrait he usually paid little attention to, because this woman wasn't actually related, except in the most distant sense. While Joshua was the one true child of the *real* Rachek Kasric and Martine Kasric, there were three portraits representing the union of the Lord of Thorns and the Lady of Sorrows. Three children: Hope, Charity, and Temperance. (He wondered, briefly, at the Lady of Sorrows and the

Bridge of Sorrows, and if there was any connection. Perhaps she'd taken, or been assigned, her name from the bridge. Or perhaps the Faerie were just a people with more than their fair share of sorrow. No matter.)

Temperance. Her hair was dark and curled—like Benedict's—her face fair. She wore an iron collar. The artist had been a Frenchwoman living in Soho whom Mother had been friends with before the invasion. Now she languished in a prison ship the Faerie maintained for Londoners they wanted to be able to put their hands on quickly. As far as Joshua knew, Mother had trotted her out of prison to do the new portraits and then sent her right back. Then she'd forgotten all about the paintings and painter both. Joshua had had them moved here and doubted that Mother even knew.

There was one portrait he wasn't familiar with, labeled "Love du Thorns." A sister he'd never known existed—slim, dark, a stranger. One more of Father's secrets. No, not Father. The Lord of Thorns, who might be father to Faith and Justice, but not him. He was the only one of Martine Kasric's children to have come from a fully human father.

He wondered when these had all been painted. He couldn't remember the painter's name. Marie something. It bothered Joshua that he couldn't remember her surname. Never mind. He put aside thoughts on the painter and the other portraits. Temperance was the important one.

He tapped one claw idly on his thigh with a raspy sound and thought about where Mother might be keeping this barely related spawn of the Lord of Thorns. That she was still alive, he had no doubt. She was important to the whole Virtues vs. Sins prophecy. But kill her, and her position as a Virtue could, possibly, be filled by someone else. Joshua didn't entirely understand the magical rules, but from things that Mother and Lady Westerly had said, he knew that the best symbols had the most power. So, the Lord of Thorns had launched his decades-long plan to introduce the symbols as ideas and then create his own embodiment of these ideas with seven daughters, hoping that the Faerie wouldn't have anyone prepared to match up. Like introducing a new game and rigging the outcome. The Virtues would have more favor from the gods, who liked symbols the way children liked sweets, and so, more magical power.

In theory. Magic had a way of adhering to slippery logic. The fact that no two magicians agreed on, well, *anything*, didn't help.

Temperance hadn't meant much to Joshua a few days ago, but Mother had crossed a line both by becoming one of the Seven Sins and by agreeing to marry that loathsome abomination, Widdershins. Any last vestige of hope that Joshua had had about Mother valuing family, valuing him, Joshua, had died inside of him that day.

So, to arrange his defection in a way to make Mother feel the betrayal the way *he* felt hers now, and also to bring an important gift that Justice and Faith couldn't possibly turn away—that was the trick. Their half-sister, Temperance. If he could free her and get out himself, they'd have to let him join the Outcasts, where his father, Rachek Kasric, was.

It also occurred to him that if he was caught, Mother would probably give him over to Widdershins and the Black Shuck. Joshua had been present during enough interrogations to see firsthand the combined effect of the Black Shuck and Widdershins to know that he didn't want to end up in the visitor's chair in that dark little room.

The last interrogation Joshua had seen had been of Lord Orismel of the Deepening Glade. Being part of the Unseelie Court, he'd likely thought that—because the uneasy truce between the two courts was vital to the invasion—he was immune to persecution from the Unseelie powers here.

But that hadn't been true.

When Lord Orismel had overstepped himself, the Black Shuck, who had never really cared what the nobles of either court wanted, took action. He'd had Orismel brought, without explanation or ceremony, to a little hole of a room in the basement of Dover Castle and kept there. After most of two days, the Black Shuck had shown up. Mother, Widdershins, and Joshua were all there for the encounter in the nasty place, with only a scarred table and rickety chair for furniture. Joshua still remembered watching the Court Faerie's face blanch when he'd faced the Black Shuck. But the man had clamped down the rest of his fear. No crying, no pleading. Joshua had to give the nobleman credit. He had as much starch as anyone Joshua had ever met, except perhaps Mother. Too bad it hadn't mattered in the slightest.

As familiar as Joshua was with the Black Shuck, the beast was still terrifying to be around. It wasn't the kind of feeling you got over with repetition, and this had been especially true in that close, airless, dank, wet, black interrogation room. The reeking bulk of the thing, or the drooling jaws that could easily tear out even Joshua's throat . . . those were bad enough. But you got the sense, always, that the monster was so hungry to kill everything it looked at that *not* ripping out your throat was causing the Black Shuck physical pain. It wanted to so badly. Joshua was a monster now, too, but nothing like the Black Shuck. It was as much as Joshua could do to not soil himself when the Black Shuck turned that unseeing but all-too-perceptive gaze on him.

Then Widdershins had moved in on the hapless Court Faerie, the dark gentleman's white gloves picking at the threads of the other man's mind. Holding up under that dual assault was impossible.

The man had tried drawing a weapon, at the last. They hadn't bothered to bind or disarm him. The Black Shuck had smashed the man to the ground with one great paw, shattering the chair the man had been sitting in, undoubtedly breaking most of the man's ribs, and pinning him to the dirt floor in one irresistible motion. The blow was so shockingly swift that Joshua hadn't even seen it. Orismel's weapon, whatever it had been, thumped uselessly in the shadows a few feet away. Out of reach.

They hadn't even asked Orismel any questions. It hadn't been about that. The man had countermanded some of Joshua's orders, rerouting food rations for his own purposes, and Widdershins had found out. That's all it had been. When they hadn't discovered any real betrayal or threat or plot, Joshua thought they might let Orismel go, but by then the man had died from the brutal interrogation. Neither Widdershins nor the Black Shuck had actually meant to kill him; they just hadn't been especially careful about keeping him alive during the process. Whether the cause of death had been something physical or just pure emotional terror, no one had bothered asking. Joshua could still see the man's white, white face, even in the weak light of the lantern. They'd all left him there, neglecting any funeral arrangements. For all Joshua knew, the man was there still.

Whatever else happened, Joshua didn't want to end up like that. Some option other than being left to the Black Shuck and Widdershins' tender mercies. If he could have gotten a gun working there in Faerie that he could turn on himself, that might be enough. Even with Mother's changes, Joshua could still feel soft places left on his body where a bullet would penetrate. Inside his mouth. The eyes. The hollow of his throat, probably. But guns or gunpowder didn't work here. He could try a gun once they'd left England, but it still didn't feel reliable enough. Oddly, Mother provided an answer, even if she didn't know it. She had a wide variety of poisons in her supply and it hadn't been hard to steal one. But knowing which one would be the best for his purposes, that was the problem. In the end, he'd stolen the most dangerous-looking bottle in her supply, a bottle no bigger than a human pinky finger. (His own pinky finger, being longer and clawed, wasn't a good comparison anymore.) The glass was clear, so he could see the fluid inside, an actively bubbling mixture the color of sewage. It had been bubbling like that since he'd stolen it weeks ago, like bad tea over an open flame. That had to be a good sign for his purposes, hopefully fatal for whoever took it. Joshua hoped so. He carried it in a vest pocket everywhere he went now.

With that provision taken care of, he was free to turn his resources and mental faculties to Temperance. It shouldn't be too hard to figure out where Mother was keeping her.

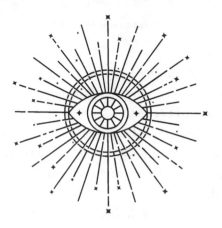

CHAPTER 9

LORD OF THORNS
The Journey Through Faerie

Making his way through the jeweled pockets of Faerie was bone-weary, grueling work, but it was also breathtakingly glorious.

Flexing magical muscles he hadn't used in too long, the Lord of Thorns summoned the mist, over and over, and moved through it, like a phantom through passages in multiple books. Through green-gold glades, shadowed cities, caverns that glowed with molten rock, along the backs of nearly submerged bog monsters, and even stranger places he walked. Several times, he passed through cities and other habitations, including one grand marketplace held underneath pale blue leaves the size of bedsheets.

He could not change his shape dramatically without serious preparation, but he could reshape his arms and horns for a short time while passing through populated areas, and he did this to avoid easy identification in case anyone was following him.

It was an exercise in heart and mind, working magic—like falling in love, and it left the same glow on him to be returning to it. For so long, it had been blocked by his growing humanity while wearing Rachek Kasric's shape. Over the years, he'd acquired magic from multiple sources—Brigid, Ogma, Cernunnos—which gave him access to a variety of it. He was not nearly as strong as magicians like Prudence or Drecovian, but he was strong, and it felt good to use that strength again.

The fit had come on him twice, and he'd had to lie helpless and twitching in strange places. (Once in the lee of a volcano and once in a deeply wooded valley, where an equine predator came, sniffed him, was disgusted, and moved on without molesting him.) He still couldn't discern what motions might possibly jostle the bullet still inside of him and bring the fits on, or how to avoid them. But it had only happened twice in seven days, and the episodes were mercifully brief, no small thanks for small favors. He chuckled at that last thought, which smacked of his time in London and had a vaguely churchy flavor, to his mind. He had never, during his time in England, considered himself a believer in the Church of England, even when using its symbolism for his own purposes, but clearly many of his human habits were still with him, despite his monstrous shape.

The realization surprised him.

Several times during his journey, when the terrain favored it, he'd paused and looked back the way he had come. The third time he did this, he was on an arid, rocky outcropping overlooking a series of dark pools flowing into one another. The lemon-yellow sky was studded with blood-red clouds, a pocket of Faerie he wasn't that familiar with. He waited for two hours, telling himself he'd get moving again after the third hour.

Sure enough, two figures came over the horizon, picking their way slowly over the ground along the same path he'd taken. He'd acquired a few things while passing through the marketplace. One of these was a spyglass, and he yanked this to its full length now and looked through it.

A large, shadowy wolf with someone much smaller riding on its back. Moving fast, for all that they were clearly following his trail.

Hope and Charity, his children, but also wrathful angels determined to exact vengeance on him. Hope could track him along the terrain while Charity would be her passage through the mist when he moved from Faerie pocket to Faerie pocket.

The Lord of Thorns frowned. He'd expected this, but that didn't make it any easier, and he couldn't imagine any pursuers who would be more dangerous.

It was time to start moving again.

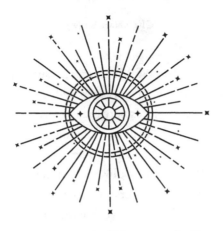

CHAPTER 10

JUSTICE
Preparations

F aith led me down to the captain's cabin, which we shared, and indicated Father's chess set sitting on a small bolted-down table.

I looked at it more closely. "Something's moved."

"A few somethings," Faith corrected. "I keep hoping this will give us some information on the Black Shuck's activities. You're a better chess player than I am. What do you make of it?"

"I can't read this thing," I said. "Father used to get information from looking at it, Sands said, but none of us have the knack of it now that he's gone." Our most obvious idea, that the game might represent the relative positions or strengths of our Seven Virtues and the invading army's Seven Sins, hadn't seemed to fit with the pieces on the board. We'd been able to confirm that our side was white, that theirs was black, that it was still in the middle of the game with only a few pieces gone, and that a whole lot of pieces were in dangerous conflict. But that was all.

"I know that part," she said. "But forget it's supposed to be an oracle. As a game, how does it look to you compared to before?"

"Well, there are more pieces here than before, I think," I said.

"There are," Faith said. "I've been keeping notes. A few weeks back, one of the black bishops that had been taken was suddenly back, and two white pawns too. Now that black bishop is gone again, but a new rook for that side has returned. Of course, when it changes, it doesn't play out like a regular game. Things just move around, usually with pieces ending up somewhere they couldn't get to in a normal game."

"It actually looks closer to the beginning of a game than it did before this," I said. "With those pieces back. Everything's deployed, and now the real conflict is about to start, which is a pretty confirmation of Queen Mab's story, as far as it goes. Black still has the edge, but white might actually have a better position. Any idea who moves next?"

"None," she said.

"Whoever moves next is going to have a decent advantage," I said. "But either way, it's going to be a real bloodbath." I'd had some difficult ideas about the upcoming battle, and some risky ones, but they were also ones I didn't want to enact. Too dangerous, too costly. But this was a cold, hard reminder that war had costs and there was no avoiding them. Even chess masters lost pieces. Often lots of them.

"Bloodbath," Faith said, shivering and making a frustrated snort. "I don't like the sound of that. I've been pondering a theory that this board is somehow tracking Father's prophecy more than the war. Meaning just the magical elements and not so much ships or troops or even battles."

"That would track, actually," I said. "But I'm not sure it helps so much. If the Black Shuck dropped dead suddenly, the board would show us, but that doesn't tell us much about the deposition of troops or ships."

"It's an oracle," Faith said. "Not a wartime field report."

"Don't you remember our language lessons as children?" I said. "The word *oracle* comes from the Latin *oraculum*, which means 'as useless as a flaming pile of wet socks.'"

"You had a very different tutor from mine, I think," Faith said with a wry smile.

There was a knock at the door and Henry's voice came through. "Justice?"

Faith opened the door and let Henry in.

"You wanted to talk to me?" he said after she'd closed the door and he'd taken the chair near the table.

"We did," I said. Faith sat on the bed and watched, apparently content to let me do the talking.

"Before that," Henry said. "There's something I need to say." His hazel eyes looked serious and I realized that Henry, my little brother, didn't look so little anymore. He'd gotten a bit leaner and looked slightly more muscular than before, but it was the seriousness in his face that really marked him.

I looked at Faith, who looked surprised. Whatever Henry was about to say, she hadn't been expecting it either.

"After... the World Tree," Henry said, "and... Father's death. I had a lot of bad dreams, seeing his death, over and over again."

I'd known he'd felt this way, but something in my blood ran cold as he went on.

"Then I started to have different dreams," he said, staring down at his clasped hands rather than meeting my gaze. "Dreams about being captain. Just me, being captain of this ship, leading the resistance. No explanation of where you'd gone, or why. Just... I was in charge. And I liked it. Then I had a few where I... deposed you." He looked up and I saw that his eyes were moist. "Some of them were violent. I won't say more than that."

"Dreams from one of the gods?" I said, thinking of how Llyr had tried so hard to motivate me.

Henry shook his head. "No, I thought of that after hearing about the dreams that you and Faith have, but I don't think it was anything like that. You haven't described your own as being subtle or sly."

"Subtle is not the word I'd use," Faith said. I couldn't agree more.

"No," Henry said. "I think this was all . . . all from inside of me." He took a deep breath. "Anyway, I started to think about deposing you in my waking hours. Pretty seriously. I'd never really understood why you shot Father. I mean, I understood what you told me about Father being forced to lead the invasion if he'd gone back. I believed all of that—I'd seen too much of the invasion myself to doubt it—but I hadn't really taken it all in on an emotional level. Not then. I knew that part about what he'd stolen from the real Rachek Kasric too, but thought maybe that wasn't so important when you balanced it against the fate of the world. I mean, one person? At least that's what I told myself."

I was suddenly struck by how dangerous an enemy Henry could be, with his strength and power.

Also, he was a member of the House of Thorns, and everyone on the ship liked him. Probably he could lead the Outcasts, if something happened to me.

"Then what happened?" Faith said.

"Then the Wild Hunt came," Henry said. "And Benedict. I'd seen them before, of course, at Newgate, but a lot had happened then and I didn't really understand. This time, seeing Benedict as one of the riders, how completely inhuman he was. Lost to us. Thinking about Father leading the invasion and looking at Benedict . . . well, I think that's when I understood, understood that you had to do what you did." He looked at me and nodded. "I just wanted to tell you that I understand now."

"Thank you," I said, my voice tight.

Just hearing those words from one person had lifted some of the crushing weight I'd felt.

Not all of it, but some.

"Thank you," I said again.

Of course, that just made what I had to ask him even more horrible.

"We need to ask you to do something," I said, rushing now to get it out. "Something incredibly dangerous and stupid."

◁▷◁▷◁▷◁▷◁▷

The *Specter* had several smaller boats for our use, the largest being the launch that I usually used to take us from ship to ship. But this time, we had the launch loaded with some handpicked crew members to transport over to *Seahome*, so Faith, Hunter, Avonstoke, Sands, and I led the way in the smaller cutter. The sun was bright, but the brisk wind was very cold, coming off the salty sea.

Tomorrow we'd likely be in battle. I had a dread feeling that not all of us would make it.

Seahome always struck me wrong. It was profoundly enormous, more of a floating castle than a sea vessel, an extremely impossible place. A clunky, unseaworthy excuse for a craft, sprawling over the ocean like a plague made of planks and beams. It should never have stayed afloat, but there it was, despite logic, science, and my complete indignation, floating easily on the choppy channel rollers. It didn't even bob like a ship, all one piece, but rolled with the waves like a god's discarded sailcloth.

Of course, that was because it wasn't a proper ship, but a raft—a few hundred rafts, really, all tethered together so that the entire structure moved with the sea. To further add to the impossible nature of it, the entire thing was cluttered with platforms, barracks, towers, granaries, mess halls, and stables, in addition to a seemingly random collection of masts and sails all set to catch their own, equally impossible and contradictory breezes. It took a team of weather-controlling magicians working around the clock to keep it all going in the same direction and to prevent *Seahome* from tearing itself apart. Just looking closely at all those structures—the kind that should normally sit on solid land—swaying and rippling along with the ocean, was nauseating.

A group of Faerie waited for us while Avonstoke moored the launch to one of the shell-like protrusions that passed for a post there. Avonstoke, Faith, and Henry all mounted the deck with me.

Lady Rue, or Queen Mab, was easy enough to recognize in the welcoming party. Tall, dark, grim as possible, and back in her steel mask with the haughty expression that so ironically matched her own. The Queen of the Unseelie Court had asked us to keep that secret for now. She feared that the portion of the Outcast Fleet that had come from the Seelie Court, their usual enemy, might not be comfortable with the dark queen in their midst.

"Should I call you Queen Mab now?" I'd asked, just before she'd left the *Specter* the day before.

"'Your Highness'? Or 'mighty worshipfulness'? You have been cursing the name of Lady Rue for so long now," she had replied, "that it would please me now to have you acknowledge me as your ally, possibly your savior."

"Just when I feel myself warming up to you," I had grumbled.

Her answering laugh had been low and throaty and just a little bit frightening.

It was a measure of the strangeness of being among the Faerie that I now felt a surprising measure of reassurance seeing her now. She was a villain, through and through, but I was convinced she was our villain. At least for now.

Everyone waiting for us called themselves allies, but they felt more like enemies.

I suppose I had to count *Seahome*'s two magicians, Prudence and Drecovian, as being on our side. They stood off to one side, waiting, isolated even among the Outcast Fleet. I knew so little about them, when it came right down to it. Prudence, my long-estranged sister, was a complete stranger to me, but I'd already seen that she could be shockingly ruthless when she thought it was called for. Drecovian was equally mysterious.

It came with being a magician, I suppose.

Of course, the sister I did trust, Faith, was also a magician now. Another difficult concept to grapple with. Almost as strange as me being an admiral, something I needed to affirm today in the strongest terms possible. Porgineau, another of the Court Faerie and *Seahome's* nominal captain, stood next to several junior officers, talking and waving his arms wildly.

He clearly wasn't happy with me. Considering he was the brilliant tactician who had called Ireland a niblet, I felt the same way about him.

Lady Rue guided me over to the waiting cluster. We all knew one another, of course, but there were formalities.

Beaudulaire, the golden-maned and feathered Sphinx from the council meetings, nodded placidly enough, but her claws dug meditatively into the weathered planks, making an unsettling squeaky sound. The dour Lady Druhagaren, leader of the Dwarves, stepped past me to shake Faith's hand.

"Well done, lass," she said, reaching up to grasp Faith's hand in a grip that made my sister wince. "We don't know how you harnessed Cernunnos's magic to keep that ship afloat, but we're glad you did. Kept our admiral from the depths, and we're all grateful."

Faith pulled her hand carefully free, then, with the kind of careful expression that told me she was about to enjoy herself immensely, said, "Oh, I didn't do anything. That was Justice."

Lady Druhagaren looked over at me, not quite understanding. "But . . . you're not a magician," she said to me.

"Didn't use magic," I said automatically. "It wasn't just me either. We reefed the sails, dropped a sea anchor, pumped the pumps 'round the clock, and still it was a near thing. Just seamanship and a lot of work, most of it done by the crew."

Beaudulaire and Druhagaren looked at each other, clearly confused. I could see I might just as well be talking wizardry to dairy maids. They had no idea what I was talking about.

Draust, the tiny, wizened old beggar-looking man who led the Jötnar, grinned. "Well I'll be blowed," he said with delight. "Wizardry of another sort, it seems." He thumped me on the back, each blow like a friendly cudgel, and that seemed to satisfy the rest of them. I had to stumble to avoid pitching over on my face. Several of the larger Trolls, subordinates of some sort, all grinned and shook their fists joyously at me. That was all terrifying enough; I tried not to imagine what it would be like if they actually meant to threaten someone.

Whatever Lady Rue had told them, it seemed I had their support now.

Behind them were a trio of British naval officers. We'd barely met, but I'd known of them, men that Father had drafted for duty aboard his ship but who had refused to serve after I'd replaced Captain Caine. As symbolic a group as you could ask for when talking about the difficulty of getting British seamen and the Faerie to work together. I'd asked for them to be there, and they didn't look happy about it.

"Ah," said Lady Druhagaren, scratching at a shock of red hair peeking out from underneath a steel helmet studded with black lumps I suspected were a fortune in uncut gems. "Your countryman, of course. Reasonably competent cannon crew, they are." She waved them over.

"Lieutenant Commander Stephens," the first man said, saluting crisply. "This here's Lieutenants Wyndham and Radcliff." We'd barely met, these men and I, but there was a hostility and tension between us that hung palpably in the air.

"How has it been, serving on *Seahome*?" Faith said, clearly trying to break the tension.

"As you'd expect, ma'am," Stephens said, which might have been an answer or no answer at all. "Midshipman Whitman is with the rest of the men, that is able seamen Bottomly and Fulson, ma'am. We man the Red Clover Tower."

"Red Clover Tower?" I said.

"Yes, ma'am," Stephens said. "Normal terminology, like aft or forward, won't serve here." His voice dripped disdain at the unnatural state of Faerie affairs. "So we had to improvise. Our tower is near the big red sail. Not sure where the clover part came in, ma'am."

"Believe that's a lady that Wyndham fancies back in the world, sir," Radcliff, an earnest, pinched-looking fellow, said, then immediately realized he'd spoken out of turn.

I turned. The murmuring among the Faerie officers had reached a fevered pitch, and Captain Porgineau was now approaching.

"This plan of yours is pure, unadulterated idiocy!" he said coldly. "Dangerous and foolish."

"Pure, unadulterated idiocy, sir," Avonstoke said smoothly. "Or try, 'Admiral Kasric, Lady of Thorns, Commander of the Fleet.' Your lady, admiral and commander, if it comes to that, but we understand if you can't fit all of that in every sentence." He had stepped in between Porgineau and me and had a hand on the man's chest, impeding his progress quite effectively.

"Well, yes," Porgineau snapped. "Of course, but this plan . . ." He tried to lean around Avonstoke to glare at me but wasn't having much luck.

"A necessity," Lady Rue said from behind him. I hadn't seen her move from the other side of the crowd, but there she was. Porgineau and most of the Faerie stiffened when she spoke sharply. If they only knew who she really was. Despite our agreement that her identity remain a secret, it was still very strange to have her support me in public, though I kept that off my face.

I took Avonstoke by the arm and gently pulled him aside, facing the Faerie captain.

"I don't like it either," I said to Porgineau quietly. "Honestly, if I had a better option, I'd take it. But we don't." For all his pomposity, Porgineau had a valid objection. My current battle plan called for *Seahome* to take the brunt of the incoming attack. But what choice did we have? It couldn't chase down any of the smaller opposing ships, and we couldn't blockade them all. I was hoping, however, that if I put out tempting-enough bait, the enemy ships would try and push that advantage and converge on *Seahome*. That might allow us some tactical alternatives, such as an ambush or flanking maneuver, assuming that the invaders would take the bait and that *Seahome* could survive an initial attack from their entire fleet, both of which assumptions were far from certain.

I had Sands' spies hard at work to try and discover who, if it was just one person, would be leading that invasion fleet, but they'd so far come up empty. If the commander or commanders were cautious, that plan didn't have a prayer. We had a few other aces up our sleeves, like a dragon and several magicians, but the enemy had those too, and if we used our few magical resources to counter their naval power, we were sunk then too.

No, we needed some way to counter their superior numbers militarily.

"Retreat is the only option," Porgineau said.

"Our way back to Faerie is blocked," Lady Rue said with disdain. "You know this." She wasn't helping. I could see Porgineau stiffen when she spoke, digging in, but his gaze was locked with mine. I could see now that I might have been able to appeal to him in private, but here, with Lady Rue goading him, I had fewer choices.

"Then we hide in the fog," Porgineau said.

"While the Black Shuck takes over the mainland," Faith said, "and then the rest of the world."

"It's not my world," Porgineau said fiercely.

"Do I understand correctly," Avonstoke said with an utterly reasonable, almost conversational tone, "that you are refusing to follow your admiral's orders?" He shot Henry a glance. We'd all been discussing this probability, along with possible steps, for most of the morning.

Porgineau drew himself up to his fullest, not inconsiderable height. "They're idiocy. I won't have any part in them." He moved toward me, ready to jab a finger in my face to fully make his point.

"Listen, girl . . ." he started.

Avonstoke moved to intercept him again, but he wasn't the first one there.

Quiet, unassuming Henry, with his easygoing, cheerful face and sandy hair that kept falling in his eyes, making him seem even younger than his fifteen years, hadn't said a word this entire time. He was one of the shortest people present and barely reached Porgineau's armpit. But he stepped neatly behind Porgineau and got ahold of the captain's artfully crafted leather belt in one hand, and a fistful of glittering epaulet in the other. He lifted the man, twice his size, easily over his head in one smooth motion. The captain flailed and gasped, but this didn't stop Henry from tossing the Court Faerie captain the way someone might throw a soccer ball. Porgineau, taken utterly by surprise, screamed as he flew, a high-pitched wail. We were about fifty feet from the *Seahome*'s raft-style edge. Porgineau cleared it, and the two moored boats, with plenty of room to spare. His scream cut off when he hit the ocean.

The British officers stood gaping at us, stunned. The Faerie milled around uncertainly.

I jabbed a finger in the direction the hapless Porgineau had flown. "When he makes it back on board..."

"If he makes it back on board," the Lady Rue added mildly. She looked completely unruffled, perhaps a bit pleased with how it was all turning out. I could see the Court Faerie around us take that in.

I nodded. "If he makes it back on board, have his military insignia stripped. Then put him to work in the galley."

"I—I'm very sorry, Lady Kasric," the nearest Court Faerie officer stammered. We had many of the Court Faerie in the Outcast Fleet, originally from both the Seelie and Unseelie Courts. The ones from the Unseelie Court had tended toward more barbaric hairstyles, and this one had his flared out in a wild black mane. I wonder if being from the Unseelie Court meant that he already knew the Lady Rue's real identity. Either way, Lady Rue or Queen Mab, she commanded respect, and I could see him shooting her glances that she ignored.

"It's Admiral Kasric," Henry said. "We've already corrected you lot once." He flexed his hands and looked to be enjoying himself immensely.

"Yes, Admiral, sir," the hapless officer said. "But we don't have a galley, as such."

The Lady Rue transfixed him with an icy glare. "Make. One."

"Yes, sir." He saluted her, then flinched, perhaps realizing that it wasn't really a proper address for a non-officer, whatever her rank, and hurriedly bowed. Then, in a near panic, he started saluting and bowing to everyone around him, in all directions.

"Belay that," I said. "Your name, it's Glaudrang, right? Lieutenant Glaudrang?"

"Yes, sir," he said, astonished.

I nodded, glad I'd gotten it right. I hadn't been sure.

"Hold there a second," I said, and turned to the others.

Now *Seahome* needed a new captain. Something I hadn't discussed with the others because I'd been hoping to avoid it. I should have been more emotionally prepared for this, but I'd hoped against hope that Porgineau wouldn't choose to fight me. But he had, in front of everyone.

"Henry Kasric," I said formally.

"Aye," he said. He stood up straighter and brushed the sandy hair out of his eyes.

"We need a new captain for *Seahome*. Will you accept the post?"

"Lor', yes!" he said. I'd been worried that he'd be upset with me, but somehow his gleeful exuberance, as if I hadn't just asked him to step into harm's way, was even worse. His place within the House of Thorns meant that he'd command the instant respect of every one of Father's sailors, a great many of which were coming aboard now. Title and birthright felt like a stupid reason to appoint anyone to anything in these uncertain times, but it mattered to the Faerie, and that was what we needed. Also, some of the Faerie tribes respected strength as much as anything else, and Henry had displayed that quite admirably. I could already see the Trolls and Goblins of *Seahome*'s crew nodding with acceptance of my announcement.

I just hoped my little brother lived long enough to forgive me.

But there was another concern. Henry had displayed a prowess in battle, true, but also a battle-rage that was shocking to see. With each battle it seemed a little worse. I hoped that my little brother didn't lose all of who he was in this war. In truth, I hoped that for all of us.

"Congratulations, Captain Henry Kasric, of the House of Thorns, on your promotion," I said, still keeping my tone formal and pitching it for all to hear. I turned to Sands.

"Commander Sands," I said. His eyebrows shot up at the title. His green eyes held an element of amusement, but also trepidation. Those eyes had glowed with the greenish cast of Faerie absinthe, once, when he'd still been a magician. Now I needed another task of him. He'd never been part of the crew, exactly, but he was going to need a title for what I was asking of him, and I wanted to make sure he had it. "My brother will need someone to advise him on the Faerie. Someone I can trust. Will you take the post as his second?"

Sands gulped, his yellow beard twitching, but he nodded. "I'd be honored."

"Good," I said. "Join the other officers here." I nodded at the Glaudrang and the other Court Faerie.

Sands did so, looking small and out of place among the officers in their respondent uniforms, but also fiercely determined.

Lady Rue had made her way to my side. Now she murmured, low enough for just my ears: "Your commander seems to have misplaced his uniform."

"Ah, yes," I said. "An oversight I'm sure you'll help me correct, yes?" I said, turning her way.

"Of course." Lady Rue fixed Glaudrang with a steely gaze. "I imagine you can dredge up some uniforms?"

"Yes m-milady," he stammered.

"Very good."

Sands, standing with the officers, decided that one of the other officers was standing too close and turned to glare at him. The woman hastily backed away. I was relieved Sands had said yes and even more relieved that he was making the best of it. The officers and crew might obey Henry because I'd put him in charge, or because he was part of the House of Thorns, but Henry would need to understand those he was commanding, and Sands could help with that. Lady Rue's tacit approval didn't hurt either. More of *Seahome*'s sailors and soldiers were lining up behind the Faerie leaders and nobles. Not summoned or at parade rest or anything, just a crowd of onlookers forming up.

Swayle and the Crow Whisper Brigade came off the launch first, in perfect formation, presenting themselves with a thunderous stamp of their spears on the deck in perfect unison.

I saluted her.

"I was told," I called out, "a story about the Crow Whisper Brigade. One of shame. Having watched these soldiers throughout this war, I must tell you, I cannot give credit to such a story. These are the bravest, fiercest warriors I have seen and have comported themselves with honor and bravery, flinging themselves into danger at every turn." I raised my voice. "But if I did believe that story, I would say that their disgrace ends. Today. Now." The tale Starling had told me, before he'd died, wasn't one of betrayal or cowardice, only that they'd gotten to a battle late. It wasn't much of a dishonor, by my reckoning.

I'd been late hundreds of times, but Swayle had moved in a cloud of barely repressed shame the entire time I'd known her and it had gone on long enough.

There was a roar of approval from the crowd. I had them with me on this, at least.

"Will you fling yourself, Colonel Swayle," I went on, "and your gallant marines into danger one more time for us?"

Swayle, already ramrod straight, stood a bit straighter and saluted again. "It would be our honor, ma'am." The middle part of her face visible through the slit in her helmet, usually stern and hard enough to crack walnuts on, now held a trace of sorrow on it. Her eyes were golden, without pupils, like all the Court Faerie, but they held a deep well of sadness in them as they seemed to say, *Nothing can erase my shame, but I thank you, profoundly, for the effort.* She wasn't about to forgive herself her shame, even if the rest of the world did.

Our sailors came next, Prowlers, Dwarves, and Goblins armed with cutlasses. I'd pulled a third of the *Specter's* crew for this detail. Though *pulled* wasn't exactly the right word. I'd had to turn volunteers away.

Next, two of our Dwarven women, Temerisan and Sorgia, led Wargan, our pacifist Troll, by the hand. I was pleased to see that our Troll had fattened up a little from the pathetic, rawboned creature he'd been when we discovered him in the hold, but that made it so much worse to send him into harm's way. Iela, the female Dwarf I knew best, had been Wargan's primary handler up until now, but Iela was also the only person I had who could serve as a medic, and *Seahome* needed that desperately, so I'd kept her back on *Seahome*. Perhaps Wargan would learn something about how to make war from the Trolls there. I had mixed feelings about that too. The gargoyle, Daccus, followed behind them, squinting in the bright sunlight.

A tall man brought up the rear, moving stiffly from months spent in the brig. He went bareheaded and squinted in the bright sunlight. Captain Caine.

He still had his pride, despite being in the brig for the past three months. Even cleaned up and with his hair and beard trimmed, there was a prison pallor that clung to him, and a darkness around the eyes.

"Are you sure about him?" Faith asked under her breath.

"No," I admitted. "But he's the best man for the job. We need all the help here we can get. Besides, we can't leave him in the brig forever."

Caine stopped in front of me and saluted. His eyes were sullen.

I waved Stephens and the other British officers over.

"*Seahome's* a sitting duck out here without cannons," I said. "Besides the ones on the HMS *Specter in the Mist*, we have only a dozen cannons capable of firing in magical areas. Like here." Caine compressed his lips tightly at the HMS—Her Majesty's Ship—which I'd used deliberately in his presence. But he said nothing.

"Four cannons, fifty-four pounders," I said. "All of them in Red Clover Tower. The gun crews are Faerie, but I'd prefer to have someone overseeing them who has an intimate familiarity with their operations. The British officers are all there, and they need a gun captain."

Caine's stony expression broke slightly into a sneer when I'd mentioned the Faerie crew. This man had been loyal to Father, a good captain commanding the *Specter*. Then Father had charged me to take command of the ship and the Outcast Fleet, and Captain Caine had stood in the way. None of that was his fault, and I'd lain awake at night more than once on his account.

There was no love lost between the two of us, but the truth was, I completely understood his position. He'd objected to Father putting me in charge without enough experience, and he wasn't wrong. But Father had asked me to take his place as admiral and I did it. That made removing Caine part of what needed to be done, so I'd done it. I knew I had a chance of saving England. Caine didn't.

But Caine was a good man, and a good sailor to boot, and I needed every able-bodied person, human or Faerie, that I could get.

He opened his mouth and I could see from his expression that he meant to refuse. Damn the man's pride.

Before he could get the refusal out, I stepped closer, so close my face was within inches of his, or would have been if he hadn't been so tall.

"Think, man!" I hissed, pitching my voice so only he could hear. "The fleet is going to war tomorrow, one we'll probably lose. Do you want to die helplessly in the brig or out here, where you can fight and possibly, just possibly, strike a blow for England? Think about what Father would want!"

"You mean," he sneered, "before you killed him?"

The words hit like a blow, but I kept my face impassive, or tried to.

"Father put his own life after England," I said. "Would you do less?"

He glared at me, but finally seemed to come to a decision. "No," he admitted. "I would not." He nodded. He didn't salute.

"You'll command the cannons?" The other rub was that four cannons, fifty-four pounders or not, wouldn't be nearly enough against even one ship, let alone four, if half of what Avonstoke had said about the Troll artillery was true. *Devastating* was the word he'd used.

"Aye," Caine said. "I'll command your cannons."

I nodded. "Good." I didn't bother taking umbrage at him not saying sir or saluting. Not with what he was going to be facing in that tower. He was just one more person I was likely sending to their death, and if he wanted to die with his dignity and will intact, well, I couldn't blame him.

After I sent Caine and the other human officers off, Drecovian appeared at my elbow. He was looking at Faith. She nodded and looked at me.

"There's someone else you need to confer with while you're here," she said.

"The dragon," I said.

She nodded. "Yes."

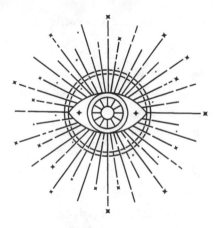

CHAPTER 11

JOSHUA
Making Plans

I n the end, it was almost too easy.

It was almost like the Faerie had holes in their minds, the way they obsessed over everything to do with the bloody prophecy and left all the details of actually winning the war to him. While the Black Shuck and Widdershins' reign of terror might have been responsible for keeping the Seelie and Unseelie forces from falling upon each other, the fact that the invasion forces still had food and shelter was undeniably Joshua's doing. He was in his office with fine pens and papers sorted in an orderly fashion on his polished desk and tea still warm in a silver service on the sideboard. The order and implements of his desk felt like his last connection to humanity, even as he shuffled and manipulated them and pondered the details of the Faerie's control over England.

The huge ships of the line were monstrosities. True, they were ideal for ferrying a prodigious number of troops, and all four carried an absurd number of cannons. Enough to turn poor *Specter* into kindling if they could ever get the smaller, faster ship with a full broadside. The problem was, they were top-heavy and ungainly, so they didn't actually sail all that well. Urguag's Windshrikes would take care of getting them across the channel at a decent speed, no matter the wind conditions, but clumsiness and lack of maneuverability would still be issues in any battle.

Mother and Widdershins had summoned him for orders yesterday morning, which they delivered, not during any kind of war council or staff meeting, but during a bizarre parody of a tea party out on the battlements of Dover Castle, overlooking camps all around as if it were some kind of living, murderous garden. There had even been little cucumber and watercress sandwiches. Widdershins bid Joshua sit, so he did, carefully, so as to not break the chair.

Then the moment stretched out. The wind brought them the sound and the scent of the sea and the smells of cooking fires and the dankness of the castle walls. Widdershins was watching Mother, his glasses gleaming, his eye sunken, dark shadows, even in the morning light. Mother kept looking out toward the water, not looking at either of them. Joshua wasn't sure she even knew he was there. Joshua sat, trying not to jitter. He could hear, could *feel*, the voices that whispered in the back of his mind whenever he got this close to Widdershins, and he tried to keep them out.

White flowers on a grave of black earth and an unburied corpse three feet away . . . emerald pine needles, glistening with frost while two men, possibly soldiers, struggle, both of them fighting for the same knife . . . one falls and the other lifts the knife . . . a spray of red on the white snow . . . a cold river and streaks of red flowing slowly, peacefully through it.

Joshua fought with his mantra, a feeble, imperfect defense, but the only one he had. *I am me and no one else. I am here now, and nowhere else . . .*

"Such pretty dreams," Mother said distantly. "The red is lovely on the snow." Joshua felt a shock as he realized that he and Mother were receiving the same visions, hearing the same whispers, it seemed. That had never happened before, or if it had, he'd never known.

Then she shook her head, as if to drive something out or shake something off. "I don't like the dreams of lists and charts. It's boring, and too much like death."

"Those come from your baby boy, dear heart," Widdershins murmured. "Should we not cherish them, if only for that reason?"

"No," Mother said. "Too much like a desiccated corpse for my taste."

Widdershins gave Joshua a brief shrug as he lifted his hands, palms up, as if to apologize for her faux pas. *Women*, the motion seemed to say, *we must allow them their foibles.* The motion was all Joshua could read, for the silver discs and shadows of Widdershins' face were entirely unreadable. Joshua's pulse was pounding in his ears. He couldn't remember ever being so afraid.

Widdershins captured Mother's hand in his pristine, white-gloved ones and kissed the inside of her wrist.

They sat a while longer, Mother still looking out over the camped army to the crashing waves beyond. Neither looked at Joshua. Mother's face took on a blank look that said little about what was going on inside her head. Joshua was reminded briefly of the many dinner farces that Mother had held with the London nobility and the Soho Shark, one of which Justice had interrupted, where Mother had used her powers to enslave many a nobleman as her whims dictated. Now, it seemed, it was her turn to play the puppet.

Then something in Mother's gaze changed, and Joshua changed his assessment of what might be happening.

"The Wealdarin will occupy the hold," Mother said finally.

"I had thought the dark would be bad for them," Joshua said.

"They will go dormant in the dark," Mother said. "Which, as it happens, will be convenient for transport. They will take up most of the hold. The rest of the floors you shall pack with troops, as many as possible, including the Pix, Kellas Cats, Hanged Dogs, and the like. Section the hold as best you can to keep them separate. Pick a select crew of Court Faerie, Dwarves, and Goblins to man the deck. There need not be many, as the Windshrikes will do most of the work. No more than a few dozen."

"The bulkheads won't hold very long," Joshua said. "Not if anything like a Hanged Dog wants out. There are likely to be more than a few fatalities."

"How many?"

Joshua licked his lips, feeling the fangs and then closed his mouth suddenly, aware again that his tongue seemed to be forked now, like a serpent's. More of the changes. He'd woken up and discovered it last week and wasn't used to it yet. "As many as twenty percent."

"Acceptable," Mother said. Widdershins nodded his agreement. "As long as the Wealdarin are kept separate, manage the rest as best you can."

"Yes, Mother," Joshua had said. He wasn't at all surprised that both Widdershins and Mother weren't at all worried about so much death among their own troops.

They had dismissed him, then, and he left as quickly as he could manage. He'd waited for three hours, keeping a large axe near at hand, wondering if Widdershins had picked up the betrayal in Joshua's mind, but no one had come for him.

He was honest to admit that his planned betrayal wasn't altruistic. He'd betrayed London, England, and the rest of the human race long ago for Mother and didn't expect any forgiveness from history. Not from Justice, Faith, or any of the rest either, though that part panged him a bit.

Mother had told him at length about how he needed to be made into an instrument of war when she started giving him the doses to bring around the change, but she hadn't given him any specifics, and he hadn't even thought to ask. By the stink of his medicine, he knew that Faerie absinthe was involved, but also that there was more in it than that. The iron taste made him suspect blood. It being a Faerie mixture, he'd assumed that she'd been turning him into one of the Faerie creatures. There was some irony in that, seeing as how she always sneered when talking about his siblings, calling them Faerie abominations. This war, to Mother, had always been about her against the Lord of Thorns, no matter what she said.

Except now he'd seen so many of the Faerie, and none of them matched what he was becoming. So, he didn't know what Mother was doing, and it was long past due to find out. He didn't have a plan of attack for that, yet, but he would.

He looked down at the shipping reports still in his hand. A trail of bread crumbs for him to follow. Mother used a great deal of unusual supplies. Things she never did without, because she used them on herself, on Joshua, in most of her magic. As a result, tracking the supplies was a reasonably sure method of tracking Mother's movements, which is how he got wind of her trips to the docks. Mother had little interest in the ships themselves, so it got Joshua looking. When he'd discovered that a number of pages were missing from the logbook of one of the prison ships there, he knew he'd found it.

So that's where Mother was holding her insurance, Temperance du Thorns. She was on the *Emerald Demise* already. The same ship that Mother and Joshua would be commanding. That made things easier.

Joshua's eyes, like hot coals, were reflected back to him in the window. His grin, fangs and all, looked wild, feral, and dangerous in a way that transcended the animal kingdom.

Just you wait, Mother, he thought. *Just you wait.*

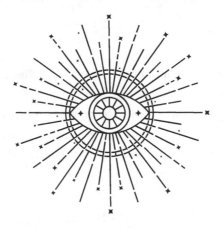

CHAPTER 12

JUSTICE
War Council

"When the battle starts," Brocara rumbled, "you will have a number of considerations beyond troops, sail, ships, or weather."

"The other dragons," I said.

Brocara turned her enormous head, and a look passed between her and Drecovian.

"Yes," Drecovian said, and there was something brittle in his voice. "We are going to do the best we can to keep the other dragons away from you, because if we can't, that will likely be the end of it for the Outcast Fleet."

Faith, Henry, Avonstoke, Prudence, Sands, and I had all come to see Brocara, the dragon, and Drecovian, our most senior magician. Faith had been spending a great deal of time with them the past few months since the two of them had taken over Faith's magical training, but it was still something of a shock to me to watch their greeting and realize that

Faith clearly had a lot of fondness for them both. The irascible magician, who specialized in the deeply unsettling shadow magic, still made my hackles stand up. That went double for the dragon, at least.

Lady Rue had come with us and brought Beaudulaire, the Sphinx, who was her second-in-command. The golden-haired woman-creature, with a lion's body and golden eagle's wings, was unnerving in her own right, but she kept licking her lips and looking nervously up at the dragon. That somehow made me feel better.

We were all seated around a polished walnut table set in the flat expanse of deck where Brocara lay. The team of Goblins had brought tea, like last time, but it was decent Darjeeling instead of the foul travesty we'd drunk before.

Brocara was nearly a hundred feet from tip to tail, but she'd coiled into a tight bundle behind Drecovian, with her wings furled, so that her horned head was only a dozen feet or so above us.

Drecovian looked pained. "We may have a problem."

"There is no question of 'may,'" Brocara rumbled. There was some reproach in her voice.

"You're sure that's who you saw?" Drecovian said, glaring up at the dragon. "From a glimpse of a shadow on a cloudy night?"

"I am certain," Brocara said. She held up one lethal claw and began to delicately nibble at the place where skin and claw met. Her teeth were the size of swords. It was intimidating as hell, and I was pretty sure Brocara hadn't even meant it to be. She looked bored, if anything.

Drecovian didn't look intimidated. He looked peevish. "Just because you're usually right," he snapped, "doesn't mean you *always* are."

"If you two need some time to be alone," Lady Rue purred, "to mend your lovers' quarrel . . ." She didn't look intimidated by dragons, either.

"Do you think me wrong,?" Brocara said.

"No," Drecovian admitted. He looked at us. "No, I think the Black Shuck has managed to recruit another dragon."

"Not just any dragon," Brocara said. "Usarador, the Red Death."

The Lady Rue leaned back suddenly, clearly surprised by this last bit of information. "The Red Death has never taken an interest in human affairs."

"Nor has he now," Brocara said. "He is interested in *me*. He wants to test me in battle. Has wanted to for eons."

"It was bad enough with the Green Trio," Beaudulaire said.

"Green Duo, now," Prudence said helpfully. "Brocara killed one, remember?"

There was a sudden, awkward pause. Drecovian looked without expression at Prudence, and a chill went down my back. Even Lady Rue and Avonstoke, the two most irrepressible people I'd ever met, looked taken aback. It was as if, back home, someone had just cheerfully mentioned defecating into the Holy Chalice. Twice.

"What?" Prudence said. "We're supposed to pretend that it never happened? Or that it might not happen again? We're at war. With dragons."

"She's not wrong," Brocara said, glaring at Drecovian. The deepest part of her voice rattled my empty cup in its saucer.

Drecovian held his empty expression for a few moments, then nodded slowly. "No, I suppose not." Brocara sniffed delicately and with great satisfaction, a sound like an enormous bellow, and looked, somehow, very satisfied, as if Prudence's statement had just decided an argument between her and Drecovian. That level of smugness was a strange and somehow entirely appropriate expression on a dragon. Next to me, I could see Faith wearing the almost blank, wide-eyed expression she used when trying, very hard, to suppress a smile.

Avonstoke, Beaudulaire, and even Lady Rue all grew silent at the thought of putting dragons at risk. You could see their minds playing out the worst possibilities.

"Now," Drecovian said, "all the dragons that exist are in the war. If we lose them, we lose everything." There was a different emphasis on *we*. He didn't just mean our side of the war. He meant all of Faerie.

"You're telling me," Avonstoke said in a choked voice, "that there are only four dragons left in all of Faerie? What about the dragon of Fenmore Glenn?"

"Dead," Drecovian said. "Ages ago."

"The Devourer of Mountains?"

"Dead," Drecovian said.

"Wasn't actually that large anyway," Brocara said. "But 'decent-sized scratcher of mountains' lacks poetry."

"What about . . ."

"All dead," Drecovian said flatly.

"The Black Shuck won't risk it," Beaudulaire said. "He *can't.* Can he? He'd have as much to lose as the rest of us."

No one bothered to answer that. No one had to. We'd already seen what the Black Shuck was willing to do. He had no limits, and we all knew it.

"Usarador will come for me," Brocara said. "He has always longed to test me, but there are rules and traditions in dragon history that prevented it. This war circumvents all of those niceties. It's his excuse. For that matter, I have longed for this too." Her claws flexed against the timbers of the deck, and wood shrieked and tore hard enough to make Faith, Henry, Avonstoke, and I, who were all closest, straighten up in alarm. "However, this is more to be considered than just the two of us. I must find a way to contend with all of them, Usarador and the Greens. I have pledged to keep them off of you, whatever the cost. Losing that battle will mean losing the war, and it is my fear that the Black Shuck, if victorious in this land, will then be in a position to take over all of Faerie, even enslaving dragons. We stop him here, or everything is lost."

"*We,*" Drecovian said, looking hard up at the dragon, "shall have to keep them off of you. You won't be alone."

The dragon growled deep in her chest, a sound that somehow managed to impart fondness and deep sorrow. "I did not want to speak for you. It will be dangerous for me."

"It will be nearly suicidal for you," the old man said flatly.

"Even more so for you," Brocara said gently. "Magic will not be much use against the Red Death."

"You're not facing him alone," Drecovian said.

The dragon dipped her head solemnly in acquiescence.

"Is there anything we can do to help?" I asked

Drecovian shook his head. "Not really. Perhaps we can drive one of the dragons close enough to receive cannon fire, but any dragon would be far more dangerous to the ships than the other way around. This is our fight. You'll have enough to do down here."

"The Lord of Thorns had two major contributions to this war," Brocara said. "The first was bringing the prophecy of Virtues vs. Sins to light."

I could feel my face twitch into a frown. Father's machinations with the prophecy had affected all of us, but not for the better. Now, the Black Shuck was playing Father's prophecy game better than he had and better than we were. They had all Seven Sins, and we had no idea where all of our Seven Virtues were, despite the fact that Father had sired all of us. Pure idiocy. Some contribution.

"The second greatest contribution," Brocara went on, "was undoubtedly the cannons on board your ship, Justice. They are the only explosive weapon lethal to Faerie and capable of firing inside of Faerie and human territory as well as the between places, like inside the mist."

"The Black Shuck's ships won't have cannons?" I said. That tipped the balance considerably. If they didn't have any real weapons, we could stay at range and easily harass a single ship without putting ourselves in danger. But could we stop four ships of that size?

"They won't be entirely without weapons," Avonstoke said, clearly reading my thoughts. "Their artillery will only have the effective range of one of your carronades, but at that range, they'll be far deadlier than any cannon. I've seen them at war. It's truly awesome and terrifying."

"Their artillery?" I said. "What kind of artillery will the Black Shuck have?"

"Trolls," Avonstoke said.

"Trolls?" I could hear my voice climb incredulously. I remembered him talking about going to war with Trolls in the distant past. He'd made them sound very dangerous.

"Trolls," he repeated. "The projectiles they'll use will be closer in size to your cannons than to your cannonballs. Devastating if they hit."

"How many rocks like that could you fit on a ship?" Faith asked.

"How many do you *need*?" Henry said.

"How accurate?" I said.

"Accurate enough," Avonstoke said.

"Well," I said. "That's marvelous." My mind was already working feverishly. Against one ship, there were lots of possibilities. Against four? I needed seven more *Specters*, at least, and about a hundred more miles of sea between England and France.

"What about Wealdarin?" Faith asked. "Can they bring them on a ship?"

"Almost certainly," Drecovian said. "But they'll keep them in the hold, is my guess. Not exposed, because the Wealdarin will be *very* vulnerable at sea. The Black Shuck will want to land them at the first opportunity. The minute he gets one on land, they will run amok, ignoring battlements and mundane wartime obstacles. The Wealdarin will stride through any French defenses like elk through grass." It was a strange image to consider, those arboreal monsters, some of them two stories tall, stuck in the hold of one of those ships.

"How vulnerable?" I asked. They'd been one of our insurmountable obstacles to retaking England.

Drecovian bobbled his head side to side, a noncommittal motion. "They'll drown with the rest of the ship if you can sink it. The ocean is not a place they are meant to be."

"There is still the matter of their full complement of Sins," the queen said, "while we have only our few Virtues."

"I'll say," Henry said, but no one laughed.

"The prophecy isn't what's going to decide this," I said hotly. "It's meaningless."

"If it is," Avonstoke said gently to me, "or if it isn't, the Faerie *believe* in it. They'll fight harder if they believe we have a chance to win, and right now, most of them believe we're doomed if we don't have the prophecy on our side."

Faith shook her head at me, clearly frustrated. "Father's prophecy is a spell. Spells don't always work as designed, but the more juice you can put behind it, the more powerful it is, and Father put a lot of juice into this one. There's no guarantee it will do exactly what he imagined, and it certainly isn't the only thing affecting our future, but it *will* do *something*. That something may be subtle and behind the scenes, but it's making an impact, I promise you. Think of it as being enormously lucky, if you will. You might be able to overcome luck with strategy and naval tactics, but it's better to have it than not have it. To ignore the prophecy simply because you don't understand it—"

"No one understands it!" I complained. "If anyone actually seemed to understand how it worked, that would be something."

She sighed. "Say you sail toward an enemy ship with cannons and you know they're going to shoot at you. The cannon might miss, yes? In fact, at anything except close range, it might miss a *lot*. It might misfire too, but it's going to do *something*, even if it takes a whole lot of shots, so you'd best include that in your plans, right?"

"It's not the same thing."

"No," she agreed. "It's not, but it's not entirely different either. Cannons are a bit of a mystery to me, but I don't ignore them. Now think of everything that Father, a magician and master tactician, put into the prophecy. My birth, yours, and all our sisters', all the years of machinations. I'd guess the thinking behind the Black Shuck's strategy, and yours, I'd guess"—she tipped her head at Lady Rue—"is that he set something powerful in motion, even if he didn't understand all the ramifications or how it would all play out." She looked back at me. "So they play the game. They'd rather subvert his magic, get some benefit from all that power, then hit it head-on or ignore it. They're both trying to build their team of Sins or Virtues, all constructed according to Father's plan, all of it rife with symbols that mean more to the Faerie than they do to us, and turn Father's own construct against him."

"Fine," I said. "Say I admit the prophecy has power. What am I supposed to do about it?"

She pushed back her hood and rubbed her scalp. "*Use* it. Would it kill us to find seven people of power and name them? We start with the ones we actually have: you, me, Prudence—give up on Hope and Charity, since we can't get them—and name some other people? Avonstoke, Henry, and the queen, to start? Then we just need one more. Say, Drecovian."

"Avonstoke, Henry, and Drecovian are men," I said.

"So I've noticed," Faith said. "Women would be better, but this isn't an exact science. It's magic. And we don't have seven women of power."

"Wait," Henry said. "Me?"

At almost the same time, Avonstoke said, "I'm no magician."

"You," Faith said, jabbing her finger at Henry, "can throw a man the length of the ship. You've ridden with the Wild Hunt and returned, and you're a Kasric and part of the House of Thorns. It all fits. Accept it. You're a perfect symbol for this." She turned to Avonstoke. "*You* are dripping with magical power, including that flaming sword of yours."

"That's Drecovian's magic."

"Doesn't matter. Also, your connection to"—her gaze flickered to me, then away—"to *us* makes you perfect for the position. Symbols, remember?"

Avonstoke looked skeptical but nodded his acceptance.

Henry spread his hands. "If you say so."

Lady Rue pursed her lips, but she didn't object either. She regarded Faith speculatively.

"Then we hold some kind of ceremony," Faith went on, "to get the attention of the gods and magic. Just to hedge our bets and offset whatever magic and luck the Black Shuck and his Sins are generating against us. Then you can win this thing with your nautical voodoo without any interference from the prophecy."

"Fine," I said, feeling childish and ungraceful. "But I won't take orders from a god I don't trust."

"No one is asking you to," Faith said smoothly. "We ask for their blessing, and probably nothing visible or impressive happens, and then you get on with the fighting."

I nodded. I didn't like it, but if we could have this ceremony and then focus on what was important, it would be worth it.

"In the morning, then?" the queen purred, and she looked so satisfied that I had to bite my tongue.

"Agreed," Faith said.

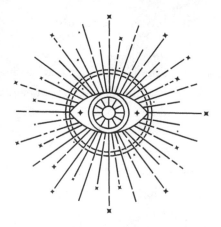

CHAPTER 13

RACHEK KASRIC
Finding Martine and Joshua

He hadn't really been sure if he could navigate the mist or not, but he'd learned a lot of magic while imprisoned in Faerie. Besides, if he couldn't get into England, then his escape from Faerie meant nothing. That might very well be true, but it served little purpose to think like that, so he avoided it. It was amazing how positive he could be now that he'd regained his human shape.

Of course, it was wildly inappropriate. Funny really, how inappropriate. He'd found, living in Faerie, that while horrible things happened, they didn't really happen that often, compared to your average human existence. In fact, the chief calamity for the long-lived Faerie was boredom. By contrast, the average human life was short, brutal, and filled, most often, with unspeakable suffering. Hunger, poverty, and all the common varieties of misery didn't happen in Faerie. And yet, he'd spent countless years in Faerie trying to get back to his home and all its sorrow, only to find it filled with the Faerie. Ironic, perhaps, or tragic. Perhaps both.

The small boat that Justice had given him had a triangular lateen sail that now hung limply in the still air while he stared at the swirling mist and tried to see his death coming. That was a strange girl, he thought, her and Faith both. His almost children, the daughters of the man who'd taken his place. They'd clearly been touched by the Faerie. They practically reeked of magic. But they were also a little frightening. Especially the girls. Meeting those two, with so much of Rachek and Martine in their features, but so much of that Faerie ferocity inside, had been more than a little unsettling. Getting out of their proximity had been a guilty relief, if he was honest. But there was also a fierce humanity to them, a fierce, bright, urgent burning antithetical to the Faerie. It didn't make sense, but there it was.

He nearly missed the first vortex when it came on him, a whirling tornado of magical energy, black in the gray half-light. It swept right for him, and he cried out and crouched in the bottom of the boat as the thing passed right over him.

Then it was gone and he was left unharmed in the slightly rocking boat.

He knew that the magical energy in the mist could take a helpless victim and carry them to other places. Other times even. But somehow, he didn't think that had just happened. It felt as if the vortex had broken over him like a wave over the rocks. It happened again, three more times, before he became sure. He was somehow immune to the magical effects of the mist. This didn't surprise him as much as it should have, perhaps. He had, after all, been living among the Faerie for a long time. That had to mark a person.

When he broke from the mist, he was in a sudden turmoil. Where the powers of the mist hadn't frightened him at all, the natural but very sudden rise and dip of the sea put a shock of real fear right through him. He struggled to get the sail aligned properly and the boat perpendicular to the waves before the little boat capsized and he dropped down unto the undertow. It was a moonlit night, same as when he'd entered the mist, so that part was a relief at least, if he didn't drown.

The water was black all around him, but the breakers glowed white off to his right. The coast. He made for it and finally worked his way in enough to get out and drag the boat the rest of the way up onto the beach.

If he had any doubts about his time and place, they were banished as he came over a rise and looked down into the area surrounding Dover Castle. There were the ships, with yards crossed and ready to go out into the channel. All around the castle and the docks and the beaches were the Faerie horde, all of it made even more unreal and inhuman by the shimmering moonlight.

Also very familiar to Rachek Kasric. The castle and teeming army seemed perfectly normal, but the roads and street signs and manicured lawns that still remained stirred feelings of strangeness and arcane awe inside of him.

He gave a tight smile at this. He'd been in Faerie a long time.

Even now, a trio of the Hanged Dogs, the Black Shuck's overseers, were driving a troop of Dwarves up the gangway of one of the ships. One of the monstrous Kellas Cats was there too, though if it was helping or interfering Kasric couldn't tell. It pounced on one of the Dwarves still on land, savaging it horribly, and the rest of the Dwarves doubled their speed up into the ship.

The Hanged Dogs chased off the Kellas Cat, though the beast took part of his handiwork with him. Kasric could see the boot dangling. One of the Hanged Dogs pushed the rest of the body into the crashing, moonlit foam under the gangway without ceremony. The boarding process went on. It would probably kill a lot more of them, this boarding and transport, but what did that matter? They had lots of bodies to give to the problem.

"Don't move," a cold voice said behind him.

He moved anyway, to the extent of turning his head enough to see who had come up behind him.

Three of the Court Faerie. Most likely from the Unseelie Court in this army, but that was by no means certain. They had thin leather armor and two of them had bows, arrows nocked. The one closest to him had a thin, delicate, and lethal-looking sword, the point of it held steady near the side of his neck.

He surprised himself then, backhanding the sword with a negligent swipe and moving, with uncanny speed, to get his other hand around the Faerie's neck. The other two shot him, then, as he broke the first Faerie's neck. The first arrow sunk into his side, near his belt, but not nearly as far as it should have, and it didn't hurt as much as he thought it should. The other arrow would have gone in under the armpit of the arm that was around the first Faerie's neck. But Rachek, almost without thinking about it, dropped his shoulder and shrugged the blow off the way a prizefighter would deflect a stiff jab.

He dropped the body, picked up the sword, and killed the other two in two quick thrusts. The whole thing hadn't taken more than a few seconds.

Now that he had half a minute to think, he turned, with growing wonder, to the arrow in his side. It came out with little effort, and the wound it left looked small, shallow, like something a penknife could have made.

Rachek was suddenly dizzy and had to sit down between the bodies of the men and women he'd killed.

So. It wasn't just what he'd seen, heard, and learned while in Faerie. His body was somehow fundamentally different. Less human. It had saved him just now, and yet the idea of it came as a staggering blow. A deep, profound loss of a part of him he hadn't even known was gone until just now.

A sudden haunting grief overtook him and he wept, there among the bodies on the fringe of an army. But not for long.

After, he got up and kept moving.

So, it seemed that the Lord of Thorns, after forcing him into that monstrous shape, had also left him with some gifts that remained in his human form. He was clearly faster, stronger, and though he was loath to admit it, probably a lot smarter. It was an intriguing thought, because Rachek Kasric had already been pretty sharp before ever meeting the Lord of Thorns. How smart now, and how best to use that? After having to deal with all the headaches of the Lord of Thorns' Faerie kingdom, his war, his subjects, his wife—not to mention being banished from his home, family, and everything that had been dear to Rachek—it seemed like the least the Faerie Lord could do.

This was an uncomfortable but irresistible line of thought. When forced into the shape of the Faerie King, he hadn't noticed any severe rise in mental faculties. But he knew, now, that the actual Lord of Thorns had suffered a long, slow decline in guile and intelligence. Rachek had been able to track it each year as they clashed over the chessboard but hadn't fully understood the source. He did now. Shapeshifting had dangers, and one of them, apparently, was assuming the properties of the thing you shaped into. So what did that mean for Rachek, living all those years in the Lord of Thorns' shape? The results seemed to speak for themselves.

The question was, had the Lord of Thorns done it on purpose?

A decade ago, Rachek's answer would have been an unconditional yes. The Lord of Thorns, as Rachek knew him then, was a creature of layered schemes and infinite cunning. He didn't do *anything* by accident. But now, after having watched the Faerie's steady decline, Rachek wasn't sure. The Lord of Thorns from years ago might have had different plans, or some way of manipulating that kind of magic, or possibly just hadn't planned on each of them keeping the other's form that long. Years of seeing magic in action, and learning some of his own, in a small way, was ample proof that magic was a messy business.

Would Joshua be the same? For all that he had been born fully human, Rachek had heard from the little ex-magician, Sands, some of what
Joshua had done and what had been done to him. Rachek cursed Martine inwardly, but not very vehemently, because he still loved her. Still,
he had always known her rabidly ambitious nature could cause her trouble. It seemed the Faerie had given that ambition unexpected and unprecedented expression. Still, according to Justice and Faith, Rachek's
kidnapping, once Martine discovered it, had been the incident that had
turned her to the Faerie. Perhaps his return could turn her back. Rachek
had to try.

Infiltrating the Faerie camp was shockingly easy. There were so many
different kinds of Faerie here, from both courts, that the place was a bubbling pool of chaos already. He could have lit his hair on fire and still escaped notice. In fact, that might have made it easier. He'd taken a sword
from one of the guards who had found him on the outskirts, and he now
wore it around his waist. He had a bow from the same source and carried
that as he walked. No one seemed to notice.

He skirted a cloud of the abhorrent Pix, feeding in the shadow of a
reddish tree on something that had probably once been human, shuddering as he did. Horrible little things, but they were too busy with their
feast to bother him. There were some campfires and tents, almost feeling
like a military camp such as he'd known in the past if you didn't know
that the figures around the fires were inhuman. He avoided the fires and
sentries carefully. They might ask questions. He was gaunt enough to
pass for one of the Court Faerie, perhaps, at some distance, but not close
up. He pulled his hood up and shadowed his features as best he could.

Gleaming eyes watched him from underneath one of the hedges but
didn't make any move to follow him. In the shadow of another tree—
not a natural English tree either, but something with reddish, waving,
hungry, fronds—stood a figure much like a man, if you didn't count the
batlike wings on his, no . . . *her* back. Rachek had assumed a man because
of how muscular she was. He avoided her too, but needn't have worried.

She seemed entirely absorbed in murmuring some kind of lullaby to the tree and didn't pay him any mind.

As he got near to the castle, a trio of black birds, storm crows, perhaps, landed near him and started to scream raucously. Rachek found that he could still work the bow without any difficulty. One, two, three shots and three dead birds, and the alarms fell silent. Several fanged lizards with saddles on them looked up as he did this but then went back to grazing.

⊲⊳⊲⊳⊲⊳⊲⊳

Rachek watched the castle for some time. There was nothing as systematic as guards or sentries, but it was swarming with a great many Faerie, many of them types he couldn't begin to identify. There was no telling what kinds of powers or senses some of them might have. Besides, it wasn't like he could just accost Martine in a hallway somewhere and expect a warm reception.

So, he watched. Mostly, all the activity was centered on preparing the ships. Rachek could see them at the docks. Four ships of the line. That was bad for the Outcast Fleet. Bad for the rest of the world too, but there wasn't anything he could do about it.

It was late on the second night of his surveillance that he saw the procession leaving the castle. All the Sins were there. The Black Shuck, Widdershins, the Goblin Knight . . . these were all easy enough to recognize by reputation, even though he'd never seen them before. The withered woman behind them was likely Westerly. He'd put a knife in her throat if he got the chance. If he dared, for honesty forced him to admit that his fear of her ran nearly as deep as his hatred. This was the woman that had taken Martine for the Faerie in the first place, and right under the Lord of Thorns' nose. He fingered the hilt of his sword while his pulse pounded in his ears.

The others he didn't know.

That was, until Joshua stepped into view. Even with Justice and Faith's warnings about his monstrous appearance, with the heavy ram's horns, it was still something of a shock. His hands and feet were monstrous too, heavy, taloned things. They stuck out of the heavy robe he wore, which was garnished with a bright sash. In fact, most of the procession was unduly formal and decorated.

Then Martine came out. If Joshua had been transformed into something that barely seemed human, Martine hardly looked different from the woman Rachek had married. Perhaps wilder, less restrained. She wore a glittering dress made of snowy droplets that exuded formal and staggeringly precious excess while still managing to leave a great deal of her actual person uncovered. It startled him as much as anything else to see his wife that way. Then his legs went weak. She was in white. It was farcical but was also clearly meant to be a wedding dress.

He followed the procession to the water's edge, where an unseeming man in a brown three-piece suit beckoned to both Martine and the sinister and shadowy Widdershins. They approached.

The man in the brown suit went through a brutally short wedding ceremony. When he was done, they both moved to kneel in front of the Black Shuck, who also pronounced them King and Queen of England.

Rachek had come just in time for Martine's wedding and for her coronation.

◁▷◁▷◁▷◁▷

He spent three days watching the Faerie prepare for war, with a growing sense of wrongness about everything. Justice had tried to get him to stay, become part of the Outcast Fleet, but he had refused. The war and the Faerie had claimed too much of his life already. He wasn't about to give them any more time. He just wanted to get what was left of his family and get out. Except that the Faerie war had already taken both Martine and Joshua.

He watched the Faerie, Trolls, Goblins, the spooky Kellas Cats, Court Faerie, and all the rest tearing and destroying everything around him. The Wealdarin particularly frightened him. He'd seen one shaped like a two-faced giant stride across a cobbled street one mile inland and the effect the creature made, wading through the earth, simply *erasing* anything manmade as it went. Ripples ran along the grass and land in the Wealdarin's wake, as if land or *this world* was just a shallow pond to them. Any man-made structure, or any other artifact of human existence, was washed over with those ripples of earth and simply *ceased to be*. Even Widdershins and the Black Shuck seemed to fear them, and it was the nondescript John Brown, the man in the brown suit, that seemed to control them. Rachek had watched them boarding the ship. Brown had had to perform some kind of ritual just to prevent the Wealdarin from erasing the ships by their mere presence.

Often he was able to watch closely enough to overhear gossip at the campfires and sometimes even a few snatched phrases inside of command tents. Martine's reign as Queen of England started auspiciously when she sent in a team of Goblins and Dwarves with orders to burn three streets in South London to the ground. What her goal might have been other than terrorizing the citizenry, Rachek could only guess. The Faerie plant life, magically augmented, had been slowly taking over most of London anyway, but had not penetrated these particular streets, which held mostly warehouses.

Perhaps some kind of insurgency was bubbling there. Certainly there had been a great many displaced Londoners holed up in that area, hiding from the changes the Faerie made as they took over London more and more completely. There certainly wasn't any sign of rebellion when the burning was done.

The air was still rank with smoke when Rachek watched Martine, Joshua, and their entourage board the Emerald Demise. He could see they had installed some kind of magical air spirit under control of the Formori, Urguag. They were preparing to launch.

Fortunately, despite their magical assistance, the Faerie still weren't very good sailors, and it was possible for Rachek to swim out while they were still hauling up anchor. He'd expected getting on board to be more difficult, but the Faerie, ridiculously, had already opened all the gun ports and it was possible for Rachek to slip aboard through one of those. There had been no gun crews manning the guns, another bit of foolishness, and there'd been no one to question him and no need for him to kill anybody.

Once on board, Rachek, who had spent many years in the Royal Navy and had a more-than-passing familiarity with ships of all kinds, had no trouble avoiding unwanted attention.

For now.

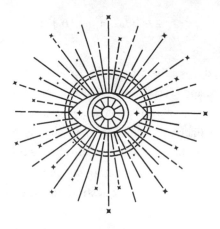

CHAPTER 14

JUSTICE
Springing the Trap

The ceremony to declare and celebrate the Seven Virtues had been a strange thing: brief, out of necessity, but profoundly important to morale. As short as it was, it had seemed a supreme pile of pontification to me. Also a profound waste of time for myself, Faith, Lady Rue, Prudence, Drecovian, Henry, and Avonstoke, who just stood there. Prudence, Drecovian, and Lady Rue had all spoken some platitudes. At least they had the good sense not to ask me to say anything.

Still, watching the crew afterward, I had to admit that it had goosed morale a great deal. Prudence, Lady Rue, Drecovian, and Henry had all gone back to *Seahome* and it had finally been time to turn the *Specter* to the wind and get moving.

But then news came from London by way of Sands' scouts. The new monarch the Faerie had installed in London had ordered a section of South London burned to the ground. I clenched my teeth as Faith read

me the report. She and Henry and I were in the captain's cabin, reviewing maps and documents.

"They estimate at least several hundred dead," Faith said grimly.

"New monarch?" I sneered, trying to blink away the tears that the
thought of London burning threatened to bring out. "That bastard the
Black Shuck! I'll . . ."

"No," Faith said with a strangled voice. "Not the Black Shuck." She
seemed unable to get out any more.

"It's Mother, isn't it?" Henry said.

Faith nodded, still unable to speak. Finally, she got out, "Mother's
never really coming back to us, is she?"

By *us*, I wondered if Faith meant the three of us, the Kasric family, or
even the human race. Either way, the answer was the same.

"No," I said.

No one had much to say after that.

As we were nearing the mist, Faith joined me on the quarterdeck.
"Can you leave topside for minute? I'd like to show you something."

I nodded.

◁▷◁▷◁▷◁▷

We were expecting the enemy fleet here tomorrow, and now, with dusk
coming, we were heading toward the mist. I was hoping desperately that
the Lady Rue's intelligence about the timing of the attack was correct.
But her intelligence and Sands' both said the same thing: tomorrow. If
they were wrong, we'd either miss the battle entirely or be fighting the
entire fleet by ourselves.

We were also hoping that my ghost eye and Faith's ability to suppress
the dangerous vortexes inside the mist could combine to not only allow
us to emerge from the mist at the right time, but also avoid the Black
Shuck's ships, which were sailing the same waters and making their way
through the same patches of mist.

Behind us trailed the *Blood Oath*, as well as the other eleven schooners Lady Rue had promised. I'd replaced most of the crew for this mission with Prowler sailors from the *Specter*, because I'd need strong swimmers for what I had planned for them. This included Nellie and Wil, which I had grave misgivings about because of their age, but they'd shown themselves extremely capable.

However, none of the schooners could operate without the storm serpents or their handlers. (I hadn't even known until two days earlier that the serpents *had* handlers. More of Lady Rue's secrecy, at least until now.) I'd been assured that the serpents were not only strong swimmers but capable of transporting their handlers through the water too.

The schooners were two-masted, smaller ships, with fore-and-aft rigged triangular sails that lay along their length, giving them a leaner, smoother look than the *Specter*. They were flush decked, with no elevated forecastle, quarterdeck, or poop deck, so the deck was much closer to the water than the *Specter*'s. Each had artillery mounted in the front, a javelin-launching scorpion. These were dangerous enough to enemy crew but lacked the devastating power of cannons. It wouldn't do much against the towering sides of the Black Shuck's triple-decker.

The fore-and-aft rigging, handled by a human crew, allowed the schooners to lie closer to the wind, but that wouldn't be relevant with the Faerie and the storm serpent sailing them. I'd had a short demonstration the day before, after meeting the *Blood Oath*'s handler, a lean, curly-haired Court Faerie named Heleena. Being a slight person with long, curly brunette hair, she reminded me irresistibly of our brother Benedict. Being trapped in the Wild Hunt, he could be literally anywhere right now, but wherever it was, he was just as likely causing destruction. I'd had a lot of bad nights thinking about Benedict, riding hard in that ghostly retinue through a smoldering, rumbling sky. I'd wanted to go back and rescue him when we got Henry, only Benedict's rescue hadn't worked out because the Wild Hunt was a lot harder to break someone out of than Newgate Prison, which was only bricks, mortar, and metal, after all. A lot of bad nights. It's easy to be tough about something during the day, but it's a different thing at night.

"This is Demet," Heleena said effusively. "Demet, this is Admiral Kasric."

"Oh," Nellie said. "It's big." Wil looked more belligerent than anything, as if he planned to single-handedly wrestle the thing into submission as soon as the rest of us turned our backs.

"He won't eat us, will he?" Nellie asked, clearly nervous. Her webbed fingers clutched nervously at the air.

"No," Heleena said. "Of course not."

I wasn't so sure. The storm serpent itself was deeply unsettling, mottled white and black, and nearly as large as the foremast around which it twined. I could see the mast had been reinforced specifically for this purpose, with a cross brace partway up for the snake to curl around. The flat head turned and regarded us briefly with dead, black eyes, and then went back to its perch on the cross brace, staring out across the water. I wasn't sure if it could understand or respond. Perhaps Heleena just liked talking to it or perhaps the thing gave lectures at Faerie University on the weekends. You could never tell, and I didn't have the heart, somehow, to ask. The mast creaked as the thing shifted its weight. The cross brace was ten feet up, and even with a third of the serpent coiled up there, there was enough snake body left for it to twine down the mast so that the lower third lay in heavy coils on the deck. Heleena stepped over the coils thoughtlessly as she led us forward. I shuddered as I followed her.

"Don't be silly," Faith said to me, following suit. "We've met dragons, after all." But she didn't sound so sure, and she stepped over just as carefully as I had, making sure of the motion of the ship before doing it. Nellie and Wil followed behind gingerly.

A soft chuckle came from above. From the snake. I craned my neck to look up at the serpent, to make sure I'd really heard it. Demet had one black eye facing us. When it comes to poker faces, dragons have nothing on snakes. I suddenly wondered if that's how people viewed my ghost

eye, which was also black. Enigmatic and dangerous, hiding murky subterranean thoughts of blood and hunger. Part of me hoped they did; part
of me was filled with revulsion at the idea.

Demet lowered his head and Heleena promptly scratched him over
the eye and talked about how wonderful he was for a minute while the
rest of us eyed him cautiously. Heleena did not offer to let any of us pet
the serpent, and none of us would have wanted to anyway. It didn't look
like a pet, in any case.

Heleena gave us a brief demonstration of the serpent's power. The
storm serpent didn't quite have the control of the breeze that I'd expected. I'd thought they could summon a breeze in any direction they
wanted, but that wasn't entirely true. They could tinker with the wind,
not commandeer it, so that a Faerie schooner had to avoid or use the
stronger gusts until they found one weak enough to bend to the storm
serpent's will, meaning they had to understand the basics of tacking into
the wind and often had to follow an unfavorable wind to get to a more
advantageous position. Not nearly as often as a human ship, but it was
an interesting hybrid of technique.

I was astonished to find a Faerie who had any idea of sailing and
how to use the wind, and I took to Heleena immediately. She'd been
the first Faerie to express an interest in learning more too, and we got
briefly caught up with the technical aspects of her craft's fore-and-aft
rigging compared to the square rigging that the *Specter* and ships of
the line used.

When I'd told her my plan for her ship, she pondered for half an instant, then nodded.

"It's a bloody shame," she said, "but a smart tactic. Makes sense." She
was eyeing me now with a careful, grudging respect for my ruthlessness.

Her reaction surprised me. The other schooner captains—serpent
handlers were all captains on these ships—had all balked at my plan and
had to be convinced. Lady Rue had made the difference, speaking with
several of them privately until they'd agreed. I couldn't be certain if she'd

told them her true identity as Queen Mab, head of the Unseelie Court, or if she'd coerced them with some other threat or leverage.

"Thank you, Captain," I'd said, and meant it. We left Nellie and Wil with Heleena and Demet.

Now, back on the *Specter*, I made further preparations. This was going to involve cunning and bold action. To that end, I enlisted the help of the crew. The sail crews most of all.

I had the sail crew captains all gathered on the quarterdeck: Étienne, Emily, and Percy from the Ghost Boys (despite Emily's being a girl), and Spear, Ruk, and Cort from the Goblins. Ruk, I noticed, was wearing a lumpy, woven facsimile of Étienne's white-and-black-checkered cap that I hadn't seen on her before. Percy had eschewed his prim blue jacket for a shaggy brown thing that, along with a little brown hood with saggy cloth horns, made him look more like a particularly small Goblin than a little boy. I'd expected some very serious problems, since the ghosts couldn't be seen when we were outside of the Faerie mist, but the Goblins, somehow honing a subterranean sense they couldn't entirely explain, had developed a keen awareness of where their spectral comrades were simply from their footfalls and the movement of the rigging around them. The sail crew didn't look like much, but I'd pit them against any British sail crew any day. The Faerie, by nature, were not a cooperative people, but the *Specter*'s crew had overcome that, and I was fiercely proud of all of them.

Faith was squinting hard at the place where Étienne, Percy, and Emily were sitting. With the *Specter* being outside the mist, the Ghost Boys and Emily were invisible to all but my ghost eye again. Étienne, seeing the direction of Faith's gaze, waggled his fingers; then, when he got no reaction, he made his eyes bulge out as best he could and puffed out his cheeks like a blowfish at her. Emily jostled him for it, but he ignored her. Faith peered as if she could just make something out, but not quite.

"Stop that," I said, struggling to keep a stern, respectable captain's face.

"Is he doing something?" Faith said, looking hard at a spot a foot to Étienne's left. "He's making a face, isn't he?"

"Not paying attention, is all," I said with a straight face. At least, I hoped it was a straight face.

I turned to the nearest Goblin, hoping to create a distraction. "Why do they call you 'Spear' anyway?" I said. I was addressing the scraggly-haired, burly Goblin, who was head of the mizzen crew. "I've never seen you carry—"

"Don't," Faith said, cutting me off, "even ask."

"She's right," Avonstoke added hurriedly. "It's far, far, better if you don't."

Spear himself was wearing a jagged grin. Cort, a female Goblin, had an entirely different sort of grin. It was a difficult thing telling the women Goblins from the men. The less shaggy ones tended to wear more clothes, but that wasn't a surefire method of telling, and, honestly, I wasn't always up for staring hard enough to see past the hair and minimal clothing to try and tell the difference. But somewhat against my will, I had most of them figured out by now.

Avonstoke jostled Faith, who had an echo of her old properly offended expression on her face. Étienne's reaction was even more comic, as he slowly and very visibly went from confusion to understanding to shocked curiosity. He blushed mightily, and then, realizing that everyone could actually see him in the mist, blushed even more. Mog, crouching behind Faith and me, chuckled loudly, a sound like grating wood.

"Right, then," I said, pushing on before I thought about any of this too much. "The important thing is to reduce our visibility as much as possible." I pointed up at the canvas. Even in the uncertain light of the mist at night, the reflection of our lanterns made the sails stand out. "We can hide the body of a ship behind land, but the sails could still be visible from a lookout. Then, when the enemy is completely past, we'll need to hoist the mainsails and staysails as quickly and as silently as possible. We'll keep everyone down on the deck until the last minute, then you'll all have to get up into the yards as quickly as possible. We'll hoist mainsails and staysails only, the minimum we need to gather way. Remember, it all has to be done silently."

Étienne, Spear, and Cort nodded, all levity put aside.

Under other circumstances, I might consider trying guerrilla tactics from inside the mist as a desperation move, but the Black Shuck only needed to get one ship to the mainland, and I couldn't afford for that to happen while our only mobile ships were fighting or lost in the mist.

"Good," I said. "To your posts. Faith, let's find that island."

We'd encountered features of the regular English coast inside of the mist, particularly farther in, but the island we'd encountered inside the mist that hadn't been part of England before fit my purposes better. The only question was: Could we find it? Was it even still there? There was still a lot we didn't understand about how the Faerie occupation was reshaping things.

We glided soundlessly across still, black water. Our lanterns gave the top of the water a diffused gleam but didn't do much for visibility. Sounds were muffled, the way they always were here, but we still caught other, ghostly sounds that didn't come from the *Specter* or her crew. They weren't always easy to make out, and that was a blessing.

The smell of salt passed and another, brackish scent replaced it.

Behind us, connected by only twenty feet of tether, was the *Blood Oath*, the first of Lady Rue's black schooners with a small crew of *Specter* Prowlers to man her and two of Swayle's marines. The other eleven schooners were farther back, all tethered in a row and all manned with crew and marines from the *Specter*.

"I would never hand my ships over to anyone," Lady Rue, the Queen of the Unseelie Court, had said before departing for *Seahome*. "Except now, for you."

"You won't regret it," I said, offering my hand.

She looked at my hand, her steel mask back on and her head tilted, as if I'd gone quite mad. She didn't offer her own.

"If I do regret it," she said with a flash of a smile barely visible behind the mask, "it won't be for long. We'll all be dead. Or wishing we were." Her smile didn't reach her dark eyes.

She had turned then and departed the ship.

"Breath of fresh air, that one," Faith had said with a completely straight face. "A delight, really."

Now, in the mist, I cursed suddenly as the wind died. I looked at Faith helplessly, who simply gave me an enigmatic shrug.

"Why don't *we* have Windshrikes?" I muttered, which earned me another shrug. Faith's wizardly imperturbability made me want to scream, but I kept my face as impassive as I could, trying to preserve some shreds of a captain's dignity, though I couldn't for certain say why.

I ordered our largest boat launched with a crew to row her and a line back to the prow of the *Specter*. Keeping all of that as quiet as possible was nerve-racking, and the unavoidable sounds of crew dropping into the boats and, finally, the splashing as the oars bit made me grind my teeth. It was a wonder I had any teeth left. I had to pass the order, through Leaf Rider messengers, for the Prowler crews of the schooners, all of them that could be spared, to get in the water and help move their ships as best they could.

That didn't provide a lot of power to move that many ships, and we crawled forward inch by backbreaking inch. The work was so grueling that I had to waste more time switching out the crew every half hour or risk them working themselves literally to death, so willing were they to endure blood, sweat, and pain on my command. That realization terrified me as much as the enormous stakes we all played for.

Avonstoke went into the boat with the next shift and wouldn't come out until I'd changed out the rest of the crew twice. I missed Henry too, who could have pulled as much as ten men, and wondered if I'd ever see him again.

We started making slightly better time, but the silence in between the pull of the oars was both timeless and endless. I had a watch from the cabin, probably Father's or Caine's, tied to the binnacle near the helm. It felt like a lie every time I looked at it.

But over two hours passed, by the watch, before I spied what I was looking for.

The Hanging Tree.

There it was, as macabre as ever, with its long, leafless branches and the Formori bodies hanging, long, solid, silent, black, grim condemnations of wars past.

"Sands said the Seelie Court killed the Formori," Faith said softly. "You wouldn't think Urguag would want to help the Court now. He must hate them terribly."

"The Unseelie Court is more in charge of the invasion," Avonstoke said, "I would guess. Uneasy allies. Something I'd never thought to see." He gave me an odd, speculative look, just a flash that I would have missed if I hadn't known him so well.

"It's me," I said bitterly. "Again. I killed the Soho Shark, the second to last of his kind and probably Urguag's kin. He'd do anything to get back at me."

"It wasn't like you had much choice," Faith said, putting a hand on my shoulder.

"Doesn't matter," I said, shaking myself free. Truth was, I'd do it again and everyone knew it. "Mog, port the helm two points. We'll lay off on that side there." I pointed. "The Black Shuck's ships should be coming from the other side."

"Yes, Captain," Mog said, moving back toward the quarterdeck to pass the order. Squinting with my ghost eye closed, I watched him disappear into the fog at midships. That was what visibility was like for everyone else here. Even with my ghost eye open, he and the rest of the quarterdeck were hazy and indistinct.

"How can you tell," Faith asked quietly, "which direction the enemy ships will come from?"

"That side's closer to England," I said.

Faith waved at the fog all around. "How can you tell?" she repeated. "The compass doesn't work in here."

I shrugged. "I just can."

She nodded as if that made perfect sense. A gift from Llyr, despite my unwillingness to serve. My uncanny abilities at sea had never faltered, even when Llyr had plagued me with storms and bad dreams. For once, I was grateful for Faerie magic and its inconsistencies.

"With the tree branches hiding our masts and the sails down," I said, "we should be nearly invisible to the invaders as they go past. If the Faerie even bother to post lookouts."

"Here's hoping they don't have anyone with your eye," Faith said softly, like a prayer. Her voice was a little distant. She was still suppressing the magic of the mist around us to keep us safe.

"Mog," I said, as he came back to the forecastle, "reef all sails and impress again on the crew the need for further silence."

"Yes, Captain." He still didn't seem to have the hang of "aye-aye," but he was an excellent second in command. Leftenant, that would have made him, in a more formal service. The eternal enmity between the various classes and factions of the Faerie made the conflicts between England, Wales, Ireland, and Scotland look like a party game, but we'd been able to band together as one crew, and that owed a great deal to Mog's fearlessness and loyalty.

But I missed Starling. Starling, for all his grousing about "human 'close-'auled, abeam to the wind nonsense," had actually been starting to get a decent feel for real sailing. He might have become an astonishing seaman, if given the chance. Something none of the Dwarven people, to my knowledge, had ever even aspired to, let alone accomplished. Starling had worked hard and should have been there, reaping the rewards, but that wasn't going to happen anymore because the Goblin Knight had crushed him with that terrifying cudgel of his. It wasn't right.

I watched Mog's heavy-shouldered form sway and lope easily across the deck. He stopped a pair of Prowlers repairing rope, correcting them using mostly grunts, hand gestures, and examples. Mog's large, clawed hands were capable of surprisingly delicate work. I hoped to be able to reward him properly when all this was over. I hoped he'd still be around to *be* rewarded. Him and the rest of the crew. Lord knew they deserved it.

I shook my head to clear it. "The schooners behind us will have to do the same," I said. "Also, we'll need people in the water to keep the ships close together, but also to keep them from bumping into each other and making noise. At least there's little current or wind here."

"They do not like it," Mog said, "being in haunted waters. But Mog explained very carefully. They will do."

"Do not like it is putting it very mildly," Avonstoke said. "How did you convince them?"

Mog shrugged. "They do for Captain Justice. They would kill for Captain Justice. They would die for Captain Justice."

"They would . . ." Avonstoke agreed slowly.

"Also," Mog added, "Mog promised to eat any who failed."

I pinched my nose wearily. "I know I'm going to regret asking this," I said, "but would you really? You know, eat them?"

Mog smiled. It was a very large, toothy smile.

"You're right," I said. "I don't really want to know."

Faith burst out in a nervous, helpless laugh. "Try not to eat anyone we need, I guess."

Mog nodded gravely. "Mog will do Mog's best."

"Well," Avonstoke said spreading his hands wide with elaborate drama. "That's all we can ask of anyone." He patted Mog fondly on the shoulder.

The orders were passed from ship to ship using the Leaf Riders, and we arranged our line of vessels against a jagged shore made of gnarled roots from the hanging tree. With many of our Prowlers on *Seahome*, we had only just enough to keep the best swimmers in the water handling the mostly stationary ships. Once collected, we roped the ships together silently, bobbing very slightly all together. We'd planned on keeping the Prowlers in the water but had to abandon that strategy once we discovered the water was bitterly cold, even for winter waters in the channel.

"The water around this island," Faith said, pulling her hand hastily from a bucket we'd had hauled up, "is not natural. Not this close to the Hanging Tree."

"Care to elaborate on that?" I said.

She shook her head. "I can't guess the full effect. But I know death magic when I feel it. It's more of a malaise than a spell. Something general about this place, not specifically aimed at anybody or anything. I'll do what I can to suppress it, but . . ." Her voice was low and serious.

I looked around for Mog, then saw his low, wide-shouldered outline looming out of the mist as he come up on the quarterdeck and moved toward me.

"Mog," I said, "Faith says there's something wrong with the water. Let's pull them out."

"Just did," Mog said, sadness in his voice. He jerked his head to indicate I should follow him, and I did, to where he had two of our swimmers out of the water. "Too cold," Mog said forlornly.

Faith crouched to where other crew members were tending to the two shivering men.

"So cold," one of them said. A Prowler named Dodson. Then he shivered once more and went still.

Faith crouched quickly and checked his neck, his face, his eyes. She shook her head. "He's gone."

"Isn't there something . . ." I started, but Faith shook her head. "No. He's gone. I'm sorry."

"Damn," I said. Prowlers could swim in all but the coldest of any waters without trouble. What kind of cold *was* this?

"This man should recover," Faith said, looking at the second man, another Prowler, named Norrell. "But we need to get him inside and warm."

"You heard her," I said. "Do everything you can to keep them warm. Get everyone else out. No one else goes into the water near this place."

"Yes," Mog said, and disappeared down into the mist again to give his orders.

That vigil lasted forever, everyone silently standing, crouched, or in many cases, sleeping on deck. I'd had to give orders encouraging sleep. We'd be on watch all night with battle in the morning, so anyone who could catch a few winks huddled next to their cannon, tether, or crowded in tight huddles around the masts had better take the opportunity.

Two more crew members died, Reese and Able, and there was nothing we could do about it.

I ordered our few lights extinguished and we settled in to wait. I went to the ship's bow, peering anxiously into the misty darkness. Nothing yet. The black glass of the water was undisturbed but gave off a soft glow visible once our lights were off. It did not rise very high off the water, though. The looming presence of the Hanging Tree was felt more than seen. The ship and crew around me were nothing more than dull shadows. Fetid swamp smell lay all around us and nothing made any sound. Time stretched immeasurably. I longed for conversation to pass the time, but I'd ordered complete silence for a reason. Faith and Avonstoke crouched beside me, silent, very close.

I took Faith's hand. "How are you holding up?" Her hands were cold and slick with sweat as she gripped mine back. Her face looked exhausted and strained. "Fine," she whispered tightly. She was a liar, of course, but what else was there to say? She'd hold on, keeping the effects of the mist at bay for as long as it took, because she had to.

Avonstoke's hand found mine, which was a much-needed bulwark against the solitary and isolated feeling building all around us.

Gray mist was everywhere and we moved through it so slowly that the *Specter* barely made a whisper through the water. There was no sense of motion and I had to lean over the side to see the water moving every couple of minutes to check our headway. Days, nights, weeks, and years seemed to pass before the word was passed in whispers that it was one bell into the morning watch. I wished desperately we could have rung the bell, just to break the silence, but that was wild foolishness. Four-thirty in the morning. I realized that I could now make out shapes above us, the bulky, monstrous bodies of the long-dead Formori, so clearly not human, and farther up, the dark suggestion of tree branches.

"Hear that?" Avonstoke whispered. His warm hand gripped my shoulder.

I'd been sitting, and now got into a crouch and tilted my head, straining to hear. Nothing. No. There. Voices?

Mog appeared suddenly, moving without sound for all his bulk. One of his batlike ears lifted halfway from its drooping position.

"Yes," Mog said. "Mog hear voices. That way."

"Just where you said they would come from," Faith said. Even with the strain on her face from her magical striving, there was an expression of wonder.

"Of course," Avonstoke said with pride. I wished I had half the confidence in myself that he had in me, but his words fanned a soft glow inside of me.

I stood up, moving to the rail, where I could peer down into the main deck where the sail crew, ghosts, and Goblins, all sat, waiting. There was no need to alert them; they were all looking at me the moment I came into view.

I held up my open palm. *Not yet. But get ready.* They all stood.

We all waited, listening, quivering with readiness, trying not to breathe, willing the enemy ships to unknowingly pass us by. Just as the tree would screen us from their eyes, so too did it screen them from ours, but then, even through the scratchy lattice of the Hanging Tree, I could make out the shadowy bulk of a ship.

A large ship, triple-decker, no doubt. Right where I'd expected it to be.

The Faerie invaders gave no care to stealth. They had no need of it, so the voices and calls from the enemy ship became much clearer as they drew closer. The snap of the lash, too. It seemed their Windshrikes required motivation. I caught a glimpse of one of them through the trees, a cobalt blue fire. Vaguely humanoid, vaguely avian, angular and elongated and easily twenty feet or so tall, impossibly thin arms and legs. It had both distinct arms and wings, brutal-looking claws, and a beak of blue flame. Even the wings looked like weapons, with thorns for pinions. The beaked inhuman face leered with pain, rage, and hate and no wonder, for it had been stretched and trapped like a fly in some kind of gossamer rigging.

Heaven help the crew members around these creatures if they ever got free. They looked terrifying.

"You ever see anything like the Windshrikes before?" I whispered to Faith and Avonstoke. Faith shook her head.

"Just what Brocara showed me," Faith said, "in dreams."

"Nightmares, you mean," Avonstoke said with a sympathetic look. Faith didn't meet his glance but gave a short nod of assent.

Avonstoke looked at me. "Never. Dreadful-looking, though."

I looked back at Mog, who shook his head.

"But there are stories," Avonstoke said, keeping his voice low, like all of us. "They are demons. Creatures so evil they've fallen to the very darkest pits of Faerie. Creatures of shadow and blood. They live only to kill." He spoke with the cadence of repetition, as if he'd learned about demons as a child. Clearly, he had. Their being demons meant they had ties with Pavor Nocturnus. It made me shudder to see this example of her home.

"Held in place by one of the Twenty Crafts of Lughus, I'd guess," Faith said. "Those thin lines, see? I think Urguag cast those."

The second ship followed closely on the first's stern, as did the third and fourth. They were keeping a tight formation and moving slowly, so slowly through the mist for the same reasons that we did. Mother was on one of those ships, and Joshua. That sent a cold, tight, sad feeling through my shoulders and belly. The Black Shuck, Widdershins, and all the other Seven Sins were there too, probably. That triggered a different tension, hot and angry.

All the time I kept my hand up and the ship waited, frozen around me.

Slowly, so slowly, the enemy ships passed.

I brought my hand down and everyone sprang into action. Goblins and Ghost Boys all swarmed up in the rigging and the sails started unfurling almost at once. I felt a burst of pride at how smoothly they all moved. I ran back to the quarterdeck, still trying to move as silently as possible, and Faith and Avonstoke fell in line behind me.

Mog was already next to the helmsman, his ears perked up, sniffing delicately at the breeze. There was just enough breeze to gather way, I thought, which was a blessing. I could feel the gentlest of motion starting. It wasn't much, but it would be enough. I wouldn't have to send out boats to tow the ship again. Leaf Riders were flying in to report that the other ships were ready and underway too. The entire operation was going off with nothing louder than a footfall.

We moved slowly around the island with the Hanging Tree, the HMS *Specter in the Mist* (and a grin split my face at the thought of how appropriate that name was, again) and all the Faerie schooners moving silently into position behind our enemy.

The mist turned lighter all around us, and then all the fog on port side ran bloody red as we came out to dawn breaking on the English Channel.

We'd done it.

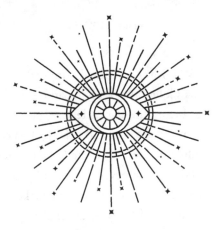

CHAPTER 15

Joshua
Traps and Surprises

Of the Seven Sins, only the Black Shuck and Widdershins could navigate the mist easily, so it was their ship, the *Descending Shadow*, that led the other three ships. Mother, Lady Westerly, and John Brown all had the barest feel for traveling through it, but it was easy enough to follow the ship ahead of them. It was very early in the morning, when everything was still gray and the white cliffs of Dover were a vague paleness behind them and the churning foam glowed in the darkness. Past the breakers, all the water was the deepest black.

The *Emerald Demise* was Mother's command, though, as she had on land, she gave orders to Joshua and relied on him to actually carry them out.

With Urguag had come the Windshrikes. Huge, avian demon-men, wailing as Urguag had them dragged aboard in silvery silk nets. Now one of those nets was stretched out between the mainmast and the bowsprit, and the Windshrike writhed, trapped like an insect. The thrashing creature had killed two Goblins and even one of the cadaverous Hanged Dogs before the Faerie learned to give that part of the deck a wide berth. Now, in the near darkness, Joshua couldn't make out anything but the flailing net, which seemed like it surely must tear and give, only it never did. Two dwarves, assigned by Urguag for just this purpose, each holding a silvery silk whip, now flicked the ends of these at the creature, very low and lazily, near what might have passed for heels on another creature. This was all happening near the forecastle and mainmast, with another Windshrike and two dwarves with whips at the mizzenmast. The pace and energy of the whipping escalated now as the Dwarves really got going, working themselves into a lather.

The Windshrikes moaned low and pulled even harder at the nets.

With a long, creaking groan that might have been the ship or might have been the Windshrikes, the ship began to move.

Joshua walked past the mizzenmast group, giving them a wide berth, and up onto the quarterdeck. He leaned over the rear railing and looked at the water behind them. His posture was even more hunched than normal. Mother's treatments were doing something to his back now. He felt as if a tumor large enough to become another full person, a particularly painful and evil one, was growing there. The burning sensation was unbearable, but as with all of Mother's decisions and "gifts," he had no choice but to put up with it. For now.

The ship wasn't moving that quickly yet, only fifty yards from the docks, and already the water was a long churn of white foam. The Faerie, even Lughus, Master of the Twenty Crafts, the Faerie god that Urguag got his magic from, didn't seem to know or care about jibs or spanker sails. Urguag had found the rudder a novel, quaint, and unnecessary component to a fighting ship, and had an entirely different solution to keeping the ship upright. Mostly, the Windshrikes held the ship up by pure brute strength, but Urguag had also instituted a series of knotted ropes to provide enough drag to keep the back end of the ship behind them.

Justice, or any other human sailor, would have called it a sea anchor and lamented the foolishness of deliberately orchestrating that much drag. Urguag called it a trifling. Joshua had thought that the ship commanders might be shuffled after that detestable farce of a nuptial ceremony. Why not combine the invasion of the modern world with some kind of blasphemous honeymoon? It made just about as much sense as anything else the Faerie did. Joshua had spent so much time explaining basic things to the Faerie—that troops needed food or that ships *without* holes in the bottom floated better than ships *with* holes in them—that he almost got worried when the Black Shuck ordered something practical.

The Black Shuck. God, that beast's mind was a fractious horror. Of all the Faerie, the leader of the Hanged Dogs was the worst of them all, and the most terrifying. That was a creature that wanted to watch things bleed. Joshua, England, the world. The Black Shuck would joyfully watch all of it die. Joshua could feel the hatred rolling off it in waves. And it was unpredictable, which made it all the more dangerous.

He and Mother were on the second ship in the line, with the Black Shuck and Widdershins on the first ship, and much bad luck to them. Joshua's most profound and dearest wish was that a more powerful ship would put a broadside into Widdershins' ship and scratch it out of existence. Problem was, Justice didn't have a much bigger ship. So much for dreams.

British ships, or any human ships for that matter, used signal flags for coordinating their movements, but the Black Shuck wasn't worried about that sort of thing. The Black Shuck's plan was simple, and the other ships had their orders that they would follow. They had the vastly superior force. Smash and utterly destroy the *Specter, Seahome,* or any other part of the ragtag collection they called the Outcast Fleet they encountered. Then, land on French soil and begin the assimilation and complete dismantling of the European nation and all of their peoples. So, it was a plan that relied entirely on brute force and couldn't adapt at all to changing conditions.

The problem was, it would probably work, for all of that.

The dwarves on the main deck lashed harder, and the groaning, ship and Windshrike both, increased.

Now they were entering the mist. Joshua clamped his fanged teeth together, hard. This was another place where they were in the hands of the Black Shuck, for only it could navigate the mist. That had been part of the Black Shuck's campaign of terror, that none of them had any way back home or off England without its intervention.

The trip through was mercifully short, guided as it was by the Black Shuck's indomitable power and force of will.

They emerged from pearly clouds into a sea resplendent with flaming blue. The lookout called out. The presence of ships. There, lying like a land mass on the blue water, was *Seahome*. Oversized and ridiculously helpless now that they had real ships. He couldn't see, squinting against the sun, any sign of Justice's ship or the little schooners that usually supported her.

Mother appeared next to him wearing an immodest black dress, as if she needed to emphasize the connection that now existed between her and the shadowy Widdershins. Over the dress, she wore a thin, intricately patched cloak, patterned with inconsistent black and gray squares, like a chess board drawn by a drunken artist and seen through a drugged haze. Still, it would have provided some of the missing modesty if she'd bothered to draw it around her. The patches were actually pockets, countless pockets holding the tools of her magical trade. Her hair was loose, wild, and crimson in the wind, despite having white streaks in it now. Her eyes had a green, feline glow to them from the absinthe she used constantly to drive her magic. If the cold wind bothered her, she didn't show it.

"The gods have given us a glorious day for our victory," she said, ostensibly to him but clearly pitched to carry to the Faerie crew around them. Playing to an audience. She always did that now. Perhaps that was a Faerie quality. He realized with a shock that he thought of her entirely as one of them now. Before, he'd harbored a hope, a fantasy, that there was some small kernel inside of her that might be saved. But he knew better now. He'd also had some thought about reconciling with Father, Justice and the rest of his family, but that wasn't very likely, either. The idea of reconciliation was one that had come to him as time passed. But it was subjective time. It had been nearly a decade for him and Mother, most of it spent in a pocket of Faerie, where time moved more quickly, and time had mellowed his position on his family slightly. But it was all still fresh for Justice and the others. Also, new betrayals kept happening. The burning of South London that Mother had ordered was well past the final straw. There would be no reconciliation.

But nor could he continue serving Mother. Not after he got his first taste of what kind of queen she would be. With that realization came the sudden decision. He'd avoided acting until now, but really, what possible purpose could be served in delay? He might as well play his gambit to try and rescue Temperance now, in the brief bit of suspended chaos before the battle. If his absence caused confusion, so much the better. It probably wouldn't save Justice, Faith, or Henry, as much as he secretly wished for this, but it would hurt Mother, the Black Shuck, and Widdershins and possibly slow down the Faerie Invasion. That was as much as he could hope for.

If the rescue plan didn't work, there was always the backup plan, which was embodied in the gunpowder he'd stashed secretly on board. It wouldn't work here in Faerie but would work just fine once they were out in the open sea.

If he couldn't rescue Temperance, he'd sink the ship. Preferably, he'd like to do both but didn't see how that could be done without a confederate, and there wasn't anybody on the ship that he trusted, let alone anyone that would cross the Black Shuck.

Mother would put Temperance in the deepest hold, he knew. Now, if he could only get there without attracting too much attention. No mean feat in the enclosed environment of a ship.

He was still pondering the details of his plan while he scanned the sea. There was no sign of Justice's ship, the *Specter*. Probably behind *Seahome* or farther down or up the channel. With the mist on one side and the French reefs, rocks, and shoals on the other, to say nothing of the hostile French guns, there wasn't any other place for the *Specter* to be. She'd come into view shortly.

"I want to check the maps again," he said, and turned his ponderous, powerful body away from the railing.

"There they are!" Mother said, her green eyes picking out things at a distance even before the lookout. She sucked in a sudden breath. "No . . . that's . . . not possible!"

Almost against his will, Joshua turned and gazed out at the sea, but his eyes were better for the dark now than for sunlight and he couldn't see what had suddenly stymied and infuriated Mother.

"The Seven!" the lookout wailed. "The Seven Virtues are there!" Echoing wails rose up on all sides, mingling with the constant low moaning from the Windshrikes.

"Not possible!" Mother said again.

And it certainly shouldn't be. Especially since Mother had been keeping one of those Seven in her dungeon and now in the ship's hold to prevent this very thing. How had Justice managed it? Was it a trick? Or had Mother made some kind of mistake?

Joshua snatched a spyglass from one of the approaching Court Faerie and trained it on *Seahome*. There, on top of one of their ramshackle buildings, were Justice, Faith, Prudence, all to be expected. But somehow, they'd gotten Hope and Charity to leave Faerie and join them, the one looking pale, ragged, and preternaturally dangerous, the other a golden-haired child. That seemed next to impossible alone, but there was Temperance, with her dark, curly black storm of hair and no iron collar. The last woman, slim and dark, he didn't know personally. *Love du Thorns*, whoever that was, Joshua thought, remembering the portrait of a stranger back in his secret room.

How could they all be here? Impossible. It just couldn't be. It had to be a trick. He almost opened his mouth to say so to Mother, but something stopped him. She knew how unlikely it was, same as he did. Still, the Faerie lived in a world of magic and daily impossibilities. How could anyone be sure of anything?

He looked again, but it wasn't enough to confirm or deny the possibility. What was more, Justice would *know* that they couldn't see well enough to decide if these were the real Virtues or not, but that the Black Shuck would almost certainly take the bait. This was a ruse that shouldn't have worked but that Justice must have known *would* work, based on the Black Shuck's personality. Joshua had to hand it to her. She knew her enemy.

Trick or not, it had clearly spurred a reaction from the lead ship. A bone-chilling howl seethed out from its bow. The Black Shuck hurling out a wordless challenge. His ship increased speed, heading right for *Seahome* and the Seven Virtues.

Mother turned away from the railing with a wordless snarl and immediately made for the hatch down to the hold. Then she stopped and looked back at him.

"It has to be a trick," she snapped at him. "I'll show you. Follow me."

So it was just that easy. Joshua had had a tentative plan to try and get into the hold that involved climbing out onto the hull and tearing his way into it, but it wasn't a good plan at all, simply the best he'd been able to come up with.

Now, gloriously, he was being invited, actually ordered, to follow her, and he had little doubt of the destination. The place he'd been trying so hard to figure out a way into. He jumped to obey while she made her way down the first hatch to the gun deck, from which they'd removed all the guns and filled with troops. The most tractable and humanoid troops, and incidentally the most numerous, were all lodged in the upper, middle, and lower decks, where the gun ports allowed a modicum of air and sunlight to filter through. The stairs on the *Emerald Demise* were staggered throughout the ship, not near each other, so Mother and Joshua had to walk across part of each deck in order to get to the next stair down. Though the conditions were miserably crowded, everyone knew enough about Martine, one of the Seven Sins, that a way appeared miraculously in front of her as she stormed through. (Joshua had often wondered why the Virtues were all named, if ineptly, after actual virtues, while the Sins were not. He had never gotten an answer. Just another example of the haphazard way the Faerie did magic . . . and everything else, he finally concluded.) Such was the fear she inspired that people seemed to evaporate out of her path. Joshua followed easily in her wake. There were a few salutes and formal, respectful greetings, but neither Mother nor Joshua stopped to hear them. Mother, her eyes blazing green, her hair flowing around in a windstorm unfelt by the rest of them, took the stairs down.

She passed quickly through the upper deck and middle decks, inhabited by mostly Court Faerie, Dwarves, and Goblins. On the middle deck, Mother stopped briefly to snatch a wicked-looking knife from the belt of one of the Goblin guards watching the stairs. The Goblin, face rusty gray with fear, did not object. She paused, despite her rage, long enough to pull out a vial and rub some kind of salve on the curved blade. She then proceeded to light the thing as if it were a torch. It cast a dancing, eldritch-green flame. Open flame on a ship was a terrifying thing in its own right, but no one, including Joshua, said anything about that, either. Holding her makeshift torch, Mother passed, with Joshua still behind her, down to the lower deck. Here were the Jötnar, Trolls, and Ogres. The subterranean dwellers had not opened any of the gun ports and there was only darkness, with the exception of Mother's pool of emerald light. There had been a few giants in the Seelie Army, but these, out of necessity, had been left in England. The Trolls and Ogres said nothing, and even their large, craggy faces showed fear as Martine passed through.

The next deck, the Orlop, was also the one that Joshua had ordered the most bulkheads installed on, so that the deck was sectioned and divided in places like a honeycomb. The real monsters were here, the Kellas Cats and the Black Shuck's Hanged Dogs. The Pix, too, and other monsters too individual and unique to fall into any of the recognized groups. But a way had been left open from the stairs up and down, and they saw no one there. She went down to the hold, the lowest level, and Joshua followed, careful not to catch his heavy horns on any of the rafters.

This section was the size of a small sitting room, cut in half by the iron bars that held its single prisoner. On this side of the bars stood a Court Faerie guard in Mother's adopted livery, emerald and black. He dropped to his knee at once. A small off-white songbird, some pet of the guard's or a stowaway, perched on one of the rafters near the lantern.

Inside the cage, Temperance stirred but did not move. There was some kind of stain and grit on her that Joshua first took to be foulness from the hold—mold, perhaps. But when he took a second look and saw the sheen of it, he revised his opinion. Some concoction of Mother's, he thought now, made from Faerie absinthe, which was the source of her magic. Something Mother had fabricated, though he couldn't imagine its purpose.

Joshua had seen the painting, had a fairly good idea of what Temperance looked like. She had the angular, lean features of the Court Faerie, which wasn't surprising. Temperance had been taken off the playing board before she'd ever had a chance to make decisions or forge loyalties. She might have joined Justice or might have followed her sisters, but Mother, Widdershins, and the Black Shuck had somehow found her well before she could choose.

Temperance lifted her head. Her hair was wild and unkempt, falling in dark ringlets. Her eyes, Faerie golden, no pupils, were clouded over with pain. Her iron collar, black iron, had to weigh fifty pounds and burn like the devil. It also did a fair job of smothering any powers she might have had. Joshua was pretty certain neither the Black Shuck nor Mother had any idea what those might be. Clearly not anything that prevented her capture.

Joshua was beside himself with fear and panic. This wasn't how everything was supposed to go. He'd imagined coming down here, quickly killing the guard and setting Temperance free. He'd imagined a face-off with Mother then, saying something clever and revealing that he'd set the captive Seventh Virtue free, before also revealing that he'd left a candle burning in the powder room.

Or, possibly luring her down to the powder room, so he could hold a pistol to one of the powder kegs. Gunpowder didn't work inside the perimeter of the mist, so many of the Faerie didn't have the proper fear or respect for it, which made it easier to tamper with than it would have been on any other ship.

But Mother would understand the danger. He'd just have time to see her face before blowing them all to hell.

Doing something now, *right now*, was the only way to enact his revenge in time to have any effect on the outcome of the war. And he was surprised to discover that that, too, was part of what he desperately needed, his only way of making his amends to Justice, Faith, Henry, and Benedict. But the instant she suspected his treachery, Mother would kill him if he didn't kill her first.

Despite Mother's magical abilities, Joshua found he had very little concern about his physical ability to kill her. He was well aware of the power in his hands and reasonably certain that she had few physical protections without her magic. But the idea of actually *putting* his own hands on her disturbed him more than he wanted to admit. Just the image of it, in his mind, brought on waves of nausea and helplessness such that he doubted his ability to carry such a thing out. Joshua was starting to wonder if Widdershins had infiltrated his mind and damaged some small but integral part of him required for taking such an action.

Mother stalked across the hold and leaned over until her face was inches from the prisoner's. "You are Temperance of the House of Thorns," she hissed. "There can be no mistake. So who is out there pretending to be you? And why?"

Temperance's lips moved, but Joshua couldn't hear the words. Then he forgot all about what she might have said, for the guard turned his way and Joshua saw that the face the guard had been wearing when they'd come in had changed.

The man, who Joshua recognized at once, put his finger to his lips, signaling for silence.

That man being the very man Joshua had been looking for: Rachek Kasric, his father.

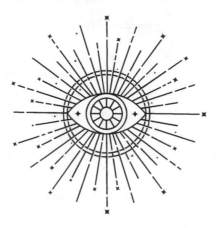

CHAPTER 16

JUSTICE
The *Specter* and the *Glorious*

The sky behind us and to the west was the cold color of a silver coin, but to the east, even with it being so early in the morning, the sun was so bright that we all blinked looking at it. The light sent a pang of discomfort through my ghost eye, but it was still welcome after a night filled with fear and gloom. Even so, I pulled my brimmed hat down lower on the left side to shield that eye a bit. The sun didn't bring any real warmth with it, and we all huddled on the cold deck every time the wind picked up.

Ordering my ship into battle was exhilarating, but also so terrifying that it might have been paralyzing if I hadn't been so busy trying to make certain that I didn't mess something up and get all of us killed. Right now, we had the advantage and an opportunity to do some real damage, but once we got into the thick of battle there would be no turning back. Even if we could sink two or three of the enemy ships, just one victory for the Black Shuck would doom the human race. We had to win not just one battle today but all of them, and my insides felt like cold water when I thought about what could go wrong.

The nearest ship was easy to spot, half a mile in front of us, and they hadn't yet bothered to look back and notice us. Probably didn't even have lookouts posted. Of course, that had been one of the reasons we'd staged that faux display of our Seven Virtues. In addition to drawing the invading fleet to *Seahome*, I wanted to keep their eyes forward so they didn't see us.

They were some bloody big ships ahead of us, all triple-deckers, huge leviathans of the sea. They rode with their gun ports closed, having no working cannons, but we knew better than to regard them as helpless. Avonstoke had already warned us of the Troll artillery, as well as archers, and whatever magic each of the Faerie Seven Sins might have waiting for us.

I swept the glass from ship to ship. Whatever you had to say about the condition of the ships themselves, they certainly had plenty of crew. The decks swarmed with figures. Easiest to pick out were the Troll artillery. It was hard to miss them, spyglass or no, huge, twenty to thirty hulking figures three or four times the size of large men on each ship. The ammunition was hard to miss too, large chunks of masonry that must have been broken off of English buildings and brought along. The deck was crammed with it. The chunks were huge. It would be more like cannons being thrown at us, rather than cannon balls. Avonstoke had said they could go as far as a quarter of a mile. Hard to imagine, but I trusted his judgment too much not to believe. I tried not to imagine what a barrage of fire from one of those ships could do to the *Specter*. I didn't get very far, not imagining. It was all too vivid in my mind.

We were looking at the stern galleries on all three decks, each boasting balconies and a large bay of windows twice the size of the *Specter*'s. But now most of them were broken and hadn't been replaced. In fact, no one had even bothered to clean out the pieces of broken glass from around the window frames. The ship looked dull and in poor repair, with the wood weathered and paint peeling. Someone barely literate had scrawled THE GLORIOUS just under the railing. That kind of name on a ship in squalid condition struck me as funny and sad at the same time. It would be downright tragic if a ship like this was responsible for humanity losing their place in history.

Past the *Glorious*, the other three ships could be seen not far ahead. They were still keeping in tight formation. Shockingly, no one had noticed us. The *Specter* had been cleared for action and the guns run out long before, and now the gun crews, particularly the crew manning the forecastle bow chasers, quivered with readiness. Mounted on the front, these two guns were aimed at the enemy, which was well within range for the long nines.

Render, the red-haired Dwarven gun captain, watched me expectantly, looking just about ready to eat his beard. But I wanted to wait and get the full element of surprise. The ship rode easily with the wind across her beam. The ship ahead was a good twenty feet taller than our own quarterdeck.

Avonstoke came down the shrouds from the crow's nest. He had a spyglass in his hand, having just scanned the enemy one more time.

"Normally," I said to Faith, "I'd think about trying for the masts so they couldn't maneuver, but they don't rely on the wind the way we do. What happens if I hit those Windshrikes?"

"Whatever those lines are made of," Faith said, "they seem to be anchored to parts of the ship, including the masts. I'm not sure you can hurt a Windshrike that way, but I'd say tearing one of the lines of force binding them or knocking down a mast would be as likely to release them as anything else. That would probably stop the ship, but might not be a good thing for us, releasing demons."

"They don't look very happy," I said, "those Windshrikes, being forced to drag around those ships that way."

"Malevolent demons aren't known for being *happy*," Faith said.

"Might be bad for us if they somehow got free," I said, "but it would probably be a lot worse for the *Glorious*."

Faith gave a slow, surprisingly evil smile. "Probably."

"And they have the added advantage of being near the Troll artillery, which I'd dearly love to reduce."

Faith frowned. "Is that the right term? Isn't artillery some kind of big gun?"

I just looked at her. "They throw rocks the size of people," I said, finally. "What else fits?"

"Fair point."

"What kind of range would you say these things have?" I asked Avonstoke, who seemed to be the only Faerie on board who'd seen them at war. "Quarter mile?"

"A little more, I'd say," Avonstoke said, looking through another spyglass. "I'm just estimating based on what I can see of the ammunition. Most of it's hidden by the railing now that we're this close. I had a better look from the crow's nest. Might need to go back up and use the spyglass."

"Um," I said, looking at Avonstoke's sightless golden eyes and the raven that gave him his vision. I was trying to decide if he was having fun with us. "How does that work, exactly?"

Avonstoke gestured with the spyglass at the raven on his shoulder. "I hold the glass. He looks."

"Mog think Avonstoke pulling Mog's leg," Mog said. "No Troll can throw big rocks that far."

"That's the part you think he's making up?" Faith said. "We're just going to move right past the raven looking through a spyglass?"

"Aren't they known for having their own farsighted vision?" I asked, against my better judgment.

"Excellent vision," Avonstoke agreed. "But he *likes* looking through the glass. He could read a newspaper on the deck if he wanted to. Not that there are any newspapers. Also, he can't read. But I can see with his eyes and I can read, of course. You understand."

"Mog understood things much better before Avonstoke started talking," Mog said.

"We don't have time for you to climb to the crow's nest when the bird can just fly up and check on his own," I said.

"I suppose you are right," Avonstoke said sadly. He said nothing and made no motion, but the bird launched itself at once into the air.

"My best guess," Avonstoke said after the raven had returned, "is that we are well out of range of the Trolls. About half this distance and we should watch out."

"Half this distance would also be bow range," I said, considering the advantages and disadvantages of trading blows. We'd seen firsthand the devastation that Swayle's archers could cause, and we knew our enemies' archers would be just as dangerous. That would be a big disadvantage for us as we only had a dozen of Swayle's archers left, the rest being with Swayle on *Seahome*. At our current range, we could hit them and they couldn't hit us. The problem was, we couldn't hit them hard enough to actually stop them if they had the stomach to just proceed with their plan under fire.

We'd discussed this ahead of time. If I'd been in charge of the enemy ships and the Faerie Invasion, I'd split them up and head for four different landings in France, trusting to the troops in the holds to take and hold their positions on the beachheads.

Once there, there was nothing in the world of man that could stop the Faerie from taking all of Europe and, from there, the rest of the world. That was what Joshua would do if he were in charge, but our best guess was that he wasn't.

I also hoped our guess about the Black Shuck was right. If he was rational enough to let Joshua proceed with a careful plan, there'd be no stopping him. That was also why I thought the "Seven Virtues" I had on display ahead of them would draw them in. Most of the Faerie on my side thought the actual war was just a backdrop for this prophecy of theirs, which would settle everything. The fact that both sides had been openly fabricating and tinkering with this prophecy, some with remark-able ineptness, didn't seem to bother anyone except me.

So, I was trying to use that blind spot to my advantage. I'd set up a target, right in their path.

Seahome.

I turned to Render, our gunnery captain.

"When I give the word, Mr. Render," I told the red-haired Dwarf, "start with the bow chasers. Aim for the middle stern gallery. That'll be the main deck level. If we can destroy their artillery or their main deck, so much the better."

"Aye-aye, Captain," Render said.

"Think they'll take the bait?" Faith asked.

By "bait" she meant *Seahome.* I wanted them very much to attack *Seahome* and I dreaded it at the very same time. The smart thing for the Faerie to do would be to just keep on sailing, even under fire, right past *Seahome* to the French coast. Even if I sank or crippled the last ship, that still left three more. But I was betting they didn't have the temperament, any of them, to keep on sailing with cannons blasting them from the stern.

"One way to find out," I said. "Mr. Render, you may fire the bow chasers when ready."

"Don't worry," Faith murmured behind me. "This is going to work."

"What part exactly?" I said. There were a lot of potential actions about to unfold in the next few hours, and I wasn't at all sure what she meant. "What part of the plan do you mean?"

"All of it," she said brightly.

"Oh," I said. "Well then. That's a relief."

On one level, it felt like slinging at giants, to shoot at a triple-decker like this. The *Specter* was only a sloop of war, the smallest ship with three masts, while all of these ships were full ships of the line. But they didn't have cannons. If the Troll artillery turned out to be as devastating as Avonstoke feared, then our offensive was going to be horribly, hilarious-ly short-lived.

The deck shook as the two bow chasers went off together, belching smoke that hung briefly around the bows and spread the stench of gunpowder that I could catch even back on the quarterdeck. I couldn't see, but we'd been pretty close range for these cannons, and a crash and screams from the other ship told me that at least one of the shots had hit. The wind carried the smoke away and we could see the bottom level of the stern gallery blown all to hell. That wasn't so good. We hadn't done anything to their deck, so they could fire back with everything they had, and we'd hit above the water line, so they wouldn't take in water from that. We had hit the gun decks, only the *Glorious* didn't have any guns, so those decks were packed to the beams with troops. The prodigious screaming floated across the water to us like a suddenly opened chasm to hell.

I could feel the blood drain from my face but kept my expression neutral.

The two bow chasers were a far cry from a full broadside, but the stern, with its gallery windows, was the weakest point of just about any ship. Cannonballs shot through there would run the entire length of the ship, pulverizing everything. Countless heads, torsos, limbs, and more would be vaporized. In crowded conditions like that, the carnage must have been terrible. But not enough to make a dent in their invasion force. The troops in the hold, below the water line, would be enough to overrun France, and so I would have to continue to stack horrors on horrors until the butcher's bill ran to completely unfathomable lengths. So much blood on my hands.

"More elevation, Mr. Render," I said. "We want the main deck, if possible. Continue firing."

"Aye, Captain," Render said, his voice pained. Clearly, he was more upset with his marksmanship than even I was. He might not have timed the shots along with the rise and swell of the ship's bow as well as he could have, or else didn't have the elevation right for this distance. It wasn't his fault. You could hardly expect miracles on the first shot.

"You stay here," I said to Avonstoke. "You've got the best eyes in the ship right now, and I'll want to know what we've hit as soon as possible." Normally, he assisted with both the deck crew and the gun crews when things started happening.

"Yes, my captain," Avonstoke said with a grin. My order had been valid. His raven could see better than anyone, spyglass or not, but it also gave me a comfort to have him near. Faith, nearby, was also a comfort, but she didn't look too happy. She was gripping the railing, leaning forward, clearly frightened, but keeping those feelings in check.

Render was still using the Dwarven crank on the port side bow chaser to adjust the elevation when the *Glorious* returned fire.

"Here they come," Avonstoke said. His voice was nonchalant, bland, even, and nothing in his face or the casual way he stood betrayed any hint of apprehension at coming under fire. He was leaning against the quarterdeck rail, barely moving except with the motion of the ship, his golden hair in its queue glistening in the sun. But I'd known him long enough to understand that this casual immobility was forced, meaning that he must have been terrified. The raven on his shoulder shifted restlessly and cawed once, softly. Its head was turned slightly sideways so that it could watch the incoming boulders.

The boulders went up, up, far slower than any cannonball, of course. It was curious how much more terrifying it made them. One boulder in the lead, followed by two more while the first one was still arcing up. Then they hit their apex and sank, falling short of the *Specter*'s position. The geysers they made hitting the green water went up several stories, spraying white foam everywhere. We were out of range, but not by nearly as much as we'd hoped. This wasn't optimal range for the long nines, but they were called the *long* nines for a reason, and could be remarkably accurate, for cannons, at this range. Certainly, it would be suicide to exchange fire at close range, where it could still take hundreds of cannonball hits to sink a triple-decker ship like that, while just one of those boulders could spell doom for us.

"Wear the ship, Mog," I said, then shook my head. "Flugelstan the ship, I mean. Away from the wind!" Somehow, I'd lost the argument on naval terminology when Mr. Starling was still alive and I knew Mog and the rest of the Faerie had gotten confused with the difference between *wear the ship* and *tack*, so I'd agreed to Avonstoke's twice-blasted and ridiculous word *flugelstan*, but I still needed to clarify which direction half the time. Avonstoke had even suggested we alternate between *flugelstan* and *stannelfloog*, but he'd lost that debate when it had become clear even he couldn't remember which was which.

"We'll turn," I told Mog, pointing to make sure he understood which direction, "and give them a starboard broadside from here. Best keep our distance."

"Aye, Captain," Mog said.

The ship exploded into a fury of repressed activity. Hands ran to the braces to turn the sail while the marine in charge, Swayle's second, started bellowing orders to the marines. He sent half of them to the rail and the other half up into the yards.

It would have been too far for human archers, but I'd seen the Court Faerie archers in action before, and they knew their business. The deck officers were shouting too, but it was hardly necessary as everyone bustled to their new positions with smooth precision. I felt a swelling of pride at the crew they'd become.

Mog turned his huge head, his droopy ears swinging, to catch my eye, and I nodded. He bellowed orders to the helmsman and the tiller went around. The *Specter* swung easily.

Render roared the command to open fire and the main deck guns all went off together, a sound like mountains smashing together. An instant later, his commands had been relayed to the gun deck and those guns went off with an even deeper and louder crash. The ship trembled with each one.

The wind had picked up so that the smoke wasn't screening our vision and we could see, two seconds later, a section of the quarterdeck and stern of the *Glorious* burst apart into planks and splinters. A cheer went up from our crew.

"Keep firing, Mr. Render," I said.

"Aye," Render said with a vicious grin. Both the Goblins and the Dwarves seemed to have a deeply unsettling fondness for battle.

Moving at a perpendicular angle to the *Glorious*, we'd only be able to get one more broadside out, perhaps two, before they drew out of range. Then we'd have to tack and try and catch up with them, but I wanted to capitalize on our good start.

"Oh, my captain," Avonstoke said, with wonder in his voice. "I think we did more damage than you know. Or, rather, we did damage to just the right spot."

"Demasted?" I asked hopefully, putting up my spyglass and trying to get an eye on the damage for myself, but the larger ship was heeling over so that the deck was away from us and I couldn't make anything out.

Then, as if in answer to my deepest desire, the ship listed to the port side, heeling in our direction so that we could see the devastation that our shots had done to their main deck. But it wasn't just that. Something was happening there now, something violent, casting crew and pieces of ship overboard as if the Faerie ship were still under fire.

"Here," Faith said, "let me see that." She snatched the spyglass away from me. I had to bite back a nasty comment.

"Is that . . ." Avonstoke said slowly.

"It is," Faith breathed. "Their elemental, the Windshrike. You must have hit the mast, like you said, Justice, and it broke the tethers keeping the elemental in place. It's loose now."

"And it is *not* happy," Avonstoke said with glee. "I'd guess being summoned to our world, tied to a mast, and whipped while you have to drag a huge ship around has made it a bit peevish."

Peevish was one word for it. Screams rang out again as half a dozen bodies went over the shattered railing. The released Windshrike was clearing the deck as well as any carronade.

"There are two magicians there," Faith said. "One of them is the Formori. Urguag. The other almost looks human, but . . . there's some kind of glamour on him, I can't tell to what extent. That's going to be John Brown. Two of our Seven Deadly Sins, I suppose."

"How do you know his name?" I asked.

"It's my job to know that kind of thing now, isn't it?" she said mildly. "Between Sands, Drecovian, and Brocara, I've been getting a lot of information. We weren't sure up until now, or I would have said something. Why won't the ship hold still?" That last bit had come with a bit more asperity. She sighed. "I can't keep the glass on him. Here. You'd better take a look. He's doing something. Maybe trying to bring the Windshrike back under control. He's on the forecastle." She handed me the spyglass.

Even though the ocean rollers moving under us weren't terribly ferocious, with both ships bobbing out of sync, it took some experience with the spyglass to keep one person at a distance in constant view, but I'd gotten the knack of that long ago. The man on the forecastle was normal-looking enough, a slightly portly figure in an expensive but slightly worn brown suit. Someone looking human was enough of an oddity among the fanged and monstrous Faerie running all around to make the scene somewhat surreal, though that word was starting to lose its meaning. He was crouching now, partly turned away from us.

"Whatever he's doing," I said, "I don't think it's about the Windshrike. He's not even looking at it."

The cannons were still thundering off in the gun deck below us, and then one of the cannons on our deck crashed too. I could see several holes in the *Glorious*'s side now.

The Windshrike, a murderous, angular form, didn't even notice but continued its rampage on the main deck. Two clawed hands seized the mizzenmast, ripping it out of the deck with horrific force, blocking my view of John Brown. Its fury was making a floating wreck of the ship.

"What happens," I asked Faith, "when that thing has done enough damage over there? Will it turn on us?"

"I have," she admitted, "absolutely no idea."

"Cease fire!" I ordered, and Mog loped across the deck to put a hand on Render's shoulder, making sure the order was heard and followed, even in this confusion. As long as the monster was doing the work of disabling the ship for us, I didn't want to anger it and bring it our way.

I went back to the spyglass. I caught a brief glimpse of the Formori, clearly of the same breed as the Soho Shark had been but much smaller. The size of a normal man but with the yellow goat's eyes, dirty gray fur, and demonic body, including backward-bending legs and cloven hooves, though these were difficult to make out over the bright orange and cobalt blue robes he wore.

He was trying to weave some kind of spell that I thought looked like the same barely visible gossamer tethers that had held the Windshrike in the first place, but he wasn't getting anywhere this time. That supported the theory that Urguag had been the one to bind them in the first place, but clearly it wasn't an on-the-fly sort of task, because he wasn't having any luck now.

The Windshrike was so busy tearing one of the Trolls in half that it didn't even seem to notice the binding attempt.

Then the Windshrike's rampage moved further starboard and I could see the man in the brown suit again. He was kneeling on the deck of the forecastle holding what looked like a cornflower blue, speckled robin's egg, which he rapped sharply on the deck.

A nightmare burst forth in a shower of bloody egg fragments. I stepped back in revulsion, even though it was nearly a quarter of a mile away. It was vaguely birdlike, like the Windshrike, but the similarity ended there. Yellow skin stretched so tight over skull, body, and wings that it was nearly skeletal. An extra set of hands, no, two extra sets, protruded under the wings and a long, barbed tail streamed behind. It threw back its beaked mouth and screamed, a bone-chilling noise that made our hackles rise even at that distance.

"What now?" Avonstoke said. "What is that?"

"Another demon," Faith said, her mouth compressed into a tight slash. "Brown's specialty seems to be summoning them. He's probably as dangerous as any of the Sins, perhaps more so."

On the other ship, the hideous creature bowed and John Brown crawled onto its back. This demon was long and lean, and while it didn't look large enough to carry a full-grown man on its back, it did so without any notice, moving as if it were completely unburdened. It pounced in a lightning-quick motion, seizing the other magician, Urguag, in its four-armed embrace.

Then, it spun and launched itself off the prow of the ship, gliding easily away from us. Several of Swayle's marines tried a shot or two, but the creature easily avoided the arrows at this range. The creature was taking the magicians to the lead ship. A tidy escape, and there wasn't anything we could do about it.

"Some kind of spell to avoid the Windshrike's notice," Faith murmured, almost to herself. "Clever." Which explained how Brown had so easily escaped from the demon rampage.

"Damn," I murmured. "Speaking of outrageously potent Faerie powers, where are their dragons? Where is *our* damn dragon, for that matter?" It would have been nice to see Brocara swoop out of the sky and gobble up a demon or Windshrike or two, but no such luck.

"Busy," Avonstoke mused, his golden eyes squinting up into the sky. "All of them. Ours and theirs. Probably with each other. But"—he turned back to me with shining eyes—"this is not so terrible a start, I'd say. That's one ship that won't be sailing to France. Not without a mizjibspanker, eh?"

"Mizzenmast," I said. "It's mizzenmast."

"What is?" he said.

"Oh, shut up." I turned to shout. "Mog! Three points to starboard. We're going to give that ship a wide berth, but we need to catch up to the others."

"Yes, Captain," he growled happily. "Mog do."

"There!" Faith said. "It's noticed us." She pointed to the Windshrike, which now, having broken, shattered, or impaled every living thing on that ship, gave a scream like a lightning crash and started winging our way.

"Bloody hell," I said. "Mr. Render, I need you to . . ."

"No," Faith said. "This is beyond physical influence. I'll have to take care of it."

"Beyond physical . . ." I said, suddenly very frightened. "What does that even mean?"

But Faith moved up into the forecastle, throwing back her hood and lifting her voice as if she meant to meet the demon with only song. Her voice had that unnerving, mismatched choir sound to it now, as if several other Faiths had been living inside of her, a sign that she was channeling the power of her god, Cernunnos. The breeze around us twitched like a living thing and I felt the ship shudder. I followed Faith up onto the forecastle, my pistol out uselessly, and waited.

The demon, a bolt of cobalt flame, was within a hundred feet of us now, moving with alarming speed.

Faith lifted her voice even higher, singing louder, and the wind picked up, visible somehow as a focused, sparkling gale. The demon screamed a challenge and flew right through it . . . and vaporized like so much blue smoke. One more scream, ascending in pitch and fury even as it diminished in volume, until wind, scream, and demon were all gone.

"That," Avonstoke murmured in awe, "was amazing."

Faith sagged at the rail and I moved to catch her. She gave me a wan smile. "Wasn't sure that that would work. It seems my connection to Cernunnos is more powerful than ever."

"You vaporized it!" I said, seeing my sister, the magician, in an entirely new light. This was a power I hadn't expected.

"No," Faith said. "I merely vaporized John Brown's spell that kept it here. I'd hate to meet that thing on its home turf."

"I'm glad you're on our side," I said. She stood up and gave my arm a squeeze and I let her go.

Off the starboard bow, the *Glorious* was heeled far over to port, presenting her deck to us. It was clear the ship wasn't making any way, with her foremast and mizzenmast gone and the remaining sails hanging in rags. She was riding low in the water, too, bobbing aimlessly on the channel rollers with the port side of the deck dipping into the water with each bob. The triple-decker was obviously taking on water too, and I could hear muffled screaming coming from the hold, which had to be partly underwater by now. It was a multitude of voices, roars and moans and wails, and sounded pitiful and desperate. Water would be coming into the hold, and the oil lamps, if they were still lit, wouldn't stay lit long. I tried to imagine what it must be like in there, the darkness closing and the cold water coming in and people screaming and thrashing and drowning next to you with no way out.

"Drop the launch and the spare rowboat," I ordered Mog. "Minimal crew, but make sure they're armed. Have them pick up who they can."

Faith nodded at me with approval.

"Tell me," I murmured to her, "that a half-drowned boatload of Dwarves or Court Faerie or whatnot can't actually overrun the entire French coast on their own, right? It's not like they're dragons or Wealdarin or whatnot."

"No," Faith said. "There are Wealdarin in the hold, but they can't get out. As we expected."

I stared over at the ship as if I might see through the water and the hull and into the bottom of the ship. "So . . . they'll drown?"

"Yes," Faith said, her voice flat. It was what we were here to do, and a part of war, but that didn't make it any less horrible.

I shuddered, remembering watching the implacable tree monsters walking through England, unmaking the modern world as they moved. Wading through the earth in one of the most bizarre sights I'd ever witnessed, they had caused ripples in the earth, like tidal waves made of dirt that had washed away the world I knew and left a Faerie landscape in its place. More than dragons, more than the Black Shuck, the sheer raw irresistible power of the Wealdarin frightened me. But they were also wondrous and rare, and we were here to kill them all, if we could.

Faith leaned onto the railing, her face twisted with rage and hate as she glared at the sinking ship. "Damn the Black Shuck for bringing them into this!"

"Is it safe to rescue the others, the people? They're just going to be regular troops, most of them pressed into service?" We couldn't afford a full-on rescue mission, but I just couldn't let that many people drown. Not when the smallest gesture could save hundreds of lives.

Faith didn't answer, but just kept on glaring.

"Faith?"

"What?" Faith said, then shook her head to clear it. "Oh. Yes. You can send in boats. Just normal Faerie in the water, if there is such a thing." Then, to herself: "Not everyone needs to die."

"Good," I said. The sun was finally bringing a little warmth now. I pulled my hat low, trying to avoid the headache that a bright sun always brought to my ghost eye.

"Get some of our Prowlers in the water to help the rescue," I said to Mog. "We need a visual confirmation, need to make certain those Wealdarin aren't going to come back and haunt us."

"Aye," Mog said.

"Message from the fleet, Captain!" one of the sailors bawled. It was Cort, the female Goblin who was enamored with Spear. She shuffled over, puffed up with sudden self-importance for her impromptu mission but also walking slowly and carefully because she had a Leaf Rider perched in the palm on her raised hand. "Message from the fleet!" she said again, unnecessarily.

I didn't know this Leaf Rider, a striking little fellow all in black, which was uncommon enough to set off alarms in the back of my head.

"Grave tidings, Admiral!" the Leaf Rider wailed. "Death!"

I shot a quick, involuntary glance with the spyglass over at *Seahome*. They were on the brink of battle. The invasion fleet was bearing down on them even as we spoke and death would come riding, but how could there be a death *now*?

"What death?" I snapped.

"Drecovian!"

"What?" I said.

"It's true, Admiral."

"No!" Faith said, and there was a catch in her voice. "That can't be! He's with Brocara and she would never let him . . ."

She staggered in place, caught by the ship's sudden motion when she wasn't paying attention. Avonstoke, his face ashen, grabbed her, and she turned and gripped his shoulders. "No, no, no . . ." she kept repeating. I could see a tear on Avonstoke's cheek. He didn't look much better than Faith. More like someone had stabbed him in the gut, which was a whole lot like how I felt.

I could feel a weight descend on me, one more to roost with all its brothers and sisters. So the dragons were fighting already. We hadn't expected that this soon, and I'd seen no sign of any battles in the sky. I swept my spyglass around, but still saw nothing. The weight settled in as I thought of it. I hadn't realized how attached I'd gotten to the crotchety old wizard until he was gone. I hadn't thought anything could harm *that* one, even dragons. He also represented the largest portion of our magical power, if you didn't include Brocara herself.

To have lost him so early into the battle was a staggering blow, and the implications of that loss would resound throughout the entire campaign.

"*How?*" I snapped. "Which dragon did it? Is Brocara injured?"

"It was n-not in battle," the messenger stammered. "It was this morning. All of *Seahome* shook this morning when Brocara started wailing, but she did not stay to explain, only took to the sky, and we have not seen her since. They found Drecovian's body a short time after that. No mark on him, merely dead. There is speculation of a wizards' duel or some argument between the dragon and the wizard . . ."

"Preposterous," Faith said, shaking her head. "What did Sands or Prudence have to say about it?"

"None of the other magicians has any idea what happened," the Leaf Rider said. "Captain Kasric, that is Captain du Thorn . . . or . . ."

"Better start calling him Captain Henry," I said, taking some pity on the poor Leaf Rider, who looked ready to wet himself just then.

"Aye-aye, sir," the Leaf Rider said. "He bid me come to this part of the water and wait for you to come out of the mist."

I could feel my jaw clenching. We would have to grieve later. Right now, we were committed to our plan, and there was no going back. Without Drecovian to help hold off the other dragons, there was no way Brocara could beat them all by herself, not if what everyone said about the Red Death was true. I couldn't imagine how we could stop the invasion fleet, either, if the Black Shuck had dragons in the skies and we didn't. We might lose a lot more than Drecovian today.

"Now we're down to six Virtues," Faith said. "That could mean a lot more deaths on our side."

"Crap. Now Brocara will have to face multiple dragons on her own," I said. The many ramifications of losing Drecovian were starting to make my head spin.

"It seems," Avonstoke said in a tight voice, "we shall have to lean a bit more heavily on strategy and naval tactics, after all." He and Faith exchanged glances and I knew they were thinking about how our side of the prophecy was broken with Drecovian gone.

We all looked at the schooner, which had been moving up and around, and had now passed on both sides of us.

Heading for the *Indomitable*.

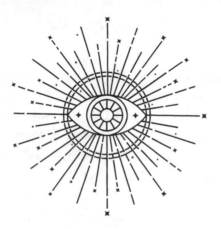

CHAPTER 17

BROCARA
Dragons at War

Brocara soared over the choppy gray water of the English Channel. She squinted, wanting to see the shape of England through the mist but failing. Even so, it was clearly not a large place, England. Funny to think that such a small place had become central to so much.

The ships beneath her had started fighting already, the cannons booming thunder and belching smoke far below her. She surprised herself by feeling an ache inside of her at the thought that some of the people she knew might be burning too. Humans, with their lightning-fast lives, were not something she was used to thinking about. At least, not specific ones. Even magicians, with their extended lifespan, still came and passed too quickly to make much more than a ripple in a dragon's life. Human countries and empires, shedding detritus everywhere, were something she thought about abstractly, but she wasn't used to even thinking about, let alone feeling fear for, specific humans.

Now, she had become attached to quite a few.

Except, of course, Drecovian. He'd been something different. The truth was, Drecovian had transcended both groups, humans and magicians, a long, long time ago. He'd been with her longer than even dragons remember easily.

And now he was gone.

She'd known it as soon as she'd woken on the morning of battle, could feel the dark, brave, terrible, and wonderful thing that he'd done. Could feel it deep inside of each foreclaw, and in the dangerous, jagged tip of her tail.

Three things he'd left her, and he'd poured every bit of his magic and his own self into them. So much so that there wasn't any Drecovian left anymore. She knew it, exactly what choices he'd made and why, though they'd never openly discussed it. Even powerful magicians like Drecovian have an end to their days eventually, and Drecovian had chosen his end at a time when it would have the greatest impact on the battle, and so on the entire world. He'd given his entire life to magic, and now, at the end, he gave magic his death so that magic would have a chance to continue.

He'd given his death to Brocara, though she hadn't asked for or wanted it. Hadn't needed it, by the gods! It made her angry enough to crush his foolish, impudent, stubborn, disrespectful body into pulp, except that he was already dead so what good would that do? It was anyone's guess if the three spells that Drecovian had left on her would even work, which was why she would have stopped him if he'd given her the chance. Damn his brave, brave stupid hide!

There was thunder and fury in the wind tonight. The Wild Hunt was not far away, from the smell of it. Cernunnos, too, favored some of the humans Brocara liked, but that would not matter. There was no telling what the Wild Hunt would do here if they rode again unfettered.

The mist roiled, agitated as if an alien intelligence inside sensed the coming events. That could be an escape for Brocara, the mist. Any dragon could navigate it, riding the thermals of place to time, and none so well as Brocara. But she didn't want to escape. She was ready to fight.

There, coming out of the very top of the mist, two shapes glittering emerald in the midday sun. Senuguhan and Sendurjihan, the two remaining members of the Green Trio. They had a moment of disorientation coming out of the mist, then they got their bearings and started winging for her at once. Brocara had killed Senestial, Senuguhan's brother and mate, and Sendurjihan's brother too, for they were all of a brood. Now the two remaining members were coming for blood, exactly as Brocara had known they would. Boldly.

Too boldly.

Brocara knew that Usarador would not come at her directly, if he could help it. He was bloodthirsty, famously so, even by dragon standards. But his heart was black and rotten and he had no interest in a real fight, only helpless prey.

So these two were the bait. The Red Death could not swim as well as she could, or navigate the mist as well. So that only left above. Brocara cast her gaze upward without moving her head in any way, so she didn't alert the other dragons to what she was thinking. Even another dragon would be unable to tell where she was looking, for her eyes were the color and swirled texture of molten gold. But the sun's glare screened anything that might be far above. That was where the attack would come from, but when? How far up was he? How long would he wait?

Then the two green dragons were closing and the bloodlust, buried for so many years until that last confrontation with the Green Trio a few months earlier, filled Brocara's heart.

She had craved battle for so long, and now she was at war. Better than magic, the bloodlust of battle, better than mating, better than friendship or love and gold, which were much the same thing.

The tactics of the green dragons were solid but predictable. Senuguhan, the female and larger of the two, postured and feinted, trying to buy time for Sendurjihan, the male, to circle around and get to Brocara's back, not so easy when in flight and everything and everyone was constantly moving.

Brocara rushed at Senuguhan and the other dragon twisted and dropped out of the way, snapping at Brocara's belly as she passed underneath. Brocara snapped too, and reached with her talons, but none of their blows found any target and then Brocara had to put on a burst of speed and drop herself to avoid the dragon behind her.

She twisted, screaming and lashing out with her barbed tail, a weapon superior to the green dragon tail, which had no such barbs. The green male screamed and spun away. Then everyone circled and did it all again.

Two more passes. Three more. Brocara kept casting glances up when she could, knowing that the Red Death was still up there, waiting.

It was the fourth pass where the female green, bloodlust clearly overtaking her, got close enough to turn and lash out with her tail. No barbs on it, true, but lethal enough. The blow hit Brocara's shoulder with enough force to shatter buildings. Pain flared all through that arm, and Brocara could feel some of the smaller bones in her wing give way in a white-hot blinding flash.

But it didn't stop her from making her own turn, which let her get a claw into Senuguhan's haunch. A small part in the back of her mind could feel whatever spell Drecovian had lain in her right claw discharge, but her lust was too high to pay it much attention in the moment. What she knew, and could feel, was the other dragon's scaled hide and flesh giving way as her claws sank in. There was a flash of powerful magic. The green dragon in her clutches was stunned but not dead. The brief purchase gave Brocara the leverage she needed to sink her fangs deep into Senuguhan's back. The green screamed while they both fell.

Brocara ripped at the other female's back, trying to rend and tear the powerful shoulder muscles that drove the wings. She tore and tore once more, all while both of them fell and both of them roared and screamed. She could hear the other green dragon's scream too, trying to get closer, but Brocara and her prey were plummeting out of reach.

One more savage tear, and Brocara pushed off Senuguhan, banking and pulling up hard, knowing that the other green and most of all the great Red Death were coming for her.

Once free, she could feel the spell missing from her right claw and craned her neck around to see what Senuguhan's state was.

The other dragon was flying despite her wound, but shakily. She roared her rage and turned, not done yet. The wound dripped red ichor that flowed off in streams with each beat of her wings. And blackness.

Wait . . .

Blackness?

Drecovian. That was his spell at work. It was a creeping shadow—he had been a shadow magician, after all—that slowly, so slowly, consumed the shoulder even as Brocara watched. In her rage, Senuguhan seemed oblivious to what was happening.

Now the male green was on Brocara, knowing that his sister was seriously injured and clearly determined to buy her the time she needed to regroup. He crashed into her, this time without guile or plan, and they tore at each other with unbridled fury. He sank his teeth into Brocara's wing, the wounded one, and the pain was a tower of flame. They were tumbling now, neither of them flying, just blood and tooth and claw and a desperate savage need to feel the other dragon's throat in their jaws, lest the other get his on their throat.

Somewhere in the flurry of blows, Drecovian's second spell discharged from her other claw, but she didn't care because she had the smaller dragon's throat between her jaws.

But no time.

The water was spinning closer.

Brocara could feel it, and reluctantly gave up her grip. She'd done enough damage that Sendurjihan was frantic to break away too, and they both desperately pulled up to avoid the water. Brocara could swim, better than the other dragons, but hitting the water at this speed would be the end of anything, even a dragon.

So she came out of her free fall and pulled, pulled, pulled up to avoid the sea. Only her tail dipped briefly in the water as she beat her wings and fought hard to gain altitude, while her wing burned like the sun. The ships were fighting now too, and some of them were burning, but she didn't have time to see more.

Senuguhan, the female, was in a shallow dive, trying to close despite her own injuries. But the dive grew shaky as the green dragon started to become, finally, aware of Drecovian's spell.

The shadow was visibly gaining speed all the time now, crawling over the dragon's chest and up her neck.

Senuguhan roared in impotent rage, knowing somehow that her revenge on Brocara wasn't going to happen. She was only a hundred yards away and closing when the shadow enveloped her completely and she winked out of sight.

Not dead. Brocara could feel it. Moved. Moved far away from here. Back to the depths of Faerie, where time moved more slowly. So far and so deep that it would take her months to make it back.

Drecovian had always been clever. He wasn't just saving Brocara from the other dragons, he was also saving the other dragons from Brocara. Saving all of Faerie from the loss of magic that would happen if all the dragons died. Even in her rage at being denied her final kill, Brocara felt a grudging respect for the magician's choice and actions. It was a worthy death for any magician. No one could deny him that.

Brocara wondered if anyone else would understand what he'd done, and if she, Brocara, would live long enough to tell them. Probably not.

The other green dragon swooped at Brocara again. Brocara could see the blackness crawling across it, but it was slow, so slow. Brocara was not as agile as she'd been a moment ago, with a wound across her stomach and back and the injured wing. She dove to avoid the other dragon. Just . . . a . . . few . . . more . . . seconds. Brocara, her bloodlust receding just a little, banked hard, in full-on flight while the green dragon pursued. Brocara tried to keep climbing, tried to keep track of the open sky and of her pursuer at the same time, and knew the pain in her wing was making her slow and stupid. She kept beating her wings, trying for more speed. The mist swirled off to her left as she kept moving, climbing little by little, her lead on the green dragon gaining just a tiny bit. Her enemy raged, screaming its fury without any seeming awareness of the shadow crawling on its back. The burning pain in Brocara's wing was hotter now. She would not be able to stay in the air much longer if it kept getting worse, and it wasn't going to get any better if she kept pushing it, but what choice did she have?

The shadow, blotting out the sun, fell on her just as she fought to take herself higher and only then did she realize that it was too late to do anything about it.

A mountain fell on her, a mountain that roared. Jaws large enough to swallow a horse whole snapped down on her neck, and she felt the bones give. Something crunched very loudly, and she could feel herself slipping away.

She fell.

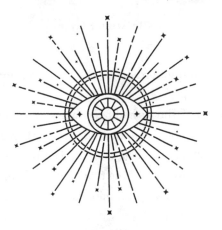

CHAPTER 18

PRUDENCE
Discoveries

It had started during the setup for Justice's ruse to display the Seven Virtues.

That's when the vision from Brigid came to her.

Of course, things had started out very early in the morning, and tragically, as a wail like a thunderstorm savaged Prudence's ears, waking her. One of the luxuries of *Seahome* was the actual beds, instead of the hammocks that English ships used, or the nests or moss piles or what-have-you that the Faerie tended to use. After her childhood among the Jötnar, sleeping on slabs of stone, the Lord of Thorns had taken Prudence on a visit to England, and she'd tried a human bed and fallen in love with it at once.

The Lord of Thorns must have thought similarly, for his quarters on *Seahome* sported a stout bed, sinfully fluffy, with a frame of real English wood. It had wooden railings, too, a concession to being at sea, so

Prudence suspected the Lord of Thorns had had it made expressly for these quarters.

When the Lord of Thorns had been taken back to Faerie, Prudence had immediately commandeered his quarters for herself, one of the few bright spots in an otherwise abysmal and calamitous war.

The railings were the only thing that kept her from falling out of the bed when the wail, a basso profundo, ear-splitting, cataclysmic thing, had torn through the ship.

Prudence had sat bolt upright as the wail faded like a bad memory and there was only the sloshing of the sea underneath *Seahome*'s raft-style timbers. The room creaked and bobbed up and down with the sea, her bed tilting slightly to the right and then left as the waves tipped up first one part of the room, then the other. It didn't move like a human ship, which mostly moved as one thing, but undulated with every serpentine motion of the sea. Prudence felt no trace of the nausea that some of the others, mostly human, complained of, however. The Faerie, as a rule, weren't susceptible to such things.

Prudence sat frozen, waiting to see if the wail was going to happen again. It didn't. There was only one place that kind of noise had come from, their dragon, and Prudence needed to find out why. Since she always slept in her layers of gray clothes and wasn't worried about looking rumpled, she only had to slip on sandals. Being able to shapeshift had taken some of the glamour out of polishing her human appearance.

In fact, it would take her precious minutes to *run* across the shifting decks of *Seahome*, so she instead pushed the curtain to her entranceway to one side and lifted her arms, letting her human form melt away; so, it was a gray-feathered bird with a nearly five-foot wingspan that rushed out into the open air and winged over to the section of *Seahome* devoted to their dragons.

As she did, she kept her eye on the sky and was quick to spot Brocara's dwindling form already two miles up and climbing. There was no point in trying to follow or catch up with Brocara. Prudence had a phenomenal speed for a bird, but that was nothing compared to the cruising speed of a dragon. So she flew to the place Brocara had recently vacated in hopes of understanding what had happened.

It hadn't taken her long to find Drecovian's body.

It took her some time to understand what she had found. Drecovian's body showed no sign of physical injury or any sign of an internal magical presence, which surprised Prudence to no end. Drecovian's core, his spirit or soul or magical chi, depending on who you asked, had been a powerful thing. Prudence had seen it when she worked serious magics, his core burning like a dark star. Even after death, that kind of power left magical residue, and it was extraordinary that the magician's corpse should have no sign of it. That discovery, and the timing of his death, precluded it being any kind of accident, and Prudence's first, terrifying thought, was that the Black Shuck had found some kind of way to reach out and snuff the magician from afar. As if this war hadn't been frightening enough. This kind of thing stank of death magic, which was what both the Black Shuck and Drecovian used. Had there been some kind of contest between them, with Drecovian the loser? If the Black Shuck had that kind of power, why had he waited this long to use it? Prudence could only hope that the price for this kind of magic would be too costly to use frequently or in quick succession.

If that wasn't true, they were already dead, all of them. What hope had they now without Drecovian and with one less Virtue?

But Prudence couldn't do anything about that and instead swore the Goblin retainers working for Drecovian and Brocara to secrecy and then sent a message to inform Henry and another to wait for Justice's ship as it came out of the mist.

Then, having no option but to continue to fight in a war effort that was probably doomed, she went about implementing Justice's plan as best she could, fabricating costumes so that seven of the people on board could display themselves while impersonating Justice, Faith, Hope, Charity, Prudence herself, as well as Temperance and the one she knew least about: Love. She knew one thing, that she'd been born to a human woman named Ashmir from somewhere in India and was raised under the name Pyar, which was a Hindi word for Love. Like Prudence herself, Love hadn't been raised in the human world but somewhere in Faerie. Only Prudence had searched England, India, and a great deal of Faerie and had never been able to locate either Love or her mother. She'd had Justice's description of the portrait of her, which meant that Martine, or somebody working with the invasion knew what she looked like. Prudence would have given a great deal to see the painting herself.

The hardest part about the ruse was avoiding the use of magic, which would be detected much more quickly than mundane subterfuge. Instead, Justice had drawn on the paltry human population within the Outcast Fleet. This would have been impossible before the occupation, as the few sailors and military personnel that the Lord of Thorns had used had been predominantly male, and the Virtues were all women. But since the Outcast Fleet had spent the last few months rescuing refugees from the invasion, Prudence had had her veritable pick of human women on *Seahome*.

"Is Admiral Justice commanding *Seahome*?" one of the women "volunteers" asked as Prudence arranged her outfit and hair to the best effect. They hadn't found anyone that matched Love's description very closely, but hopefully, this woman would do.

"Justice is on the *Specter*," Prudence replied absently.

"The little ship?" the woman said.

"Yeah," Prudence said. "She seems to think she can do more damage that way. I don't know. Perhaps she's right. I don't know ships."

"So we're not going to be in the real fight, then?" the woman said with some relief.

"Certainly we are," Prudence said, putting a tricorn hat on the woman's head. Prudence frowned. The woman's hair probably wasn't dark enough, either, but the hat did an adequate job of hiding that. It would do from a distance, which was all it had to be good for. That was as fine a faux Love as she was likely to get.

Prudence, a deep believer in the prophecy, for all of Justice's reluctance and disbelief, had searched for as much information on the missing Virtues as she possibly could. She still prayed desperately that Hope and Charity, back in Faerie, would change their minds and come to their assistance. Anything was possible. Prudence had pleaded to them directly for their help before the war had started, but to no avail. The Lord of Thorns, for all his cunning, had made enemies of all the wrong people, including the Lady of Sorrows, Hope and Charity's mother. They had nothing but disdain for the father who had abandoned them and weren't likely to come help his cause or the humans he cared for anytime soon.

"I hear she defied the Faerie gods and everything!" the young girl they'd found to imitate Justice herself said, then. Faux Justice.

"I heard that, too!" Faux Love said. "I would love to hear the story of that from her own lips, I would."

Prudence wasn't really paying attention to their conversation. But then she turned slowly and looked at Faux Temperance, and flashes of vision suddenly hit her like a storm of the mind.

This was not a sudden recollection or inspiration. This was coming from somewhere else, somewhere *outside* of Prudence's mind.

Every magician, or any other potent force within Faerie—if you didn't count dragons; they were their own source of power—traced their magic back to one of the Faerie gods. That included the Virtues, and Temperance, Prudence suddenly knew, was sourced with Taranis, the god of the sun. But it seemed that Brigid and Taranis had decided to join forces to send Prudence a vision.

The vision hammered Prudence's mind and heart with images of a dark place, but not just images, for Prudence could hear and feel the clink and cold weight of manacles. And the stink of it: cold bilgewater around the ankles.

That stink was unmistakable, and Prudence had been in enough human ships to recognize it. Which meant that Temperance was in one of the ships the Black Shuck had brought to sea.

And with Brigid's help, Prudence now thought she knew which one.

It was a good thing she'd created a Faux Prudence too. She had other things to do.

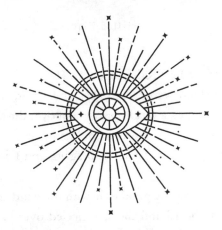

CHAPTER 19

JUSTICE
The *Specter* and the *Indomitable*

The *Indomitable* lay ahead, with our smaller schooners closing on them.

"Send for Golden," I said.

Golden was the new leader of the Leaf Riders, in place since Dream's death. He was a tiny Faerie with a great mane of golden hair like a miniature lion's. He landed on the railing, his red-speckled leaf dancing underneath him restlessly just as Dream's used to do. Leaf and rider together could have easily sat comfortably in the palm of my hand.

"Send riders to the lead four schooners," I said. "Have them close with the *Indomitable*. The rest stay back for support and to pick up anyone in the water. Tell them to rescue who they can of the enemy but save room for our people."

"Aye-aye, admiral!" Golden piped up at once and then launched his leaf steed off the railing, making his way down to the front gun port, where the rest of the Leaf Rider tribe was. He'd send one rider to each ship, making sure there were no mistakes, and would have them all back in three to four minutes, a vast improvement over the flag signaling system. I was amazed that a Leaf Rider could outpace a ship running with the wind, but they'd done it again and again, and I'd come to rely on them more and more.

The *Specter* was making good time with the wind coming down the channel off to starboard and the ship heeled over to port with foam creaming past the bow. My face was wet with the spray.

Even so, the schooners were moving a lot faster. In a few minutes, the four lead schooners had broken out from the rest. With their fore-and-aft rigging, they could move faster through the water than either the *Specter* or the invading triple-deckers and lie closer to the wind, even if they only used the wind available to the rest of us. Of course, they had the storm serpents. The fore-and-aft rigging accounted for some of the difference in speed, but the storm serpents were clearly bending the wind to their will too, and the schooners nearly flew, heeled hard over to their port sides, skipping easily over the waves, each ship leaving a long trail of churned foam. They bore down on the *Indomitable*.

One of the schooners attacking was the *Blood Oath*, Heleena and Demet's ship, with Nellie and Wil on board. The schooners were approaching two each from either side, and Heleena's ship was one on *Indomitable*'s starboard side. The schooners had just about drawn even with the *Indomitable* and were starting to edge their way closer.

The first chunk of rock sailed through the air in their direction. I was deeply glad that the Faerie didn't seem to understand or care about coordinating their fire. They'd had at least twenty Trolls hurling missiles on the *Glorious* and I had to assume that the *Indomitable* had a similar complement. Twenty boulders launched at once would have been far more potent than the haphazard arrangement they were using. Even so, it was terrifying enough, one at a time. The first missile flew at Heleena's ship but was too high. Heleena's ship turned neatly and swiftly toward the *Indomitable* so that the boulder sailed over, coming within a dozen feet of the topmast.

"Neatly done," Avonstoke breathed. We could have put cannons on the schooners, of course, and allowed them some chance of retaliating in a situation like this, but there would be no guarantee that this would be enough to disable the *Indomitable*. We couldn't rely on that kind of luck. Also, the *Specter* couldn't possibly operate effectively with a dozen cannons missing, and I wanted to keep them together to concentrate their effect. Even further, the thinner decks of the schooners would have broken and fallen in with repeated shots. There was a simpler answer.

I had another task in mind for the schooners, and the reason that I hadn't told anyone on the *Specter* besides Faith and Avonstoke was that I hadn't wanted to listen to everyone else's outrage.

The *Indomitable* fired again. These Trolls were better marksmen, or else picking their ammunition better, because they were coming a lot closer to their targets now than they had to the *Specter*, even though the schooners were smaller and faster. I could feel the muscles bunching in my jaw. I ground my teeth and my hands were like clamps on the railing until I forced myself to let go.

"Spread sail on the topgallants, Mr. Mog!" I called out. "We need to get closer and give them some support." We were at long range for our cannons, but I wanted to give the crew on board the *Indomitable* something else to think about other than using those schooners for target practice.

"Just Mog, Captain," Mog said. "But Mog do." I'd forgotten his objection to "Mr." in the heat of battle, but he hadn't. Despite that, he immediately had the sail crews up in the rigging spreading the extra sail. It was a risk on our part, running that much sail in this wind, but we needed speed, and we needed it badly. I only hoped that the extra sail didn't snap a spar or a top mast and slow us down.

"Three points to port," I called out. "Mr. Render, fire the bow chasers as they bear."

"Aye-aye, Captain," Render replied.

Another volley of boulders soared out from the *Indomitable*, three of them arcing toward the nearest schooner on the port side. Knocknaguer, an older, shrewd, and slightly cantankerous Goblin, captained that ship. I had met and learned the names of all the captains, and now I almost wished I hadn't.

Knocknagur's ship turned away from the group of boulders, using the long travel time to try and get out of the way. The first boulder fell far ahead of the ship, which wasn't dangerous in itself, but a stone that size dropping into the water threw up a geyser of water that drenched the deck of Knocknagur's ship, captain and serpent both temporarily blinded. Even worse, the ship floundered in the sudden wave and lost its way. It never had a chance to recover. The next two boulders found their marks and what had moments before been a lean and beautiful ship with a lively crew became an empty bit of tossed sea with a few shattered planks floating in it.

I swept the area for any sign of survivors but didn't see any. Knocknagur, his serpent, and the crew were gone

"Gods," Avonstoke whispered.

"Good God," Faith said in almost the same moment.

I stared at her momentarily, the sudden wild and random notion rattling around in my brain, entirely against my will, of the incongruity and conflict in taking the Christian God's name, in vain, no less, on a Faerie ship. For that matter, Faith was a wizard drawing insight and power from the Wild Hunt, which was almost the same as a pagan priest. Did that make her unconscious blasphemy better . . . or worse? Did she even believe in the teachings of the Church of England anymore? Did I? Did the very real existence of magical Faerie, many of whom felt an enmity for the Christian church, alter our views? Should it?

Father had borrowed, somewhat haphazardly, the names of the Seven Cardinal Virtues for his own purposes, and the Black Shuck had done the same with the Sins. Those names and titles had power for them, which almost made them better believers, in a strange fashion, than most of England.

My refusal to follow the Faerie gods had nothing to do with English piety. The truth was, the Church of England was part of England I wanted to save, same as Big Ben and the House of Parliament and London's bridges, and Christmas, Guy Fawkes Night, Boxing Day, Stonehenge, tea, biscuits, scones, fish and chips, and bowler hats, and all of it was wrapped up together and supported by all the rest. I wanted to save it, even if I didn't know how I felt about the Church of England and their teachings anymore.

"Mr. Render!" I bellowed. "Where are my bow chasers!"

"Coming, Admiral!" Render said in a strained voice. The *Specter* was closing on an intercept course, but wasn't quite pointed directly at the enemy, which was forcing Render to constantly re-aim the bow chasers. He stood up finally and yanked the lanyard on the port-side bow chaser and it roared, a small, bright gout of flame shooting out of the barrel with the black acrid smoke.

It seemed as if I'd always had the taste of it in my mouth. The Dwarf forecastle lookout with a spyglass shook his head. There were lookouts higher up too, where there wasn't so much smoke, but none of them called out a hit.

"Keep firing, Mr. Render," I snapped. Possibly, Render was aiming *too* carefully. With the variance between powder cartridges and imperfect ammunition and the way the *Specter* was moving on the waves, there would always be an element of luck to each shot and too slow a rate of fire could be a grievous mistake.

But I needn't have worried. Render was already moving back to the other cannon while the gun crew started reloading the one he'd just fired.

The Faerie archers on the schooners were starting to create casualties on the big triple-decker, but the archers there were returning fire, most of them aiming to try to neutralize each other.

I was constantly scanning the other ship through the glass and stopped when I caught sight of a familiar cadaverous figure on the quarterdeck.

Mrs. Westerly. Or rather, Lady Westerly. The woman who, along with Father, had helped push Mother into madness. I hated her down to the bottom of my heart. She looked older now, far older, with her sunken black eyes, long, greasy brown hair, and hooked nose.

Standing next to her was another of the Seven Sins, the Goblin Knight.

He was bigger than even Mog, who was the biggest Goblin aboard the *Specter*. The Goblin Knight had short, stubby ears, unlike Mog's droopy batwing ears, but those were the only comparisons possible since the Goblin Knight also wore a giant bear's skull as a mask. He carried the giant morning star as before, the one that smoldered red when he used it, and trailed black, oily smoke. The same one he'd used to kill Mr. Starling. But that was at his belt, hanging inert like an infernal torture device waiting for victims. At the moment, the Goblin Knight bore an enormous shield to fend off the arrows.

Next to me, Avonstoke stiffened, and I knew that he and his raven had spotted the Goblin Knight too. That same Goblin had also killed Avonstoke's father.

"*Him,*" was all he said.

"Westerly and the Goblin Knight are over there," I called out to Swayle's second. "Make them primary targets."

"I *have* been," he called back, just as he loosed another arrow. I went back to the spyglass in time to see the Goblin raise his shield a few seconds later, deflecting the shot that would have otherwise gone right through the bear skull and into the Goblin's eye.

The archer swore and snatched another arrow out of a makeshift basket in front of him. "Get me a little closer and I'll pierce that shield. But at this range, in this wind?" He shook his helmeted head. It seemed there were limits even to Court Faerie archery.

"Perhaps a bigger bow?" Avonstoke said lightly, but I could see that his jaw was tight, and his blind eyes narrowed as they glared at his enemy on the other ship. Even his raven looked intent. Avonstoke didn't have to say it, but he was clearly content to see his enemy evade the arrows for the simple reason that Avonstoke wanted to kill the Goblin himself.

Mog had come up next to us. "Mog heard somewhere, probably an old book, that war the great idiocy."

"I said that," Avonstoke said. "Right here on this deck."

"Yes," Mog said, grinning. "Avonstoke did. But does war need to take everything? Dangerous path revenge? Is personal war, yes? Maybe personal idiocy too, Mog thinks."

Avonstoke turned around, looking hard at Mog, then finally shrugged.

"You're not wrong, Mog," he admitted.

"Mog hardly ever wrong," Mog agreed.

"Two points to starboard," I said. "Don't let the sails luff." I wanted the best speed possible. "Best get the topgallants out too."

"Yes, Captain," Mog said. He patted Avonstoke on his arm in a gentle, almost fatherly gesture, and then turned and bellowed at the helmsmen with the power of a foghorn, baring fangs the size of knives. The helmsman, a Prowler with green skin, scrambled to comply.

Now Heleena's ship was closing from the other side. The archers on her ship had lit a small fire on deck in a burning brazier and started firing fire arrows into the side of the *Indomitable*. Under ordinary circumstances, no sailor, human, or Faerie, would ever use fire in battle, or even bad weather. Even with constant drenching of sea spray, the use of tar and pitch made sail, cordage, and even the ship's hull far too ready to burn, to say nothing of the powder room or the various powder charges that were required for the cannon. The smallest spark could ignite any of these and overtake the ship before any crew, especially one in battle, could hinder it. No matter how fearsome a weapon, fire was always a danger to everyone and just as likely to burn the user as the victim.

But that hadn't stopped me from ordering its use on the schooners, since I'd been planning on setting those ships on fire anyway.

The *Indomitable*'s Troll artillery took two more schooners before Heleena's ship darted in and closed with the triple-decker. By then, the schooner's archers had already peppered the side of the enemy's ship with burning arrows, but the ship was heeled over in their direction, so none of them caught.

"Oh," Faith said at my side. "Here they go."

With a sharp turn of the helm, Heleena turned her ship and rammed the triple-decker. I cringed at the crunch of wood on wood and screams from both ships. At the same time, the archers had spilled their brazier and several others like it, and their own ship burst into flame around them and their captain. The array of fearsome hooks we installed on the prow, masquerading up until now as anti-boarding measures, buried themselves into the partly staved-in hole that Heleena has just made in the side of the *Indomitable*.

Demet, the storm serpent, was the first to slip off the boat and into the turbulent water, moving with a liquid grace but surprisingly fast. Heleena, Nellie, Wil, and the Court Faerie archers followed, diving neatly, one, two, three, as if they'd rehearsed the move.

Behind them, Heleena's ship, the *Blood Oath*, was already sending tongues of flame up the side of the *Indomitable*. Small packets of gunpowder scattered around her deck now sent up more messy gouts of flame. More gunpowder and firewood in the hold would ensure that once the *Blood Oath* was lit, there would be no putting her out. The deep booming cough of that small explosion and another rush of fire and hot air, visibly rippling up and over the railing of the *Indomitable*, signaled that the fire had found it.

The *Blood Oath* went up like a torch, and a column of flame crawled over the hull and railing of the *Indomitable*, which caught quickly and thoroughly. Flame licked over every surface and the air shimmered all around. The *Blood Oath*'s sail caught with a massive, soft implosion of air. A wide, black, oily trail of smoke curled up into the air. I'd had some concern about a magical method of counteracting the flame, but nothing like that was happening now. It seemed the Faerie, as a rule, were better at starting fires than putting them out.

"Good," I said. "Now don't let up, Mr. Render. Keep firing. Helm, two more points to starboard. Take us in closer." The wind had backed a little, so our speed had picked up. A favorable turn for us, as long as it lasted.

"Aye, Captain," Render said.

"Aye-aye," Mog said, gesturing at the helm to comply, which they did.

Render had just finished aiming again and suited actions to words by pulling the lanyard, which sent the spark to fire another shot. The cannon banged and belched more smoke while the deck shook. The shot exploded the quarterdeck this time, raising an outcry of screams and wails. That would slow any fire crews, bowmen, or Troll artillery, for certain.

"Good shot!" Avonstoke said, gripping the rail. His raven cawed agreement.

But the *Indomitable* was still shooting back. I'd taken a risk getting this close, and now the *Specter* was well within Troll artillery range. Fortunately, they were foolishly aiming at the *Blood Oath*, pretty much just dumping masonry over the side. The chunks of stone fell right through, tearing out the hull for certain, but that didn't matter. It wouldn't stop the fire and she couldn't fully sink while she was hooked into the *Indomitable*'s side. Not without tearing out more of the *Indomitable*'s hull, anyway.

Even as the cannon's echo died, another of the schooners was coming at the *Indomitable*, closing from the other side. The *Indomitable* herself blocked most of the action from our point of view, but another plume of smoke appeared streaming from that side almost at once, indicating they'd done their work. Screams and smoke were coming from her, but no more boulders. Render fired another of the bow chasers and another hole appeared in her side. She was listing and burning and helpless in the water.

"Mog," I called out. "Bring us one more point to starboard."

"Aye," Mog replied.

"Render, ready for a port-side broadside. Aim for the masts. We want to demast her and set that Windshrike loose. She'll be dead in the water for sure after that."

"Aye, Captain," Render said.

"Avonstoke," I said, "can that raven of yours get closer and get us a better look?"

"Yes, my captain," he said, and the bird launched from his shoulder at once.

"Don't get *too* close, in case there are any archers left over there."

"Yes, my captain." His smile was thin. He'd probably already thought of that. I'd never forgive myself if he got blinded a second time on my account, and yet all war was risk. Ironic that Avonstoke, who'd once been blind, now had a vision that none of us could match.

It took us almost a full minute to get the ship into position for our next broadside, and by then there was no need. We didn't need Avonstoke's raven to see that The *Indomitable* was a burning inferno. The Windshrike was long gone, though freed or destroyed I wasn't sure. The mainmast groaned and fell in a shower of sparks, causing a flash of heat we could feel even this far out.

"Look," Faith said, appearing at my elbow, though I wasn't sure when she'd left. She pointed.

There on the quarterdeck, barely discernable in the flames, was a familiar shape. Lady Westerly. She stood, unmoving, as the walls of fire climbed all around her, until the mizzenmast, too, fell, and she disappeared.

A scream drifted across the water, audible even over the roar of the fire, horrible to hear, no matter how badly I hated Lady Westerly and what she'd done to Mother. The mast must have broken into the aft part of the hold, because some inrush of air caused the flames to spark and dance anew.

"Look there!" Avonstoke said, pointing with urgency. "Heading for the bow."

I didn't see it at first and my ghost eye was no help for this, since it wasn't a matter of peering through Faerie glamour or any kind of magical trickery, just the fiery flickers and shadows of the massive fire. But then I saw it, a dark shape moving quickly from fore to aft, bounding along the deck, his shield screening his head from the worst part of the fire, at least from one side. The Goblin Knight. I remembered the last time we'd done battle with him, he'd killed Mr. Starling, almost killed Mog, and then jumped over the side. Now he was about to escape the exact same way again. Wearing armor as he did, he should have drowned that time, but obviously hadn't. So either he was some swimmer or had some other aquatic ability that we didn't know about.

"Marines!" I shouted, but they were already shooting, letting loose arrows as fast as they could draw and fire in a blur of motion. The Goblin Knight wasn't an easy target, weaving through and around obstacles as he was and shrouded by flame. Even so, I saw, through the dance of flames, at least three arrows bounce off that shield of his. As the Goblin Knight, moving faster than I would have given him credit for, bounded up the stairs to the *Indomitable*'s quarterdeck, he cleared the greatest mass of flames and smoke, though wisps and tendrils of it still swam around him, and headed for the railing He still bore the smoldering morning star in his hand, the weapon he'd killed Mr. Starling with. That was a dark irony as its own smoke was completely lost in the conflagration all around him. Another arrow hit his burning shield, this time piercing the metal and drawing some blood from his shoulder or neck, I couldn't tell. Probably only a minor wound, at best. Then he was over the quarterdeck railing and falling into the water.

"Damn!" the marine nearest me said.

"There's something in the water," Avonstoke said, his face taking on that blank look he had when his raven wasn't near him. "Prowlers, I think."

"Our Prowlers?" I asked, though that didn't make any sense. I'd had Mog send out some of our Prowlers to confirm the death of the Wealdarin, but they should still be in the *Specter*'s wake, if I was any judge of nautical speed. They could catch up to the *Specter* easily enough when we were forced to tack often and they could swim a straight line, but as it was, that hadn't happened, and it would be a surprise for them to have caught up with us now, let alone be ahead of us that way.

"Not ours, I think," Avonstoke said. "Not Prowlers either, now that I get a better look. Something else. Bigger, humanoid still, but perhaps twice their size. More like Trolls with fins and flukes."

"Deep Ones," Faith said.

"I didn't think that the Black Shuck had any Prowlers or Deep Ones under his command," I said.

"He doesn't," Faith said. "At least I didn't think he did. But it seems he does now."

"They've taken the Goblin Knight," Avonstoke said, "and are heading, at impressive speed, for the lead ship."

"Damn," I said.

"Lady Rue said she had a pact with the Deep Ones," Faith said, "but either she's lied, or she's wrong, or some of them aren't adhering to it."

"Some kind of splinter group," Avonstoke hazarded.

"That may have something to do with Lughus throwing in with the invasion."

"Damn," I said again. The weight of Lughus's joining the enemy still felt like my fault, and the ramifications of that shift kept haunting us in more and more ways.

Then there was nothing to do about the *Indomitable* except watch it burn to the waterline. We lowered boats for the survivors, who all surrendered immediately, according to the Leaf Rider reports. I wasn't going to stick around. We had to catch up with the *Emerald Demise*. In theory, I should have been thrilled. Two enemy ships down, both of them far larger than anything we had on the water.

But that still left two more to go and the entire world in the balance.

"This may change things," Faith said. "We don't have a full complement of Virtues, despite our ruse to the contrary, but now . . ."

"Now the Black Shuck doesn't either," I finished.

"Precisely," Faith said. "It makes me wonder what the Black Shuck will do about that."

"I don't think the Black Shuck is formulating his own strategy," I said. "Who else? Widdershins?"

"I was thinking of the dreams that Llyr sent you. I'd guess the Black Shuck is getting his own marching orders from above."

"Hmm," I said. "The Faerie gods."

"But they aren't infallible either," Faith said. "They get foiled all the time. They have petty misunderstandings, temper tantrums, all the rest. All the stories agree on that."

"Fallible," I mused. "Like Father."

Faith's eyebrows went up, since this went very much against my statements about this topic in the past, but then a lot had happened lately. His original plan had been brilliant, cold, and immoral. Horrible, in fact, sacrificing the real Rachek Kasric, a near stranger who had done him no harm. I'd refused. His backup plan, having me shoot him to take him out of commission, was a stunning display of self-sacrifice for our benefit, perhaps proving that humanity, possibly us, had taught him more than a little about morality. But it was a move of desperation against impossible odds, and now his own original plan was being turned against him, none of which smacked of "brilliant tactician." So, his plans went from cunning and cruel to selfless and desperate. Neither plan was doing us much good right now. All of which meant that he wasn't perfect, or perfectly trustworthy, something I'd been grappling with, I think, for a long time. This was the first I'd expressed that thought out loud, though.

Faith nodded, slowly, carefully, with understanding, and I knew instinctively that she'd followed all of my reasoning on this precisely. After all, she'd been trying to convince me of that very thing for some time now.

"Lady Faith?" one of the crewmen, a Dwarf, came up and saluted quickly. "Leaf Riders are back. The ships picked up survivors from the *Blood Oath* and the *Florimell*, the two ships we lost, but not everyone made it." In Sands' absence, Faith was collating the Leaf Rider reports as they came in.

"Who?" I asked in a tight voice.

"Nellie, Wil, and Heleena are safely on the *Cambina*," Faith said. "But we lost the rest, including Demet, the Storm Serpent. Our best guess is that one of the last boulders got him while he was in the water."

I sucked in a deep breath. Losing one of the Storm Serpents was a terrible blow to the fleet, in addition to being a tragedy for poor Heleena.

Almost against my will, I pulled out the spyglass again and turned to see if I could pick out Heleena on the deck of the *Cambina*. Sure enough, there she was on the main deck. Even from here, I could see her heaving and sobbing. Of course she was. They'd had a bond more than coworker or ship's mate or pet. She was bawling as if a lover or parent had died, and I'd been the one who had ordered them to perform the fire ship maneuver knowing full well what it might cost. At least I could confirm to myself that Nellie and Wil were still alive. It had been a close thing.

I snapped the spyglass shut. Avonstoke had left the deck for the gun deck when I'd ordered port-side broadside readied, but I wished he was here to lean against. My legs didn't feel up to the task of balancing on a moving ship right this moment.

"What about the dragons?" I asked.

"Scouts thought they saw some movement, but it's too far up. There's no way to tell what's happening."

"Great."

Faith reached out and squeezed my shoulder. No more than that, but it was a lot. Then she was gone.

"Open up the sail a bit more and take us three points into the wind," I told Mog. "Let's get those long nines into range on the *Emerald Demise*."

ACT III

PROPHETIC
CONFRONTATIONS

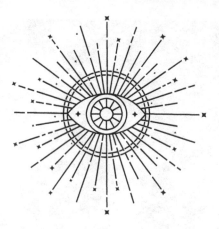

CHAPTER 20

JOSHUA
Rachek Kasric

O n board the *Emerald Demise*, Joshua looked at the man he'd been trying to find for nearly all his life, even before he'd known to look. The man he'd thought was dead. The man nearly *everyone* had thought was dead, now posing as a guard in the hold. How he had managed it, or why he was still here after getting this far, Joshua could not fathom.

Rachek Kasric, in his role as guard, had opened the metal prison gate without needing to be told.

Mother stalked past her one-time husband without paying him any attention whatsoever. Her feet splashed in the vile and moldy bilgewater, soaking her boots and the bottom of her checked and patched cloak, but she paid it no mind. Her dress, shameless as it was in Joshua's estimation, wasn't long enough to get soiled. Some kind of parable there, he thought. But watching the bilgewater stain Mother's legs, leaving bits of mold, debris, and probably rat dung, made him shudder. Not that his own bare and heavily taloned feet were clean, but it wasn't the same thing. Or was it? Joshua could feel his mind running off the rails, drifting on effluvia when he should be focusing on the matter at hand, and he wondered yet again what kind of damage close proximity to Widdershins had done to his brain. What had it done to Mother's, which had been exposed to so much more of it?

When Joshua looked at the guard's face, his Father's face, it already resembled a Court Faerie's again. It was a minor bit of Faerie glamour, but so smoothly and effortlessly done that Joshua wasn't at all surprised it had escaped Mother's attention. Joshua gawped, feeling overwhelmed and mentally inadequate to the shock of it all. That Father was here was astonishing enough. That he clearly had some kind of plan, and the magic to back it up, was just as surprising. Rachek Kasric's recognizing Joshua, after all the changes that Mother had wrought on him, was even more impossible, but clearly that was exactly what had just happened. Not counting the shabby light thrown from Mother's magical torch and a dark lantern hanging from one of the rafters, the hold was a lightless, airless place. The air lay fetid and close about them. The songbird fluttered once and went still.

Temperance was chained against the bulkhead. One chain that ran through loops forged onto a collar and a manacle on each wrist. Her head rolled listlessly. Mother selected one of the many pockets in her patterned cloak and took out a vial of . . . something, uncorked it, and carefully dabbed it on each closed eyelid. As a smiling afterthought, she also dabbed a little on her exposed collarbone, as if she'd forgotten where she was and was preparing for a ball, bilgewater notwithstanding. Then she seized a fistful of Temperance's hair, examining her face carefully, as if expecting some kind of glamour. She stared for long moments, then grunted and let Temperance's head go. The prisoner stayed unconscious.

"You have not escaped," Mother murmured to herself, which was just as well since Temperance seemed mostly unconscious. "Why? What is she up to?"

This answer he knew. It seemed an overly obvious question to Joshua. Justice wanted to prevent the Black Shuck from getting to the coast, where the Wealdarin could awaken and overrun everything. Her subterfuge was a distraction to delay them, and an obvious one at that. But the Black Shuck would fall for it. And that wasn't Joshua's problem anymore.

His next thought was interrupted when the crash of a cannonball tearing into the deck above them thundered overhead, followed quickly by muffled screaming. So Justice had dealt with the *Indomitable* already, somehow, with her smaller ship and was now firing on them, probably from out of range of their Troll artillery. He felt a cold, inward smile crawl over his fanged mouth.

"Damn her polluted flesh!" Martine growled, turning from the prisoner. "I'll skin her myself!"

The guard, Rachek Kasric, grabbed her arm as she went past.

"Unhand me!" she snarled.

Rachek made a subtle gesture and revealed his true face. "Martine, it's me. We *have* to talk. You're leading an invasion against your own people. This has to stop!"

"You?" she said, looking him full in the face for the first time. She didn't seem much surprised or impressed. "What could I possibly have to say to you? You gave up any right to speak to me when you left and didn't come back."

"I was trapped in Faerie!" Rachek said, a note of pleading had come into his voice.

"Oh yes," she said. "I know the entire story. I also know that a real man would have found a way to return to his family. You were dead to me before. You're just as dead now. Get out of my way." She yanked her arm free and turned to level a murderous stare at Temperance.

"Would you really harm your own child, Martine?" Rachek said. "Are you really that far gone? You have to try and find yourself and come back to me." He took off his helmet and let it splash into the water at their feet. "Can you find a way to do that, Martine?" He was Rachek Kasric again, older and wiser, perhaps, than Joshua remembered, but the same man he'd longed to find. Joshua's heart leapt.

"Bah," Martine said, pulling her arm free. "You know nothing!" It seemed impossible that Father had come back and revealed himself and Mother wasn't the least interested. Had Widdershins addled her mind so completely that the memory of Rachek meant nothing? She took two strides for the door.

"Martine?" Rachek said, and his voice cracked. His face was so filled with loss that Joshua felt something inside of him break. He flexed his claws, stepping to intercept Mother as she headed for the prison door. If this wasn't going to be the reunion that he'd dreamed of, then it was time for Joshua himself to end things.

Then Martine stopped and slowly, so slowly, turned back to face the room.

"Did you think I would not notice?" she said softly.

But she wasn't looking at Rachek Kasric. Or Joshua, or Temperance. She was looking, instead, at the songbird sitting on the rafter. Several decks overhead, another cannonball crashed into the deck, and there was more yelling.

With a motion too quick to follow, Martine yanked a vial out of the sleeve of her outfit and flung it against the bulkhead. A foul-smelling explosion of yellow gas billowed through the room. Joshua had time to register Rachek's astonished expression and the man's swaying stagger. Joshua himself was feeling woozy.

The songbird fell. As it fell, even in the very short distance from rafter to bilgewater, it *unfolded*, expanded, blossomed into something very different from a songbird . When it hit the water, it was a woman, one Joshua thought he recognized. Only his mind wasn't working right.

He, too, fell. He felt the vile stench of the water hit his face, then he knew no more.

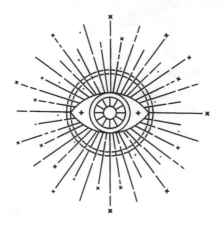

CHAPTER 21

LORD OF THORNS
The Return

He came out of the mists of Faerie wearing his cloak of grass and loam, which he'd drenched in spells so that he could walk unseen through the remnants of the Faerie army that had been left on the shores by the Black Shuck. The few were growing fewer as he passed, for their masters had gone with the ships, and they had begun, in short order, to war among themselves. This included some Goblins, Court Faerie in disfavor, and Dwarves of the wrong clan, none of whom were faring well because the largest population was from the Jötnar—Trolls, Ogres, and no less than a dozen giants—all too large to travel by ship. The eldest of these, an ancient Ogre with the unlikely moniker Stoneheart Stevens, had inflicted a nearly mortal wound on himself to avoid being part of the invasion armada, healed himself with arcane arts, and had begun his small rebellion before the Black Shuck's ships had even passed from sight. The other Jötnar had gathered under his banner, and now, a dozen hours after the ships' departure, he was in process of either binding or eliminating anyone Faerie, human, animal, or vegetable. If the Black Shuck did get across the channel, it was almost certain he would have to conquer England all over again.

The Lord of Thorns shook his shaggy head, the tines of his large antlers swaying as he did so, lamenting the tragedy, the waste. The enormous stone sword was on his back, but he could not help anyone here with it.

He knew that.

He walked under a cloud of Pix fleeing Dover for more heavily forested areas, skirted around a small but terrifically bloody skirmish between Dwarves and Trolls on what had once been manicured lawn, and finally, had to pause briefly as a Giant (one of the Bramble family) lumbered by to weigh in on the Troll and Dwarf skirmish. The Lord of Thorns would have liked to stop the fighting, but he knew the futility of trying.

The unprecedented compulsion of the combined powers of the Black Shuck and Widdershins had been the only thing holding the myriad Faerie together. Now the Seelie and Unseelie, all the major races, and the Solitary Faerie, had all left the shores of England.

The true fate of England would be decided out on the water, not here on land. He'd done everything he could on that score. Others, more capable, probably, now fought that battle as best they could. He had other duties back in the human world.

The delays he'd had to endure in order to shake off his pursuit through Faerie had nearly cost him dearly. But Hope and Charity were not to be trifled with, and it had been necessary to lose them before crossing over here.

Steeling his heart and ears against the sounds of battle behind him—which were growing, not diminishing—he approached the cliffs of Dover and pulled out his spyglass to get some idea of what might be happening out there. He had a fair number of enchantments on this tool, for no normal spyglass would suffice for this distance.

He heard a scream that didn't match the battle and turned to look behind him. Several other creatures had joined the fray, coming from who knew where, including an honest-to-gods unicorn. Where had *that* come from? It fell underneath a wave of Trolls even as he watched, and there was nothing he could do to save anyone or anything.

Not here.

Trying to keep his eyes clear and his gorge down, his wooden mask of a face still etched with grief, he made his way carefully down the cliffs and away from the battle. If he could not find a boat, however small, he would have to craft one, but he had come prepared for that.

He was only partway through the climb down when some part of his exertions must have jostled the bullet in his back, and a fit seized him, sending lancets through his spine.

The pain was all encompassing and he clung to the cliff face, help-less, his wooden face grimacing and covered with sweat, gasping in great gulps and trying not to fall.

Which was, of course, when they struck.

They came in a swarm of blood-red spiders, shining like jewels in the sun on the white cliff, skittering over the chalky stone, and then over *him*. As bad as the pain of the fit had been, this was far, far worse, and when his hands spasmed he could no longer hold on and fell forty feet down to the rough gravel of the beach.

The world swam in a bloody haze around him, but he managed to struggle, still gasping, to his feet. He'd lost his sword somewhere in the fall and couldn't see well enough to find it. He did manage to trigger his magical wards in a semi-reflexive motion with one hand, but he knew they would not be enough.

He never even saw the first blow, which hit him like a freight train. The impact sent him flying into the cliff, which put him in danger of blacking out.

As it was, he had no breath to scream with when the spiders found him again. More fire stings of indescribable pain, which also had the effect of evaporating all his wards and passive magical protections. The spiders bit him a few more times for malice and good measure before receding, leaving him a panting, shattered and helpless wreck at the base of the cliff.

"Hello, Father," a soft, piping voice said. "You have led us on a merry chase, haven't you?"

He raised his head painfully and squinted to make out the tiny figure of Charity sitting on a rock a short distance away from him, sheltered from the sun in the lee of the white cliffs. Then he saw Hope, an immense, bristling shadow of a wolf in the sunlight, only there was no actual wolf to cast that shadow. Both of them sat, watching him, waiting. He was pretty certain the delay wasn't altruistic but boded ill for him.

Charity laughed softly, her golden curls catching the sunlight as she left the rock and walked over to see if Hope would need any assistance dispatching him, their estranged and negligent father.

So he hadn't lost them in Faerie after all. They could ruin everything, and he wasn't at all certain he had the strength or magic to fight them off.

"Wait," he gasped. "I'm not here to fight, you or anyone else."

"Of course you are, Father," Charity said. "You're here to throw in with the humans and help them drive us out again."

"No," the Lord of Thorns panted, his wooden face a picture of desperation. "I'm not here to take part in the battle, I swear. I'm here to pay a debt." He kept any expression off of his face. While technically true, that statement was a bit deceptive too.

"What do you know of duty, honor, or debts?" Hope spat out of her wolf's black, black mouth.

But Charity's head tilted as she looked at him. Good. She was curious. It was the last appeal he had with these two.

"We can always kill him *after* he explains himself," she said to her sister. It had the cadence of a question.

"We have waited this long," Hope said slowly. Blood dripped from her muzzle and the Lord of Thorns realized he was more injured than he thought. Part of his armor was hanging off his chest and blood was dripping slowly down the verdigris-stained copper plating and pooling in the black and white sand.

"If the explanation is *very* entertaining," Charity said, "I suppose another three minutes will do no harm."

So he told them.

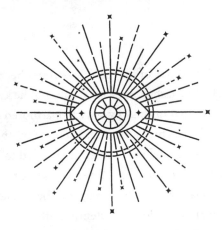

CHAPTER 22

BROCARA
The Fall

Brocara blacked out for the briefest of instants with the impact but struggled back to consciousness.

She was falling . . . Even worse, she was falling with her back to the sea, and with Usarador, the Red Death, on top of her, grappling with her. His claws grasped at her wings so she could not break her fall, while his own wings were furled so that they plummeted, plummeted down. That small amount of drag wasn't breaking their fall but ensuring he stayed on top of her, so that she fell helplessly with her back to the water. She could feel the flaring pain of her wing, broken during his initial attack, and a savage wound on her shoulder. She twisted, fought, mostly on instinct, trying to deny him her neck. The sky, the sea, the sky, pinwheeled so she could not tell how close they were to impact. A dozen seconds, perhaps, not more. Usarador was still trying to get his jaws around her throat for the killing bite while Brocara barely fought him off. Flame, a gift that she did not possess, licked out of his maw, scorching her arms, chest, and neck as she fought. She lashed out with a claw, but he kept his neck bent and his head low so that his heavily muscled, armored shoulder caught the blow. She didn't even break the skin. There was nothing she could do to keep him off. She needed to breathe, she needed to break free of his savage, incendiary grip, or she needed her wings free to slow her fall. She needed to keep those jaws off her throat, and she needed to strike some kind of blow, any blow, to slow his relentless attack, only none of those things were ever going to happen unless . . .

Drecovian's spell!

Her tail was twisting and lashing at the air, trying to get some kind of extra leverage to fend Usarador off, but she could still feel the spell there, the shadow magic that Drecovian had given his life to cast.

She lashed out, bringing the tail up and around to his back, like an upside-down scorpion. While her tail could be a fearsome weapon to lesser things, she didn't have the leverage for any kind of blow that would bother a larger opponent, unless Drecovian could save her.

She hit, felt the spell discharge into the blood-colored dragon, and . . .

Nothing . . .

Usarador, his jaws finally getting a purchase on her neck, paused for the barest of half instants to chuckle. Of course. He was as old as she and had his own magic more than equal to the dead wizard's. The spell had distracted him for a half second, no more.

At the last instant, while the Red Death was bringing his jaws to bear on her throat and end her life, she changed tactics. She twisted, lashed out, and got her own teeth on the edge of his wing. He roared, slackening his grip slightly, and she twisted again so that they spun, locked together. She still couldn't breathe, and red and black spots swam across her vision. It was anyone's guess who would hit first now, and she knew something about Usarador that she had learned over the years. Something obvious, really, about fire dragons.

They didn't like the water.

Usarador roared again in pain and fear while Brocara kept her jaws locked on his wing, savaging the leather membranes. But he hadn't, for all that roaring, completely let go of her neck. He just needed a slightly better grip, and she would die. They might both die yet, two writhing serpentine shapes, shedding flame and blood in all directions as they fell to the sea.

They both hit and plunged, down, down, down into the water.

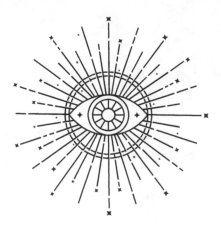

CHAPTER 23

Justice
The *Specter* and the *Emerald Demise*

The *Specter* had closed on the *Emerald Demise* and was hammering away with cannons shot into her aft.

But now the Black Shuck's strategy had become clear. He managed to surprise me again with his ruthless simplicity. No feints, no attempts to make the most efficient use of the incredible speed afforded him by the Windshrikes and escape to the coast. He wanted to smash everything in his way.

He headed the *Descending Shadow* straight for *Seahome*. So I guess my Seven Virtues ruse had done the job of antagonizing him into the response I wanted. I just hoped *Seahome* could survive. The Virtues themselves, our fakes, had gone into hiding.

Joshua or Mother were playing a safer game. We had injured the *Emerald Demise*, but not severely, and they were on a course that could take them close enough to *Seahome* to shower them with artillery or head on toward the French coast to land their Wealdarin. I had my spyglass out, conning the deck of the *Emerald Demise*, trying to assess the damage, which wasn't making me happy. I did not see any sign of either Joshua or Mother, which didn't make any sense. Had they joined the fight at *Seahome* already?

I turned to view the *Descending Shadow*.

This was my first time laying eyes on the Black Shuck, and it made my blood run cold. Henry had told me everything, of course, as had Avonstoke and Sands, but the Black Shuck, standing in the prow, was terrifying, nonetheless, an impossibly huge wolf with horrid eye sockets and a scarred neck and waves of black terror rolling off him. None of that prepared me for seeing those eye sockets slowly turn and regard me, even from that distance, knowing, somehow, that I was watching at that moment; the expression on the thing's face was pure malice and triumph. Widdershins, with his moon-gleam spectacles and pretentious top hat, was right beside his leader.

"There are some among the Faerie," Avonstoke, standing suddenly next to me, said softly, "who believe that this will all come down to a final confrontation between the Black Shuck and . . . you." He turned, his long golden hair shining in the sunlight. "Promise me if that happens that you will be careful." He sounded so sincere that I wanted to comfort him. Faith, also standing nearby, cocked her head as if she, too, was interested in the answer.

"When have I *ever* been not careful?" I said, which sounded pretty laughable, even to my own ears, but I just couldn't think of anything more comforting that wasn't an outright lie.

He snorted to himself softly and addressed the raven on his shoulder. "And I thought *you* were the funny one." The raven cawed indignantly.

"You couldn't have expected a satisfactory answer," Faith said, shifting slightly closer to us with one hand on the rail while the other held on to her staff. Avonstoke and I both moved easily with the motion of the ship, but it still wasn't second nature with Faith yet.

"I suppose a true promise would have just been a lie," he said wistfully. I was mostly used to the loss of the black tattoo he'd had on his face, but it was still occasionally jarring. The golden Faerie pupilless eyes, too, were always striking. I realized, with something like a familiar surprise, that none of this, all together, added up to much compared to how damnably, unreasonably handsome he was. Somehow, that made me proud and irritable all at the same time. I couldn't think of any way to answer him. Besides, the battle required my attention.

Several dozen Court Faerie archers lined *Seahome*'s edge, peppering the sailors on the prow and deck of the oncoming ship. I thought I saw Sands' smaller form with his wild mane of yellow hair among them, giving orders, but I couldn't be sure in the multitude. There was no sign of Henry, but I knew he would be there somewhere, and the thought terrified me, especially since both of them were there at my request.

On the Black Shuck's ship, I saw several Faerie fall, but our main targets, the Black Shuck and Widdershins standing in full display on the prow, seemed impervious to harm. Arrows passed through Widdershins' spectral form, while forty or so found their mark on the Black Shuck. But they might have been hitting a mound of earth for all the reaction the Black Shuck gave. He shook himself, shedding arrows the way a dog sheds rainwater and with even less concern.

Three Dwarven catapults were launching missiles, but the *Descending Shadow* was moving too quickly for them to make a good target for these.

The cannon on Red Clover Tower, with Caine in command, boomed, and part of the *Descending Shadow*'s quarterdeck exploded into splinters, taking a dozen or so enemy Faerie with it. The cannon rang out again, and the top mainsail crashed to the deck. It looked for a moment as if Caine's small group of British gunners would succeed where the rest of *Seahome*'s defenses had failed.

But the Troll artillery was in range now, and Widdershins was among them, pointing with a white-gloved hand at the tower that had done so much damage. The first two missiles, boulders that had to weigh five hundred pounds each, went sailing in deadly and ponderous arcs toward the tower. They both impacted at its base, and the three-story structure collapsed like a pile of matchsticks, tearing a hole in *Seahome* and sinking so rapidly it was out of sight in seconds. Another few boulders fell into the devastation, putting any question of survivors to rest. Damn. Caine had been a good man, for all that he and I had been at each other's throat.

"Caine and his crew are gone," I told Faith, "and so are *Seahome's* cannon." Yet more people I'd sent to their deaths.

She squeezed my shoulder but said nothing.

Then, the Black Shuck showed us what real ruthlessness was.

The Black Shuck didn't move his ship into position to send in landing boats or try and board using lines. He sent the *Descending Shadow* right into the much larger *Seahome*, ramming it with all the speed his Windshrikes provided him.

There was a horrible crunch as the ship crashed into the floating city. I could see, through the spyglass, the surface of the raft, timbers lashed together and made by design to be flexible and to move with the sea waves, crumple like tissue paper as the prow of the triple-decker ship hit, plowing its way into the floating city and leaving a furrow of wreckage on either side for at least a hundred feet. The *Descending Shadow* was now wedged so firmly into the portion of the floating city closest to us that the two were locked together. It was going to take giants with crowbars to separate them now. The Black Shuck's plans were clear. He meant to storm *Seahome* and either take it or burn it to the waterline; then, with the Outcast Fleet removed, he could invade Europe at his leisure. Besides, he still had Joshua and Mother's ship, the *Emerald Demise*, to try and make landfall.

None of that stopped the Black Shuck's Troll artillery, who kept hurling boulders on Widdershins' instructions. I watched as Faeries from my Outcast Fleet on *Seahome* ran in all directions while buildings and fortifications, including what looked like a makeshift healing ward and three of the multicolored sails in that impossible and ridiculous construction, crumpled and sank. Screams floated across the water, and a black, oily column of fire started up at once. The worst part was that I wasn't sure that impacting *Seahome* had done all that much damage to the *Descending Shadow*, which looked fully intact, if wedged into place. Once the Black Shuck destroyed the area around him, it may well still be a force on the water.

Now came the real danger as the gun ports of the *Descending Shadow* flew open and hordes of enemy Faerie poured out. Others were streaming off the deck too, and in less than a minute, the Black Shuck had disgorged a small army, nearly a thousand troops or so. I could see Court Faerie, Goblins, a small contingent of Dwarves, come first. The ponderous Jötnar followed, Ogres and more Trolls.

The defenders of *Seahome* were in full rout now and I finally spotted Henry in there trying to organize a more orderly retreat. And I couldn't do anything about it. Not until I'd finished off the *Emerald Demise*. Henry, Sands, Prudence, and the rest of that fragile, beautiful, impossible floating city that was *Seahome* would have to fend for themselves for the moment.

An immense cloud of murderous little Pix winged out of the *Descending Shadow*'s hold, going after the hapless defenders. These were followed by the half-human, half-wolf, cadaverous shapes of the Black Shuck's own Hanged Dogs, then by the sinister Kellas Cats. Both dogs and cats were easily twice the size of a normal person, and I shuddered to think of the damage they could do.

Then the Black Shuck threw back its head and howled, a blood- and bone-chilling sound I heard almost as clearly as if he'd been right in front of me. He and Widdershins followed their troops down onto the ruined deck of *Seahome*. I couldn't see either Henry or Sands, or any of the other defenders either, who had all fallen back. The horde of enemy troops blocked any sight of anything or anyone else.

I yanked the spyglass away and stepped back, crying out despite myself. How could anything stand against that?

"We need to get over there," I said, my voice sounding half strangled.

"You said we need to take care of Mother and Joshua first," Faith said, her voice sounding tight too, though she had better control of herself than I. She was waiting in reserve, standing ready to counter whatever magic Mother or Joshua could throw at us. Only there wasn't any sign of either of them. She should have been with *Seahome* too, and so should I, where we could do more good.

The *Emerald Demise* turned and we followed. They were circling *Seahome* now, battering the edges with pure devastation, yet still threatening to turn at any time and head for France. This forced us to follow, also circling around *Seahome* as we kept putting cannon shots into them from behind. But it wasn't enough, and they kept on hammering away. *Seahome*, almost a mile across, was large enough that both sides often referred to it as the floating city, but it wasn't built for durability, and the Troll artillery was doing terrific damage, breaking off immense portions. The floating city wouldn't be floating for long if they weren't stopped.

But if the *Emerald Demise* could make landfall . . .

"Yes," I said through clenched teeth. "Mother and Joshua first." We knew this could happen, but it didn't make the prospect any less painful to watch. This was the second time, at least, that I'd put my little brother into danger. And Sands, too, for that matter, who'd already given more than any of us to this war. I thought of his glorious pale horse, Acta Santorum, the mate to my own nightmare, Pavor Nocturnus. But Sands had lost Acta when he'd given up his magic and now she ran with Cernunnos and the Wild Hunt, never to return to him.

"Tell me again," I said to Faith, "what influence do you have over the Wild Hunt?"

"Virtually none," she said.

"Great," I said.

"In fact," she said, "I have a deep concern about them."

Something about her voice made me turn to look at her. This had the feeling of something she'd been wanting to tell me for a while.

She was looking out over the water, avoiding my gaze.

"I thought," she said, "that there wasn't any chance of it happening, that I or Father could somehow prevent it, but now it's looking . . ."

"Father's dead," I said, my voice sounding strained and flat.

"Yes," she said. "He played a dangerous game with the Wild Hunt, and so I thought I could too. But now he's gone and I just don't have the power to influence them."

"We knew that," I said. "I'm not relying on the Wild Hunt to help us. You know that."

She finally looked at me. "But you weren't planning so much on fighting them either. I'm concerned they will fall in with the invasion forces if it looks like you're winning. They won't do anything before that, but if we can somehow stop the Black Shuck's ships—"

"Why are you telling me this now?"

"I didn't think they'd side with the war," Faith said. "They don't care who wins, only if they can run free in the sky. But if it looks like you're winning—"

"Me," I said, something clicking in my head.

"Yes," Faith said. "The gods know you won't be pushed, and your hatred of the Faerie is known to them, including Cernunnos, who is probably worried you'll not only find a way to win the war but also banish Faerie out of our world forever. He won't want that."

"Damn," I said. This was yet another legacy of both Father's treacherous manipulations and my harsh actions—shooting him under the World Tree, which was sacred to Cernunnos. After all, it was Father's theft of magic from Cernunnos and the World Tree that started all these events, long before I was born.

"We'll have to fight that battle when we get there," I said flatly.

Avonstoke, in a strange voice, suddenly pointed behind me and said, "Sweet father of the tree!"

I turned and looked behind me to see the answer to where Brocara was.

She was in the sky, fighting for her life, locked in a homicidal embrace with the largest dragon I'd ever seen. Cragged like a mountain and easily half again Brocara's size. Usarador, the Red Death, Brocara had called him. He was the color of burnt blood and awe-inspiring in his majesty. He was also trying to tear our dragon's head clean off, as best as I could tell.

Neither of them was flying either, but tumbling end over end through the sky. Usarador's mouth was like a furnace gone awry, not spewing fire so much as scattering it in gusts and puffs in all directions as he twisted and fell. Both dragons seemed to have their claws in each other's wings, which explained the falling.

"No!" Faith breathed.

Shouts went out over *Seahome* and from the other ship. It seemed both sides had seen the dragons and the war paused to watch, wait, and see. They were falling such that they would land nearly a half mile away, I guessed, into some of the sea we'd just come through.

"Pull away," Faith breathed. "Come on, Brocara, pull away!"

"Come on," I echoed, feeling more helpless than I ever had before. They were falling at a terrible speed, easily fast enough to smash Brocara into pulp.

"Pull up!" Faith said again, her eyes locked on them both.

Avonstoke, saying nothing, leaned forward and gripped the rail as if his life depended on it. His face had gone from pale to chalk white, his eyes flared as wide as I'd ever seen them, for all that he couldn't actually see through them. The raven on his shoulder was staring just as fixedly.

Usarador, the big dragon, roared but didn't pull away. Perhaps lost in some kind of dragon bloodlust? It was the grandest, most tragic thing I'd ever seen, and it made me feel small and frightened and sad.

They hit, and a geyser of water the likes of which I'd never seen rose up. It scattered and fell in the wind. Over what had to be two miles away, I could feel the cold mist of it.

Nothing came out.

The world and the war held their breath for ten seconds, twenty . . . thirty. A full minute went by and nothing surfaced. No sign of any dragon. They were gone.

Avonstoke sagged in place and would have been knocked over by the motion of the ship if I hadn't reached out a hand to steady him.

"I'm sorry, my love," I said softly. "I'm so sorry."

"Damn, damn, damn the Black Shuck for making war with dragons," he whispered. "If *you* don't kill him, *I* will. I swear it."

"I'm sorry," I said again, knowing that no words could ever soften a blow like this, but not knowing what else to do.

Then the world around us seemed to recover and move on, including the battle. A roar came up from *Seahome*, and I saw another of the towers shudder and fall. Most of the fight was occluded by buildings now, so I had no idea what might be happening, only that it probably wasn't good. I wished, for the thousandth time in the last few minutes, that I had some idea of how Henry and Sands were.

"Mother and Joshua first!" Faith snapped at me. There was a fury blazing in her eyes now that was unmistakable and more than a little frightening.

She was right, of course.

"Keep firing!" I shouted at Render, at the bow chaser cannon. The gunner crews had all gone still, watching the dragons, just as we had. Render, still staring at the place where Brocara and Usarador had fallen into the water, jumped at my yell. He jerked back to himself and turned to his crew.

The crew fired at once, miraculously exploding a section of the *Emerald Demise*'s aft railing, along with a few crew members who had had the terrible luck to be standing next to it. Even so, the Troll artillery on board their ship was still taking a terrible toll on any part of *Seahome* they could reach, and their reach was considerable.

"This is too slow," I decided aloud. "Besides, they're essentially ignoring us and wreaking havoc on *Seahome* unchecked. Time to make them pay for that." I conned the deck again. Still no sign of Mother or Joshua. Where in the hell where they? Meanwhile, the *Emerald Demise*'s Troll artillery kept mindlessly unloading into *Seahome*, completely ignoring us. *Seahome* was ridiculously huge, but even it couldn't take this kind of destruction. Not counting the hundreds who had been killed before they could get out of range, I could see that the nearest two acres of raft were broken and so shot full of holes and burdened with wreckage that it was no longer floating at all but sunk three or four feet into the water. Another ten minutes or so of this, and the broken sections would drag more sections down, and the cascade would sink the entire place.

"Mog!" I shouted. "Bring us two points to starboard and open as much canvas as the ship will stand. No more playing it safe. Bring us up alongside and we'll put a full broadside into her." I glared hatefully at the ship. "Let's see them ignore *that!*"

"I thought," Faith said mildly, "that you said the Troll artillery could sink us in a couple volleys if we were, and I'm using your words here, asinine enough to get close to them."

"Yeah," I said. "I did, and they could."

"Ah," Faith said.

"I'll need you ready to counter anything Mother might do. Can you do that?"

"I will do what I can," she said. "Is she on deck?"

"No," I said, wishing I knew exactly where she was.

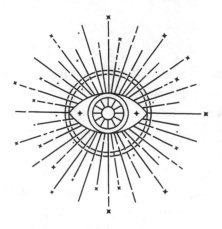

CHAPTER 24

JOSHUA
Family Confrontations

Joshua slowly came to, with the feeling that something terrible had happened to his head. Falling bricks, hammers, bombs . . . something.

He couldn't force open his eyes. Someone had glued them, perhaps, along with whatever damage they'd done to the rest of his skull. But he heard a voice, Mother's voice, and the love and hatred swelled up inside of him in almost equal measure. Almost. He thought if he could get his clawed hands around her throat *now*, now he could do what needed to be done. But, of course, his hands weren't working either. He could smell the stink of the hold and thought that his feet lay in bilgewater. So, they hadn't moved him. But he could also smell something burning, which didn't fit.

"We've done enough damage to their glorified raft," Mother said with a sneer. "Set a course for Cape Gris Nez. We'll land the Wealdarin there. The Black Shuck will have the Outcast Fleet in submission before too long, but even if he doesn't, it won't matter once we've taken France and have access to the continent."

"Is it wise to proceed without him?" the mild voice of John Brown asked.

"It would be unwise to disobey him," Mother said, and an oily note of violence crept into her voice. "Just as it is unwise to disobey *me*."

"Heavy lies the mantle of power," Brown said placidly. "As you wish." "Leave the guardian of the pit here."

A timeless drifting came over Joshua, and he heard Rachek Kasric pleading with Martine, the woman he had married, not for his own life, but for that of Joshua, their mutual son, and for Temperance and Prudence's lives. Prudence, too, was Martine's child, and Temperance had committed no crime upon Martine, but these last two were both children of the Lord of Thorns. Martine's response, a derisive laugh, did not sound promising.

Joshua could hear the roar of flames now, in addition to the scent of fire, but was certain they still had to be in the *Emerald Demise*'s hold. Not only was fire death to any ship, but they weren't all that far from the powder room, where he'd smuggled in all that gunpowder and his makeshift bomb, and that final element of terror roused him enough so that he could force open his eyes.

They *were* still in the hold, where Mother had imprisoned himself, Father, and a grayish woman who had to be Prudence. She must have been the sparrow. Some kind of shapeshifter? But her powerful magical transformation had clearly tipped off Mother when Father's weaker but more subtle illusion had not.

They were all installed next to Temperance, four prisoners in a row. Joshua could see, both on himself and the others, the same greenish, gritty paste that Mother had put on Temperance, and now he had a better idea of its purpose, because something was keeping him woozy and helpless. Mother's concoction must be dampening his powers as well as the rest of him. That would be in addition to the cold iron collar and manacles he now wore. He had to wonder how Mother could have managed it all so quickly. He could barely breathe for the smothering effect of the collar and paste together.

He could see Mother and John Brown, and also the source of the burning smells and sounds standing behind the both of them. Well, floating behind them. A horned, powerful, graceless shape, wreathed in flame, with bat wings and cloven hooves. Two realizations struck Joshua like knives to the heart.

The first knife was the fact that the creature was obviously a demon from hell, or from one of the infernal pocket worlds within Faerie, depending on who you asked.

The second was that Joshua could almost be looking into a mirror.

It shouldn't have been a surprise, really. Horns, clawed hands, fanged mouth. He should have known back when Mother taught him the "spell" he used to breathe enough heat out of his mouth to melt the hinges on the gate to Stormholt. The fact that he hadn't sprouted batlike wings yet just meant that he still had some time. He now knew, instinctively—had already known, in truth, in the dark recesses of his brain where he refused to look—that while the first ingredient to the potion that Mother had been feeding him for so long was the Faerie absinthe, the second ingredient, which tasted like copper and something not of this world, had to be demon blood.

A sudden, cataclysmic thunder came from somewhere outside the ship, like a hammer the size of Camberwell. This was followed immediately by a series of crashes directly above them. And screams. So many screams.

For an instant, Joshua thought that his makeshift bomb, with the slow match fuse that he'd never even lit, had somehow gone off. But then his mind made sense of the data. The first crash had been cannons—not just one or two but twenty or so, at least—quickly followed by the noises that twenty or so cannonballs make when they tear a ship from bow to stern. Justice—for it had to be her—had somehow gotten her ship close enough to shoot a full broadside into the *Emerald Demise* and wreak untold damage on ship and crew. Joshua could feel a sickly smile crawl across his fanged face.

"Damn that hell-spawn child!" Mother spat, which would almost have been comical, considering the circumstances, if their situation wasn't so twisted and dire. She pointed at the demon. "You! Watch them! Kill anyone that escapes while I help that imbecile Brown deal with this!"

The demon didn't make any acknowledgment that Joshua could see, but perhaps Mother wasn't expecting one, because she sloshed through the bilgewater and climbed out of the hold.

"She was a good woman, once," Rachek said softly, and Joshua realized with a start that he wasn't talking to himself, but to *him*.

"I know," Joshua said. "But that was a long time ago." He shook his head to clear out the last of the cobwebs and, pulling the chains on his wrist manacles as far as they would go in order to get his clawed hands out of the way, he craned his head to get a good look at his father. Prudence and Temperance were both still unconscious.

The man looked tired and in some pain, and his temples had a bit more gray in them than Joshua remembered from his childhood, but otherwise it was remarkable how little the man had changed, for all he'd gone through.

"How did you recognize me?" Joshua asked him. "I've . . . changed a bit since I was a child."

"I've watched you," Rachek Kasric said. "Watched you all. As much as I could."

Joshua frowned as he thought about the implications of that. "Mother too?"

"Of course," his father said.

"Then you had to know that she's changed too. Why ask for mercy? You couldn't have expected any, not if you've been watching the person she is now."

Rachek Kasric thought a short minute before he answered. "I spent years, decades in fact, as a shambling monster in Faerie, and I know the magical theory that spending time in a shape is an experience that changes you. Yet, to my astonishment, I am back now and feel that while my time in Faerie changed me, it did not, necessarily, change the entirety of the person that I am. I believed, for all those years, that a path *back* to the person I was existed, and now I have found that it was true. I wanted that for you, and for your mother. I had to believe that you and your mother could come back too. Come back to me."

"Even if there was a way back for Mother," Joshua said, knowing in his heart that it was true, "she wouldn't take it."

"No," his father said ruefully. "No, I see that now. But I could never forgive myself if I hadn't tried."

"Even though it may cost you your life?"

"I had to try," Rachek Kasric said simply.

Then Joshua knew with a certainty what he had to do.

"I'm going to break out of these chains," he said, looking at the demon as he said it. But, as he suspected, the demon was adhering to Mother's orders precisely.

Talking about breaking out didn't trigger any response, though the action itself surely would.

"Can you?" Rachek said.

"I think so," Joshua said, still watching the demon. "Then, I'll have just enough time, I think, to tear your chain free of the bulkhead, then I'm going to have to handle this monster here. I have a contingency plan to sink this ship and then escape, but I'll need you to get Temperance and Prudence clear. Everything is going to be either on fire or underwater in short order. Can you get the other two free?"

"Yes," Rachek said. "One hand free is all I need. I can take care of all the chains then."

"If you can get me out of these," Prudence said, "I can get us out of the hold and clear of the ship. Very quickly."

Joshua actually jumped, not having seen that Prudence was awake. She'd been playing at unconsciousness, clearly.

"There won't be time to climb up five decks," he told her.

"I wasn't planning on it," she said. "Get these chains off of me and tearing through this wall and taking the others through the water won't be a problem at all."

Rachek chuckled, then looked at Joshua seriously. "What about you? What kind of contingency plan do you have?"

"It's too complicated to explain," Joshua lied. "I'll be right behind you." He couldn't quite make himself believe that, like his father, he had any path back to a normal life. But at least he had a path back to redemption, and he felt good about it. It would be enough.

Rachek reached out, pulling against the chains, and took Joshua's clawed hand in his own.

"You're a good man, son," Rachek said. "Don't take any unnecessary risks."

"I won't," Joshua said. "Ready?"

Rachek and Prudence nodded.

Joshua closed his eyes, mustering his strength. The trick, he thought, would be to stop fighting the changes that Mother had been forcing on him all this time and to instead *lean* into them. She'd been making cryptic comments about him being ready just in time for their final battle, and Joshua knew his biggest metamorphosis had been waiting just beneath the skin.

He took a deep breath, twisted his head, and breathed heat and flame on the spot where his father's chains were bolted into the wooden bulkhead. It blackened and scorched immediately and Joshua seized the chain with one heavily clawed hand and, muscles bulging, yanked it free.

Then came a soft grunt, like fire spreading, and Joshua knew the demon was coming for him. It couldn't be more than twenty feet away.

But Joshua was ready to meet it. Feeling his back writhing, burning through the effects of cold iron and Mother's smothering spell, he powered through, using all his anger, his hate, his rage against the injustice, that he had been keeping penned up every time Mother had done yet one more terrible thing to him, to their family, to England.

He could feel the flames burst from his hands, from his shoulders and chest. From everywhere, in fact. The tumor that had been causing such pain along his back suddenly wrenched itself free and he actually laughed as he felt his flaming bat wings unfurl themselves.

He hadn't been exaggerating about the entire ship burning or drowning shortly. After all, they weren't really that far from the powder room. But even as he completed his transformation, out of the corner of his eye, he could see his father make a subtle gesture, and his chains fell away. Another gesture, and Prudence and Temperance's followed. Almost at once, Prudence was changing into her own monstrous shape, something reptilian with webbed claws, a long serpentine neck and tail, and a mouthful of lamprey teeth.

With this much magical power, they might almost be able to make a stand against Mother and John Brown in equal footing. Probably Rachek and Prudence would want to, Joshua guessed, if they knew his plan. But Joshua saw his path to redemption clearly now, and he wanted, needed, *yearned* to take it. He wanted the world to know that Joshua had set the world afire and hadn't just been a servile worm all this time. In an ideal world, Joshua would get to see Mother's face as she saw what Joshua had done, but since when was the world ideal? This would be enough. Justice would be able to explain it to his Father if he didn't understand on his own. He'd always understood Joshua at least as well as he'd understood himself.

He turned to face the onrushing demon. If you couldn't rely on a battle between two fire demons to set off a room full of powder kegs, what could you rely on?

"Come on, then!" he told it.

He just needed to buy Rachek, Prudence, and Temperance a few minutes to get away.

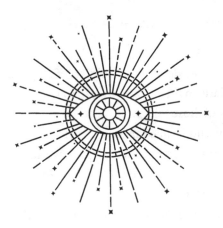

CHAPTER 25

JUSTICE
Seahome

"**F**lugelstan the ship!" I shouted. "Bring us around! I want to hit her again!" The *Specter* was a whirlwind of furious activity between the turn and the gun crews reloading and the wails of the wounded. Iela, one of the women Dwarves who'd been in charge of Wargan, our Troll, was our doctor and she had plenty to do. We'd done terrific damage to the *Emerald Demise* on our first pass, but we'd taken plenty of our own as well. I saw Bartlebottom, the young blond Dwarf with the fuzzy head and permanently surprised expression on the deck, and I had to turn away. He looked surprised in death too. We'd paid for our attack in dearest blood.

The *Emerald Demise* was a long way from being finished off, but we'd fired grapeshot across the deck, and even Trolls fell to cannon. But not all of them. There didn't seem to be any real leader among them now, what with Mother and Joshua still missing. But they would regroup, given time. The *Emerald Demise* could still fight, could still sail, could still land Wealdarin in France, and we had to keep battering her until she couldn't do any of those things.

For the thousandth time I missed Swayle and her Unforgiven. With a full complement of archers, we might have taken out more of the Trolls and suffered less. I missed a lot of the soldiers and crew I'd sent to *Seahome*, Henry most of all. The *Specter's* crew were slaving their hearts out to keep everything moving quickly, but everything on the ship was moving just a shade slower, and that added to the butcher's bill.

Faith, standing at my side on the quarterdeck, was an eye of stillness in the hurricane of battle. She'd been standing by to try and nullify any magic that Mother or Joshua could send at us. Only there hadn't been any. So Faith was largely just waiting, her face strangely calm under her hood, holding the staff that one of the Dwarves had carved. The top was adorned with the charred pieces that remained of Sands' shattered violin, which Father, before that, had carved from Cernunnos's World Tree.

Where were Mother and Joshua? I'd dreaded facing off against them, but there hadn't been any sign of either of them. We hadn't seen them leave the *Emerald Demise*, but they must have abandoned their ship in order to participate in the attack on *Seahome*. I couldn't imagine any other reason for their absence.

Another Leaf Rider landed on the railing near the two of us. Lop ears bobbing, he started reporting to Mog, who nodded. He'd bring me the information once he correlated everything, and he was surprisingly good at the task. All we knew now was that the Black Shuck's forces had penetrated farther into the wide sprawl of *Seahome*, killing and burning as they went. Henry and Sands had been forced to fall back to the center of the mile-wide raft and were even now being surrounded. We had to get over there.

Mog had just bellowed the skeleton sail crew through the turning of the ship when the *Emerald Demise* exploded.

The crashing sound tore across the ocean along with a concussive burst of hot air that hit all of us, even this far away, with a blow like a fiery locomotive in the chest. I hit the deck, hard, feeling another wave of hot air flowing past. I was stunned and dripping blood on the deck, though I couldn't tell from where. My brain wasn't working right, rattled by the impact. Faith and Avonstoke were on the deck too, looking just as dazed and bloody as I felt. A fragment of what had to be a piece of the *Emerald Demise*'s deck plank, charred and smoking, fell onto our own deck an inch away from my hand. Many other pieces were falling, sizzling, into the water around us.

The main blast seemingly over, I climbed warily to my feet, probing at my head where I thought the injury was. It didn't feel like anything serious. Faith had some blood running out of her nose, but that was the worst of it. Avonstoke—his hair mussed and wild—ignoring a gash on his arm, climbed to his feet, his face a mask of astonishment. I looked too.

There wasn't anything left of the *Emerald Demise* except bits of wood and sailcloth, most of it burning.

"What in the *hell* was that?" Faith said, as rattled as I'd ever seen her.

"Gunpowder," I said, though that part seemed obvious. I was babbling but didn't know what else to say. "They didn't have any cannons but they must have had gunpowder on board and something set it off." I narrowed my eyes, a sudden, terrible idea occurring to me.

"Do you think Mother and Joshua were on there?" Faith asked.

I squinted with my ghost eye, but everything was the same regardless of how I looked at it. "Could it be some kind of trick, or Faerie glamour powerful enough to fool my ghost eye?" I asked. "So they could sneak off to France without us being any the wiser?"

"Some glamour," Avonstoke said with wonder.

"What?" Faith said, still staring at the place where, a moment ago, a ship filled with people had been. "What? Oh, no, there was nothing magic about that." Now, it was flaming debris, none of it all that big. Nothing could have lived through that, Faerie or otherwise. Faith's hood had fallen back and her impassive wizard's expression had completely crumbled into tears and grief. Her face was smudged with black too, like soot.

"I am truly sorry if your brother and mother were on there," Avonstoke said, standing up and reaching out a hand to each of our shoulders.

"They were the enemy," I said automatically, but my voice sounded flat and insincere. I was too rattled to feel anything at the moment but could sense a growing wave of horror and sadness, disconnected for now, but there all the same.

"We didn't see them on deck," Faith said. "Maybe they weren't on board at all?"

"I was going to ask *you*," I said. "I thought perhaps you had some way of sensing them."

"No," Faith said, shaking her head. She couldn't bring herself to look away from the wreckage. "Not unless they were performing some kind of magic."

One of the pieces of flaming wreckage had landed in one of the spars and I had to wrench myself away from my conflicted feelings about the possible death of Mother and Joshua for a few precious seconds to issue orders to deal with it. Emily, up near the crow's nest, was the closest, and she ran across one of the spars to the place where the fragment, about the size of a cricket ball, was causing a rope on the spar to smolder. Balancing on the spar, Emily reached down for it, then snatched her hand back. But it was a reaction. The fire wouldn't be hot, not to her. Out here, outside of the mist, which meant outside of the influence of Faerie, she was mostly invulnerable again. Grabbing something in our physical world required concentration, but hours on the sail crew had made certain that all our ghosts were pretty good at that by now. She made a visible effort to quell her normal reaction, picked up the chunk of wood, and, waiting a few seconds for the sway of the ship to tip the mast a little to one side, tossed it down into the water. There was a nauseating moment while the sail nearby smoldered, but Étienne and Percy joined her and the three of them beat at the spot with Étienne's checkered cap and their sleeves. Étienne sighed and gave us an okay sign with his hand. I had Mog send the crew scurrying with buckets to drench the sails, rigging, and deck in case we missed something or we had another explosion coming.

"Captain!" the lookout, one of the Goblins, bellowed. "Something in water!"

"There!" I said. For an instant, it looked like an enormous creature, like some kind of aquatic dinosaur, then there was a shimmering effect, and it became three people swimming awkwardly off the port bow.

"Prudence," I said. "What's she doing out here? And who is that with them?"

"I believe," Faith said in a strangled voice, "that is the man who would have been our father. Rachek Kasric."

Prudence's shapeshifting magic seemed to have failed her and the other woman I didn't know still seemed to be nearly unconscious, so it became necessary to send Nellie and Wil and one of the other Prowlers into the water to retrieve them.

When we finally got them onto the deck, the unfamiliar woman was still unconscious and Prudence nearly so. One of the Prowler crewmen had arrived with blankets. He threw one around each of them.

"Get them into our cabin," I said, "and into some warm clothes before they die of the cold." Avonstoke lifted the unconscious woman while several other crew members sprang to assist Prudence and Rachek Kasric, who could both walk, if just barely. Faith and I followed in their wake.

"Mog," I said. "Get us to *Seahome*. There's a war happening there that we need to be part of. And ready to launch for a landing party."

"Aye," Mog said.

I followed the rest to the cabin.

Iela, our female Dwarf medic, was there, slim and competent and completely unruffled as she always was. She proceeded, without comment, to strip the three of them of their wet clothes, ignoring modesty in favor of expedient medical care. The woman I recognized suddenly as Temperance remained unconscious, and Iela's treatment showed a crisscrossing network of scars on her pale body. Other than her face, there was little portion of her skin that was not covered. Faith and I shared a look. Who had inflicted this on our sister, and why? Was it the Black Shuck or Widdershins, or had Mother had a part in it? How far had she fallen, to do this to another person, even if they didn't share actual blood?

Étienne showed up at her elbow, juggling three hot beverages. Prudence and Rachek took them gratefully. We were out of the mist, so Étienne couldn't have been visible to them, but if either of them had a comment about floating beverage mugs, they didn't bother with it.

"Mog will need help," Avonstoke said, making it a question. I nodded and he left.

Prudence looked even more gray than usual. Rachek Kasric sat looking stunned, still tall, thin but athletic, with raven-black hair that hung loose and now showed a bit of gray about the temples. As before, meeting the true Rachek Kasric, the man who looked like Father but wasn't, was a surreal experience, one that spoke to a weight of debt impossible to completely articulate and even more impossible to redress. There was the debt accrued by our actual Father, who had stolen Rachek Kasric's shape, life, marriage, rank, and station all before we had even been born. I could imagine no set of circumstances where Rachek would be able to rejoin Mother, his true wife, and resume any semblance of a real life, to say nothing of the years lost and the turmoil the world was in now. The blame for all of this lay squarely on either the Lord of Thorns' shoulders, or on the shoulders of his people. I also couldn't shake the feeling, seeing this man, looking like this now, that he had somehow stolen our Father's true human shape, even though I knew for a fact that the opposite was true.

"How is she?" I asked Iela, pointing at Temperance. My half-sister, born of Father, the Lord of Thorns, and the Lady Dierwyn, or the Lady of Sorrows. Like Hope and Charity. Three half-sisters and I knew virtually nothing about them.

"She'll probably live," Iela said. "Exhausted past all endurance, probably by some kind of magic."

"Martine had something on her to suppress her magic," Prudence offered.

Iela nodded. "But if this lass made it through all of that, the magic and explosion and the water, she'll probably be fine now if she's kept warm and allowed to sleep. Can't say how long it might take. I wouldn't hold your breath."

"He got us out," Rachek said, gesturing vaguely in the direction the *Emerald Demise* had been. "He told us that he would follow and I believed him, but *damn*, I should have known better. Why didn't I know better? What kind of father am I? Now I've lost him and I'll never have a chance to make it right."

"Joshua," Faith said. "Joshua got you out?"

He nodded, looking as wet and bedraggled and grief-stricken as anyone I'd ever seen.

"Out of what?" I said. "The ship?"

Rachek nodded. "Yes. I'd snuck in, thinking to find a way to appeal to Martine, get her stop all this. But I saw that it wouldn't work before I ever spoke to her. I slipped past her, but she smelled the magic from *you*." He turned and glared at Prudence.

Prudence nodded, looking ashamed down into her tea. "I had an idea that Temperance was prisoner there in the hold, and I was right about that, but Martine caught me and imprisoned us. I didn't think she'd be that sensitive to magic."

"I wanted to get Joshua out," Rachek said. "After seeing Martine, I gave up on that, like I said. I've seen people gone over to the Faerie enough to know what it looks like. She'd even married that shade . . . I don't know his name."

"Widdershins?" Faith said, her voice rising up a notch towards hysteria. "Mother *married* Widdershins?" Her eyes were wild, her unflappable magician's visage completely broken. She crouched, looking as if she was about to seize Rachek by the blanket and throttle the rest of the story out of him, but a sudden shifting of the ship caused her to slip and she fell hard into a sitting position on the floor with her back against the wall. She looked up and tears were in her eyes. "Mother married Widdershins?" she repeated.

Rachek nodded miserably. "She did. She's as good as a Faerie now, or was. What she did to our boy, to Joshua. That, as much as anything, demonstrated who she is now."

"A demon from the Pit," Prudence said. "I think that sent him over. John Brown was using a demon summoned from the Pit, and once Joshua saw it, like two demonic peas in a pod, they were, he probably couldn't deny what Martine had done to him. I knew as soon as he sent us away that he wasn't coming back. Didn't know about all the gunpowder, though. Bit of a shock, that."

"Mother, Joshua," I said, "and this other magician or Sin . . . John Brown . . . they were all on the ship when it exploded. You are sure?"

"They'd left the room," Rachek said, "but they wouldn't have had time to climb up to the deck, let alone get off the ship, before it exploded. So there was gunpowder there somewhere and Joshua fought with the demon and the fight got out of hand, perhaps, and . . ."

"No," Prudence said. "He knew what he was doing. I saw it in his eyes."

Rachek looked at her again, a slew of unvoiced accusations in his eyes, but then he looked away and slumped, defeated. There were tears in his eyes.

"Perhaps you're right," he said softly. "Perhaps he couldn't go on, the way she had shaped him. I know something about how hard it is to lose your human shape. You lose so much of yourself with it."

"Oh," Faith said, still on the floor and clearly not absorbing any of this very well. I knew how she felt, but was keeping a firm hold on my heart, at least as best as I could. I remembered Joshua when we'd met in the foyer of Stormholt. He'd been holding an enormous axe. He'd done virtually the same thing then. Helped us escape, even helped us fight the Soho Shark, but then Joshua had refused to leave Mother. He'd been only partway through the transformation then, but already had the horns, and you could tell Mother was turning him into something inhuman. Funny, in the end. Joshua could destroy her but couldn't leave her. Somehow that made perfect, twisted sense to me.

"Mother and Joshua," Faith moaned, putting her face in her hands. She made a noise like cold wind through a dying, hollow tree.

Then several things happened at once.

A crash of thunder boomed through the room. Not like a storm suddenly appearing in the sky, but more like all the noise and chaos of a storm suddenly and magically appearing in our small room. I thought for an instant that the *Specter* had suddenly fired all her guns, but even that would have been more distant.

The door to our cabin burst asunder, two halves and various fragments blowing inward so that we all had to cover our faces.

Temperance, who'd been unconscious since we pulled her out of the water, suddenly sat bolt upright, her eyes snapping open.

A figure stood in the doorway, framed by sullen blackness, and there was thunder in the voice that boomed, "You will release your prisoner to me!" A black haze crawled into the room from her fingertips, like the wet fury of a storm at night. We could even smell it.

I was struggling to get my pistol out, completely taken by surprise, barely able to see the threatening figure. Most of the others around me were in a similar boat. Squinting into the haze, I discovered I could see better with my ghost eye, while my normal eye was virtually blind. Prudence had fallen over entirely and was struggling to her feet.

The black figure causing all of this took two steps into the room.

Faith, suddenly standing with her back against the wall across from the door, lifted her own voice into a song sung by many voices. The bright, textured noise, like a chorus of bells, streamed through the room and the fury dissipated.

"No one is a prisoner here, you fool!" Faith intoned and her voice rang through the small cabin like her own thunderbolt.

It was like storms battling for supremacy, one of darkness, one of light, and while Faith seemed to have the upper hand, I could feel the darkness recoiling to strike again.

But the fury had given me time and some cover for rolling across the room, and I was able to come up next to and slightly behind the threatening figure. I pressed the barrel of my pistol to the soft spot behind her right ear.

"Stop," I growled, "trashing my *ship!*"

Just as I did, Avonstoke appeared in the doorway, also behind the intruder, with his blade out. He saw me and stood poised, waiting to see what would happen next. He always did catch on to everything quickly.

The figure stiffened, and darkness brewed around us. "Do you think me stupid? I know you want your Seven Virtues and will do anything to get them, but we'll not be your playthings!"

"No one," Faith repeated, "is prisoner here. She can leave any time she wants. We merely rescued her from her prison."

The figure turned her head slightly to look at me and in a more normal voice said, "You expect me to believe that?" Now that the fury was gone I saw an angular face with a strong, straight nose and dark hair down to her shoulders. Welcome to the party, Pyar. I guess we're all here now.

"Believe what you want," I snapped, "but she's free to go. We made our own Virtues in a ceremony a few days ago, but honestly I could care less."

"But we lost Drecovian," Prudence said. "We'll only have six Virtues."

"I don't care," I snapped. "We'll fight our war on our own terms, thank you." I glared at the newcomer. "In the meantime, *you* are trashing my ship, and if you don't stop I'm going to shoot you in the leg and leave you in a rowboat."

"Justice," Faith said.

I looked at her. "A few bandages, some water. She'll be fine, right?"

"Pyar," Prudence said. "The Hindi word for love. She's a Virtue, too. And our sister."

"I know that," I snapped.

"That explains a lot," Avonstoke said.

"Love?" Faith said. "Here I was rooting for 'Punctuality.'" She shrugged.

"I thought 'proper table manners' was your favorite?" Avonstoke said, a small smile playing around his lips. A few locks of his golden hair came loose from his queue.

Temperance was staring at us, but still hadn't said anything.

"Truly?" Pyar said. "You would let us go?"

"Whenever you want," I said. "We were waiting for her to wake up, but now that that's happened there have to be a hundred places safer for her than a ship of war. You can take her if she wants to go with you. In fact, I'd recommend it, as we are about to sail into extreme danger and it won't be safe here. I imagine Prudence would like to give you her pitch to stay and fight, but you won't be compelled to do anything if you don't want to."

"Of course," Prudence said. "Any help you could offer would be—"

"It's not their war," I said. "It never was."

"I will go with her," Temperance said, standing up. "Her presence brings me strength."

"You *are* both champions of Taranis," Prudence said, "the God of Thunder, Lightning, and War. You'd be invaluable in—"

"Not their war," I snapped. You could just look at Pyar and see a lifetime of hostility in her eyes. I wasn't sure what kind of situation she may have grown up with in Faerie or England or India, but having myself discovered that my entire life was a thread manipulated by others, I can imagine her feelings about the matter. She'd be more dangerous in the war if she hated us that much, and who could blame her?

Prudence looked at Pyar, then Temperance. "No," she said. "I suppose not."

"If it was our war," Pyar said, "Taranis, the Faerie God of War, Thunder, and Lightning, would want to pave the way for the Faerie to return to this world. Taranis would be on the side of the invasion."

Prudence opened her mouth to speak. I could feel my hackles rise. Things were so finely balanced, another Faerie god on the side of the invasion could make all the difference.

"But," Pyar said, "the invasion is being led by honorless butchers, so we avoided any of you . . . from either side. As you say"—she caught my eye—"it is *not* our war and I will not dance to the Lord of Thorns' tune."

Prudence nodded.

"I understand," I said.

Pyar turned to look at me, her dark eyes wide and amazed though she didn't even seem to notice the gun. "You actually mean it, don't you? You'd let us walk out of here without trying to recruit us?"

I lowered the gun, since she'd stopped breaking things and didn't seem to find it much of a deterrent anyway. "That's what I said. Hell, I don't even know you."

"Although," Faith said, "it would be nice to get to know you during other circumstances, us being related and all. Of course, things are a little save-the-world and all-out-war right now. Come visit in a month or so, if we're still alive and England's, you know, still there."

Temperance stepped over to join Pyar, but still didn't say anything. I wasn't sure how well these two even knew each other. They'd had the same father, sure, but so had we all. Prudence, Faith, and I shared one mother, the one that had just died while trying to murder nearly everyone around us. Temperance, Hope, and Charity were all born to the Lady of Sorrow. If Pyar was born to yet another woman, as it seemed, Father would have had a little bit more to answer for, in my book, if he'd still been alive.

"Come," Temperance said. "Let us away."

Pyar held up a hand, still looking at me. "What of the gods?"

"I don't know them either," I said. "Not sure there are *any* I trust."

Pyar looked shocked and then thoughtful at this. Then she looked at Temperance and nodded. Temperance lifted her arms, and lightning flashed where the two of them were standing.

Then they were gone.

"Damn it," I said, seeing a tongue of flame licking the floor where Temperance had been. I seized a skin of water and poured a stream onto the blackened wood. "Is it too much to ask to *stop* trashing my ship?" But the sudden danger and questions about the presence of Pyar and Temperance were gone.

"How close?" I asked Avonstoke.

"Launch is ready," he said at once.

"Let's go," I said.

"You're going into battle?" Rachek Kasric said, standing up. "If you don't mind, I'd like to help."

Faith, Prudence, and I all exchanged glances.

Rachek, seeing the hesitation, said, "I'm not a Faerie lord, but I'm quite recovered from my brief ordeal and I'm sturdier than I look. Also, I do know a little thing about war and ships."

I still hesitated, though I couldn't have said why. Part of me wanted to protect this man who had gone through so much at Father's hands and shared our name. His trials should have been over by now. Also, his presence disturbed me, but that was no fault of his. And he certainly knew something about ships, war, and the Faerie, having lived for years with all of them.

"Please," he said. "England and the world around it is my home. I've already fought for it once. I can do no less this time."

"Of course," I said. I looked at Avonstoke. "Better find him some kind of weapon."

"That," Rachek said, "will not be necessary." He reached out, grabbed something that didn't exist in the air in front him, and from nothing pulled out a long, heavy blade. The same trick produced a wool cloak, tunic, boots, and a sword belt.

"That," Prudence said, "is some very handy magic for someone that *isn't* a magician."

"Magic is just something the other person doesn't understand," Rachek said, "and I spent a long time among the Faerie. Always was a quick study."

We went out onto the deck, and there was a brief moment while everyone got down into the launch where Faith and I stood slightly apart, watching the proceedings. Avonstoke was a few feet away, ushering the landing party into the boats.

"Do you think," Faith said quietly, "that if Father's plan had come off, and he was here, in all his ruthless and amoral Faerie glory, do you think he would have kept the Faerie out of England entirely? Do you think that it would have been worth it?"

I could feel the surprise on my face, thinking of what all that would entail. I saw Avonstoke's gaze flicker up and meet mine.

Our family would still be shattered, just as it was now, but Father would be in charge and certainly more successful than I'd been at stopping the Black Shuck.

On the other hand, as much collateral damage as Father's plan had inflicted, the original plan had included a great deal more, including the life of Rachek Kasric, who was now busily engaged helping people land in the launch.

"Probably would have worked out better for London," I admitted. "Might seem worth it to the ones not paying the price."

"That's probably war in a nutshell," Faith said. "Worth it to the ones not paying the price, but not everyone else. And the generals hardly ever pay the price."

"No," I said. "They usually don't."

"So is war ever worth it?" she said. "For everyone, I mean?"

"You want to live under the rule of the Black Shuck for a few years and see?"

"No."

"Me neither." I pulled out my spyglass and conned the *Descending Shadow* once more, then turned to the quarterdeck behind me. "Mr. Render?"

"Aye," Render said, running to the railing to lean down and look at us.

"I'm leaving you in charge of the ship," I said. "Stay at long range and start hammering at that ship. If they ever find a way to wedge it out of there, I want to make sure it sinks. Even better if you can batter at the parts of *Seahome* holding it and sink it now. Should be an easy target."

"Aye, Captain."

"Ms. Justice," Mog said, appearing at my elbow. It was an unusual address for Mog.

I turned, curious. "Mr. Mog?"

"Just Mog, Captain," he said glumly. "Mog is just Mog."

"Yes, of course. What is it, Mog?"

"Mog has request, Captain."

This alone made my eyebrows hoist themselves even higher. Mog's manner, normally so matter-of-fact, was starting to alarm me more than hysterics would in someone else.

"What is it?"

"More a favor, Mog wants," Mog said. He still wouldn't look up. A bad feeling settled in my gut. Faith and Avonstoke, along with a great many of the crew, had noticed the unusual exchange too. Avonstoke was openly staring, which was a pretty good trick for a man technically blind. The rest of the crew were pretending to busy themselves with other tasks, but not very well.

"For the love of *God*, Mog, what is it? Spit it out."

"Mog need Justice to throw Mog off of the crew."

"You're my first mate, Mog, the second in command and a damned fine one. Why would I throw you off the crew?"

Mog sighed. "War."

"You're not making any sense. Of course we're at war. That's why I need you."

Mog sighed again and lifted his gaze. It was filled with anger and resolve. "The Goblin Knight," Mog said, and spat onto the deck. "He will be on *Seahome*. We go there now, where Mog will fight. Fight the Goblin Knight. Mog made blood oath to kill Goblin Knight."

I looked over at *Seahome*, which was burning now. It was just as likely as not that Mog and the Goblin Knight would never get close to each other before the ship sank or one or the other of them got killed. I remembered too, that Mog had sworn to kill the Goblin Knight after he'd killed Mr. Starling. Hell. I wanted him dead for that too. Most of us did, and we were about to enter battle. Killing each other was pretty much the point. But I got the distinct impression that this was a lot more personal with Mog.

"We're going into battle, Mog. You'll get your chance."

"No. Blood oath will take Mog." He sighed, took a deep breath. "Mog not just Goblin, but warrior of the Sazurwood clan. When Sazurwood clan warrior go to battle, they see only the enemy. No friends next to them. No war to win. No wounds or fear. Only enemy to kill. Understand? This even *more* true with blood oath. When Mog go into battle, Mog will not be part of ship or first mate or Justice's friend. Not even Starling's friend then, and Starling is why Mog make oath in first place. But that not matter when Mog fight. Mog will not even be Mog. Not really. Mog will only be a thing to kill the Goblin Knight. Mog can't be first mate then. When the Goblin Knight is dead, Mog can be Mog again." Mog's eyes got darker and darker as he talked, talked longer than he ever had before.

"Didn't you call," Avonstoke said, "revenge a complete idiocy?"

"Mog did," Mog said. "But that not change blood oath. Blood oath is how Mog know revenge is an idiocy, but Mog is still Mog. Mog never say Mog smart."

I had to blink back angry tears. I only just now realized how much I'd come to rely on Mog and how true a friend he really was, despite this damned blood oath. I could feel my face stiffen as I tried to keep the hurt off it. This Mog, the blood-oath Mog, frightened me more than a little. His heavy shoulders flexed and his talons twitched. His fanged mouth was open and he panted heavily from the emotions his speech had stirred up.

"If I commanded you to forego the blood oath, would you?" I asked quietly.

"Mog . . . does not know," he said.

I bit my lip, but then nodded. "All right. I won't ask. I will respect the blood oath you swore. For Mr. Starling's sake. When it is done, will you come back to us?"

Mog frowned, as if this thought hadn't occurred to him. His eyes cleared a bit, and the talons stopped flexing. "If Mog not dead."

"Very well," I said, stiffly, still struggling with all this. "I'll have to think about your temporary replacement. Is Mr. Render up for it, do you think?" I didn't want to take Render off his current station, but it seemed I had little choice. Then I'd need a replacement for *him*.

"Avonstoke," Mog said.

"Avonstoke?" I said, unable to keep the surprise out of my voice. "*Our* Avonstoke?" I turned to look over at Avonstoke to see if he'd put Mog up to this, if perhaps this was some carefully orchestrated joke. Avonstoke wore a serious expression, but I could see the slight hint of smirk at my surprise. It was true he was supremely competent at most of the actual tasks on board a ship, but by his own admission, he couldn't seem to keep any of the nautical terminology straight and had a hopeless feel for how the wind and ship interacted.

"Mr. Avonstoke," I said formally, "I trust your judgment and bravery as much as my own, *except* when it comes to keeping my ship afloat." I turned back to Mog. "He referred to my cabin door as a *spankenmizzen-whistle* the other day. A bloody door!"

We really shouldn't have had this conversation on deck in front of the crew. Avonstoke's smile had turned to surprise of his own and he was looking at Mog curiously.

Mog shrugged. "Avonstoke not know the words, but he know the ship. Everyone listen to Avonstoke. Goblin, Dwarf, Court Faerie. Everyone."

I blew out a shocked breath. Well. All right. There was an extra complication of having your lover serve as your first mate, but if anyone could handle that honorably, I trusted Avonstoke to do it. In fact, I simply trusted him. Solid, competent. Also, Avonstoke would be coming with the war party and I'd be leaving Mr. Render in charge of the *Specter* regardless, but this was more than a mere formality. War had a way of advancing people quickly. If something went wrong and the Black Shuck took *Seahome* and I and Mog were both lost, who would carry on the fight? I didn't want to see him in harm's way, but Avonstoke was a clear choice, for all the reasons that Mog had just stated.

I sighed. I could feel my eyes close as the realization hit home that his competency or the dangers weren't the only reasons for my reluctance at all. It was another piece of me, my relationship with Avonstoke, that I hadn't wanted to give over entirely to the war. Making him my second in command might ruin whatever relationship we had. Bad enough that this war put him at risk, put all of us at risk, but this was something else on top of that, a risk to the connection we had now. We'd just have to deal with the conflict between his duty and our personal connection if it came up.

I opened my eyes and turned to Avonstoke. "Well, Mr. Avonstoke, what do you say? Will you stand in as Mog's replacement?"

Avonstoke was still looking curiously at Mog, and I realized, by the expression on his face, that with the considerations of ship and war and love, I'd completely forgotten something.

Avonstoke had sworn his own oath to kill the Goblin Knight. If he took Mog's place as first mate, it was an implied but tacit promise to put the ship's needs above his own personal revenge. To let Mog take the danger of his blood oath on his shoulders while Avonstoke took Mog's responsibilities, forgoing his own vengeance. It also meant making the way for Mog to possibly get himself killed, though there was clearly no stopping Mog on that score.

Mog and Avonstoke held each other's gazes for a long moment, and I could see a clear understanding pass between them. "Yes, my captain," Avonstoke said, turning finally to me. "I'd be honored."

There was something difficult in my throat. "Thank you . . . Mr. Avonstoke."

Avonstoke couldn't help a broad wink. "My pleasure."

"I'll be down in the hold briefly," I said.

"Yes, Captain." He threw a terrible facsimile of a salute. More like someone flailing with a sausage, really, and I just knew he did it on purpose. I sighed.

This was going to be a long day.

Down in the makeshift stable, Nocturnus whickered softly as I approached. Even without a light, she always seemed to know when it was me.

"It's our time, girl," I said to her softly. "Battle. You and me."

She snorted affectionately. A clear yes. At least, that's how I took it.

"Problem is," I said, "we're still at sea and what with the Black Shuck blowing holes in half of *Seahome* it's going to be uncertain footing. But we need to promise each other not to let you get wet, right? We both know you get . . . a little monstery when that happens. So we're not going to let that happen, right?"

She blew another soft, horsey snort. Another yes, I thought, but not quite as enthusiastic as the last.

"I know," I said. "I don't like it either. Even worse, I'm going to have to unsummon you to get you over there."

Another snort, this one even softer and more uncertain.

"I'll be as quick as I can to bring you back," I said. "I promise. I won't leave you in that demon place any longer than I have to." Was the demon place hell? It seemed that Faerie magic and human religion had some overlap, managing to agree on much, and this was no exception. It seemed today was a day of bitter events and was going to get a lot worse. Best to get this over with.

I got out the chess piece, the worn bit of black wood shaped like a horse that I'd had since the very beginning. In a small, strange way, everything that had happened, my entire experience with the Faerie world, all started with this chess piece.

"Pavor Nocturnus," I said. "Pavor Nocturnus, Pavor Nocturnus."

I'd known it was coming, but the change still shocked me. My beautiful, fantastic steed whinnied once—in anger or fear, I couldn't tell—and *collapsed* in on herself. Then she was gone and I was in a stuffy room filled with smoke. The chess piece was hot to the touch.

"Hold on," I said. "Hold on."

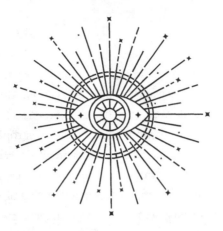

CHAPTER 26

JUSTICE
The Final Battle

We landed on a part of *Seahome* some distance away from where the *Descending Shadow* was lodged. While it was the outermost portion of *Seahome* now, it hadn't always been. It looked like the battle had claimed a section of *Seahome* a few hundred feet long. If the scorched and broken bits of *Seahome* hadn't clued us in to the fact that the battle had come and gone in this section, the bodies lying around would have done the trick. Smoke and the reek of gunpowder mixed with the iron tang of blood in the air. The air was cold with a hard breeze coming in from the north, from France. The light was bright and brittle, making everything stark and mercilessly brilliant.

This section of the raft was still intact, with elaborately carved planks laid to form a convenient and elegant walkway across the lashed beams, with bark still artistically clinging to the walkway edges. Buildings on three sides used to form a courtyard of sorts, open to the ocean on the fourth side, but those buildings were smoldering ruins. The stink of smoke and blood and seawater lay over everything. At least the fire was mostly out, having died when it reached the water line. I saw that the construction of the raft, with sections connected by wet rope, however artful it might be, also formed natural firebreaks on all sides, so at least it had afforded some protection against the fire spreading from one section to another. The motion of the raft felt different than that of a ship and it took my legs a minute to adjust before they stopped feeling wobbly.

Screams and monster roars came from our left. Avonstoke pointed, and we could see a chunk of building fly out toward the *Specter*, followed by what had to be a dead body, though if it was attacker or defender, I couldn't tell. Probably didn't matter to them. I could think of nothing more gruesome or dehumanizing. The Black Shuck's Trolls flung chunks of *Seahome* itself, which included the dead, who were now just *things* in our world.

The *Specter*, having dropped us off some distance away as ordered, opened fire. Mr. Render had the range right, I was relieved to see. The Troll missiles were falling short, but they were well within cannon range. On the other hand, it might take all day for Render to follow my orders and sink the *Descending Shadow* in her current position.

We could hear the fighting right off. Mog, for his part, seemed content to stay with us for now, but it was clear from his expression and twitching hands that he was slavering for battle. He hadn't exaggerated at all about the Sazurwood way of war. If anything, he'd undersold it. He looked ready to chew his way through half of *Seahome*, buildings and all, and most of the Black Shuck's army, to get to the Goblin Knight.

Avonstoke and Mog led the way, the smoldering black fire of Avonstoke's sword an eerie counterpart to the smoldering raft. Wil and Nellie were with us too, and the enigmatic and grim-faced Rachek Kasric, his heavy broadsword out.

"Wait," I said, and went through the now familiar ritual of summoning Pavor Nocturnus. Fire, smoke, and her name chanted three times while holding the chess piece over the fire. The slowly coagulating demonic shape then poured itself, at the last moment, into the now familiar shape of my horse. Sands' words echoed in my ears: *Above all things, do not take Pavor Nocturnus into the sea.* Well, I could only hope I lived long enough today to regret it.

Leading Nocturnus, I followed Avonstoke and Mog inward, with Faith and a hundred and fifty of the crew, mostly Prowlers and Goblins, following us. A cloud of Leaf Riders circled over our heads.

What I wanted was to drive our way into the center of *Seahome*, to a heavily defended structure called the Bastion, where Henry, Sands, and the rest would be making their stand.

Picking my way across the raft on horseback was unnerving, especially when I thought of the danger of Pavor Nocturnus falling in, so I didn't allow myself to think about it. Nocturnus was smart and graceful enough, despite her size, to avoid most pitfalls. I just had to trust her—or admit that I should never have brought her in the first place. The Faerie had built *Seahome* in a series of floating platforms, narrow bridges, ladders, buildings, and terraces. It wasn't quite glades and waterfalls floating on the sea, but they'd come surprisingly close.

We passed over something that had once been an honest-to-God brook built into the slope of a series of buildings, some two stories tall, probably fed from rainwater, except that some part of the assault had shattered the thing into bits so that we had to go around. None of the platforms were uniform, none of the bridges from one to the other the same as the last. My ghost eye picked out a fair number of magical spells, all of them minor and all of them cast to keep *Seahome* floating and intact. Seemed like a good smashing or burning overcame that magic easily enough.

We climbed up a series of ramps, hearing shouts and screams the whole while, and stared down into a valley of ramps, most of them a hundred feet wide or so, a great sloping open place that led to the Bastion, the fortress in the middle.

It was very much a fortress under siege. The base was a frontier-style log wall with parapet above so that the defenders could hurl down all manner of deadly discouragements. The area around it, easily the size of two football fields, was filled with struggling figures, most of them murdering each other. Immediately in front and below us, a row of the Hanged Dogs were trying to bring down Swayle and her Unforgiven and looked to be doing a fair job. At least half of the Court Faerie looked to be missing while the rest fought for their lives in pitched battle with bladed spears.

I took a precious thirty seconds to assess the battle. There was a tight knot of fighting underneath the Bastion and I could see Henry and Sands on the ground with their backs against a wall, with the Black Shuck only a few dozen feet away. The parapets above them had been filled with defenders, but enemy arrows were taking the toll and it was nearly overrun. A short distance from them, I saw the Sphinx, Beaudulaire, flutter her snowy eagle's wings and pounce at Widdershins like a lion after a black rat. But Widdershins slipped to one side and somehow got on her back. He stuck his fingers into her wild golden mane and she stumbled and fell. The snowy wings twitched once and went still.

Another hundred feet away, the Lady Rue, or rather Queen Mab, ruler of the Unseelie Court, stood in her own elevated position in full regalia. No more hiding her identity, it seemed. Everyone would see who she really was now. She gripped something in her hand that leaked falling smoke. The smoke, in a maneuver strangely reminiscent of Pavor Nocturnus's summoning, poured down until it formed the shape of a squat gargoyle, which then launched itself a dozen feet away into the battle. A line of Court Faerie, probably from the Unseelie Court, stood in defense, while two parties of the Goblins, including the hated Goblin Knight and some of the Kellas Cats, were battering their way in. Clearly they wanted to bring down the queen. Among the defenders, I also saw the inhuman shapes of Wargan, the Troll, and the leathery wings of Daccus, the gargoyle, two of my crewmen from the *Specter*, still whole and fighting. I started to scan for Mother or Joshua before remembering they'd been killed when the *Emerald Demise* exploded. The idea of their deaths kept rolling around in my head without any real acceptance.

I looked again, seeing one of Queen Mab's Court Faerie fall without a clear cause, and realized a giant cloud of the deadly Pix were there too.

"Golden!" I shouted and the Leaf Rider leader was at my shoulder.

"Pix," I said, pointing. "You're the best equipped to handle them."

"Assuming you can't find a giant spray bottle," he piped, followed by a cascade of high-pitched laughter. "Aye, Captain, we're on it!" He shook his tiny, shaggy mane, lifted an equally tiny bone horn, and it rang out, piercing, clear and sharp.

"To war!" he screamed and the Leaf Riders swirled away to the other side of the battlefield.

"Mog," I said, "Take a dozen warriors and skirt around the edges to assist the queen." I gestured at a section of our group, indicating about a dozen Goblin and Dwarven warriors.

Mog peered up a me curiously, as if I'd asked him to serve tea.

"The Goblin Knight is there, Mog," I said.

Mog flexed his claws and made a noise like a bloodthirsty purr. He nodded and headed off.

"The rest of us," I shouted, "straight ahead." I pointed down at where the Unforgiven were fighting for their lives.

I spurred Pavor Nocturnus down into battle, and Avonstoke, Faith, Mog, and Rachek kept pace on my flanks. We crashed into the rear line and everything turned to screams, death, and blood.

Leading troops into battle was ghastly and horrible. My jaw hurt already from clenching it, and my mouth was dry and my hands clammy. My heart was pounding in my ears, but it was also the most exciting thing I'd ever done. I'd never felt more alive, which was disconcerting because it was just as likely as not that I was heading for my death, as well as leading the others to theirs. Pavor Nocturnus reared and spun, coming down on a Kellas Cat with devastating results. I shuddered as the thing, back broken, twitched and died. But even as that shudder went through me, I drew aim and used my pistol to send a Hanged Dog to the same place. Avonstoke was to the right of me, Nellie, Wil, and a burly black-maned Dwarf named Fyodor on the other. Faith walked behind me, as planned, to deal with any incoming magic and the possible disaster if Nocturnus fell into the water. Her sword still hung at her side, but she brandished her staff openly. She would play shield while the rest of us played sword and hammer.

A roar came up from the Unforgiven as they became aware of our assistance, which attracted the attention of a few nearby enemy Trolls. I fought my way toward the Unforgiven banner, a white spear on a field of green dark enough to be almost black. A Troll reared up on our left and Avonstoke intercepted it with a leap and swing of that deadly blade of black fire. The Troll howled, terrified when Avonstoke lashed out twice and put deep gashes across its chest and upraised arms. It spun and fled, while one of the Hanged Dogs sprang up on Avonstoke's right. I put a bullet into its head from behind.

Faith's triple voice sang out, drowning out the battle for a thundering instant. Then she stamped her staff on the platform and it crashed like a cannon. The three cadaverous Hanged Dogs nearest to us stopped, stock-still, for an instant and then fell bonelessly.

Nearly a dozen other of the zombie dogs farther into the battle did the same.

"They're not like other Faerie creatures," Faith said behind me, her smile grim. "The Black Shuck's magic was the only thing keeping them alive, and magic can be dispelled."

"Remind me," Avonstoke said to me, while lashing out at another of the Kellas Cats, "to never make you angry." The Kellas Cat dodged Avonstoke's strike and crouched, but I was able to put two shots into its body. It staggered and Avonstoke was there, plunging his sword into the creature's heart. It went down.

"You *always* make me angry," I said with a smile, and he laughed.

There was a sudden respite as many of the enemy around us fell or retreated. One of Swayle's Unforgiven lieutenant colonels, a man called Swift, stood over a fallen figure.

Swayle.

I slipped off Nocturnus's back and ran over. Even as I did this, I shook open the cylinder on my revolver and fed new cartridges in. This lull wouldn't last long. One of the fallen bodies caught my eye as I passed. Porgineau. There was a dead Hanged Dog on top of him and another nearby, which suggested he had acquitted himself admirably before the enemy had finished him.

I snapped my cylinder shut as I reached Swayle's side and crouched.

"Swayle?" I said. A makeshift bandage covered most of her chest and stomach, and blood was everywhere. I looked up at Swift. "How bad?"

Swift had a long queue, similar to Avonstoke's but sable black. His face looked ashen. He shook his head, tears running down his angular cheeks.

"It is all right," Swayle said, gripping my arm. "I know a death wound when I feel one. But you gave us back our honor, before the end. I will always love you for that, my captain. Don't grieve, this is a good death."

I brushed away angry tears. "The *kind* of death doesn't matter. We're going to get you a medic and prevent it."

"When death is all that is left," Swayle said gently, "the how matters a great deal and this *is* a good one. Give my Whisper Crow Brigade a place of honor, my captain."

"Always," I whispered, but her yellow, pupilless eyes had stopped the subtle, almost imperceptible shifting of golden shades within. They had gone still. She was dead.

"Mog and his Goblins have reached the queen and the Goblin Knight," Faith said, standing over me. Avonstoke stood next to her, panting heavily and looking around.

"I see," Avonstoke said in a singsong voice as if this were all a game or a children's rhyme, "the Black Shuck and Widdershins. They are trying to get to Henry and Sands."

I wanted to rush to the aide of Mog and the queen too, but I could only be in so many places at once.

"Then the Black Shuck and Widdershins are our primary targets," I said, standing up. "We kill them, this invasion force will crumble."

"Agreed," Faith said, though she cast a longing glance over to where Mog was fighting. "Agreed," she said again and this time there was a rumble of thunder in her voice and flashing light in her eyes. I looked to the sky, overcast and filled with darkness though still afternoon.

"Swift," I said, "fall in on our left flank."

"Yes, sir," he said.

We pressed on.

On horseback, I had an elevated position compared to most, so it fell on me to forge the way, at least in my mind, and I didn't bother to discuss it with the others. With Avonstoke and the remaining crew from the *Specter* on my right, and Swift and the Unforgiven on my left, I pressed further into the chaos.

Very far on my left, I could still see Queen Mab, alternately sending more smoke gargoyles into battle and lashing into the fray with a rain of magical spears when she thought the moment opportune. Mog and the Goblin Knight would be in there somewhere, but I couldn't see where in the mass confusion of Goblin and defender either might be, and I could only spare a glance.

To my immediate right I saw a group of Dwarves fighting with more Kellas Cats. When I saw one of the Kellas Cats tear one of the smaller and closer Dwarves from their feet and wrestle on top of them for a killing blow to the throat, I took the shot, putting two magical bullets into the side of the beast. It reared and snarled at me, which gave the victim below it a chance to put a very serious sword into the Kellas Cat's chest. I recognized her as Lady Druhagaren, the leader of the Dwarves on *Seahome*, as she pushed the three- or four-hundred-pound cat off of her with one arm and got to her feet. The Dwarven women still surprised me. She gave the briefest wave of thanks before putting her short, heavy-bladed sword into the back of another Kellas Cat about to spring onto Nocturnus and I. She scooped up a shield, used it to pin the fallen cat and finish it off. Then she turned and was immediately back into the fray.

We surged into ranks of the Hanged Dogs from behind, and snarls and howls filled our ears. We were less than a hundred feet from Henry and Sands now, who were hemmed in by more Hanged Dogs and what had to be at least two platoons of the misshapen and Deep Ones, similar to Prowlers, but only in the same way that Trolls were similar to humans. They were huge and barbed all over, and I saw several of the defending Court Faerie fall to their hands. The enemy was trying to drive into the place where Henry and Sands were making a last stand.

"We're coming!" I hollered, but Henry was too busy fighting to see or hear. I saw Widdershins dispatch an enemy Goblin and turn his silvered gaze on Henry, a dozen feet away and unaware of him. Widdershins hesitated, then slid along the timber barricade that was the foundation of the Bastion. Henry had his back to the same wall, dealing with another group that had broken through on the other side.

Aiming as carefully as I could, I drew a bead on Henry, then drifted my aim two feet to his left and put a bullet into the wall.

Henry jumped at the impact, then looked at me, his sandy hair a mess and nearly in his eyes, both amazed at my presence and confused as to why I'd shot near him. I pointed with my pistol at Widdershins and I saw Henry's understanding gaze.

I shot two enemies in front of me, urging Nocturnus forward. She managed to obey and trample the fallen enemies in the same motion, surging to close the gap between us and what was happening ahead.

I knew that Widdershins and the Black Shuck had both presided over Henry's interrogation in Newgate Prison. Hard to imagine how terrible that must have been; it probably gave Henry plenty of sleepless nights.

My unassuming little brother, who was always something more than his appearance would suggest, tightened his jaw, loosened his shoulders like a prizefighter, and strode to intercept Widdershins.

Widdershins, for his part, saw Henry coming, and something in that usually open and friendly face made Widdershins twitch and then turn and flee.

But several combatants got in his way and Henry leapt a dozen feet, landing so that he could put his hands on Widdershins' fancy and sinister cloak. The Deadly Sin struggled again, clearly in an absolute panic, but Henry hauled his previous tormentor in with the cloak and seized his neck in his iron grip. Widdershins kept struggling, but Henry twisted, and the shade of a man went limp.

There were tears in Henry's eyes, but a satisfied expression on his face that made me shudder to look on it. We were none of us children anymore.

Then a horrid, scarred bulk that I recognized all too well reared up from a swarming mound of combatants between us and my skin ran cold and my face ran hot.

The Black Shuck. It roared, swiping with a massive paw that sent Outcast warriors of all sizes flying, and lifted its head and howled. The howl reverberated through the air and waves of fear came with it, echoed off the metal of swords and shields, filled the entire makeshift valley we fought in, and shook the timbers of the Bastion. I could feel the vibrations hit my chest and clenched my eyes shut as everything went blurry. My brain buzzed like an engine on overload.

It was almost over just that quickly.

The blast of magical energy that had disoriented me had done the same to everyone, including all the defenders. Through blurred vision, I could just barely make out a huge black shadow bounding through standing defenders and attackers as if they weren't there, rushing directly at me with appalling speed. I lifted my pistol but couldn't see anywhere near well enough to take any kind of shot.

The Black Shuck would have shot past Avonstoke and taken me right off of Nocturnus's back, only Nocturnus had recovered more quickly than the rest of us and reared up, hooves flailing. I felt the shock of a jarring impact, like two locomotives colliding, and dropped my pistol as I clung fiercely to Nocturnus's back, knowing my life probably depended on it.

Faith's triple-note voice cut through the fog in my brain, driving the last effects of the Black Shuck's howl away. A dozen feet away, I could see Prudence—in her gray bird shape, only this time far larger—battling with what looked like Urguag and one of his Windshrikes. Rachek was there too, hacking at the demonic air creature.

My clearing vision showed me the Black Shuck's jaws closed on Nocturnus's neck. The teeth scraped on Nocturnus's iron-hide skin, setting off sparks and a high-pitched screech. This was joined by Nocturnus's scream. The wolf bore down. There was no blood, but the Black Shuck wasn't letting go either, and was bracing to fling my steed down, while she scrabbled frantically to stay on her feet. With no pistol, there wasn't much I could do besides direct Nocturnus. I needed to find it or get myself another weapon.

Avonstoke was behind the Black Shuck but having little effect. It seemed his black flaming sword, sourced in shadow magic, didn't work very well on a creature of shadow.

I could hear Faith chanting and saw her erect some kind of circle of power, encompassing all of us. The minute it was up, I could feel the terror howling in the back of my brain, the Black Shuck's aura of fear, decreasing to a dull whisper.

Avonstoke abandoned his weapon, flung his arms around the Black Shuck's neck, and tried to throttle the creature with sheer brute force, which seemed a laughable idea until the Shuck coughed and snarled, letting go of Nocturnus's neck.

It spun on Avonstoke, determined to rip his throat out quickly so it could finish me off.

Henry appeared on the other side of the Shuck with one of the wide-bladed spears carried by the Unforgiven. He jammed it with terrific force into Black Shuck's side. The weapon went in, ripping dead flesh, but it just seemed to make the Shuck angrier without doing any significant damage. Still, Henry bore down harder, his jaw clenched, his muscles bulging.

I slid off Nocturnus's back. She reared and hit the Black Shuck again, thundering strokes on the beast's head and shoulders. They rang out like hammer blows. I saw my pistol, wedged between two broken sections of raft boards, teetering as if it might drop into the sea at any moment. I leapt, landing with my hand on the gun handle. Just another inch . . .

Faith, still maintaining her suppression spell, had circled around behind Avonstoke and now shouted as she tossed him her Faerie sword. Avonstoke, guided by the eye of his raven circling only a dozen yards overhead, plucked it easily out of the air. It was a sword with some magic of its own and when Avonstoke slashed the attacking Black Shuck across the face with it, the beast flinched and reared back.

It threw back its head back for another howl, but this was what Faith had been waiting for, and she stamped her staff, once, twice, three times, lifting her own voice and drowning out the Black Shuck's howl, which became soundless and ineffectual.

It reared again, launching itself onto Faith and dealing with her magic in a more direct and physical fashion. I got my pistol up and fired twice into the creature's dead flesh. The bullets made the Black Shuck snarl in pain, but that was all. Nothing we'd done to the monster yet had significantly injured it, and I was starting to wonder if we could.

The Black Shuck lunged at Faith, jaws wide, with death in its eyes.

And came up short. In fact, it had barely moved at all.

Henry had driven his spear even further into the Black Shuck's back, angling downward now, and had transfixed the beast entirely, driving the head into an enormous log that was part of the raftlike deck underneath us.

Trapping it.

The Black Shuck tried to twist to get to the shaft sticking out of its back, but Henry kept a fierce hold. Avonstoke, meanwhile, kept slashing at the head and shoulders while I got to my feet, took two swift steps and emptied the rest of my revolver's cylinder into the beast's skull.

Again, the Shuck howled, and again Faith's own spell smothered both sound and effect.

I saw, out of the corner of my eye, that Queen Mab was part of the fight with Urguag, the Goblin Knight, and Mog. The Formori artificer went down under a swarm of gargoyle shades. I caught the barest glance of Mog and the Goblin Knight, stalking each other, and then the fighting shifted, blocking my view.

The Black Shuck was staggering and shuddering as our combined efforts started to take their toll. My pistol was empty now and I hurriedly reloaded while Avonstoke and Nocturnus continued to slash and pound away from all sides.

The Black Shuck staggered and fell.

Henry, sensing victory, yanked his spear free to deliver a death blow to the head.

But the Black Shuck had been waiting for this, it seemed, and twisted to get its jaws on Faith. Apparently, it was tired of the magical suppression spell that blocked all its more fell and terrible powers.

Faith met those jaws with her staff, chanting as she thrust her weapon deep into the Black Shuck's throat. Obvious panic infused the Black Shuck for the first time as Faith chanted and lightning flashes sparked and flared in the wolf's mouth. Avonstoke chopped at the neck, laying open enough dead flesh to partway accomplish a separation of the head entirely.

The Black Shuck's black and empty eye sockets eyes were flashing now with whatever magic Faith was releasing down the beast's gullet, and Henry used this as a guide, driving the spear down through the socket to meet the lightning and thunder.

The Black Shuck shuddered once more and went still. Faith's lightning began to consume the corpse, the way a fire can consume a building from the inside. When large gaps appeared in the cadaverous hide, we could hear the sound of distant rolling thunder, as if Faith had spawned entire worlds of thunderstorms inside of her enemy.

The lightning licked the corpse like flame, and in seconds, it was gone.

I turned around, dazed. Henry had a few bandages but was otherwise unhurt. Avonstoke, too, would need some small attentions, but looked whole. Faith looked exhausted but unhurt. Nocturnus was fine. It seemed beyond astonishing that we all could have come through this without serious injury.

"Mog and Queen Mab," I said. "We need to . . ."

"No," Avonstoke said, "it's all right." He gestured.

Queen Mab was staring down, looking at a flaming corpse that I took to be what was left of Urguag. Mog, Prudence, and Rachek Kasric were there too. Mog looked injured, with blood dripping down his scalp, but it didn't look life-threatening. Queen Mab, or the Lady Rue as she had been, wasn't wearing the silver mask anymore but looked no less regal and inscrutable for all of that.

"It's done, Admiral," the queen said to me in a voice pitched to carry. "Our enemies have broken and now it is a rout." It only took a glance across the battlefield to see that, not counting a few small pockets of fighting, she spoke the truth.

Mog staggered over to our dazed little group, stumbling as he did so until Avonstoke caught him.

"Mog," I said, "are you all right?"

"Mog is clearly injured," Mog said with a very serious face, "but more than that, he is confused." He glared at Queen Mab with a hurt expression.

"The queen," Rachek explained, "killed both Urguag and the Goblin Knight."

"And Windshrike," Mog complained bitterly.

Rachek nodded. "Mog seems to feel cheated."

"Mog was in duel!" Mog shouted, he sat down on the wooden slope, looking defeated.

"Yes," the queen said, "which was why your opponent's attention was elsewhere. A very convenient time to kill him."

"Shadow spear," Rachek provided. "Right through the back. Transfixed him all the way through. Very nasty."

"Mog had blood oath!" Mog said.

"I made no oath whatsoever regarding the enemy, my young Goblin," the Queen said with perfect equanimity. "You'll find most such oaths are nonsense. War is too messy a business for oaths."

"That true," Mog admitted.

Avonstoke knelt next to Mog. "It wouldn't have brought Mr. Starling back, you know. And you're still alive, which is the best you can hope for after a battle. In fact, most of us still are, and we can all return to the *Specter* and drink to his honor. I'm afraid all the closure we can get is to remember our friends that are gone."

"You pour out honey wine over the railing," Mog accused, "when you think Mog not looking!"

Faith burst out laughing, then quickly stifled it.

"Perhaps we could both drink beer then," Avonstoke said quickly. "To honor Mr. Starling?"

Mog nodded. "Yes, that would be good."

"Come on," Faith said, holding out her hand to Mog. "Let's get someone to look at that."

Mog agreed and levered himself up. He allowed Faith to take his huge reddish clawed hand in her small white one and lead him a short distance away. Prudence, I knew, was a healer of no small skill, but she had already drifted off and likely had more pressing injuries than Mog's.

"All that expectation of the prophecy," Henry said, "and it didn't work out at all the way we'd imagined, did it? No massive face-off between Seven Sins and Seven Virtues, like what so many people thought would happen. Some of them"—his voice took on a profound note of sadness—"were dead before I even saw the Black Shuck."

"Everyone was expecting some great battle between the Black Shuck and me," I said, "and the rest of you did most of that."

"You got us here," Henry said. "Your plan kept the Black Shuck from landing troops on the continent and brought their forces here."

"You took out two ships of the line with only the *Specter*," Faith said. "I didn't think it could be done."

"My plan and Joshua," I said. "We couldn't have done it without him. That last ship would have made all the difference."

"Yeah," Henry said, lowering his head.

"I'm glad *we* made it," I said softly to Henry. "I wasn't sure we would."

"You too," he said with a lopsided grin, seeming to realize that he was surrounded only by friends now, and the enemies were gone. "We did the right thing here," he said after a moment, "thanks to you, but it cost . . . so much. And could have cost us so much more."

"Promise me we'll never do something this stupid again?" I said.

He laughed and we embraced. Faith did the same and it was just about the most important thing in the world, to see that they were all right.

"Where's Sands?" I asked him.

"I am here," Sands' slightly accented voice came from the other side of Nocturnus. He limped past Nocturnus toward me, taking a moment to pet her nose and softly whisper something to her. "I *am* frightfully glad to see you."

"Yes," I said, and we, too, embraced.

"You all right?" Avonstoke said when I was done, putting his hands on my shoulders and looking me over.

"I am now," I said, collapsing into his arms. If I hadn't earned that by now, when would I? He held me, clearly surprised but pleased. His strong arms were all I needed right now.

At a nod from Avonstoke to one of the Whisper Crow Brigade members, they moved to collect Nocturnus's reins. Smart move, that, and I was grateful for Avonstoke's common sense, as much as he tried to bury it. There were a lot of holes in *Seahome* right now and it would be a poor job to have Nocturnus fall into the sea through an accident, now that the fighting was mostly done. At least here. I could see trails of smoke and still hear the clash and screams of combat outside of this valley surrounding Bastion. Skirmishes closer to *Seahome*'s border.

I reached up to sink my hand into his golden hair and pull his face down toward me.

"Dwarven beer," I murmured into his ear, thinking of his promise to Mog. "But you don't like beer?"

"Better than honey wine," Avonstoke murmured back.

"Especially since you'd better actually drink it this time!" I laughed.

"I will, I will," he said, laughing.

"You're a good man, Raythe Avonstoke," I said, just before I pressed my mouth to his.

"It's a burden," he agreed after coming up for air a few seconds later.

"Lor'!" Henry said, laughing at the two of us, reminding me for a second of the young boy he'd been when all this had started.

Faith returned, having seen Mog to the medics.

I cast about the suddenly still battlefield, catching what faces I could and wondering about the rest. Nellie was with Wil a short distance away, tending to what looked like a broken arm. His face was white with pain, but I felt relief that it wasn't something worse. Closer to where Queen Mab had made her stand, I could see Wargan, the Troll from *Seahome*, still looking unharmed, though the enemy Trolls around him suggested this had been a near thing. He sat with a crumpled, broken thing in his arms, tears rolling down his face. Daccus, the gargoyle, well past any help, from what I could see. Another casualty. Farther away, I picked out Heleena, still among the living even if her Storm Serpent, Demet, was not.

"Word from the *Specter*, Admiral!" A tiny voice said near my ear.

I turned to regard Golden and offer him my wrist to perch on.

"The *Specter* reports the *Descending Shadow* dislodged and sunk, Admiral," he said.

"Any casualties on our ship?" I said, thinking of my loyal crew, including the ghost boys.

"All is well," Golden said. "Prowlers also report that the Wealdarin went down with the *Descending Shadow*. All perished."

A roar of many voices in alarm from the east caught my attention. Then, I saw what had caused it. Rising from the sea, shedding seawater in a shower of glitter and snow-white seafoam, was a black shape that rose, rose into the sky.

"Brocara!" Faith said. "That's a relief. I don't think I could have handled one more loss today."

Henry looked at her as if she was crazy to tempt fate by even saying something like that, then took another look up at the black dragon.

"She's circling," he said. "Probably looking for a place on *Seahome* that will hold her without sinking. Raft has got so many holes and breaks, we're probably halfway sunk already. I better get some repair crews on that." He gestured at one of the Dwarven guards, but another voice cut in.

"I think I can arrange that," Lady Druhagaren said. She caught my eye and nodded, almost certainly thanking me for when I'd saved her. She nodded at one of the officers, who rushed off.

"What of Draust?" I asked her. Last I'd seen the wizened leader of the Jötnar, he'd been in her company.

She shook her head. "Enemy Troll, one of his own kind, though it took nearly a dozen of them to do it. Not sure if that makes it better or worse. Same group of Trolls killed Lieutenant Glaudrang, too."

"I'm sorry," I offered. Add those names to Swayle, Mother, Joshua.

"Usarador, the Red Death," Avonstoke said, possibly as an addendum to my own thoughts.

"What?" I said.

"The enemy dragon," Avonstoke said. "They both went into the water. Brocara came out. Usarador didn't. One more death."

"One death I can't regret," Faith said, her profound relief at seeing Brocara apparent.

"I am more glad that Brocara is alive than you can know," Avonstoke said, "but I cannot celebrate any dragon's death, as it lessens us all."

"Well, I won't miss him!" Faith said with no sign whatsoever of the magician's perspective and poise she usually tried to cultivate.

Brocara gave a cry that seemed part challenge, part celebration, and part warning and decided the question of a landing spot herself by settling on top of the Bastion. The wood creaked but held. I could see the huge wounds from here, across her chest and wings and neck, most of them still bleeding. Henry looked in a panic at the water sloshing through the gaps in several of the broken sections of *Seahome*, clearly in fear that the extra weight might sink this entire section.

"Don't worry," Lady Druhagaren said with a hearty slap to Henry's back, which made even him stumble. "I'll have crews on it immediately."

"Sure," Henry nodded, not looking at all reassured. "Better make it quick."

"We are not quite finished, I'm afraid," Queen Mab said, pointing. "We have one other visitor, but whether they are enemies or not, I cannot say."

I followed her finger and saw a sight that chilled my very soul.

Black clouds moved toward us, hanging very low in a sullen, bruised sky and swarming with storm crows. On top of those black clouds came dogs the shade of bone, their hungry eyes like embers. The horses were black, and smoke billowed around their clawed feet. The riders were equally fearsome, shades and specters, all of them led by the god with the great sweeping horns.

"Cernunnos," Faith said. "Leader of the Wild Hunt."

Damn. Damn, damn, damn. We weren't ready for another fight, and if what Faith had told me earlier was true, that's exactly what this was going to be. *Seahome* was barely floating, Brocara was wounded, the *Specter* was damaged and likely low on ammo, and most of us couldn't fight if our lives depended on it.

But our lives *did* depend on it. I started bawling orders, knowing already that we didn't stand a chance.

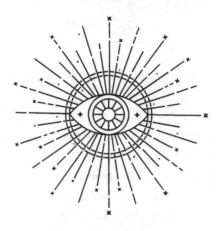

CHAPTER 27

JUSTICE
The Wild Hunt

"I have come for what is owed," the voices of Cernunnos intoned, spilling out of the mouth of every crow, hound, horse, and rider. He was as regal as I remembered, more so, regal as only a god could be; for all that I wasn't certain *god* was even the correct term. His enormous spread of antlers did not seem cumbersome to him but wild and dangerous, and were graced with a beautiful mane of hair. His face was bestial but also elegant, handsome, and refined, with fangs and a short beard and mustache, and eyes with horizontal slits, like a goat's. Down his bare and muscular chest, past his flat stomach, was the place where man stopped and stag began, an impressive stag, larger than any in our world.

His two lieutenants rode in his wake, men both, two personages that Faith had called the King with the Eye Patch and the King with the Sword, as if those were titles, rather than descriptions. Certainly they did look like kings. I remembered, too, that the last encounter we'd had with Cernunnos and the Wild Hunt, Faith had said that they'd be claiming a new hunter soon. Someone from our world. I felt a cold chill down my spine and tried not to think on who that might be and how we had no real way to resist them.

Brocara, nearly on a level with the Wild Hunt, reared up and roared, but it looked like it cost her something, moving like that.

"Come for what is owed?" I asked Faith.

She shook her head. She didn't know either. But she hefted her staff, clearly ready to go to war with her patron god. What did it say about Faerie magic that a god's own powers could be used to fight that very same god? My mind was spinning, trying to absorb what was happening, but it was too much. Far too much. I looked around, seeing Avonstoke and Faith and Henry and everyone else I knew or loved getting ready to battle with the Wild Hunt, even though we were in no shape for it. I checked the ammunition in my pistol, trying to ignore the voices in my head telling me how pitiful and ridiculous that was.

"I am here, mighty Cernunnos," a new voice said, "to repay an ancient debt!"

On the rise behind us stood another antlered figure.

My world spun as I regarded it, then my gaze slid to Rachek Kasric, wondering if there had been some kind of trick. Faith did the same, then looked at me, equally rocked by the sudden news.

Father! Father was alive! He hadn't died when I'd shot him after all.

Father's head was horned, like Cernunnos's, his spread of antlers smaller and heavier than the god's. His mane of hair was enormous, brown, tangled, and mixed with a heavy beard, all of it surrounding a face like a wooden mask, except when it moved. He still wore the copper armor stained with verdigris and the grass and loam cloak that bristled from his back. The stone sword was absent, but then, I did not think he had come for war. His right hand, monstrous and larger than the left, hung at his side, a weapon in its own right. A small part of an enormous, impossible weight that had ridden me for such a very long time fell away. Not all of it—I *had* shot him, after all—but some.

"Blood and birch," Avonstoke whispered. He was still holding me up as he stared into the sky, which was now more necessary than ever.

"Can't you just," Henry said in a low, awed voice, "say bloody hell like everyone else?" He was still staring, the words spilling out of his mouth as if by their own volition.

"Very well," Avonstoke whispered. "Bloody hell!"

"Will you two *shut up?*" Faith said in an equally awed whisper.

The Wild Hunt stood and stamped in the sky, watching with the rest of us. I remembered them chasing us to Stormholt and crashing our carriage; when they'd taken Benedict, again at Stormholt; when they'd freed Henry . . . Hell, Henry and I had even ridden with them, before Nocturnus had broken the rules and we'd dropped down to plunge into the ocean, but they still terrified me. Perhaps there are some things you never get used to.

My eyes kept tracing a path from the horned god, Cernunnos, stopped now on his mound of black thunderclouds, looking down over a battlefield at his descendant. (That is, if the rumors were true, though *that* raised questions no one had been able to answer for me.) A man who had seen this battle coming generations ahead and had prepared for it with many underhanded and dishonorable machinations, including stealing from Cernunnos.

"I have come to you," Father said again, "to repay an ancient debt!"

"Then you are welcome, my son," Cernunnos said. "Come!" The rich, deep voice poured from the throat of crow, hound, horse, and hunter. His goat's eyes flared and he reached out his clawed hand, and a wispy trail of smoke extended out and down, connecting the elevated mound of the smoke to the lower rise of *Seahome* on which Father stood.

The entire battlefield had fallen to stillness, watching what transpired on the rise and in the sky. I was unknowingly holding my breath, and felt the others had to be doing the same.

But Father hadn't moved. "You have taken my son, Benedict, oh mighty Cernunnos," Father said then.

"You stole from me," Cernunnos boomed with many voices, "then used that same magic to both avoid my judgment and raise up powers against me. Now, you barter?"

"You have taken Benedict," Father said, "to redress my transgression. Surely you do not need both of us, now that I have come to submit myself to you. Surely holding both of us for one transgression would be . . . less than honorable?"

As he spoke, the host of riders behind Cernunnos shifted slightly and I could see my brother. Benedict's dark curly hair was wild and his eyes spectral, but I saw understanding and recognition there too.

Cernunnos shifted, his stag's feet moving slightly in what in another being would have been called restless indecision.

"Very well, my son," Cernunnos said, and this time he spoke with his own mouth. "I will release him if you return."

Return? Had Father run with the Wild Hunt before? That was an interesting bit of information I hadn't expected.

"As to raising up powers against you," Father said, "my daughters and sons merely fight to take back their home, to drive out the evil of the Black Shuck. They do not wish to fight you."

"Understatement of the year," Faith murmured.

"This is true?" Cernunnos said, and suddenly everyone was looking down at us.

I looked around, realized that everyone next to me was looking at *me* and tried clearing my throat, still struggling with the feeling that all of this was so far past any normal experience and couldn't possibly be dealt with.

The first attempt at clearing my throat didn't work, so I tried it again and raised my voice. "We fight against those that would ravage and seize our home, Cernunnos," I said. "If you have no war with us, we have no war with you."

I could see Faith, Avonstoke, Henry, and Sands all nodding at me and couldn't help but feel that I'd somehow made a deal for all of humanity with all of Faerie. *Don't shoot at us and we won't shoot at you.* Who was I to speak for all of the human world? The only person who could, I guess.

"Agreed," Cernunnos said and just like that we weren't at war with the Faerie anymore. At least, that's what I thought was happening.

"Will you give me a moment, God of the Wild Hunt?" Father said. "I would bid farewell to my children."

"As you wish," Cernunnos said, nodding his mighty head.

So saying, Father seemed to see us again. He wrapped his grass and loam cloak about himself a bit more tightly and started picking his way down the ruined and scarred wooden slope.

Faith, Henry, Prudence, Avonstoke, Rachek, Mog, Queen Mab, and I all met him at the bottom of the slope.

"My children," he said, taking in Faith, Henry, Prudence, and myself. "You are better than I deserve."

"You're not, I hope," Faith said tartly, "going to pretend that you foresaw and planned all of this." She stepped forward to regard him.

"No," Father said, taking the last few steps down to a flat deck with the rest of us. "But I did foresee, among a host of wrong predictions, that most of my children would be decent and moral people as well as powers among the Faerie. That one prediction, it seems, drove everything else. I could also see, here at the end, that Cernunnos was my responsibility to deal with. You have all done enough."

Faith's expression softened and she nodded.

Father stepped forward and put a hand on her shoulder, using the smaller, left one. "I am deeply, profoundly sorry that your mother and Joshua perished. It is a great tragedy and I am sorry for your loss."

"Me too," Faith said, "but we lost them a long time ago." There was still accusation in her voice when she talked of Mother's fate, for which I could not blame her. Part of my stomach sank. I'd still been hoping against hope that Mother and Joshua had somehow survived and could, perhaps, repent for their actions and return to us, only now that could never happen.

"As you say," Father said to Faith, nodding his antlered head. "I only wish it had been different."

"We can only control our own actions," Faith said, "and even those are not guaranteed. Part of their fate, of course, rests on their shoulders."

"Even so," Father said, "whatever else she was, she was still your mother."

There were tears in Faith's eyes and pouring down her cheeks, but she reached out and embraced Father. His large right hand nearly spanned her back as he returned the affection.

"Prudence," Father said, releasing Faith and taking Prudence into his arms. Prudence, visibly uncomfortable with open emotion, hugged back in a perfunctory manner and seemed deeply relieved when she was released.

"You always believed," he said. "No doubts."

"Well," Prudence said. "I might have to rethink that now. Prophecy didn't really come true at all. At least, not the way we'd envisioned it."

"Didn't it?" Father said.

"No," Faith said. "Justice was right all along. Tactics, strategy, and luck had a great deal more to do with it than anything else."

"Things did not come out the way I envisioned either," Father said, stroking his shaggy beard, "but I think you'll find that you and Justice have been working a common strategy far more than any of us realized."

Prudence looked doubtful.

"Henry," Father said. "It seems I have, partly on account of your age, largely underestimated you. Forgive me. I'll not make that mistake again."

"S'all right," Henry said with a grin. "Honestly didn't think I'd make it to the end of today, in truth."

"Seems like you need to change your assessment of Henry Kasric too," Father said gently.

Henry nodded, a grin splitting his face.

Father turned to me. "Justice. How can I ever thank you?"

I rushed into his arms. "I'm just sorry I shot you!" I sobbed.

He pushed me back so that he could look down at me. Up until now, I still hadn't been able to shake the feeling that shambling monster was only partway my father, that Rachek Kasric was *also* only partly my father, and that the soul of one and the shape of the other would have to recombine to produce the man I'd grown up with and admired all my life.

But there was a tilt to the antlered head and a wry and rueful semi-smile on the wooden face that felt more familiar than any part of Rachek Kasric's face. I could suddenly and completely see the father inside who had raised us and had also given up everything to save England.

"I seem to remember the shooting being my idea more than yours," Father said. "Besides, while I *hoped* to survive, I would truly have rather died than lead the Faerie Invasion and preside over the deaths of all of you, not to mention England. It was the best choice of a bad lot, a lot that fell out the way it did because of my mistakes. No, you gave me the best choices I had, with that bullet, and I thank you."

I sniffled again, getting tears on his beard, I was certain, and then stood up straight.

"My children," Father said. "Even when we fail, our children rise up and succeed. I could not be prouder of all of you. I hope to see all of you again someday, but it will not, I think, be soon."

I could feel tears in my eyes. Faith and Henry were both sniffling next to me.

"The rest of you," Father said lifting his voice. "England, the human world, *and* the Land of Faerie owe you a debt that can never be repaid."

"Hopefully," Queen Mab said, "it won't be for lack of trying."

"As you say, Your Highness," Father said, bowing low. "Of course, the Black Shuck and Widdershins had their eyes, as it were, on the Unseelie Court. You know this as well as I."

"Are you saying," the queen replied, her tone frosty, "that I should be grateful to retain possession over that which is rightfully mine?"

"In a word," Father replied, "yes."

"Well," Queen Mab said, "perhaps there is some truth in what you say."

"I, at least," Father said, bowing yet again, "have the profound gift of having been of inestimable service to the Unseelie Court."

"Oh," the queen said, "a dangerous and syrupy tongue with pages and pages of tactical thinking behind it. They have not exaggerated about you, Lord of Thorns. But I do not think that tongue or any plans will assist you when it comes to Cernunnos."

"No," Father said. "Nor do I, and it has come time to pay that final debt. I bid all of you a fond farewell."

"Father!" I said. "Is this forever? How long will you be trapped there?" Here we had just gotten him back, and now he was going to the Wild Hunt. It wasn't fair!

"Who can say?" he said. "But time is different among the Faerie. If I have given you no other gifts, I have at least given you that. We have time."

He turned and climbed the wooden slope; then, at the top, he set his feet on the wispy trail of smoke that Cernunnos had created, but he did not climb.

"Send down Benedict," he said. It seemed he did not trust the god or the Wild Hunt, even now.

But the horned god did not take offense, only smiled a thin, beatific smile filled with fangs and nodded to the king on his right, the King with the Eye Patch. The king, in turn, nodded at the host behind him, who parted enough to let Benedict through.

Faith gasped beside me. "Is that . . . ?"

"It *is*," I murmured. I looked over at Sands, whose eyes were gleaming with recognition and yearning.

Father and Benedict were nearly abreast now and they paused. Benedict, on horseback, looked down, but only slightly, as Father's monstrous form was far taller than a man.

"I am sorry," Father said. He spoke softly, but somehow his words carried in the storm-laden air. "You should not have had to bear my burden and I should have come long before this. Forgive me." He reached out his hand, the left, by necessity.

I found that I was holding my breath.

Benedict nodded and clasped Father's hand. Benedict said something to his horse and they started down.

Faith, Henry, and I were there to welcome him back to a normal world, such as it was on floating Faerie raft, much of it in ruins, in the middle of mist-ringed waters, with a dragon perched overhead.

He dismounted, holding on to the reins of his horse as he embraced us.

Benedict had, somewhere along the path down, shed his spectral light and now stood as I remembered him, hair the same raven's-feather black as Rachek Kasric and Father's had been, alternately, but falling in curled ringlets. The same Kasric glacial blue eyes, but his face was smaller and leaner, with that ascetic expression often ruined when his mouth quirked in an irreverent half smile.

"Are you all right?" Faith said after kissing him.

"There are some horrible nights I would like to forget, but that was true before I ever rode with the Wild Hunt. There are a few more of them now, but I can live with that. Still, it was a bit like an apprenticeship with the Faerie. I learned a lot, some through Cernunnos, some through others of the Wild Hunt, and not a small amount watching all of you."

"You could see us?" I said, surprised.

"You can see a lot from the sky," Benedict said cryptically, and he winked. That was a bit more like the old Benedict, whom I found delightful and frustrating at the same time.

The deck trembled and I turned, surprised as Nocturnus dragged the Court Faerie soldier holding her reins a dozen feet in order to nuzzle at my shoulder. The guard, one of Swayle's people, now under Swift, looked at me helplessly, but I nodded my acceptance and took the reins from him.

"What's into you, girl?" I said, though I was pretty certain I knew already. These two horses had a history, after all.

"Well," Benedict said, as if seeing Nocturnus reminded him of the reins in his own hand. "I've been holding on to something that isn't mine for a long time now. It's time I returned it." He held up the reins.

Just as the spectral glamour had left Benedict when he had come down from the Wild Hunt, so, too, did that glamour leave his steed, and the shadows fell away. The stallion now shimmered brightly in the hard, brilliant sunlight. He whinnied, tossing his head back, looking past all of us. I looked back . . ."All right, boy," Benedict said, dropping the reins. The horse quivered and took three quick steps, causing almost everyone around me to crouch as he sailed easily overhead. Being shorter, but also more trusting in this particular instance, I merely held my hat on tightly as he went over. Nocturnus huffed once, as if she were only grudgingly impressed, and that just barely. She hadn't ducked either.

"Yes, girl," I said to her, petting her sable nose. "I know you can jump like that too."

"Perhaps not quite like *that*," Avonstoke said with wonder, straightening up.

"Shh," I said, covering Nocturnus's ears and glaring. Avonstoke laughed, his smile brilliant in the sun. No one laughed with more heartfelt joy than Avonstoke.

The new horse landed easily on the section of raft behind us, cantering to a quick stop in front of the one he'd been staring at since he'd been released from the Wild Hunt.

"Acta Santorum," Mr. Sands breathed, like it was a benediction. His hands reached up wonderingly.

"He has been in our keeping," Cernunnos said through the voices of his host. "But there is no debt attached to this one and it is time he returned to the world."

I jumped, having almost forgotten about the presence of a god in this one, shining moment.

"Acta Santorum," Sands said again, and as his hands touched Acta Santorum's white coat, the little ex-magician's eyes blazed green, as they once had.

Something I hadn't noticed before was draped around Acta's neck and now glowed fiercely. Sands made a soft, incoherent noise and unclasped it. When he'd worked something free from the tether and held it up to look at it more closely, I saw it was a pale horse-shaped knight from a chessboard, the white twin to my own black token for Nocturnus. Sands' eyes were still bright but also moist. The white chess piece had flared like a sunrise, settled into a softer, more burnished gold, then dimmed even further, as if, having gotten our attention, the magic lying inside was content to slumber.

I made a little noise of surprise and stared at Faith, who was openly weeping happy tears. She nodded at me.

"Well, I'll be damned," I said happily.

"Too much magic has passed out of this world today," Prudence said. "Drecovian, the Wealdarin, all of the Deadly Sins, the dragons Usarador, Senuguhan, Sendurjihan, for all that they were evil. It is good to see a magician returned to the fold."

Prudence had been disparaging of Sands' lost magic before, but you could see she meant precisely what she'd said. It was not often that any magician had such contact with the powers of magic themselves, the gods and the dragons of Faerie. I had a hunch that Sands would rise now to become a magician far more powerful than he had ever been in the Lord of Thorns' service.

There was a rumble from the top of the Bastion. Brocara. I'd nearly forgotten about her too. What kind of profoundly overwhelming day was it when you lost track of dragons?

"Ah," Faith said, as if she'd understood that rumble as something more than words. "The green dragons, Senuguhan and Sendurjihan, still live. Drecovian, somehow, put his life into a spell to transport them back to Faerie. They live?"

"Usarador?" Avonstoke and Prudence both asked together.

Brocara gave another rumble, this one filled with dark satisfaction. She still lay with her head resting on the top of the Bastion, her eyes closed.

"No," Faith said. "Drecovian's spell would not work on him and it came down to bloody tooth and claw in the sea. Usarador the Red Death will never come out of the sea." She spoke with a cadence, as if Brocara were sending her thoughts in bursts of dark dragon poetry.

"Well," Prudence said, looking at Faith and sounding somehow satisfied, as if a plan of hers long in the making had just come to fruition. "It seems as if Brocara has chosen a new magician." She inclined her head briefly. "Dra-Faith."

"Are you the new DrecoviFaith?" Avonstoke said, delighted. He held up his hands as if viewing her through a picture frame. "No wrinkles, no wizened, dour expression . . . I'm not sure you fit the part yet. Can we make wrinkles? Makeup, paint?"

"Wait," Faith said, "I haven't agreed to anything here."

"Haven't you?" Prudence said. "Would you really wish to refuse?"

"Well . . . *no*," Faith said, "it would just be nice to be *asked.*"

Brocara, still not lifting her head or opening her eyes, rumbled again.

"*Now* you ask?" Faith said, rolling her eyes at the dragon. "And like *that*? Oh, I'll accept, all right, if only to teach you some manners!"

"This is a great honor," Prudence said, a little concerned. "I'm not sure the word *manners* is entirely appropriate."

"You talk to *your* dragon the way you want," Faith snapped, "but as long as mine"—she lifted her voice to a shout—"has the manners of a goat, well . . ." she took a deep breath and resumed in a calmer voice. "We'll just see about *that*."

"So magical," Avonstoke said. Prudence snorted and gave up.

"It is time," Cernunnos intoned, reminding us that many, many profound and magical things were happening on this day.

"Yes," Father said, his feet still on the wispy path up to the Wild Hunt. "Be well, my children."

We stood, Faith, Henry, Benedict, and I, with our hands in each other's as we watched Father go to Cernunnos and the Wild Hunt. He mounted up and the host cawed, bayed, whinnied, or shouted, each according to their nature, to welcome him into the fold.

A steed came out for Father, a huge, black, fanged creature easily large enough to carry such an oversized passenger. The Lord of Thorns mounted up effortlessly. I was surprised to see the King with the Sword and the King with the Eye Patch make room for him between them.

"Cernunnos had three kings," Prudence whispered. "The King with the Sword, the King with the Eye Patch, and the Antlered King, son of Cernunnos himself."

Faith looked at her sharply. "Where did you read that?"

But Prudence shook her head and said nothing.

"We fly," Cernunnos said, "but know this: the champions of Taranis, the God of Lightning, Thunder, and War, have returned to Dover and scattered the remnant of legions that the Black Shuck left there. The British Isles, her cities, and the ruling of these places belongs to humans again. But make no mistake, the Faerie *have* returned to this world. We shall haunt your forests, the glades, the rivers, turbulent seas, and stormy skies of this world again, as we did of old. We shall have to learn, I think, to live with each other."

"You will also need, I think," the Lord of Thorns, the Antlered King of the Wild Hunt, boomed, "to select a new monarch. The old line has passed, and it would be best chosen from those here, with an understanding of both worlds."

Cernunnos lifted his horn to his lips and blew, sounding a call wild and free, and then he leapt, followed by his host, into the sky. Storm clouds rolled, black and oily, after them, leaving behind the tingle of power and the scent of dangerous weather. Once in the sky, the horn rang out again, and Brocara lifted her head and roared in response.

"A new monarch," Prudence said musingly, once the noise had died down. "With no surviving members of the royal family left."

"Don't look at me," Faith said jokingly. "I've got a dragon to babysit."

"The Kasric name, combined with the House of Thorns," Sands said, his green eyes still luminescent, "would help. Stories of the House of Thorns fighting to free England have paved the way quite nicely, I believe." He was eyeing the four of us, Faith, Benedict, Henry, and I, with open speculation.

"There are even a few songs," Avonstoke said helpfully.

"Shut up, you!" I said, thumping him in the ribs. "Perhaps someone older," I said, looking at Rachek Kasric, who certainly had an understanding of both the human and Faerie world.

"Oh no," Rachek said. "I've been drafted into a monarchy once, remember? Not again."

"A visible face from the resistance would be best," Prudence said. She'd moved over next to Sands and the two of them were looking at the four of us Kasrics like someone at the butcher's counter.

Rachek Kasric moved to stand next to them. He was looking at me and thoughtfully stroking the stubble on his chin. "Would that ghost eye be a commanding presence under a crown?"

"Undoubtedly," Prudence said.

"No!" I said. "I did Admiral and General, no way. My turn's over."

"She does have a point," Prudence said. "Also, I'm not sure the eye is the right . . . face . . . for this."

"Oh, thanks!" I said.

"Magician," Faith said quickly. "Dragon. Far too busy."

"They don't know Benedict's face," Sands said. "But . . ." He was looking steadily at Henry.

"Honorable," Prudence said. "With an open, honest face. Marriageable age. Well-known face of the resistance. He's perfect."

Faith looked down at Henry and ruffled his sandy hair. "Congratulations, Your Highness."

"Wait," Henry said. "What?"

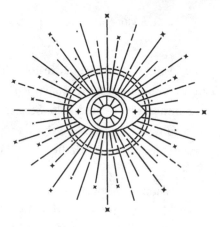

CHAPTER 28

JUSTICE
A New World

The coronation of King Henry the IX, or the Faerie King, happened at the newly rebuilt (and, in the case of some portions, newly grown) Westminster Abbey. Henry broke with tradition and insisted on holding the ceremony outside on the lawn, rather than in the chapel. This was also, by consequence, underneath the Faerie Tree, as it is now called. The significance of having both the prominent British and Faerie landmarks in view was not lost on either Faith or I. Henry was getting a good handle on such things even faster than I'd expected. Thankfully, the Faerie Tree that had been part of the changes thrust on London, is now diminished to less domineering dimensions and no longer threatens to tear London into rubble. It is still a marvel among trees, however, three hundred feet or so tall and one of the new wonders of the world.

The ceremony was long and not overly exciting, and both Faith and I had an engagement to get to, so it wasn't more than an hour after this when we caught Henry's eye and he nodded. We had an important appointment to keep. Avonstoke caught my eye too, and smiled. He made a slight bow, imitated carefully by the raven on his shoulder in perfect unison. I had to stifle a laugh. Benedict and Sands, as Henry's two advisors, stood next to him. Sands had a hand absently on the shining, white neck of the glorious Acta Santorum, standing next to him, who nickered softly. Since being reunited, the two had hardly separated, and no one had even considered suggesting that they should, even for important coronations. They both saw us looking and nodded. They knew where we were going.

Having made our good-byes, Faith and I both slipped away to change into better traveling clothes. Then, we sought out the side of the tree away from the ceremonies and stood under it for a brief space while Faith collected herself. Whichever person was speaking at the ceremony now, the drone was distant and barely audible over the wind rustling through the innumerable leaves above us. Peaceful.

Faith pushed back her hood and rolled up her sleeves, then stamped her staff on the ground next to a gnarled root the size of a buffalo. The wind responded and I found myself lifting in the air and rising majestically into the tree above us. Or at least it might have been majestic if I hadn't had to keep my hand on my hat to keep the wind from carrying it away. In the mysterious and symbolic way that Faerie magic had about it, the Faerie tree had started blossoming today, huge orchidesque flowers of bright orange, lemon yellow, and pale ivory among the emerald leaves. The trip up, carried on Faith's docile wind through the boughs of the Faerie Tree, was slow, stately, filled with wondrous beauty, and a bit tedious.

It's funny the things you get used to.

Our rendezvous was at the very top of the Faerie Tree.

Faith set us gently down on one of the topmost branches, and we were there less than two minutes when Brocara's form appeared like a massive ghostly bat in the clouds above us and began plummeting.

Another two minutes, and we watched her bank gracefully in a downward spiral and light on the branch next to us.

She trumpeted in greeting and leaned her enormous, craggy face down to nuzzle Faith's shoulder, nearly knocking my sister off the branch and ending the promising career of Dra-Faith Kasric, one of Faerie's most powerful magicians, by sending her tumbling. But Faith survived Brocara's affection and we mounted on Brocara's spiked back.

Flying by dragon was a little bit like sailing a ship with the wind, so it wasn't the turbulent wind tunnel I'd expected, and as we watched London, and then England, dwindle in size below us, I thought of the past few weeks and how they'd been busier than just about any other time I'd known. Even war hadn't been so busy.

Brocara entered the Faerie mist, moving us into Faerie. The sun, blazing overhead, was shrouded but not diminished so that we moved through a shining pearlescent fog while I thought about the past week. The air was cold on my face and smelled of salt and the sea. So many funerals: Drecovian, Beaudulaire the Sphinx, Draust of the Jötnar, Swayle of the Crow Whisper Brigade. Demet, Daccus, Porgineau, Glaudrang, Captain Caine, and British officers Stephens, Wyndham, Radcliffe. A private ceremony for Joshua and Martine Kasric. Even funerals for the Deadly Sins—the Black Shuck, Widdershins, John Brown, Urguag, Mrs. Westerly, the Goblin Knight—and another funeral for Mother in Faerie. But we hadn't been invited to those.

With the Black Shuck's demise, the Faerie mist segregating England from the rest of the world has retreated once again to the deepest forests, hidden grottos, and other forgotten, shadowy corners of our world. In England, many of the less solitary Faerie, Dwarves, Goblins, Prowlers, even a few Jötnar and Court Faerie, have remained in the open and taken up occupations as clerks, merchants, sailors, newsvendors, cooks, or craftsmen, as their nature dictated, and King Henry has made them welcome. There are others who have taken up less savory occupations, but then London has never had a shortage of criminals, and they've fit in as well there as anywhere else. The docks of our port cities now swell with visitors from Europe, the Americas, and the rest of the world to see and meet the many remaining Faerie. The flow, of course, has gone both ways, and stories of the Faerie reappearing in the rest of the world have abounded.

The Faerie army might have been shattered, but the remnants of that army have scattered throughout our world. The Faerie are, however, excellent at remaining elusive, and there are many people who haven't journeyed to London who still don't believe, despite the occasional sighting of the Wild Hunt.

No matter. They'll learn soon enough. The Faerie are truly here, and here to stay.

Brocara dipped and started a gentle glide downward. The wind picked up, bringing with it the smell of wild, green things. When the mist slid away on all sides, I beheld the World Tree again in all its frightening glory.

We sailed over an expanse of blue and landed on a stunningly bright white beach. From here, we would have to make our way through the tangle of branches—a forest made of one tree, and one tree only—to get to the agreed-on meeting place. The very same spot where the Lord of Thorns and Father had once played chess under the World Tree.

The dragon, after we'd dismounted, craned her serpentine neck to bring her massive head down as close to Faith's as she could. "Do not," Brocara rumbled, "take overly long. We have other errands to run."

"Yes, dear," Faith said and patted the dragon fondly on her snout. Seeing my look of curiosity, she said to me: "There have been no less than three dragon sightings in places where we hadn't expected them. There may be more dragons left alive than we realized. She wants to see."

I could feel my eyebrows rise. "More dragons? But Faith, that's *amazing*! You're just telling me this now?"

"I just found out," Faith said, with a sly look at Brocara. Was she getting waking dreams from the dragon now? Or did they have other, more subtle ways of communication? Certainly, I hadn't heard them talking during the journey. I decided not to ask.

"Wyrmlings!" Brocara said excitedly.

"She means dragon babies," Faith said. "We've gotten report of some solitary adult dragons in remote areas in Faerie, but that's secondary to the reports of wyrmlings. Those are coming from Africa. That'll be our first priority."

"Don't take too long," Brocara said. Then she yawned, exposing enough teeth to chew up castle turrets, and stretched out on the beach to sleep and wait.

Faith patted the dragon again and we left.

We made our way through the forest, walking silently through the verdant and solemn maze. The air shone a mottled green and gold all around us and we walked in silence, each alone in our own thoughts, through the briar mazes and tunnels of the World Tree. After we were inside a short distance, the forest opened up on a mossy green expanse, much more open than the last time we'd been here. I summoned Pavor Nocturnus for the last few miles, and it was a very short time before she bore us down into the mossy hollow under the World Tree that I remembered so well.

It was only moments before a mottled gray falcon landed in the hollow. The shape shimmered and grew until Prudence, looking as gray, mundane, and out of place as ever in Faerie, stood in front of us.

"Great entrance," Faith murmured.

"Well," I murmured back. "She's faster than before. The shapeshifting is a lot less gruesome to look at when she does it more quickly."

"Why don't we have a cool entrance like that?"

"We came here on a dragon and a nightmare," I said. "What more did you want?"

She sniffed, not looking at all satisfied.

Prudence walked across the moss and bowed low. "Greetings from Queen Mab and the Unseelie Court."

"Greetings," Faith replied gravely, "from King Henry and England. We look forward to the queen's scheduled visit next month."

"As do we," Prudence replied.

Queen Mab's, or Lady Rue's, adoption of our sister had been a bit of a surprise to me, but Faith had said it made sense. Faith would represent the Unseelie Court in her visits to the Seelie and British courts. Mab and Prudence had developed a working relationship during the invasion, and Mab needed to open relations with England and reestablish the same with the Seelie Court. It felt like the last dwindling effect of Father's prophecy, since the new ambassadors to each of the courts were all sisters. Who was I to fight it? Faith was the primary assigned ambassador, while I was something more of a backup ambassador, part-time, since Avonstoke and I had some travel plans that wouldn't allow for a permanent assignment in England.

The formalities honored, Prudence grinned and embraced us both.

A small dip in the mossy terrain near the edge of the clearing shimmered and shed what looked like moonlight up into the branches. Two shapes appeared suddenly, outlined and limned in a blueish glow: one large wolfish black shape and a much smaller, childlike one. There was a liquid sheen at their feet. Blood. Even if I hadn't known their shapes, I recognized the particular sheen that characterized Charity's blood magic.

"Greetings," Charity said in her piping voice, "from the Seelie Court."

Wolf and child stepped out of the blood and the glow, both of which promptly shimmered out of existence. The shadowy wolf shape collapsed on itself as it moved, changing, until Hope's slender form stood next to her sister.

"Another cool entrance," Faith said. "We really need to work on ours."

I rolled my eyes at her, even though I was pretty sure she was only half serious.

Again, we all went through the formalities. The Seelie Court, not to be left out or outdone, had wooed and won the Lady of Sorrows and both her daughters as ambassadors. The Lady Dierwyn of Thorns—no one called her the Lady of Sorrows anymore—had gone to the Seelie Court. With both courts eager for relations with each other for the first time in untold ages, it was an interesting time.

This decision from the Seelie Court had come from King Oberon alone. Queen Titania, having been, as it turned out, mostly responsible for approving and assisting the Black Shuck's plans and the invasion, had essentially abdicated and now lived under palace arrest.

The Seelie and Unseelie Courts' seeking relations with not only each other but also Britain heralded an age of human and Faerie cooperation that had never been seen before. It all seemed very hopeful. Both the Faerie courts even had plans to approach the other nations of Earth, but that was for the future.

Lightning flared above us, then shot down and struck the ground, showering the mossy glade with light. When my eyes recovered, Pyar and Temperance stood in that spot.

Faith caught my eye again and I sighed. I had to admit she might have a point. It was a hell of an entrance.

"Sisters," Pyar said. "I hope we find you well. Taranis bless you all."

There was a subtle shifting among us. Or, at least, the rest of my sisters. No one's expression changed and no one actually moved, but where the five of us had been a representation of three different governments, there were also other allegiances represented. I could see Faith's eyes grow thoughtful as she considered, in her role as Cernunnos's champion, the other champions before her and the Faerie gods they represented. Prudence stood for Brigid, the triple goddess, as she always had. Charity and Hope represented Lughus and the horse aspect of Morrigna. Arawn and Ogma, the main forces behind the initial invasion, no longer had a living champion. Lughus had been against us at the end but now seemed to be enjoying a careful truce with the others, especially since Charity had refused to side with anyone, and Urguag was now dead. Lughus, for his part, was probably pleased.

After all, the Faerie had come back to the world. A happy ending for the Faerie gods in general.

Of course, no one dared call me a champion to Llyr, which was just as well. Llyr leaves me alone and I do the same for him. However, I have some very serious plans to take the HMS *Specter in the Mist* and her crew out to visit as many of the magical seas of Faerie as I can. The Shimmering Seas, Lichen Bay, the Caves of the Deep, they all called to me. Perhaps that was as close a celebration of Llyr's domain as anyone could hope for. I hoped so. If you want Llyr's opinion, you'll have to ask him. We don't speak.

"King Henry," I said to Pyar and Temperance, "extends his heartfelt thanks to you for the service you've done the crown. He hopes you will allow him a chance to repay you, should you ever come to England."

"That is very kind," Pyar said.

Service was perhaps too small a word for it, but I didn't know what else to call it. Having refused to fill out their assigned roles as Virtues, they had avoided any involvement with our battle with the invasion fleet but had instead gone to England and attacked the forces that had still remained at Dover. Pyar and Temperance hadn't bothered anyone who fled, but any group still waving the flag of any Sin had been struck with enough hurricanes and lightning to effectively end that portion of the occupation once and for all.

Had they not, it was likely that the minor generals remaining would have directed their forces to raze all of England into ruins, and we would have had to cause even more damage trying to retake our home, costing uncountable loss of life. Taranis, Pyar, and Temperance didn't help us win the war, but they *did* make sure that we had a country and home to return to once we won.

"Why?" Faith said. "Why did you do it? If you didn't want any part of the war, why did you help us? I wouldn't have expected England to have your sympathies."

Pyar and Temperance exchanged glances and hesitated.

Finally, it was Temperance who answered. "That's because you don't know us very well. After being their prisoner, I had no love for the Black Shuck and was happy to help punish him, but neither of us wanted to dance to the Lord of Thorns' tune, either."

"I grew up in India," Pyar said, "and then Faerie. With no love for the British Empire. But Temperance convinced me that it, and the rest of the human world, was worth saving."

"Besides," Temperance said. "We *are* sisters and you'd just helped me without trying to entrap or enslave me. It seemed the least we could do."

"You are," Pyar said, "a more honorable leader than the Lord of Thorns. Your actions deserved respect." She nodded to me and I smiled back. It hadn't all gone perfectly, but we *had* saved England, with help, and I was as proud of that accomplishment as anything I'd ever done in my life.

"Thank you," I said.

"So," Faith said, looking at Pyar and Temperance. "It seems that while the rest of us have gotten drafted into political duties, you two have wisely avoided that. What are your plans for the future?"

Pyar and Temperance exchanged looks. It seemed that for only being together a short time, they had already developed an impressive bond.

"We've been talking about that," Temperance said. "We've both lived somewhat sequestered lives and now have many new places to explore, both in and out of Faerie."

"I had a similar thought," I said. "Avonstoke and I are going to take the *Specter* to as many different Faerie waters as we can find."

"Would the *Specter* have room," Pyar said quickly, "for the two of us to join you?"

I felt a slow smile cross my face. "Quarters are cramped on a ship, but there's always room if you don't mind that."

Clearly, they had discussed this between themselves first, because they both nodded at once.

"As long as I'm not chained in the hold," Temperance added quickly.

"I promise," I said. "No chains." I could certainly think of no better way to get to know my new sisters, and they would be infinitely useful to have along.

"As sisters," Prudence said, "it seems we should get to know one another better today, yes? I mean for those of us that have duties and can't afford the time for pleasure cruises."

"I have an impatient dragon waiting for me on the beach," Faith said with a gentle smile. "But I also know she'll be sleeping for hours, perhaps days. I have some time. Besides, when are the seven of us going to be together again?"

I had to admit, there was a part of me that wanted to get back to the *Specter*. The HMS *Specter in the Mist* and her crew—Avonstoke, Mog, Render, Étienne, Percy, Emily, Nellie, Wil, Wargan, Iela, and all the rest—waited for me. The crew of humans, Goblins, Court Faerie, Dwarves, Prowlers, Trolls, and the like—for even given the option of departure, almost the entire crew, to a person, had opted to stay on board—were united by a burning desire to sail the Faeric Seas. King Henry declared the *Specter* a gift to the Kasric family for services rendered to the crown, but we are still very much emissaries of London. It is our quest to take word of the peace between human and Faerie to all corners of the Faerie world, now that I have trained my ghost eye to find and traverse the Faerie Mist. I was already thinking about where to put Pyar and Temperance. Without Faith, Henry, or Sands, there would be plenty of room.

But, I also had sisters to get to know. I could take a few days here.

"So," Charity piped up in her high voice. "Did anyone think to bring food?"

ACKNOWLEDGMENTS

First thanks go to my daughter, Katie, who inspired this story so long ago.

Also to my wife, Kimberly, for constantly believing in me and for her long-term understanding.

Tremendous thanks also to Sarah Zettel, Steven Piziks, Cindy Spencer Pape, David Erik Nelson, Diana Rivis, Mary Beth Johnson, Christine Pellar-Kosbar, Jonathan Jarrard, Erica Shippers, and Ted Reynolds of the Untitled Writer's Group who suffered innumerable versions of this story with grace and patience. Ink is love and I received a lot of both. Also to Janine Beaulieu, Heath Lowrance, Ron Warren, and Carole Ward for helping nurture the original version of this, even if it's likely evolved into something they no longer recognize from those days.

Also to my agent, Lucienne Diver, and editors, Elana Gibson, Helga Schier, and Cassandra Farrin over at CamCat Publishing, who have provided outstanding editorial assistance over the course of this entire series.

To my parents, Craig and Pam Klaver, and my mother Suzanne Klaver, who always encouraged my creativity and imagination.

ABOUT THE AUTHOR

Christian Klaver has been writing for over twenty years with a number of magazine publications, including *Escape Pod, Dark Wisdom Anthology,* and *Anti-Matter.* He's the author of *The Supernatural Case Files of Sherlock Holmes, Shadows Over London, Justice at Sea,* and the Nightwalker Series, and has written over a dozen novels in both fantasy and sci-fi, often with a noir bent. He worked as a bookseller, bartender, and martial arts instructor before settling into a career in internet security. He lives just outside the sprawling decay of Detroit, Michigan, with his wife, Kimberly; his daughter, Kathryn; and a group of animals he refers to as the Menagerie.

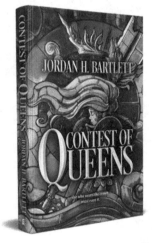
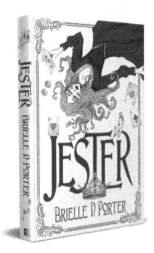

CamCat Books

VISIT US ONLINE FOR
MORE BOOKS TO LIVE IN:
CAMCATBOOKS.COM

FOLLOW US

CamCatBooks   @CamCatBooks   @CamCat_Books

CPSIA information can be obtained
at www.ICGtesting.com
Printed in the USA
LVHW020819110922
727532LV00003B/3/J